THE FLACK

Also by Brad Parks

STANDALONES

The Boundaries We Cross

Unthinkable

Interference

The Last Act

Closer Than You Know

Say Nothing

CARTER ROSS SERIES

The Fraud

The Player

The Good Cop

The Girl Next Door

Eyes of the Innocent

Faces of the Gone

THE FLACK

A NOVEL

BRAD PARKS

OCEANVIEW PUBLISHING
SARASOTA, FLORIDA

ISBN 978-1-60809-647-3

Published in the United States of America by Oceanview Publishing

Sarasota, Florida

www.oceanviewpub.com

10 9 8 7 6 5 4 3 2 1

This is dedicated to all my former colleagues at The Star-Ledger *and* The Washington Post, *and to all the newspaper people out there who are now doing something else with their lives.*

May the truth teller within us never die.

CHAPTER 1

IN A LIFETIME of breaths—most of them automatic, unconsidered, and unappreciated—he was down to his last treasured few.

He knew this. His injuries were too grave. He could feel the blood pulsing out of him, its warmth strangely at odds with his rapidly cooling skin.

The men who attacked him were gone; thinking, not altogether incorrectly, that their job was finished.

So he was by himself in the darkness of a deserted park in Oakland, California, his life leaking out onto the weed-clumped grass.

With little comprehension, he looked down at his outfit: a $4,000 custom-made suit, slashed into ribbons.

There was a street a few hundred feet away, but it might as well have been a mile. He couldn't summon the power to stand, much less walk. A car sped past, its windows rolled up, its stereo thumping.

"Help," he moaned toward it.

His voice was lost in the gloom.

On the other side of him, also several hundred feet off, there were houses, some of them with lights on.

And there was a church, though it was dark.

It was just as well.

God wouldn't be answering his prayers.

"Help," he croaked again.

He shivered violently as the shock gripped him. His mouth had gone dry.

There was little point in continuing to cry out. No one could hear him.

Really, there was only one thing that now filled his mind.

He had to warn the people he loved.

With his remaining strength, he propped himself up, pulled out his phone, and composed two texts. The first was to his wife.

Run. Take Elijah and run. I'm sorry. I love you.

The next was to his best friend, who appeared simply as "C Note" in his contact files.

Don't take the job. Just run. They are

Two words into the third sentence, the phone slipped from his grasp. He groped for it, but he could no longer make his eyes focus, much less control the finer functioning of his hand. He was shaking too much. His vision was failing.

The blackness was closing in.

With a guttural sound, he collapsed.

He died before he could hit SEND.

CHAPTER 2

ANGEL REDDISH ALWAYS could talk me into anything.

We met as freshmen at Northwestern University; a pair of randomly assigned roommates who, on paper, didn't have much in common other than that we indicated we liked to go to bed early and considered ourselves "neater than average."

He grew up on the southside of Chicago. I had multiple generations dead and buried in rural Tennessee.

I came to Northwestern for its vaunted journalism program. He was pointed toward its world-famous business school.

He was six-feet-three inches tall and 220 pounds, with the muscles of a linebacker and the cheekbones of a model, and seldom needed to exert himself to find romantic attention. I was two inches shorter, forty pounds lighter, rather plain-looking compared to him, and needed to put in the work.

My learning was bookish, intellectual, a grind. He was a natural polymath who seemed to absorb knowledge just by being around it.

We spoke in different accents and disparate dialects, his voice an urgent tenor and mine a plodding baritone. He had been raised bilingual by his mother, who was born in the Dominican Republic. My Spanish came from a book.

Our music collections had no overlap. We were frequently baffled by the other's cultural references.

You wouldn't have figured us for anything more than forced acquaintances; but, somehow, like a Hollywood buddy flick come to life, we became best friends.

Maybe it was that, in the sea of privilege that was Northwestern, neither of us came from much. I was there by the grace of a generous financial aid package. Angel was on a football scholarship.

Or maybe it was that he loved to talk and I loved to listen.

Or that neither of us had much of a father, leaving us to be reared by strong women who insisted on simple, steadfast values from their sons: kindness, integrity, humility, loyalty, family.

Whatever the case, Angel Reddish and I quickly became this dynamic duo who went everywhere together.

There wasn't much question about who was Batman and who was Robin.

Angel could convince me to buckle down and hit the books for hours; or put off studying in favor of a late-night convenience store run.

When Angel decided we were only speaking Spanish in our room—so I could become fluent and he didn't get rusty—that's exactly what we did.

If there was a cello concert, a guest lecturer in the physics department, or a special exhibition by the indigenous artist in residence, Angel would describe the opportunity with incredible earnestness—this was *the thing* we absolutely *had* to see—and then cajole me into tagging along.

His interests were as broad as my curiosity was deep.

But here was the funny thing, the thing that no one except us knew: For as much as I've made myself sound like the passive partner, there was a codependence to our relationship. Angel only went somewhere if he knew I would go with him.

It's like I was his security blanket, his comfort human.

That's why he was always talking me into things: He needed a follower as much as I needed a leader.

He was also just *interested* in what I had to say. While I was nowhere near as voluble as he was, he always responded to my observations with great enthusiasm.

"Curt Hinton, you are so money!" he'd declare. "You're *so* money!"

He said this often enough that he quickly decided my nickname should be "C Note."

Like the hundred-dollar bill.

Neither of us drank much. For him, it was about being an athlete and staying sharp. For me, it was somewhat because of all the fire and brimstone sermons my Southern Baptist mother had dragged me to.

But mostly it was that my dad died of cirrhosis when I was twelve.

I told Angel—and only Angel—about that one night early during our freshman year. He shared things with me about his dad, who would show up now and then, but only to beat up his mom; at least until, when Angel was fifteen and had finally outgrown his old man, he set matters straight.

If you ever lay a finger on my mama again, I'll break your neck.

So, yeah, in addition to being constant companions, we were also confidants. We'd gab into the early morning about our hopes and ambitions, as only starry-eyed college students on the verge of world domination could do.

He dreamed of going into business and becoming a millionaire so he could buy his mother a house. I talked about doing the kind of journalism that would make a difference in the world and maybe even win a Pulitzer.

After freshman year, it was only natural we'd continue on as roommates the next three.

We went our separate ways after graduation, though we stayed in touch, talking every few weeks and texting more frequently.

While I toiled at a series of successively larger newspapers, he pursued a career in corporate America. He earned an MBA in supply chain management, which became his passion.

It figured someone like Angel would be attracted to things in constant motion.

His rise was, unsurprisingly, meteoric. In addition to his intelligence, Angel dripped with charisma. Football had taught him the value of hard work, and he rechanneled that ethic into his career.

It seemed like every six months or so, he was telling me about another promotion. His titles became increasingly more impressive-sounding. He had future CEO written all over him. He just needed a little more seasoning—and the right opportunity.

We both met our future wives around the time we turned thirty.

For me, it was Page, a warmhearted educational consultant who was five-feet-two inches of curly red hair and blue-eyed spunk. Our first date was pure fireworks, and I spent the early days of our courtship amazed someone so smart, sensual, and gorgeous wanted anything to do with me. I proposed after just a year of dating, before she could come to her senses.

For him, it was Aiysha Miller, a razor-sharp cybersecurity consultant who he seemed similarly taken with.

When Angel and I got married within a few months of each other at age thirty-two, mutual college friends joked that they were surprised we weren't marrying each other.

Naturally, I was his best man; and he was mine.

When their son, Elijah, was born two years later, Angel asked me to be the child's godfather. I was planning to reciprocate when our first child, who was due soon, came along.

Angel's most recent exciting career opportunity was when he was recruited to become Chief Operations Officer at Bay Area Logistics Company, aka Balco, located in Oakland, California. I hadn't given it much consideration until one day he called me up with an unusual request.

He wanted me to interview for a job there.

It wasn't totally out of the blue. He knew that Page was pregnant, that she despised her imperious twit of a boss, and that she was dying to stay at home with the baby after her maternity leave ran out; but, also, that we couldn't really make ends meet on my salary alone.

I was making $58,000 a year as a reporter at a well-respected Midwestern newspaper that was, much like the rest of the legacy media business, dying.

The position he wanted me to apply for was vice president of corporate communications, which meant I would be responsible for all company messaging, both internally and externally.

It paid $350,000 a year.

Plus a generous stipend to help with the exorbitant cost of Bay Area housing.

Plus a medical benefits package that would, among other things, pay the entire cost of having a baby without a single dime in copays.

Plus a $50,000 signing bonus, which I got to keep as long as I stayed for six months.

Plus a brand-new Rivian SUV to zip around in, just because.

Balco was privately held and still owned by its founder, a publicity-shy billionaire named Gehrig Weiskopf. It prided itself on taking good care of its people and didn't have to deal with shareholders carping about excessively generous executive compensation packages.

Still, I demurred. After all, the job was essentially public relations, a field I had been trained to view with skepticism. The way I saw it, journalists existed to search for and tell the truth; and PR people existed to manipulate and obfuscate it.

They were paid mouthpieces, spin masters, shills.

Old-school reporters referred to them as flacks.

It wasn't a compliment.

Also, I didn't know a thing about logistics, other than that it was probably a lot more complicated than moving stuff from Point A to Point B.

Angel insisted there was nothing he couldn't teach me.

"I need someone who knows how to think and how to write and how to do it fast," he said. "That's you, C Note. You've always been money."

Then he added: "And I need someone I can trust."

I agreed to at least throw my hat into the ring. For 350 large a year, why not?

There were three candidates, and I was definitely the dark horse. The only one from outside the logistics industry. The only one from outside industry, period.

Angel gave me a crash course in 3PL (third-party logistics) lingo, teaching me what a bill of lading was and how to read it; or how much easier and more profitable it was to deal with FTLs (full truckloads) than LTLs (less-than truckloads); or about the importance of OTIF (on-time in-full) metrics.

Balco flew Page and me first-class out to California and put us up in the Four Seasons San Francisco. While I visited company headquarters near the Port of Oakland, Aiysha took Page and showed her around beautiful Marin County, a paradise for families that boasted some of the best schools in California.

Page was sold. She loved everything about it.

Before my interview, Angel had given me an extended briefing on Balco, a company with $3.2 billion in revenue, fourteen thousand employees, and just as many problems.

In addition to the constant series of headaches that all logistics companies faced—clogged canals, collapsing bridges, aging infrastructure, and disasters both natural and human in origin—Balco was facing a new threat.

Three thousand of its employees in California were about to vote on whether to certify as members of the IWW-Local 37, the International Warehouse Workers union. The lead-up to the vote had been rife with tension, threats, and even violence.

Coming from the Midwest, I was familiar with the many issues surrounding organized labor—both pro and con. I felt like I did a surprisingly competent job expounding on that and Balco's other challenges as I met with a series of high-ranking executives.

I was also the only candidate who spoke fluent Spanish, which was a big advantage. A not-insubstantial portion of Balco's operations were in Mexico.

Afterward, I was given a writing test with several facets to it—a press release, a blog post, an internal email, and an executive speech—and also told to record something for a hypothetical social media video. I had two weeks to complete all the elements.

In the world of daily journalism, two weeks isn't a deadline. It's practically a paid vacation.

I turned it around in four days. And, apparently, what I sent was more convincing—more thoroughly researched, better written, and better performed—than what the other two candidates provided after taking the full allotment of time.

That, along with Angel's boosterism behind the scenes, was enough to land me an offer.

I remained reluctant. I knew that newspapers had no future, but I was really enjoying the present. At thirty-five, I had paid my dues in journalism. Having covered all the car accidents, house fires, and schoolboard meetings that one man could possibly tolerate, I was finally being trusted to take on bigger projects.

Investigations. Features. The chance to do truly important work that shaped the conversation in the communities I covered.

But, ultimately, Angel outsmarted me. He had Page present me the offer sheet along with a photo of her eight-week ultrasound, our first glimpse of the miracle inside her.

Like I said, he always could talk me into anything.

Across six whirlwind weeks, Page and I gave notice to our employers; sold our townhouse and my aging Chevy, while arranging for Page's Honda CRV to be shipped out to California; and stepped aside as white glove movers (paid for by Balco) loaded our mismatched, dinged-up, secondhand junk onto a truck.

That Page did all this while also dealing with first trimester exhaustion only served to confirm something I already knew: She was way tougher than me.

I was to start on May 2, a Tuesday—because Balco's biweekly pay periods started on Tuesdays. The Friday before that, we flew into SFO, where a Balco-contracted car service whisked us out to Marin County.

There, a relocation specialist (again, courtesy of Balco) met us at the new home we had picked out sight-unseen: a single-family, four-bedroom, two-and-a-half-bath rental. Its main downstairs space consisted of an open concept kitchen/dining area, which flowed into a generous family room. Sliding glass doors then opened out onto a massive deck that offered sweeping views of Mount Tamalpais in one direction and the San Francisco Bay in the other.

Our new address was 27 Buena Vista Drive, *buena vista* being Spanish for "good view." It was a quiet street that ran along the top of a ridge and dead-ended at an open space preserve. Angel and Aiysha lived just a few minutes away.

The house was mid-century modern, much to Page's approval. It came fully furnished, so we didn't need to wait for the moving truck to arrive to get comfortable. The furniture was all new, expensive, and perfectly coordinated.

We called it the Barbie DreamHouse.

Balco had thought of everything. A company-issued phone, ID badge, and laptop were sitting on the counter, all loaded up and ready to go. Balco had even installed high-speed internet for us—which it was paying for, naturally.

It wanted its executives to be well-connected.

Angel and Aiysha had us over for takeout on Saturday. For whatever reason, Aiysha and I had never gotten along all that well. It was almost like she was jealous of the history I had with her husband and viewed me as a rival for his affections. I had tried to go out of my way to include her in things, to explain the backstory of the many private jokes he and I shared.

It never did much good. There was always this uncomfortable awkwardness that hung over every interaction we had, like we were forever doomed to misunderstand each other.

But on this night, it was almost like she had decided to start over. We took turns chasing around Elijah, eighteen months of chubby-cheeked, hell-on-wheels energy. Once we got him to bed, when Angel and I got to telling old stories, she was laughing right along with us.

It was all so perfect.

Before I knew it, Tuesday morning had arrived. My first day at Balco. I had just put on one of the new suits I had bought with my signing bonus, though I could scarcely believe what I saw when I looked at myself in the bathroom mirror.

Curt Hinton, corporate stiff.

My one concession to my old life was tucking a reporter's pad in the breast pocket.

Honestly, I felt naked without one.

As I knotted a blue silk tie Page had picked out for me, she sidled up behind me.

I loved the way my wife moved. She had been a dancer as a kid. Every step she took looked like it had been choreographed.

"Nervous?" she asked, looking at my reflection.

"A little," I admitted. "But I'll be okay. Angel will have my back. He always does."

I turned to go, but she grabbed me by the lapels, lifted herself on her tiptoes, and kissed me.

"Hey," she said. "I know you're making a big sacrifice for me. For us. Thank you."

I smiled weakly.

"And I know that being a flack isn't exactly what you always dreamed of," she added, as tears started pooling in her eyes.

"My love," I said, pulling her into an embrace. "*You're* what I always dreamed of. This is going to be great for us."

"I know, but . . . There are no Pulitzers waiting for you at Balco." She sighed into my chest.

"That's okay," I said. "Some things are bigger than a Pulitzer."

She pushed away in mock offense. "So now you're calling me big, huh?"

Now at fourteen weeks, there was barely a hint of an extra curve on her slender frame.

"Absolutely, positively *huge*," I said. "If you get in the bathtub, we're going to start getting visits from those whale-watching tours."

She gave me a playful swat on the ass as I departed the bathroom.

Driving my new Rivian across the Richmond Bridge and toward Oakland, I could feel the impostor syndrome settling in. Was I in over my head? Could I really handle this job?

Whatever the case, it was too late to back out now.

Balco corporate headquarters were located just off Interstate 880 in Oakland, not far from the Bay Bridge. In addition to the executive offices, there was a massive warehouse—one of two the company operated in the state—where fifteen hundred employees worked round the clock to keep products coming and going.

Balco specialized in electronics and electrical components, all of which were extremely valuable. Security was tight.

There was only one way to enter the facility. I had to touch my ID badge to one of those old-school magnetic card readers—the non-digital kind that predated fancy phone readers, but was also therefore harder to hack.

That, in turn, sent a stout, twelve-foot-high chain-link fence rolling slowly into the open position. Then there was a shack where I had to show my ID to a guard, who had to hold down a button to raise a boom barrier that swung up. Only then could I enter the nearby detached parking deck.

The guards were armed. The fences were topped with imposing coils of razor wire. There were cameras everywhere.

Angel and I had a meeting set up for nine o'clock. He had promised to clear his schedule for the remainder of the morning so he could continue my crash-course orientation in all things Balco.

At 8:58, I entered the elevator. My office was on the fourth floor with the rest of the communications staff. Angel was on the fifth floor, where all the C-suite executives had their offices. I punched the button for 5.

The elevator opened onto a small lobby. There, the Balco logo—really, just the company's name written in a retro script font—was etched into a wall of smoked glass. The design motif up here was industrial chic, with metal beams, exposed brick, and other touches that were meant to suggest the kind of warehouse a logistics company of yore might have used.

I pushed through the double doors into the reception area.

And that's when I became aware something was terribly wrong.

I had spent time here during my interviews, and it was a bustling place, the humming nerve center for upper management.

Now it was muted. Somber. From down one of the hallways, I heard someone bawling.

The receptionist, who was sitting behind a sweeping semicircle of an elevated desk, was sniffling into a tissue. She barely seemed to register that I had entered.

She finally lifted her head as I approached.

"What's going on?" I asked.

She looked up at me through bleary eyes. "Didn't anyone tell you yet?"

"Tell me what?"

She inhaled sharply, her hand flying to her mouth. After taking a moment to compose herself, she resumed.

"I'm so, so sorry," she said. "Angel Reddish was killed last night."

CHAPTER 3

HER WORDS WERE concussive, knocking me backward.

I had to reach out and clutch the edge of the desk, just to keep myself from falling over.

All the air had vacated my lungs. The colors in the room had gone blurry and strange, like I was looking at them through a kaleidoscope that was being turned too fast. I couldn't make myself focus on anything.

Angel couldn't be dead.

It wasn't possible.

He was too vibrant, too dynamic, too strong.

How could someone larger than life no longer be part of it?

His whole life flashed before my eyes. I was seeing him when he first walked into our freshman dorm room, this huge guy with an even larger smile. When we met, we didn't shake hands or fist bump or do anything that might have been bro-cool like that.

He hugged me with both arms, crushing me into his block wall of a chest.

Next, I saw him hunched over his desk, his face rigid with intensity and altogether too close to his book as he crammed for an econ test late at night.

Then I saw him stretched out at the Lakefill, a popular Northwestern student hangout, totally at peace, soaking in the warmth of a breezy spring day as the waves pounded the painted rocks nearby.

Then I pictured him standing next to Aiysha on their wedding day, perfectly erect in his black tux, his entire body like an exclamation point.

Then I thought about Elijah, that vivacious, cherub-faced little boy who was never going to know his father.

I heard myself moaning, "Oh God."

My breathing had turned short and shallow. I was worried I was going to pass out.

The receptionist must have been worried, too. She was on her feet. Her mouth might have moved like she had said something; but, whatever it was, I didn't catch it.

"I'm sorry, I just . . ." I said.

And then I managed: "Killed?"

The word felt like an obscenity. The whole concept of a world without Angel was obscene.

"The police said it was a carjacking. It happened last night, after he left the office. They found his body in a park a few blocks away first thing this morning."

His body.

"Oh God," I said again.

"I'm terribly, terribly sorry," she said. "I know you were close."

More than close.

We were brothers.

But I just nodded. Or maybe I grunted a word or two at her, I'm not sure.

"Can I get you something? Water, or—"

"No, that's okay."

Tentatively, I released my grip on her desk. I was reasonably certain I wasn't going to fall over anymore.

I just felt like I wanted to vomit.

Her eyes flitted to the right.

"They just went into a meeting about it down the hall, in the main conference room," she said. "I don't know if you feel up to it, but if you wanted to join . . ."

"Yeah, that's probably a good idea," I said. "Thanks."

By "they," I knew she meant Balco's other top executives, who were suddenly one less in number. They would be reeling personally from Angel's loss, just like I was; except, for them, this was also a professional crisis.

As COO, Angel had a big job at Balco. They would need people to step in immediately and take over his various responsibilities.

Balco had thousands of trucks and millions of goods circulating around the world at any given moment. It had already been impressed upon me that nothing—not even death—could be permitted to hold them up.

I walked unsteadily down the hallway to the conference room door. As soon as I opened it, every eye inside went toward me.

These were people whose names and faces I knew, though barely, from my interviewing and from studying rosters Angel had sent me. It was mostly men—not a lot of women in the logistics business—and I was pretty sure all of them were older than me. They were seated around a long, polished granite conference table.

At the head of the table, there was a man standing in front of his chair. He was a shade under six feet tall and stocky, though his suit hid his bulk nicely. His fashionably cut side-parted hair was a mix of blond and gray.

This was Lorne Murphy, Balco's CEO. When I interviewed, I had a fifteen-minute slot with him—though he was running slightly late, so it was more like ten. We spent seven of them talking about the long-beleaguered Northwestern Wildcats.

Lorne Murphy went to Texas A&M. College football was his alpha and omega. I have no doubt that's part of the reason he hired Angel, the ex–Big Ten linebacker. Being from Tennessee, I was not unfamiliar with this worldview.

The briefing Angel had given me about Lorne was that he was a genuinely good guy—humble, down-to-earth, as egoless as a man in his position could possibly be. After running Balco's Mexico operations for a decade, he had been a natural to take over when Balco's founding CEO, Gehrig Weiskopf, had decided to retire four years earlier.

According to Angel, Murphy was almost universally beloved. Lorne truly cared about his employees. One of Balco's main points of pride was that it had never, in its roughly forty-year history, had to lay off anyone. Lorne told people one of the reasons he was so driven to keep the company successful was that he wanted to keep it that way.

He was known for having three large, engraved bronze plaques in his office. One read, "PEOPLE FIRST!" The next said, "Balco: Family." The third was the famous Peter Drucker quote, "Culture eats strategy for breakfast."

Lorne stared at me blankly for a long moment and I watched his face go through a round of *who the hell is this?* Then something clicked.

"Curt. Lord, I forgot you were starting today," he said in a gentle Texas twang. "I should have called you as soon as I heard. I'm sorry, it's just . . . we're all . . . we're all . . ."

The sentence wouldn't come out. He shook his head and choked out, "Come on in. Have a seat."

He pointed to his immediate right. Not knowing what else to do, I walked over to the chair and eased myself into it.

Once I was down, it occurred to me—a moment too late—why it was empty. The COO was the CEO's right hand. This was probably Angel's seat. Everyone in the room was staring at me like I had just sat on a ghost.

"It's a good thing you're here," Lorne continued. "We were just trying to figure out how we should get the news out. Got any thoughts?"

It was a simple enough question, and it was my $350,000-a-year job to be able to answer it.

My first official act as vice president of corporate communications was going to be managing the messaging surrounding the death of my own best friend.

"Right, right. Of . . . Of course," I stammered. "Well, I think . . ."

What the hell *did* I think? I was still too shocked to have any thought beyond the urge to curl up into a ball and weep uncontrollably for several days.

But that wasn't going to do anyone much good.

Part of what being a newspaper reporter had taught me, for better or worse, was how to compartmentalize. If I allowed myself to be overwhelmed by the emotion of what I was covering—the school shooting, the triple homicide, the toddler drowning—I would turn into a useless basket case.

Especially on deadline, I had to set my feelings aside and focus on the task in front of me.

So that's what I did.

I cleared my throat and said, "We have three main constituents we have to consider here: our employees, our customers, and then the public. We need to tailor our approach for each one."

"Go on," Lorne urged.

"With our employees, it needs to be a personal note from the CEO that acknowledges the extreme difficulty of this loss. Angel was a member of the Balco family, first and foremost. When you lose a family member, you don't just shrug it off. You mourn. This is a time when the CEO has to take the lead in showing everyone it's okay to grieve, and that the company will support them in that."

Lorne nodded.

"With our customers, we have to remember that they're going to hear about this one way or another. Angel was known within the industry. I'm sure some of the trade publications will write about this. It's better they hear it from us first. We say that this is a devastating loss and we're all shaken. But we also have to tactfully reassure them that the business of Balco will stop for nothing."

"The business of Balco will stop for nothing," Lorne repeated, almost like it was an advertising slogan he was trying out.

"I think it makes sense to have the Sales Team reach out individually to each of their accounts with an email or phone call, whatever they prefer. I'll write some boilerplate language that they can use, but they should customize it so it seems personal."

Now heads around the room were bobbing.

I continued: "And then with the public, we start by putting out a press release for legacy media and something softer for our socials—probably a tribute video about Angel. Do we know if the police are going to release anything?"

"We spoke briefly with a detective this morning, but I don't remember him mentioning anything about that," Lorne said, then looked toward a mustachioed man sitting midway down the table. "Sal, did I miss something?"

I recognized this was Michael "Sal" Salcedo, Balco's chief safety officer. He was responsible for minimizing risk at our facilities—as much as was possible in an industry where not all risk could be eliminated—and also for corporate security. He hadn't been on my round of interviews, but Angel had mentioned that I would probably interact with him now and then.

Toughest job at Balco. Everything that you could never anticipate going wrong becomes his fault.

"He didn't say anything about a press release, no," Sal confirmed.

Lorne turned to his executive assistant, a handsome, bearded, dark-haired man named Lucas Chandler.

"Can you send Curt the officer's contact info?"

"Of course," Lucas replied.

"Thanks," I said. "I doubt the national media will care, but the local media will pounce. A high-level businessman from Marin County killed during a carjacking in Oakland is red meat for them. A release will be enough to feed the midday news cycle, but we're going to need more for the afternoon and evening cycles. We should probably schedule a press conference—either in conjunction with the authorities or, if they're not playing along, on our own. I can certainly handle it, if you want, Lorne. But you're the face of the company. It should probably be you up there in front of the cameras."

"I hear you," he said. "Just let me know where and when."

"Good. Thanks. All three of these things need to happen, like, now. If any of you have feedback on specific things you think we should say, I'm ready to hear it. Otherwise, I have to get to work."

I pulled out a pen and my reporter's pad.

"Dang, son, you come prepared," Lorne said.

I showed no reaction. This was hardly the time to preen.

Lorne sighed noisily. "Okay, on the personal note from me, I just want to make it clear that . . . Look, everyone here loved Angel. He was a special guy. Oh, hell, look who I'm talking to. You know that better than anyone. I'm sorry."

"It's okay."

"Well, don't be afraid to lean into that. Sounds like you got a handle on the second and the third thing, too. Anyone have anything else to add?"

Across the table from me, I heard, "Are we going to address the elephant in the room?"

The question came from Chief Financial Officer Sidney Graves, a tall, Ichabod Crane–like figure with an angular face and a jutting chin. My interview with him had been brief and awkward. It wasn't just that he didn't have time for me; he was so full of his own self-importance, he wanted me to *know* he didn't have time for me.

Angel had told me two things about Graves that had stayed with me. One, he was, of all things, an amateur botanist. Two, he was among Angel's least favorite people at Balco.

Don't trust a word he says, Angel had warned me. *He has no integrity. He'll say one thing and then do something completely different, like the conversation never happened.*

"And what's that?" Lorne asked.

"That crime in this city is completely out of control," Sidney snapped. "That's what happens when you have a total joke for a district attorney who treats the police like they're the problem. We need to make that clear in whatever we put out. Angel Reddish paid the price for this DA's incompetence."

I was aware there had been a recall campaign against the DA here. The complaint was that in her zeal to reform the police, she had lost her focus on prosecuting bad guys. But she also had a lot of supporters who claimed that her critics were being racist and probably sexist: The DA was a Black woman.

It was ugly. And it was the last thing Balco needed to be weighing into at this moment.

Maybe a flack who had come up in the corporate world would think twice about contradicting the CFO in front of everyone who mattered in the company.

This flack came up in journalism.

We believed in speaking truth to power.

"All due respect, Sidney, this isn't the time to play politics," I said. "I don't want to make it look like Balco is using Angel's death to score points in a debate that no one has even invited us to."

"So we're just supposed to sit back and accept that a man can't drive home from work at night without being killed? That's ludicrous."

"That may be, but suggesting the district attorney is personally responsible for every crime that gets committed in this city is even more ludicrous," I shot back. "Listen, if Balco wants to enter into a thoughtful discussion about public safety at some point, let's do that. But that's not the conversation we're having today. We need to keep the focus on Angel."

"And ignore the larger issue?"

"For now? Frankly, yes. Especially when we don't necessarily have all the facts. I once worked at a paper where the story of the day was a quadruple homicide, and our lead op-ed columnist dashed off a piece about the urgent need for gun control. The next day, we learned the people had actually been stabbed to death. That's the problem with knee-jerk reactions: You never know what you're going to kick."

Sidney inhaled and was just launching his retort when Lorne held up a hand.

"Okay, okay," he said. "Everyone just cool it."

He tented his hands and closed his eyes. I knew I was out on a limb here—the new guy, arguing with the CFO, who had been here for years. Lorne's reaction was going to tell me a lot about whether I had a future at Balco or whether I was going to be looking for a new job before the moving truck even arrived.

I could have been imagining it, but I felt like everyone around the table was holding their breath.

Or maybe that was just me.

When Lorne's eyes finally opened, he had turned toward his CFO.

"Sorry, Sidney," Lorne said, "but I'm going with Curt's gut on this one. Let's resist the urge to editorialize and keep this about Angel."

Graves crossed his arms and pouted, shooting me a contemptuous glare.

My first hour on the job, and I had already made a powerful enemy.

"Anyone else have anything they want to add?" Lorne asked.

No one spoke.

"Okay," he said, now looking at me. "You mind letting me take a look at the note to the employees before you ship it out?"

"Not at all."

"Then we have a plan," he said. "Make sure you cc Lucas so I don't miss it."

Taking that as my cue to dismiss myself, I lifted myself out of my chair—Angel's chair—and departed the room.

As soon as I was out of the room, I stopped and called Page. She needed to know what had happened. She also needed to know she probably wouldn't be seeing her husband until very, very late.

The first words out of her mouth were, "Oh, Aiysha." The last were to tell me she loved me. The middle was mostly a lot of shock.

What was there to say, really?

We ended the call quickly. She knew that when breaking news upended my life, I didn't have time to linger.

I was halfway down the hall when I felt a sob working its way up my throat. I stopped for a second and leaned against the wall.

Then my phone dinged.

It was the contact information for an Oakland detective named Mando Fierro. I swallowed hard, straightened myself up, and continued down to the fourth floor.

I could cry later.

For now, I had a job to do.

CHAPTER 4

FOR ALL HER power, for all her wealth, for all the loyalty she inspired—and all the ruthlessness she commanded—the woman was invariably soft-spoken.

She never lost her temper.

She didn't roar or fume or carry about theatrically when she was upset.

No one could remember a time when she had raised the volume of her voice beyond a basic speaking level.

She simply wasn't someone who needed to yell to be heard or understood.

Or feared.

So, even though he was clearly displeased, she maintained a low, even tone.

"They killed him," the quiet woman said simply. "That wasn't the assignment."

There were others around, but the quiet woman ignored them. She was focused on a large, round-shouldered man with tattoos running up his neck to his face—the most prominent of which was a winking lizard that ran up one of his cheeks.

"It wasn't their fault," the large man said.

"You're making excuses?"

"He had a gun."

"So? Didn't they check him for weapons?"

"I guess not."

"That was careless. And stupid," the quiet woman said. "In which case, it *was* their fault. And if it was their fault, that means it was *your* fault."

Lizard Man shuffled his feet and looked down at the ground.

"But no one knew he'd be armed," Lizard Man said, his panic rising. "He was a businessman, not a soldier or a—"

"More excuses. You know how I feel about excuses."

"Yes."

Lizard Man was now looking down at his feet.

"Move on," the quiet woman said. "So he was armed. He still shouldn't have been killed. I said he was to be detained, not disposed of. This is going to create more trouble than it's worth."

"But he shot one of our men."

"So?"

"Well, what were they supposed to do?"

"They were supposed to follow their instructions."

"But he shot—"

"Yes. We've covered that. He shot one of them, and they lost their minds and started hacking him apart like animals. What were they possibly thinking?"

"We needed to make an example out of him. No one defies us like that."

The quiet woman grimaced, then gave a slight nod to others in the back of the room. It was the signal they had been waiting for. They moved in fast, clamping their hands on Lizard Man's shoulders and arms.

"No," the quiet woman said. And—again, without even the slightest rise in her voice—she clarified the matter: "No one defies *me* like that."

CHAPTER 5

THE OFFICE OF Corporate Communications at Balco was referred to as "the Comms Team," because everything in Lorne Murphy's company was supposed to be about teamwork.

It consisted of a dozen people, all of whom reported to me.

When I rounded the corner of the stretch of hallway where those people worked, I was quickly spotted by a woman with a loose bun of dark hair low on her head.

This, I knew from having spent many hours studying my team members—their job functions, their performance reports, their résumés—was Korynne Vuong, who had the title of communications coordinator but also served as my assistant. She had previously held a similar position at one of our competitors. Just like me, she was new on the job, having been hired a week earlier.

"Good morning, Curt," she said, standing up.

She said it loudly enough—almost like it had been a preordained signal for everyone else—that there were soon heads peeking up from cubicles and out of offices.

I had given a great deal of thought to the delicate task of managing this group. Most of them were older than me. All of them were more experienced in logistics. I knew they would be skeptical and more than a little leery of me, given that they would surely know I was primarily here because of my friendship with Angel.

It also didn't help that my predecessor had been fired because, as Angel had told me, "There was a Comms Team mutiny. He just didn't play well with others."

Given this—and the scar tissue that had surely formed because of it—my plan had been to traipse delicately at first, to defer whenever possible, to try to win them over by asking a lot of questions and listening carefully to their answers.

All that was now out the window.

We had a crisis to deal with.

"Good morning, Korynne," I said. "Good morning, everyone. Why don't we all gather 'round. I suppose you've all heard the news about Angel Reddish."

I could tell from their grim expressions that they had.

"All right, I was just up on the fifth floor, talking with Lorne and the others. We have a strategy, and we need to move quickly."

I walked them through the three-pronged approach and delegated various aspects of it to the appropriate team members.

Then I turned to Bob Brunato, the director of public and media relations and the No. 2 person on the team. A full generation older than me, he had a thick, side-parted mop of gray hair and an unassuming mien. He wore a blazer that was at least a size too big and looked like it had been purchased while I was still in high school.

Bob was probably as good a consigliere as I could have hoped for. He had been with Balco for thirty-three years—almost since the beginning—and therefore had a wealth of industry and institutional knowledge.

He also hadn't been a candidate for my job. The first time we spoke, he flatly told me he didn't want the position or its responsibility. His kids were well out of college, so he didn't need the money. He was on a downward slope toward retirement and had no interest trying to reach for another rung on the corporate ladder. He and his wife loved to spend time with their young grandchildren. He had accrued the maximum six weeks of annual vacation, and he intended to take every second of it.

"I'm at the age of life where I know what matters," he told me proudly. "Family is everything."

In short, he was unthreatening and unthreatened. I could already tell we were going to get along great.

"Bob, I was thinking I'd ghostwrite the piece by Lorne, which leaves the press release for you. Are you game?"

"You got it, boss," he said.

"I was going to call the detective assigned to the case so I could get the details and coordinate strategy. You want to come into my office with me and hop on?"

"Let's do it," he said, brandishing a yellow legal pad—no reporter's notebook for him.

He followed me into my office, which had a glass wall separating it from the hallway. There were a lot of glass walls around here. One of Balco's company values was "transparency." Whoever set up the space around here had taken that literally.

On the far side was a floor-to-ceiling window that let me look out at the Port of Oakland below, and the San Francisco skyline beyond.

Balco's interior design consultant had helped me pick out all my furniture, which was new and sleek and surely cost more than every desk I had used during my newspaper career combined.

Bob took one of the chairs on the other side of the desk. I sat down, pressed the speaker button on my desk phone—so he could eavesdrop—then dialed the number I had been given for Detective Mando Fierro.

"Fierro here."

"Detective Fierro, this is Curt Hinton. I work in Corporate Communications at Balco."

"Hello."

"I have my colleague Bob Brunato sitting here with me. We're putting together a press release and some internal communications about the death of Angel Reddish and I want to make sure we get all our facts straight. I should also disclose that Angel was my . . . my . . ."

Once again, the urge the break down rose up in me with surprising force.

I took a deep breath and hoped the officer didn't note my faltering. But for a few long seconds, I couldn't actually get any words to come out of my constricted throat.

Bob saved me by saying, "Curt and Angel were best friends. I considered Angel a friend, too. We're all pretty emotional today."

I nodded at Bob gratefully.

"Understood," the detective said.

I finally managed to recover use of my vocal cords and said, "Are we catching you at an okay moment to ask a few questions?"

"Sure."

"What can you tell us at this point about what happened?"

"Let's see. The victim—sorry, Mr. Reddish—was driving a Tesla Model S. According to your guys' security log, he left the Balco parking lot at nine-oh-three last night. He was then accosted at the intersection of Adeline and Third Street at nine-oh-seven. I don't want you putting this out to the public, but just for your own information, there's a freight company at that intersection that has a camera mounted on the corner of its building, so we got a pretty decent view of what went down. The freight company contacted us first thing this morning when they saw what happened and gave us the footage. What I'm about to tell you is solid."

"I appreciate that."

"There were at least four perpetrators. One of them blocked the intersection with a box truck so Mr. Reddish couldn't move forward. We didn't get plates on the truck and the DOT number was blacked out. These people weren't planning on being found."

"Right," I said.

"There appeared to be another vehicle blocking Mr. Reddish from behind, though it didn't show up on camera. All we could see were headlights. Mr. Reddish was approached by two perpetrators on foot. They were wearing ski masks and dark clothing. Both were armed. One pointed his weapon at Mr. Reddish and ordered him to get out of the car. Mr. Reddish complied.

"The second perpetrator opened the rear door for Mr. Reddish and appeared to order him to get into the back seat. The second perpetrator was also pointing his weapon at Mr. Reddish. Again, Mr. Reddish complied."

I had been scribbling notes furiously the whole time, as was a reporter's habit. But this made me stop.

"Wait, why would carjackers want Angel *in* the car? Wouldn't kidnapping him just slow them down?"

"Good question," Fierro said. "I have a theory on that. But let me just finish. As they got Mr. Reddish in the back seat, the first perpetrator went up to the driver's seat. The box truck moved out of the intersection and they drove off. From start to finish, the whole thing took about ninety seconds."

"So we're talking about a well-coordinated attack," I said.

"Yeah, these guys were pros," Fierro confirmed. "Anyhow, it's a straight shot from that intersection up to Lowell Park, which is where we found Mr. Reddish's body. He was . . . Are you sure you want to hear this part?"

I inhaled sharply. Bob gave me a worried glance.

"No, go ahead," I said.

"Okay. They cut him up pretty good. Crowded area like that, the perpetrators didn't want to risk bringing attention to themselves. They probably know we have ShotSpotter, so they did it with knives instead."

I was familiar with ShotSpotter, which had been deployed by some of the departments I covered. It used sensors along with GPS technology to isolate where a firearm had discharged, allowing police to respond quickly to gunfire.

My chin dropped to my chest. I could practically feel those blades as if they were cutting into my own skin.

I don't even know why it mattered. Dead was dead.

But somehow, if it was even possible, I felt the trauma of Angel's death all over again.

"We're still canvassing for witnesses, but it was dark by then," Fierro continued. "Not a lot of folks out at that time of night. We're also looking for cameras, but it's mostly private homes and churches surrounding the park. And he was found in the middle of the park, a few hundred yards from any structure. I don't know if we're going to get anything. We'll do our best."

"Sure."

"Now, just so you understand, what normally happens with carjackers around here is that they take the vehicle straight to the Port and get it loaded into a container before the victim can alert the authorities about what's happened. We're talking five, ten minutes tops. Those containers are thick steel, so even if there's a GPS tracker on the car, we can't find it. The container then ships out to Asia or Africa, where the car is sold on the black market. That's why our recovery rate on carjacked vehicles is so pathetic. Wherever it's going, it's a place where U.S. authorities have no jurisdiction."

Fierro paused for a moment, then said, "But that's not what happened here."

"Oh?"

"We found the car about ten miles away, in Eastmont. You familiar with the neighborhood?"

"Not really," I said.

"Well, it's pretty rough. The car was left by the side of the road with the windows down and the key fob in plain sight. It might as well have had a neon sign that said 'steal me.' But no one did. My guess is that thieves in Eastmont are too smart. They knew something that easy had to be a trap. So the car was still just sitting there when the sun came up. Someone who was out walking their dog spotted it. They knew it was way out of place and they called it in."

I could feel a thick blanket of confusion settling over me.

"What kind of carjacker goes through all the trouble to take a brand-new Tesla and then just leaves it somewhere to get taken by someone else?"

"My guess? Because that's exactly what the original perpetrators wanted to happen. Someone else takes the car—some stupid kid in the neighborhood or whatever. Eventually, they get caught, because they're not actually professional carjackers and they're not that smart. And then we're all over them for killing Angel Reddish."

"While the actual killers are long gone."

"Exactly," Fierro said. "This wasn't a carjacking. It was a murder made to look like a carjacking."

CHAPTER 6

THEY HAD BEEN sitting in a black Ford Explorer all morning, two men in plain suits, parked alongside Buena Vista Drive, just down from No. 27, where they could see the house—but not be seen from it.

The first one, the bald one with the bullet-shaped head, shifted in his seat.

He was originally from New Jersey. So he uttered an expletive; which, for him, was essentially just a way of clearing his throat. He finished the thought with, "This is boring. That pregnant bitch isn't going anywhere."

The second one looked like he had spent too much time outside, and he had the sun-damaged skin to show for it. He was from Utah, so the use of coarse language caused him to shake his head.

"You shouldn't call her that," Sun Damage said. "It's misogynistic."

"Massage-a-what?"

"Misogynistic. My daughter taught me that word. She's taking a course called 'Gender and Society' right now."

"That's one of those classes where they teach girls how to dress like boys, right?"

"I'm not sure about that. But she said the b-word is 'misogynistic,' which means you hate women."

"I don't hate women," Bullethead countered. "I like sleeping with them too much."

"Yeah, I don't think that counts."

"What? I'd sleep with that one," he said, jerking his head toward the house they were watching, No. 27. "Wouldn't you? Cute little redhead?"

Sun Damage grimaced. "Come on. She's pregnant."

"So? She's hot. I have a thing for preggos. I mean, hey, it's not like you gotta worry about getting them knocked up."

"That's inappropriate. You shouldn't say things like that."

"That I like preggos?"

"Yeah."

Bullethead scoffed. "You ask me, it's inappropriate if you don't. Didn't you bang your lady when she was pregnant?"

"Come on. Stop that."

"What are you going to do, report me to the FBI?"

It was a rhetorical question. But he still pulled out a gold FBI badge and waved it around.

"Relax. I'm just talking here," Bullethead said. "Besides, it passes the time until they finally decide the Reddish widow isn't coming anywhere near here."

"She might. You know how wives stick together."

"Please. We ain't never gonna see her or her ten million bucks ever again."

CHAPTER 7

MANDO FIERRO DIDN'T have any more pertinent information to share, but he promised to keep us informed if there were any significant developments in the case.

In the meantime, he gave me the number for his PIO—public information officer—with whom I'd coordinate efforts on media releases and press conferences.

As soon as I ended the call, I tossed my reporter's pad on the desk in front of me, leaned back in my ergonomically perfect chair, and buried my face in my hands.

"Good Lord," I said, releasing a long breath. "I can't believe this."

With my eyes still closed, I rubbed my temples for a few seconds. When I opened them again, Bob Brunato was looking at me with concern.

"You okay?" he asked.

"No," I said honestly.

"Sorry."

I felt my head shaking. "Who would want to murder Angel? He was . . . He was one of the nicest guys you could ever meet. He never raised his voice. He always had a smile on his face. I realize this sounds like all the clichés you'll ever hear at a eulogy rolled into one, but it's all true. I could tell you a hundred stories about him going out of his way to help people, just because that's who he was. He wasn't someone who made enemies."

Bob's face turned into an expression I couldn't quite read.

"What?" I asked.

"I don't know. I'd just be speculating."

"About what?"

Bob looked down at his yellow legal pad. "Nothing. Forget I said it."

"Bob, my best friend was murdered last night, and I don't have the slightest idea of why. If you know something . . ."

"No, no, I don't *know* anything. That's my point. But . . ."

He stopped himself. He was studying that legal pad intently.

Then he finally looked back up.

"Logistics can be a tough business, you know? Whether you're talking about trucking, or warehousing—or, hell, even the sales staff here. You wouldn't want to know about some of the stuff they do to get business coming in the door. We bid on these huge, multimillion-dollar contracts where there frankly isn't a lot to differentiate one company from another. Most of our clients have gift acceptance policies, and yet somehow they end up at the Super Bowl on Balco's dime. You get what I mean?"

"Sure, but what does that have to do with Angel? He's bribing people, or . . ."

"No, nothing like that. I'm just trying to paint the picture for you. Our job on the Comms Team is to put this shiny veneer on everything for the press and the public. But the reality is . . . more complicated than that. Every truck that comes in and out of here has its own story. Every warehouse worker here is . . . They're good people, but you're not talking about class valedictorians."

He lifted his eyebrows at me. I graduated first in my small high school class in Tennessee, which Bob must have gleaned from reading my application materials.

I really needed to take that line off my résumé.

"My point is, the warehouse isn't Sunday school," he continued. "We've had supervisors bail people out of jail when they need an extra body for a shift. We've had warrants served on people while they were at work. They've literally been dragged off the warehouse floor. Some of these guys are coming from Latin America, where they were in MS-13. God only know what they've done."

"Okay, but even if they're the most brutal gangbangers on the planet, what did Angel do to piss them off?" I asked. "What's the 'why' here?"

"Isn't it obvious?" Bob shot back. And when I shook my head, he said, "The IWW vote."

The International Warehouse Workers-Local 37. The union that roughly three thousand of our employees were possibly going to join.

"What does that have to do with Angel?" I asked.

"What *doesn't* it have to do with Angel? Lorne was using Angel as a front man for the company. It was his job to talk those guys out of joining the union—to convince them that Balco had treated them well and whatnot."

"Isn't that our job?" I asked.

"Well, yeah, the Comms Team was involved, too. But, honestly, look at me. Look at you. Not a lot of people like us in the warehouse."

I was going to object—part of being a newspaper reporter is learning how to connect with anyone—but I understood his point.

There was no such thing as color blindness in America. Anyone who said so was peddling a myth.

Bob continued: "Angel had real influence with those guys. The Black guys, I mean, of course they'd listen to him. And the Hispanic guys, he'd whip out his Spanish and talk about his mother's *la bandera*. They knew he was from management, but he'd really *talk* to them. And listen. And even work with them. He'd go in wearing his Carhartts and his Timberlands. He wasn't afraid to get his hands dirty, and you know Angel. He was strong as an ox. Guys in the warehouse idolized him. They knew he had a tryout with the Patriots and met Tom Brady and all that."

I had sort of forgotten that chapter of Angel's life. He was a starter by his senior season at Northwestern. He hadn't distinguished himself enough to get drafted in the NFL, but he had still appeared on enough game film against the likes of Michigan and Ohio State that scouts had noticed him. After the draft, the Patriots invited him in for a free agent tryout.

It never went anywhere. It certainly didn't help that Angel had been more focused on improving his GMAT scores than his 40-yard-dash time.

Still. Tom Brady.

"So some pro-union person in the warehouse killed Angel to shut him up?" I asked.

"Or someone from IWW itself," Bob suggested. "You're talking about three thousand new members. That's millions of dollars in dues revenue. Plus, you know how these unions think. Everything is win-at-all-costs. This Balco vote, it's a big vote for them. It's getting a lot of attention. They lose it, and it looks bad. Other places where they're thinking about unionizing say, 'Eh, screw it. Balco didn't, why should we?'"

I turned out the window and watched for a moment as a super-Panamax container ship glided toward one of the unloading cranes.

"Should we call Fierro back and tell him?" I asked.

"I'm sure he's already looking into it, but it couldn't hurt."

I let out a gusty sigh. "Okay. I'll do that, and then I'll start on Lorne's statement. You got enough to get rolling on the press release?"

"Sure."

"Good. Let's each get a rough draft together and circle back in . . ."

My voice trailed off. I didn't want to be the new boss, making unrealistic demands. How long *did* it take for a typical flack to write a release?

"Give me an hour," Bob said, reading my mind.

"Perfect," I said.

I called up Fierro and quickly informed him of Angel's anti-union efforts. The detective thanked me and said he'd keep it in mind.

Then I did my best to put that out of my head and concentrate on Lorne's note to the employees. I didn't really have time to get picky with words; and, in any event, no one would be expecting Lorne Murphy to suddenly sound like Shakespeare. So I kept it simple and wrote from the heart. Ultimately, it wasn't very difficult to find nice things to say about Angel—whether it was in my voice or someone else's.

I just couldn't believe what I was writing. The whole thing was so surreal. There was this childlike part of me that kept trying to wish it away, like this was some terrible dream and I'd soon wake up.

With fifteen minutes to go before Bob and I were scheduled to reconvene, I had a reasonably competent draft. I sent it off to Lorne Murphy for his review, cc'ing Lucas, as requested.

What Bob had said about Angel and the union was still bouncing around in my head.

Out of curiosity, I googled IWW-Local 37 and navigated to its website. The union had forty-two thousand members across California. Its offices were located in San Francisco, in a historic building in the city's Mission District.

The home page was filled with headlines about the union fighting the good fight on behalf of its members. There was a video titled "Heroes Arrested in Bakersfield," where IWW-37 workers were blocking trucks from entering a warehouse in protest of what they said were dangerous working conditions. There was other verbiage on the page about advocacy efforts, worker solidarity, anti-discrimination initiatives, and so on.

My eyes scanned the top-of-page navigation, and I clicked on "About Us."

That led me to a page titled "Leadership," which was dedicated to IWW-Local 37 president Rudy Szymanski. He was a middle-aged man with a paunchy face, slicked-back dark hair, and a neatly tended goatee.

According to his bio, he had started as a rank-and-file member who then became steadily more involved in union leadership. Eventually, he joined IWW's staff, where he specialized in collective bargaining negotiations.

Seven years ago, he was elected to his first term as IWW president. He was now serving his second term. He boasted of winning concessions in salary, workplace safety, and benefits from the likes of Amazon, Sysco, and FedEx, and he pledged to work tirelessly on behalf of workers.

At the bottom of the page, there were "Statements from IWW-Local 37 President Rudy Szymanski."

The very first one actually made me gasp.

Szymanski warns of big lies from Balco brass

I clicked the link. The piece covered how there was a vote scheduled to certify IWW-Local 37 to represent the three thousand Balco employees who worked in the company's two California warehouses. It went on to say:

> Even though workers are exercising their PROTECTED LEGAL RIGHT to organize, management will do ANYTHING to prevent this from happening! This includes spreading lies and deceptions to intimidate workers and convince them to vote against their own best interest.
>
> **MANAGEMENT LIE #1:** Worker salaries won't increase, because the company already pays top-of-the-line wages.
> **FACT:** Collective bargaining works! The average new IWW member received a 12 percent raise in their first union contract.
>
> **MANAGEMENT LIE #2:** Worker take-home pay will actually decrease because of union dues.
> **FACT:** Dues average just 1.5 percent of your salary per month. The improvement in your wages, benefits, and working conditions will be far greater!
>
> **MANAGEMENT LIE #3:** IWW will make workers strike, causing them to go weeks or months without paychecks.
> **FACT:** IWW will never force you to do anything. Only YOU can vote to strike. 98 percent of our negotiations are resolved without labor stoppages. In the unlikely event of

a strike, the IWW Strike Fund is available to cover your lost wages.

MANAGEMENT LIE #4: Workers will be better off if they are "team players" and don't certify as a union, because then the company will continue to treat them like "family."
FACT: Management only cares about itself and the exorbitant bonuses it collects when it squeezes more profits out of workers. If they're such team players, why aren't they getting Rivians for everyone? The family you need to be looking out for is your own.

It irked me that instead of simply acknowledging that Balco and IWW-37 had differing viewpoints—perspectives that both could be arrived at quite honestly—they had to call us liars. And the line about the Rivians was nothing more than a cheap shot.

It was the kind of inflammatory language that didn't help anything.

I suppose it was still fairly standard pro-union, anti-company rhetoric. And I would have dismissed it as such.

Except at the very bottom of the statement, beneath a headline that read, "Paid to Push Management Lies," there was a picture of Angel.

CHAPTER 8

THE ROOM WAS windowless.

Its recessed lighting had been carefully aimed so as not to cast a glare on the banks of flat-screen monitors that covered one wall, stretching from waist level up to the top of the twelve-foot ceilings.

On a long desk in front of the monitors there was a computer with its own curved fifty-seven-inch screen. It was wired directly into a nearby mainframe, which controlled the many cameras that captured the images appearing on the screens.

Some of the cameras were meant to be seen. Others, not so much. Racks of servers assured that all the images being captured were kept and could be reviewed at any time for up to a year.

A single command chair was perched in front of the computer.

Several more chairs flanked it so that others could also sit and observe.

That was the primary purpose of the windowless room.

To keep watch.

On everything.

And everyone.

Few people knew of the room's existence, or of how extensive its network was, or of just how many people it observed at once.

This was the nerve center.

The monitors flickered at varying levels of brightness, each showing a different place. They were in color—except when they went into thermal mode at night—so the effect of the dozens of screens during the day was to merge into an ever-shifting mosaic.

Any screen could, at any moment, be changed to any camera in the network.

But the man at the command chair was only looking at the curved screen in front of him. He had an image zoomed in as far as it would go.

After a few moments, he lifted a nearby phone, a landline with the most sophisticated encryption on the market.

"Yes?"

"You told me to keep an eye on the new guy and whether he made any moves with regard to the union?"

"Yeah? And?"

"He's on the website right now."

"What's he doing?"

"He's looking at the statement from the president regarding Reddish."

"Is he?"

"Yes."

"And how is he taking it?"

"He looks upset."

There was a pause on the other side of the landline.

"Okay. Once he's done, send me the whole thing. I want to see it for myself."

"Will do."

"Thanks. And keep watching."

CHAPTER 9

I WAS STILL lost in the photo when Bob Brunato returned to my office a few minutes later with a single sheet of paper in his hands.

He took one look at my distressed expression and asked, "What's up?"

I swiveled the screen so he could see it.

"Wow," he said, after he was done reading. "That just about says it all, doesn't it?"

"Do you think I should show that to Fierro?"

Bob pondered this for a moment. "Let's see what else he finds. In and of itself, you can't make too big a deal of one photo. If it turns out to be part of a bigger pattern, then it becomes evidence."

"Okay. Agreed."

"Anyhow, here's the release," he said, sliding the paper across the desk.

This was one of the generational differences between me and Bob. It never would have even occurred to me to print out something like that.

I read it through quickly. It was letter-perfect. After thirty-three years of doing this, it probably should have been. Then again, I had definitely bumped across some newspaper reporters with thirty-three years of experience who still couldn't write a coherent thank-you letter, so I didn't want to take this for granted.

"This is great, thanks," I said.

"For something like this, we normally use PR-Newswire in addition to our own distribution channels."

"Yes, of course," I said.

The clicking of heels interrupted whatever I was going to say next. Through the glass wall, I could see Korynne Vuong coming toward my office. This was the first time I noticed she was wearing a relatively short black skirt. It showed off her legs, which were lean and powerful—runner's legs.

She poked her head through the doorway. Her dark eyes were wide.

"Lorne wants to see you in his office right away," she said.

My stomach lurched. There must have been something wrong with the piece I had written for him. If he had liked it, he would have just replied to my email and been done with it.

"Yeah, no worries," I said, trying to sound nonchalant and failing. I stood and announced, "I guess I should be on my way, then."

Korynne seemed appropriately stricken. Bob just nodded grimly.

I marched off to the elevators, my dread rising along with the car that took me back up to the fifth floor. I presented myself to Lorne's assistant, Lucas Chandler, who looked up and said, "Curt, hi. He's waiting for you."

Lucas stood, turned, and lightly tapped three times on a polished stainless-steel door that was set into the surrounding brick. No transparent glass walls here.

He opened the door a crack and announced, "Curt is here."

"Send him on in," Lorne's voice twanged.

His space was very different from the industrial chic outside. The room was all plush carpet, cherry paneling, and rich leather sitting surfaces, like it had all been plucked off the pages of *Cigar Aficionado*.

There was a desk on the far side of the room. To my left there was an eight-person conference table. To my right was a seating area, which consisted of a leather couch, love seat, and recliner set around an oval coffee table.

That's where Lorne was. He stood as I entered.

Nearby, staying seated, was another man, a rather odd-looking creature. He was in his seventies but still rail thin, with well-creased tawny skin, effervescent blue eyes, and ringlets of white hair. He wore a Hawaiian shirt with the top two buttons undone, board shorts, and flip-flops.

I had no idea who he was, but he came off as a certain California archetype: the boomer surf bum.

"Got the thing you wrote for me," Lorne said.

I inwardly cringed, waiting for him to destroy me with his next sentence.

Then he said, "It's great. I just wanted to say thanks in person. You hit all the right notes. Made me sound pretty good for a dumb ol' Texan."

I was still absorbing the compliment when the surf bum piped up from the couch and said, "Don't pay attention to the country bumpkin act. It's usually around the time he convinces people how stupid he is that he's actually outsmarting them."

The surf bum's voice wasn't what I expected. It was high and nasally, almost like it belonged on a Muppet.

Lorne chuckled, then said, "Curt Hinton, meet Gehrig Weiskopf."

It was all I could do to keep my eyes from bugging out of my head. *This* was Gehrig Weiskopf?

At least now I knew why I had never seen a picture of the man. No one would believe that someone who looked like a roadie for the Beach Boys had created a $3.2 billion company.

I flashed back to the story Angel had told me about Balco's founding. The company spent its early years bumping along, barely clinging to existence. Then along came NAFTA, the North American Free Trade Agreement, which went into effect starting January 1, 1994.

Weiskopf made a huge bet: that the burgeoning computer and electronics companies in Silicon Valley would take advantage of the new deal and start assembling many of their products in Mexico, where the labor was cheaper.

He sold a collection of investors on his plan, and leveraged himself and the company to the hilt to establish a presence south of the border, where few American logistics companies had a significant foothold at the time. He carved out a niche for Balco, shipping printed circuit boards, electrical components, and other direct materials down to Mexico; then shipping finished products back.

The gamble paid off. The surfer essentially rode two waves: the rise of NAFTA and the explosive growth of Silicon Valley.

As a private company, Balco didn't release quarterly profit statements. But even if it was operating with lean margins—I had learned that low single digits wasn't unusual in the logistics industry—it had to be making at least a hundred million a year, and it had been doing it for a long time. Gehrig Weiskopf was surely a billionaire several times over.

It obviously hadn't changed too much about him. Certainly not his clothing. His entire outfit looked like it could be purchased at a Salvation Army thrift store for ten bucks.

He stood and reached out a sinewy brown arm to shake my hand.

"Call me Rig," he said.

"Hi, Curt Hinton."

"Someday, you should sit down with Rig," Lorne gushed. "He's got a lot of great old stories about the early days of the company. Tell him the one about Las Vegas."

Rig waved him off. "Oh, he doesn't want to hear about that. I was a very different person back then."

"If you don't tell him, I will," Lorne threatened.

"Fine. This would have been early on . . . Ninety-four? Ninety-five? We were barely making it. I couldn't get anyone to pay me on time. The bank where I had a line of credit had informed me it wasn't going to give me another dime. It was a Friday. I was down to my last four thousand bucks and I owed thirty grand in rent on a warehouse that was already past due. The landlord told me that if I didn't pay him by Monday, he'd kick me out and liquidate everything inside to pay what I owed him. I don't know if legally he could do that, but I didn't want to find out. That would have effectively been the end of Balco.

"I had already tapped out every investor, every friend, every contact I ever made trying to keep things afloat. I didn't know what else to do. So I withdrew all four thousand bucks from the bank and drove overnight to Vegas, figuring I'd just have to get hot. I lost three grand at the blackjack table before I even knew what hit me. I was so pissed. I figured it was all over. But I thought, what the hell, I might as well go down in a blaze of glory. I went over to the roulette table and, from out of nowhere, the number seventeen floated into my head. So I put everything I had on seventeen and prayed like hell."

He paused, then hit me with the punch line: "And now you know why all company Wi-Fi passwords have the number seventeen in them."

Lorne smiled broadly. "That story aside, Rig built this company with a lot of foresight and a lot of hard work."

"And a lot of luck," Rig added. "I've come to believe Balco is something the universe wanted."

"Anyhow, take a load off for a second," Lorne said. "In addition to thanking you for that piece, we wanted to run something by you."

He sank into the love seat. Rig took the couch, leaving the recliner for me.

"We were just talking about Angel," Lorne continued, shaking his head. "This is so tough. So tough. It was Rig's idea to hire Angel, you know. I thought he was too inexperienced to be COO. But Rig convinced me. He said sometimes you just have to go with the most talented person, no matter their age. As usual, he was right."

"Angel would have made a great CEO someday," Rig said. "He was very wise."

"We've been talking about what we might be able to do to honor him—his memory," Lorne said. "I know we've got time to figure out what feels right. But we were kicking around establishing a scholarship at Northwestern? The Angel Reddish Scholarship. It could go to an underprivileged kid who wanted to study business. What do you think?"

"I'm sure Angel would love that," I said. "But I have to be honest. I've also been thinking a lot this morning about his family. He had a son, you know. Elijah. If you were feeling generous"—and here, I knew I was really talking to the billionaire in the room—"maybe set up some kind of educational trust for Elijah?"

"Well, I don't know if that's going to be necessary," Lorne said.

"Why not?"

"This is . . . maybe not something you should put in a release or anything, but part of his compensation package was a life insurance policy that Balco paid for. Everyone in our C-suite gets one. Angel's was worth ten million dollars. His widow and son are well taken care of."

"Oh," I said, sounding more surprised than I perhaps intended.

Angel had never mentioned that to me, though it wasn't like we had detailed conversations about his financial planning.

"A carjacking like this ought to make collecting pretty straightforward," Lorne said. "I'm sure she won't have any problems."

"Yeah, about the carjacking, though," I said. "I spoke to the detective working the case. He seems to think there's something else going on."

"Like what?" Lorne asked.

I walked him and Rig through the car being found in Eastmont, leading Fierro to believe the carjacking was really a smoke screen.

"My God," Lorne said, shaking his head. "Okay, so if it wasn't carjackers, who was it?"

"Bob Brunato seems to think it's connected to the certification vote. Either someone from the union or someone who wants to see the union win."

"Does Sal know about this yet?" Lorne asked.

"I haven't spoken to him, no."

"I'll talk to him," Lorne said.

Rig, who seemed to have only barely been paying attention to our exchange, sang out, "Or, you could just let it go."

Lorne's head whipped toward Rig, who continued, "There's no sense in fighting this. If the employees want a union, we should let them have it."

I could practically hear Lorne's teeth grinding as he said, "Rig and I have a bit of a difference of opinion on this one. To me, unions are like ants at a picnic. They're a nuisance. And once they show up, you'll never get rid of 'em."

"Now, Lorne, you're showing your againstness," Rig admonished, as if it made him sad. He turned to me and explained, "We cannot be *against* things in this world. We have to find a way to be *for* things. Our universe abhors againstness."

Lorne cleared his throat in a way that hinted of agitation. "We don't have time to get into that right now. Why don't you have Curt go out to your place in Stinson Beach sometime soon and you can share your theories then?"

"I have a little surfing hut there," Rig confided in me. "You'll love it."

"Great," I said, because what other response could I give?

"Anyhow," Lorne said, clearly trying to change the subject. "I don't want us to jump to any conclusions prematurely here. But if it turns out the union is involved, you better believe we're not going to take it lying down."

"Which will only create more againstness," Rig said.

"Yeah, well," Lorne said, and then seemed to sequester whatever he was about to say somewhere in his throat. "I'm going to have Legal nose around on that scholarship. Meanwhile, Curt has a lot of work to do. Let's let him get to it."

Lorne stood, so I took the hint and did the same.

"Thanks again for the beautiful piece you wrote for me. Feel free to send it out to everyone as soon as you're ready. And if you feel like we need to do a press conference, just let Lucas know what time."

"Will do," I said.

I pivoted toward Rig and said, "It was very nice meeting you."

Rig murmured something in reply that I didn't quite catch. He was now gazing out the window, seemingly at peace, content to not be against anything.

Lorne, on the other hand, was still simmering.

CHAPTER 10

THE CALL HAD been arranged through channels, as these calls always were.

As far as the wider world was concerned, the entities taking part in the call weren't supposed to have anything to do with one another.

Their partnership, while mutually beneficial, was secret.

And illegal.

On one end of the line was a man who was essentially a messenger. He would faithfully relay what had been said to a higher authority on his side. He had power, to a degree, but only so much; and both men on the call understood this.

On the other end of the line was Balco CEO Lorne Murphy. He had power, too.

But also only to a degree.

Both men were well aware of this fact, even if neither would acknowledge it explicitly.

They went through a terse exchange of greetings that they recognized as necessary, though neither relished it.

The messenger just wanted to get on with it.

"My boss wants you to know that what happened to Reddish was an accident," he said. "All we wanted to do was talk to him. Things went wrong. This was not our intention. We sincerely apologize."

"Yeah, well, you tell your boss I'm still pissed," the CEO fumed. "What happened here is completely unacceptable. Completely unacceptable. This may be how you do business. It's not how we do business. That needs to be respected. Am I making that clear?"

The messenger said, "Yes, I understand."

He did not like being lectured. He also recognized that his job was to listen.

And, in this case, to take it.

"You guys doing something like this, it jeopardizes everything," Murphy said. "Angel Reddish wasn't some hick off the farm. He's our damn COO. He's known and respected in this community. You can't just kill someone like that and expect it won't be noticed. An incident like this invites a lot of questions from a lot of people we don't want asking questions—is that clear?"

"Yes," the messenger said.

"Something like this cannot happen again. Absolutely cannot," Murphy said. "We can't do business with y'all if this is the kind of partner you're going to be."

"Understood."

"Also, tell your boss the terms aren't changing. Not after this. We have a deal and that's that. We don't negotiate at gunpoint."

The messenger took in a sharp breath. His boss would not like that at all.

"I will relay your thoughts," the messenger said.

"Good. That's all I have to say. Anything on your end?"

“Yes. What about Gillespie?”

“What about him?”

“Has the matter been dealt with?”

“The matter is contained,” Murphy said. “We have no indication whatsoever it’s going to become a larger issue.”

“And how do you know this?”

“Because we’ve been watching him and we’re taking care of things on our end. That’s all you need to know. Are we done? Is there anything else?”

“No.”

“Good,” Murphy said.

The line went dead.

The messenger took a moment to collect his thoughts, then walked down a hallway covered in magnificent, handmade tile.

After knocking on a door, he heard a soft, “Come in.”

The quiet woman was sitting on an ornate Queen Anne–style couch in a room that could have been hewn from Windsor Castle.

She had been reading a book.

“What is it?” she asked in her usual understated tone.

“Lorne Murphy is angry,” the messenger said.

“I expected as much.”

“He says something like this cannot happen again.”

“Of course. Did he threaten to end the arrangement?”

“Yes.”

“Do you think he’s serious?”

The messenger thought on this for a moment. Beyond merely listening, part of his job was to understand Balco’s business.

"No. He cannot afford to do that."

The quiet woman took this in thoughtfully. "Good," she said.

"One more thing. You won't like it."

"Yes?"

"He says the terms aren't changing. He seems to believe what happened with Reddish has given him a certain amount of leverage to make demands."

"Does he now?" the quiet woman said. "Well, I guess we'll see about that."

CHAPTER 11

I SPENT THE remainder of the morning and into the afternoon compartmentalizing, ignoring the pain of Angel's death, dealing with inquiries from the press and from within Balco, forcing myself to disregard that the subject matter was my dead best friend.

As it turned out, the Oakland Police did not plan on putting out a press release about the murder of Angel Reddish. The city averaged 120 homicides a year and was not particularly keen to announce another one.

Department policy was to only put out a release about a homicide when there was an arrest.

That left Balco as the only voice doing the talking. And there was enough interest in the story from the local media—as predicted—that we decided it made sense to hold a press conference.

We scheduled it for four o'clock outside the entrance to Balco corporate headquarters.

Korynne was able to dig up a temporary backdrop for us that had the Balco logo screen-printed on it. Between that and a podium for the microphones, my hope was that we looked competent and professional without making it seem like this was a company branding event.

All of the local stations sent someone, including several that planned to do live remotes, which meant their trucks had to come inside the Balco compound. Print and radio were represented, too. It made for a madhouse atmosphere and it drove the Balco security people wild.

I had to explain to Sal Salcedo, the chief safety officer, that reporters might not look all that reputable, but they truly weren't in the business of hijacking FTLs of semiconductors.

We got underway more or less on time, which I considered to be a small miracle. I had never actually conducted a press conference in my life. But I had attended more than enough of them that I knew how they were supposed to look and feel.

I stuck with the facts of the crime, not mentioning any theories about who was behind it. Because that's all they were at this point: theories. I couldn't exactly go slandering IWW based on a hunch and a photo.

Next, I asked that anyone who might have seen anything—either at the scene of the carjacking, or at the park where his body was discovered, or near where the car was found—to please contact the Oakland PD's tips line.

Then I turned it over to Lorne, who quickly became the star of the show. He was poised and polished, extolling Angel and talking about what a loss this was for the company and the community.

Lorne had obviously gone through media training at some point in his life, and he had absorbed its lessons well. He understood how to deliver sound bites in a succinct, coherent fashion. His Texas charm played well on camera.

Together, we fielded a few questions. But those petered out pretty quickly, because we really didn't have a lot of answers.

When it was over, Lorne cornered me just offstage.

"Hey, glad I caught you. You did a nice job here," he said. Then he surprised me by saying, "Now it's time for you to go home."

"Excuse me?"

"Go home," he repeated. "Hug your wife, drink some whiskey, have a good cry, do whatever you gotta do. You lost your best friend today. You gotta give yourself some time to process that."

I took in a deep breath and began my objection with, "But I have to—"

"I already talked to Bob Brunato," Lorne cut me off, resting a hand on my shoulder. "He's an old pro. He can handle anything else that comes down the pike. There'll still be plenty of dragons to slay tomorrow. Go home. That's an order from your CEO, you understand?"

"O-okay," I said.

"Good man," Lorne said, giving me a paternal smile. "And I don't want you checking emails or taking calls when you get there, either. Got it?"

"Yes, sir."

Lorne released his grip on my shoulder and made his way back inside the building. I defied his order for a little while, just long enough to make sure the TV people doing stand-ups had everything they needed. But eventually, Bob shooed me off.

Rush-hour traffic—and the fact that I had never driven the route before—kept my brain occupied during my return home.

But when I turned onto Buena Vista Drive and drove up the ridge until the Barbie DreamHouse came into view, it suddenly struck me as absurd.

Honestly, what were we *doing* here? We didn't belong in this extravagant house any more than I belonged making this exorbitant salary working at a logistics company, a business about which I was essentially ignorant beyond a few simple talking points.

With Angel by my side, backstopping me every inch of the way, I might have been able to fake my way through it until I actually knew what I was talking about.

Without Angel? I stood no chance. It was like my very foundation had been swept out from under me.

I was suddenly exhausted and scared. I wanted to quit, run, and hide, in roughly that order. I briefly allowed myself to give in to the fantasy of returning to the Midwest and my going-nowhere job; to our modest townhouse with its shabby furniture; to the known, the comfortable, the sensible.

Then, as I clicked the button to open the two-car garage that I couldn't afford and parked the Rivian that wasn't mine, I reminded myself it was too late to go back.

My newspaper wasn't going to rehire me; it was constantly shedding jobs, not adding them. Our townhouse now belonged to someone else.

Without Balco's housing stipend, we couldn't afford the rent on the Barbie DreamHouse for more than about six seconds. Without my Balco salary, we couldn't afford to live, period.

We had already spent more than half my signing bonus on clothes, living expenses, and paying off credit card debts. I had to stay at least six months before that money was technically mine, and I certainly couldn't afford to pay it back. The money we had netted from the sale of the townhouse wouldn't cover it.

So, basically, without Balco, me and my pregnant wife would be unemployed, broke, and homeless.

Which meant I really had no choice but to buckle down and find a way to get through this. Quitting couldn't even enter my thoughts.

If Lorne Murphy and Balco came to their senses and decided to get rid of me, so be it. Unless and until that happened, I just had to give this job everything I had.

With that resolved, I pushed through the door from the garage, which opened into the back of the kitchen.

Page was sitting at the island, perched on one of our brand-new mid-century modern barstools. The hanging pendant lights above were casting a soft glow down on her, catching some of the natural strawberry blonde highlights in her red hair, which fell perfectly around her face. She was wearing an old long-sleeve crewneck T-shirt with horizontal stripes that hugged her chest just so—and was now getting tighter around her belly.

She didn't have on a smudge of makeup, had clearly put zero thought into her appearance, and it didn't matter. I was, as usual, dumbstruck by her beauty; and by how lucky I was to have her.

"Hey," I said.

She looked up from the crossword puzzle she had been doing and, without a word, crossed the kitchen to wrap me in a fierce embrace.

That hug was easily the best thing that had happened to me all day.

She smelled faintly of cocoa butter, which she had taken to rubbing on her stomach because she had read it would help ward off stretch marks.

I had already grown to love that smell.

The other aroma now filling my nose was the familiar combination of garlic, oregano, basil, and tomato pouring from the warm oven. Page had made lasagna.

It suddenly occurred to me the two Clif Bars I had pulled from the fourth-floor vending machine were long since metabolized. I was famished.

I went to separate from her, but that just made Page pull me even closer. I gave into it for a little while longer, until she finally released her grip.

"How are you?" she asked, her blue eyes already filling with tears.

If I gave into the urge to cry with her, I feared we'd never stop. So I said, "Too hungry and tired to talk about it now."

"I made lasagna," she said. "Actually, I made two lasagnas. One for us and one for Aiysha. I texted her earlier but she didn't answer. I don't want to be a bother, but I figured we could run it over later and just slip it through the door or something."

Page was originally from Wisconsin, a place where they believed that grief was best handled with food that had cheese slathered on top.

As we waited for the lasagnas to finish cooking, I filled her in on the details of my day. She had just removed the baking dishes from the oven when the doorbell rang.

We took a moment to exchange puzzled glances. Other than Angel and Aiysha, we didn't know anyone here yet.

I went to the front door to find two men dressed in dark suits on our front porch. One was bald. The other was darkly tanned.

"My name is Agent Frisch," the first one said in an accent that sounded like it came from somewhere in the New York area. He held up a gold badge with an eagle perched atop it.

He then gestured to his partner. "This is Agent Bastian. We're with the FBI. Can we come in and ask you a few questions?"

CHAPTER 12

DURING MY TIME as a newspaper reporter, I talked to cops on a near-daily basis. Interacting with law enforcement didn't faze me. Cops were just people.

That said, I had never dealt with the FBI. And I certainly never thought two of their agents would show up at my doorstep unannounced at six o'clock at night.

"Uh, yeah, of course," I said, stepping aside. "Come on in."

Page was a step or two behind me as Frisch and Bastian entered our foyer.

"This is my wife, Page."

"Good evening, Mrs. Hinton," Bastian said. "We're very sorry for the intrusion, ma'am."

"Good evening, gentlemen," Page said back.

Frisch handed me a business card with his name and the FBI logo embossed on it. I held out my hand and pointed to the left. "Why don't you come into the living room and have a seat?"

"Thank you, sir," Bastian said.

Frisch nodded his smooth egg of a head at me as he passed.

That we resided in a house with a living room—a sunken living room, no less—was still bizarre to me. This one featured a stone fireplace, two recliners, and an aircraft carrier of a sectional couch that occupied an area roughly equal to what our bedroom had been back in our townhouse.

"I already talked to Detective Fierro from the Oakland Police this morning," I said as everyone settled in. "I really don't know much of anything beyond what he told me."

"Right, right," Frisch said. "We just want to make sure all our bases are covered."

"Of course, but . . . I'm not trying to give you a hard time, I just don't understand: How does Angel's murder concern the FBI?"

"Murder is a federal crime, Mr. Hinton," Bastian said.

"Well, I know that, but you guys . . . My understanding is the FBI doesn't usually take jurisdiction over something like this. Are you helping the Oakland Police with their investigation somehow?"

Frisch looked to Bastian, who returned Frisch's glance.

A brief but awkward silence ensued until Bastian said, "As I'm sure you know, Balco is involved in interstate commerce. If someone crosses state lines in the commission of a crime, that comes under FBI jurisdiction."

"So the people who murdered Angel came from out of state?"

"That's a line of the investigation we're exploring, yes."

Frisch added: "The Oakland PD is not yet aware of our interest in this case. And if it's all the same to you, we'd like to keep it that way."

I didn't think a turf war between the Oakland PD and the FBI was in anyone's interest, and I already didn't like the feeling that I was somehow in the middle of it.

"So I'm not supposed to tell the Oakland PD that we've talked? I'm not sure I . . . I don't know if I'm comfortable with that."

Bastian and Frisch again exchanged wary looks.

"We'd never tell you to lie to the local authorities," Bastian clarified. "We're just asking for a little bit of discretion. These are parallel investigations that may or may not intersect. If the time comes when they do, everything will be aboveboard. But for now, we're just saying there's no need to pick up the phone and call Oakland PD and tell them we talked. Is that fair?"

"I guess so," I said.

It still felt a little strange.

"Thank you," Bastian said. "Glad we could get that cleared up."

"Now, if you don't mind, we're just trying to get a better sense of . . . I guess what you might call the victim's state of mind," Frisch said. "You and Angel talked quite frequently, did you not?"

"Every day. Or almost every day. He was my best friend. And I was going to work for him."

"Right."

"We're very sorry for your loss," Bastian inserted.

Frisch plowed forward: "Since you know him so well, help us get into his head. Especially in the last few days before he . . . before his passing. Was he nervous about anything? Upset about anything?"

"Not really. Angel had a big job. I'm sure you guys know that. So he was busy. But Angel wasn't a worrier by nature. The way he approached things, nothing was insurmountable. He was very practical. It was just: Here's an obstacle, how do I get over it, around it, through it, whatever."

"Did Mr. Reddish say anything to you that indicated he might be in trouble in any way? Did he think that someone might be after him or wish him harm?"

"No, nothing like that."

"Do you think he would have said something to you if he had a concern?"

"I would think so. Angel and I had confided in each other for a long time. It's not like he picked up the phone and told me every little thing that ever happened to him, but we also didn't keep secrets. Not about anything big."

"So there was nothing that stood out in the last few days? Nothing he told you that alarmed you in any way?"

I searched my memory once again and came up with a total blank. "No. Sorry."

Frisch yielded to Bastian, who asked: "And what about Balco? What kind of things did he tell you about Balco?"

"Wow. The better question is, what didn't he tell me about Balco? He was trying to get me up to speed about everything—the people, the customers, the industry, you name it. I'm afraid you'll have to be a little more specific."

"Did he mention any illegal activity?"

A spurt of alarm shot through me. "Are you guys investigating *Balco* for something?"

"No, no, nothing like that," Frisch assured me quickly. "Again, we're just trying to cover our bases. Balco has hundreds of customers. One of them might be involved in something it shouldn't. If Balco had—completely inadvertently—brushed up against illegality, it could have exposed Angel to a criminal element. Maybe some rough characters. Did he talk about anything like that?"

"Not exactly, but—"

I stopped myself for a second. As a journalist, I had learned to be cautious with unsubstantiated accusations. If you weren't careful, loose talk could find its way into an article and cross the line into libel real fast.

But I wasn't a journalist anymore. And this wasn't going into print.

Frisch and Bastian were hanging on my next words. I still chose them carefully: "You guys know about the union certification vote that's coming up, yes?"

The agents exchanged quick glances.

"What about it?" Bastian asked.

I explained Angel's involvement, and told them about the photo of him on the website.

When I was through, Bastian said, "Local 37 is on our radar, yes."

Frisch added, "There have been problems with them in the past—threats, intimidation, that sort of thing. We have a file on them that's about a foot thick. It's always stuff that's hard to substantiate. Who really did mangle that conveyer belt? Why did that guy suddenly call in sick? Rudy Szymanski seems to think he's Jimmy Hoffa or something."

"So you're investigating IWW?" I asked.

Bastian shot Frisch a look like he had said too much.

"We can't really comment on that either way," Bastian said. "Department policy."

"Is there anything else that you can think to tell us?" Frisch asked. "Anything at all? Maybe even just the smallest thing Angel mentioned?"

I shook my head. "Nothing that comes to mind. Is there anything else you guys can tell me? Any leads you're following?"

Bastian cut in with: "Again, we really can't say. I'm afraid we have to leave it at that."

He stood, and so did Frisch. After some perfunctory goodbyes and promises to be in touch, they were out the door, leaving Page and me alone in the foyer.

"That was weird," she said.

"What about it? I mean, besides everything?"

"They just seemed . . . vague. Like they didn't really know anything. Don't you think?"

"I don't know. I'm used to local cops who fall over themselves bragging about how sophisticated their investigation is because they want to look good in the paper. The FBI is a different animal. They're all about discretion and secrecy."

"I guess," she said. "Anyhow, let's eat."

After we shoveled in some lasagna, Page put tinfoil over the second one she had made for Aiysha, and we hopped into the Rivian.

"Are you sure we should be doing this?" Page asked. "What if she doesn't want to be bothered?"

I began backing down the driveway as I talked.

"Everyone is probably avoiding her right now because they think she doesn't want to be bothered, so she's sitting home alone, lost and scared, in a world of hurt. A little human outreach is exactly what she needs. Her family is in Virginia. I'm sure they'll come out as soon as they can get here. But for right now, we're her family. And sometimes family has to just dive in and help."

"Yeah, but she didn't answer my text."

"I'm sure her phone has been swamped. She probably didn't even see your text. This is a simple, loving gesture at a time when she desperately needs all the love she can get."

"But what if she really, *really* just wants to be by herself?"

"Then she'll tell us that, or we'll figure it out, and we'll act accordingly. You have to remember, she's not by herself. She's also got Elijah tearing around. If nothing else, she could use a little help with him. I feel like I owe it to Angel to do *something*. If this were somehow reversed and you were the widow, I'd be looking down on Angel and Aiysha pissed off that they didn't come over and try to comfort you, whether you asked them to or not."

"Please don't talk like that," she said quietly.

"Like what?"

"Saying I could be a widow."

"What's that mean?"

"You really need me to spell it out? Angel was killed and you don't know the first thing about who did it or why. Now you're messing around in the same sandbox without the faintest clue who is there. What if you're next?"

Maybe it speaks to my naivete—or my still-youthful sense of invulnerability—but I had never given that a moment's consideration.

I still couldn't. Some things were just too much for my brain to handle.

"You can't think that way," I said.

Without a word, she grabbed my hand and placed it on her baby bump.

"I can't help but think that way," she shot back.

She went quiet after that.

My thoughts turned to Aiysha. For as wrecked as I was to lose my best friend, she had to be feeling a million times worse.

I just hoped the détente we had shared on Saturday was able to continue. There had been so many times in the past when we had these dumb misunderstandings.

As just one example, I thought back to a hike the three of us had taken a few days before their wedding. We were in the hills of Marin

County when we came across this huge herd of goats contentedly chewing their way through a meadow.

Angel explained that this was actually a wildfire suppression effort, and that local communities paid money to have the goats come in and clear away the tall grasses so they wouldn't become fuel.

"Man, just watching them makes me hungry," I said.

"That's cruel," Aiysha snapped angrily.

I was so taken aback, I almost didn't say anything. But then, finally, it came out that I was just making a joke about wanting to eat the grass.

She thought I wanted to eat the *goats*.

We always seemed to miss each other like that.

I hoped this would be a time when we could avoid that. We needed each other like never before.

The sun was getting low when we arrived at Angel and Aiysha's place. They lived in a large house that was situated on a cul-de-sac along with two others.

We pulled into the empty driveway, walked up to the front stoop, and rang the doorbell.

Nothing moved inside the house. There were no lights on. Other than the echoing of the chime, there was no sound.

The place hard that empty feel to it. Which didn't seem possible. It was an hour or so before Elijah's bedtime. He was at an age—and a mobility level—where he would be active at this time of night.

We should have seen him. Heard him.

"I don't think anyone's home," Page said at last.

"Yeah. I guess not. But where else could she possibly be?"

"I don't know," Page said. "Wherever it is, she's not here."

CHAPTER 13

THE MAN WHO called himself Frisch was really named French.

He was a garden-variety sociopath, the kind whose lack of intelligence was only exceeded by his lack of morality.

That's why this job suited him. He didn't have to think. He just had to follow orders. What those orders were concerned him less. His compensation bought his unswerving allegiance.

The man who called himself Bastian was really named Boston.

He had a full-blown gambling addiction and a tendency to bet with his heart rather than his head.

There were times when he had qualms about what he was being asked to do. But he also had several unpaid bookies and a kid in college, which was basically like being on unsupervised release from debtor's prison.

Frisch and Bastian. French and Boston. Maybe they could have come up with better aliases, but at least they wouldn't forget these.

They had returned to their Ford Explorer, which was now around the corner from 27 Buena Vista Drive, out of sight of the house.

At least for the moment.

"So what do we do now?" Boston asked.

"I don't know," French answered. "I think we're done, don't you? They're not going to make us stay here all night, are they?"

"Probably not. But you better make a call," Boston said.

French pulled out his phone, jabbed at it for a few moments, and brought it to his ear.

"Yeah?" he heard.

"Hey, it's me," French said.

"I know it's you. What's going on?"

"Nothing. I talked to your boy. He doesn't know squat."

"You sure?"

"Sure as I can be. We grilled him pretty good. It was nothing but blank stares and I-don't-knows."

"So his best friend really told him nothing?"

"Seems that way. You had to see the kid. He was eager to help. He was really trying his best to answer our questions. I really don't think he was hiding anything. No one is that good an actor."

"And he believed you were FBI?"

"No doubt. We had him hook, line, and sinker. I flashed the badge and he didn't question it for a second. At one point, he asked why this was FBI business and we came up with this great line about crimes crossing state lines. It was brilliant. Trust me, he didn't suspect a thing."

The person on the other end of the line absorbed this for a moment, then asked: "What about the wife?"

"What about her?"

"You think she knows anything?"

"If he doesn't know anything, how is she supposed to know anything?"

"Because wives talk. And we still don't know where the widow is."

CHAPTER 14

TRUE TO THE orders of Lorne Murphy, I stayed off my phone and away from my email the rest of the evening.

Instead, Page and I huddled on the couch, and I stopped holding back the tears I had been on the brink of the whole day, giving myself over to a good, soaking cry. Page cried right along with me, and was a good sport about listening to a lot of old, boring stories about our college exploits.

I still couldn't believe he was gone.

The next morning, I was in front of my Balco-issued laptop by 6:00 a.m. Coverage of Angel had made all the local news programs, newspapers, and websites. It was all pretty standard stuff, with no big surprises.

Nevertheless, I also had a long email from Bob Brunato, summarizing his interactions with the press and the various follow-up that entailed. It sounded like a busy night.

I wondered whether the coming day would hold more of the same. I showered and was dressed by six thirty, kissing a still-slumbering Page on my way out.

Near the end of the drive, I realized I was passing through the intersection at Adeline and Third Street, where the carjacking had taken place.

Before I even knew what I was doing, I had eased the Rivian to the side of the street and was having a look around.

The overall feel of the area was desolate, despondent, semi-abandoned post-industrial. There were buildings on all four corners, each of them architecturally unimaginative rectangles made with brutalist materials and pockmarked by dirty, heavily barred windows. The only attempt at color, decoration, or human expression came from the graffiti that covered their walls.

Angel would have been driving north on Adeline Street, descending into the intersection via a ramp. The road coming from that direction was divided, with two lanes traveling in each direction.

I studied it more closely. There was no shoulder on either side—just thick concrete barriers, topped with iron railings. The divider in the middle was a solid section of concrete that a Tesla couldn't clear.

The carjackers had chosen their place of attack well. With a truck blocking his path forward and a vehicle behind him, Angel had nowhere to run. He was driving into a turkey shoot.

Not even sure of what, exactly, I was hoping to accomplish, I climbed out of the car to have a look around.

To be clear, this was not a nice neighborhood. If Page had been with me, I probably wouldn't have even stopped the car, much less gotten out.

In a strange way, though, I felt at home. Every major city in America has a part of town like this. They're places unvisited by the civilized gentry; places worn down by decades of use and neglect; where huge amounts of freight moved in and out at all hours, unseen by the people who would someday benefit from it; and where those forgotten by society—or who had chosen to abandon it—could exist with minimal interference.

I had been to this part of town in every city I had covered. I daresay I was even drawn to it. There was an old saying about how it was a reporter's job to "afflict the comfortable and comfort the afflicted."

And now here I was, in my fancy new job, back in the same kind of place, because the logistics industry thrived here, too—even if it operated in parallel worlds that almost never had cause to interact.

Looking around, I was reminded of a lyric from a Simon & Garfunkel song my mother liked to play, one that talked of "the poorer quarters where the ragged people go, looking for the places only they would know."

Sure enough, on the far side of the intersection from where I had parked, there was a row of campers, vans, and cars, all of them in varying states of disrepair.

They were no longer being used for transportation, of course; they were now residences. Some of them had tarps or improvised lean-tos attached to them. Subtle signs of habitation—an ancient barbecue grill, a battered water jug, a bucket filled to the brim with cigarette butts—could be seen here and there throughout the makeshift encampment.

There were also huge piles of trash and debris strewn about: shredded tires, old furniture dollies, a car's bumper, crumbling pieces of plywood, mattresses, halves of mattresses, chunks of concrete, piles of matted clothing, empty boxes, bulging black plastic bags, and more, and more, and more.

It was as if several garbage trucks headed toward a landfill had decided to quit and drop their loads early; and then human beings had descended and given some bare hint of order to the rubbish.

The whole area smelled like urine.

I crossed the street and stopped in front of a shopping cart overflowing with trash. I stared dumbly at a pink plastic water bottle, an old high-top sneaker with no laces, the elastic band of some seriously dirty sweatpants, and a worn-down piece of asphalt roofing tile—all of which formed the upper crust of the cart's contents.

Someone, at some point, had decided to toss all this junk in here. For what purpose, it was impossible to discern.

I was just pondering that mystery when, no more than six feet from where I was standing, I saw a human hand.

It was attached to an arm; which I then followed to a torso; which allowed me to discern that, yes, sleeping atop a pile of debris, mostly hidden by the refuse, there was a person.

A man. Or at least it looked like a man. I would have missed him were it not for that one protruding hand. His head was covered by a towel. He was wearing a checkered flannel shirt that camouflaged into the surrounding detritus. I couldn't see his bottom half, which was submerged in the pile of garbage that served as his bed.

He was perfectly still and not making a sound. It was entirely unclear whether he was sleeping or dead.

"Excuse me, sir," I said, tentatively.

No response.

"Hey, buddy," I tried again, a little louder.

Still nothing. I didn't dare touch him, in case he really was dead.

At that moment, a tremendous snore emanated from underneath the towel.

Not dead, apparently. I gently touched his wrist.

"Hey, friend, wake up," I said.

He came to with a start, his bushy hair and Rip Van Winkle beard spreading out in every direction, his eyes wide and wild.

"This is my place, my place," he hollered. "You can't make me move. It's mine."

His accent was southern. His voice contained a shovel full of gravel.

"Relax, I'm not trying to make you move and I'm sorry to bother you. I just wanted to ask you a question."

He had finally managed to make his eyes focus and I could see the gears clicking into place. A well-dressed man wanted information. This was not a threat. It was an opportunity.

"Depends. You got some money so I can get me some breakfast?"

"I don't have any cash on me," I said, which was true—like a lot of my generation, I didn't carry any. Then I jerked my head down Third Street. "But I think I just passed a taco truck that probably takes credit cards. I'll get you whatever you want."

"Yeah?"

"Sure. Just tell me, were you here two nights ago?"

"I'm here all the time. This is my place."

"Did you see the carjacking? It went down probably an hour or so after sunset?"

"You a cop?"

"No. Just a friend of the guy who got carjacked."

"Yeah, I was here."

A spurt of excitement ran through me. Fierro had said he'd canvass for witnesses, but maybe he hadn't bothered with this guy. Maybe he hadn't even seen him.

This was the feeling I used to get when I found a great source for a story—especially when I knew I was the first person to talk to them.

"What did you see?" I asked.

"Get me breakfast. Then we talk."

I obliged him, walking with him down to the taco truck and paying for his breakfast burrito. He then slathered enough hot sauce on it to render it completely inedible. But given that the majority of it ended up in his mouth—with only a minority on his beard—I guess he found it tasty enough.

As he ate, I learned he was originally from Mississippi, that he had been out in the Bay Area for twenty years, and that his name was Johnny.

When he was done, he wiped his face on his sleeve.

"Okay, what do you want to know?"

"What did you see?"

"I didn't see nothing," Johnny declared, and I felt my hopes sag, until he added: "But I heard stuff."

"Like what?"

"Well, those dudes, they were there for a while. They were definitely planning something."

"What dudes? How many?"

"I don't know. There were a few of them. They were all Spanish, so I couldn't understand nothing. But they had one of them, what do you call them things . . . you know, where you talk into them and other people talk back and stuff?"

"Walkie-talkies?" I suggested.

"Yeah, yeah, walkie-talkies. They were talking to some other dudes on their walkie-talkies. They were doing it for a while, and I got the feeling they were waiting for something. I didn't know what they was saying, but I kept my head down, you know? I don't need no trouble."

"Right, sure."

"When the thing went down, it happened fast. There was a truck and a lot of errr"—he made the sound of squealing breaks—"and dudes were shouting. And the dude who was carjacked, you said he was your boy, right?"

"Yeah."

"When he was out of the car, your boy kept saying something about '*veinticinco*' and one of the dudes was all '*treinta*.' They were all saying other stuff, too. But that was the thing it kept coming back to. *Veinticinco* and *treinta*. It was like they were having an argument or something. And those dudes, man, they were pissed. They was just yelling at him. Then, like that, they drove off."

He snapped his fingers to make his point.

As we walked back to his corner, I asked Johnny more questions. But he didn't seem to have heard anything else all that useful—at least nothing that made sense to him. I thanked him for his time and completed my tour of the area, which didn't do much to heighten my understanding of what had happened.

Before long I was back in my Rivian, completing the short drive to Balco headquarters that remained.

Veinticinco was Spanish for "twenty-five." *Treinta* was Spanish for "thirty."

What was significant about twenty-five and thirty? And why did they keep yelling those numbers back and forth?

CHAPTER 15

I WAS STILL trying to make sense of what Johnny had told me when I arrived in the office.

It seemed unbelievable it was just my second day on the job. The previous day had felt like a year.

There was no time to ponder it, though; a new email from Lorne Murphy was sitting atop my inbox.

> Curt,
>
> Can you do a 9:30 in my office?
>
> Lorne

I wrote back a quick, "See you then."

Summoned to the CEO's office for the second time in two days. What was it now?

When the appointed time came, I entered Lorne's office to find him parked at the head of his conference table.

Seated next to him was Sal Salcedo, the chief safety officer. He was petting his mustache, which dominated his face like an enormously hairy caterpillar on a sidewalk.

"Come on in," Lorne said. "I believe you've met Michael Salcedo?"

"Yeah, I went a little *loco* on him when I saw the mob he was letting in for the press conference," Sal said, his mustache dancing above his grin. "No hard feelings."

"None taken," I said. "Nice to see you again."

"Sal does get rather particular about who gets on the lot," Lorne confirmed.

"That's what you pay me for, remember?" Sal said, and the mustache danced a little more.

"All right, well, let's get going here," Lorne said. "You ready?"

The question was for Sal, and he gave his head a quick bounce. On the wall opposite Lorne, a screen was descending from the ceiling.

"Great," Lorne said, turning his attention back to me. "I need to make it clear that I'm showing you this against Rig's orders. I told him I was gonna do it anyway, which didn't make him real happy. We do tend to have our disagreements from time to time. Sometimes he forgets he's not CEO anymore."

"I don't want to get you in trouble," I started, but Lorne waved me off.

"Oh, he'll get over it. For all his hippy-dippy 'don't be against this, don't be against that' nonsense, he's got a shark's fin glued to that backbone of his when he needs it. I guess the main point is, this is not something we can broadcast. Rig doesn't want to escalate the situation with Local 37 and I have to respect that—unless we get hard evidence that we can really use to move against them. But, for now, you have to keep this close to the vest and not tell anyone you saw this. Fair?"

"Of course," I said, even though I didn't know what, exactly, I was agreeing to keep quiet.

"Okay, maestro, play on," Lorne said.

Sal touched a button on his computer. I was soon looking at security camera footage of the main gate to Balco headquarters, which I—and every other Balco employee on the premises—entered and exited each day. The view was from the inside, looking out.

In this video, it was nighttime. Everything was cast in the greenish hue of a thermal imaging camera.

Nothing was happening. It was just the guard shack, the boom barrier, and the twelve-foot-high rolling gate beyond.

Just as I was about to ask what I was supposed to be looking at, a vehicle came into view. It was a Tesla with a Northwestern University Wildcats frame on its rear license plate.

Angel's car.

"This is from Monday night?" I asked.

"Yeah," Sal said softly.

He knew what I was thinking: that these were among Angel's last moments.

There was no sound, but I'm not sure it would have added much to the understanding of what was happening. I watched as Angel rolled down his window and exchanged a greeting with the person in the guard shack.

In typical Angel fashion, it wasn't just a quick wave. He probably had a relationship with the guard—Angel had this natural way of storing tidbits about everyone he interacted with—and he said something that triggered a brief exchange of friendly words.

Once their chat finished, the boom barrier swung up, and Angel drove beneath it. Then the rolling gate slid open and he passed through, with his right turn signal blinking.

There was nothing extraordinary about it until just after his tires hit Adeline Street. Then I saw something flash across the very upper portion of the screen.

A person. Man or woman? It was hard to tell, because all you could see was basically from the stomach on down.

Whoever or whatever they were, they were in a hurry. Their legs scissored quickly as they cut across the street. Neither their origin point nor their destination was included in the fixed frame of this camera, but their presence alone was certainly odd.

The area outside Balco headquarters was not a pedestrian zone. And, in any event, not many pedestrians moved at a dead sprint. This had all the hallmarks of someone up to no good.

"Who was that?" I asked.

"Excellent question," Sal said. "We were wondering the same thing. We have another camera that catches a larger swath of the area outside the building. I'm not going to show it to you, because you'd just see the same person even smaller. They run to a vehicle and—"

"You might as well show it to him," Lorne suggested. "We're here."

"Okay, if you want," Sal said. "Hang on."

He worked the touchpad on his laptop, clicking a few times, then said, "Here you go. Same time frame: Monday night, just after nine."

The new video was from a wider angle, higher up, and farther away. My guess was that it came from a camera mounted on the roof.

Sal Salcedo had a lot of cameras.

The footage now appearing on the conference room screen showed the same scene I had just witnessed. Except now I could see the entirety of the person—it definitely looked to be a man—and I was able to watch him get into a pickup truck and drive off in the direction Angel had just turned.

"You still can't tell who he is," I said.

"You can't. And I can't," Sal said. "But the computer could. We had it sharpen up the image and then fed it into some AI facial recognition software that can do a reverse search across the internet. It came back with a hit. That man you saw running across the screen is this guy."

Sal brought up a professionally shot portrait of a man with neatly combed brown hair and blue eyes, and a face set in neutral, neither smiling nor frowning. There was nothing menacing about him. He looked more like a high school math teacher than anyone I expected to be stalking Angel at the Port of Oakland after dark.

"Who's that?" I asked.

"His name is Neil Rees," Sal said. "This photo comes straight from IWW-Local 37's website. His job title is listed as 'member education specialist.'"

"What does that mean?"

"Anything you want, basically," Sal said. "He may not look like much, but my people tell me they've seen him hanging around outside the facility a lot. He's known as Rudy Szymanski's attack dog. They say his nickname is, get this, 'the Mad Bomber.'"

"Why do they call him the Mad Bomber?"

"I'm sure we don't want to know. I think it's just because he's the chief rabble-rouser. It's his job to talk up the union, foment discontent, stir the pot. I've never heard about him getting caught doing anything illegal, but . . ."

"Well, we've nailed him this time, haven't we?" I asked, feeling myself growing excited as I turned to Lorne. "You said you needed hard evidence. You've got this guy Neil Rees hopping into a pickup truck and chasing after Angel moments before he's killed. And we know from the video of the carjacking that there was another vehicle directly behind

Angel. That *had* to be Neil Rees in the pickup. There's no turnoff between here and the intersection of Adeline and Third. It's a straight shot. This is about as close to a smoking gun as you can get."

There was an awkward silence as Lorne and Sal exchanged glances.

I was obviously missing something here.

"What?" I asked.

"The Oakland Police Department is not allowed to use facial recognition software owing to its well-known problems with racial bias," Lorne said. "The city council banned its use around the same time San Francisco and Austin and some other progressive cities did. Beyond that—and I'm sure Sidney Graves would love to tell you more about this—the Alameda County DA made a campaign promise that she wouldn't allow her office to use any evidence from facial recognition software in criminal prosecutions. So we know it's Neil Rees. And we can tell the police it's Neil Rees. But the police can't do anything about it."

Sal added: "All they know is *someone* was running around outside our facility, and *someone* got into that pickup truck. But, in a way, they knew that already."

I just sat there, stumped. I had written a story about an African American woman who was subjected to an eleven-month nightmare in the criminal justice system when facial recognition software wrongly tagged her for felony shoplifting. Her pleas of *But that's not me!* fell on deaf law enforcement ears until finally a judge took one look at the video and the defendant at the same time and tossed out the case.

Still, this felt incredibly unfair. A ban meant to protect innocent people was now allowing a guilty one to remain free.

"Well, even if they can't use it at trial, can't they at least question this Neil Rees guy?" I asked.

"To what end?" Sal asked. "Neil Rees can say, 'Balco headquarters? I wasn't anywhere near Balco headquarters on Monday night. I was at home in bed with my blowup doll.' We know he's lying. The cops suspect he's lying. But there's no way to prove he's lying. There's also the problem that even if he did admit that was him getting in the pickup truck, it's still circumstantial. He could just say, 'Oh, yeah, I pulled off and took a nap another fifty yards up the road. I never made it to Adeline and Third.'"

I just sat there with my hands still resting on the table. Except now they were balled into fists.

"It's frustrating, I know," Lorne said. "I'm sorry. We're gonna get these guys. We just have to be patient."

"The good news is, even if we can't use the facial hit, we still have the pickup truck. It's a Ford F150," Sal said. "I've got someone reaching out to some of the other companies between here and Third Street, asking them if they'll share their security camera footage with us. Maybe we can get another image of the truck that has a license plate, or a better shot of Neil Rees.

"We're going to keep working it," Sal assured me. "Something will shake loose. It always does. No one commits the perfect crime."

CHAPTER 16

THE MESSENGER HAD been awake for more hours than he cared to count, stoked on adrenaline, energy drinks, and fear of failure.

A metal cooler, which had started the journey in his trunk, packed in amidst his luggage, was now sitting next to him in the front seat.

He didn't know what was in the cooler.

He was just as sure he didn't want to know.

The quiet woman had impressed on the messenger that this delivery was as urgent as it was sensitive; and that he should complete it without delay, and without attracting undue attention to himself.

As a result, the messenger had stopped just three times, and only because his gas gauge was low. Otherwise, he had driven straight through, not even pulling to the side of the road when his bladder was full.

That's what the Gatorade bottle next to him was for.

His journey was now nearing its end. He was eager to be done with it, so he could report back to the quiet woman that all had been done exactly as she had asked.

The messenger pulled his car up to a rolling gate topped with razor wire and pressed a buzzer.

"Welcome to Balco—can I help you?"

"I have a delivery for Lorne Murphy," he said.

There was no immediate response.

Then: "Is Mr. Murphy expecting you?"

"No. I'm a courier."

"Drive up to the guardhouse, please."

The gate in front of him slowly rolled open. He proceeded to the small house, where a boom barrier blocked his progress.

He rolled down his window as a guard approached.

"I'll take whatever you've got," the guard said. "You need me to sign for it?"

"I have to deliver it to Mr. Murphy personally," the messenger replied.

The guard's head jerked backward. "I don't think we can do that. We'll make sure he gets it."

"Sorry, I'm under orders. Please take my picture and tell Mr. Murphy I'm here."

"Do you have a name?"

"My picture will suffice."

The guard reacted like this was the strangest thing he had heard in a while, but he took out his phone and snapped a photo of the messenger.

"I can wait, but I have to hand this to him myself," the messenger said. "I'll lose my job if I don't."

The messenger suspected he would lose more than just his job. But that wasn't something the guard needed to hear about.

"Uhh, okay," the guard said. "Why don't you pull over there and wait in your vehicle. I'll see what I can do."

The messenger did as he was told, driving through the boom barrier as it raised, then parking his car next to a security truck.

There, he waited. When he began nodding off, he chugged another energy drink. He filled his Gatorade bottle, pouring it out on the pavement when he was done.

After a half hour or so, three men—two armed guards and a man in a suit—came for him and indicated he should get out of the car. He grabbed the cooler on his way out.

He was subject to a weapons search, and to a swab of his exposed skin. He transferred the cooler from one hand to another so that it never left his possession.

Once he passed inspection, he was escorted into the main headquarters building, and up to the fifth floor. The messenger tried to remember every detail, so he could later relay it to the quiet woman.

This would be evidence that the job had been done correctly.

There was more waiting, and then he was led into a lavishly furnished office with cherry paneling. There, sitting behind his desk, was Lorne Murphy.

His first words were to the guards: "Thanks, guys, we can take it from here."

The man in the suit remained. The courier had already seen a handgun winking out from his shoulder holster.

Lorne Murphy's next words were for the messenger: "Okay, what's so goddamned important? Let's have it."

The messenger placed the cooler on the CEO's desk.

Murphy opened the lid.

The first thing he encountered was a note:

> *I apologize for the mishap. As you can see from the enclosed, I have rectified the situation. Reddish was one*

of your top people. This was one of mine. I now consider the matter closed.

Next, there was a layer of freezer packs surrounding a cardboard box. Murphy removed the packs and lifted the lid on the box.

"*Je*-sus *Christ!*" he exclaimed, immediately turning away.

Inside the box was a severed head with a lizard winking up from its cheeks.

CHAPTER 17

IN THE HOURS and days that followed, the media's interest in the murder of Angel Reddish rather quickly flamed out.

Another rich guy had been killed in a bad part of town. It was interesting enough for a start, but stories like that needed fuel. Hot leads. New clues. An arrest.

And there was little to report. At least not that I was allowed to make public.

I had heard nothing more from the FBI. I was in regular contact with Mando Fierro, who had given me two updates—though he asked me not to share them with the press.

The first was that some municipal workers recovered a gun from a storm drain not far from where Angel's body had been found.

It stood to reason that an abandoned gun may have been used in a crime, so it was dusted for fingerprints. According to Detective Fierro, it had one very clear set all over it.

But it wasn't a suspect's prints.

It was a victim's.

Angel's.

When I heard that, I was floored. *Angel* had been carrying a gun? He had grown up in a Chicago neighborhood ravaged by gun violence. One of his former childhood playmates had been crippled by a stray bullet from a nearby gang shoot-out.

Angel abhorred guns.

The only reason he would have carried one is that he knew he was in danger.

But from whom? And why?

The answers were becoming no clearer.

The second development was that the forensics report came back on Angel's car. For the most part, it had been wiped clean. There were no fingerprints or hairs.

Except, in the crevices of the back seat, they found some dried blood.

It wasn't Angel's. They were able to run a quick blood-typing and determine that it was A-positive blood. Angel was O-positive.

Fierro told me he had sent the sample to the Jan Bashinksi DNA Laboratory, which the state Bureau of Forensic Services operated in nearby Richmond. Unfortunately, he said, it had "a backlog."

"How much of a backlog?" I asked.

His reply: "Weeks. Months. We'll get it when we get it."

Whose blood was it? Did it belong to Neil Rees? Or another one of the attackers? What had happened back there? Why were they the ones bleeding and not Angel?

Add it to the pile of mysteries.

As the uncertainty continued to swirl, my grief kept coming at me in fits and spurts. At times, I succeeded in keeping my head on relatively straight. And then a thought about Angel would come barreling in at me from around a blind corner and flatten me.

In the meantime, the Comms Team had taken on planning a public memorial service for Angel. How this came to be was a combination of factors.

It started with a conversation I had on Wednesday morning with Angel's mother in Chicago. She was distraught, as expected. And she asked what arrangements were being made for Angel.

I said I didn't know, but I would find out. That, of course, involved contacting Aiysha.

But Aiysha remained weirdly incommunicado. She wasn't answering texts or calls. And repeated visits to her house made it clear she wasn't there, either.

I had even reached out to her family in Virginia. I had met them during the wedding, so they weren't strangers. They lived in Staunton, a small city nestled in the Shenandoah Valley. I had the same kind of awkward interaction with her father that I usually had with Aiysha.

He told me Aiysha was "traveling" and wouldn't be available.

When I asked what that meant—Traveling? Where? And for how long? When did she plan on returning home?—I was met with a series of ambiguous non-answers.

It made no sense. It was like she had taken her ten million dollars of life insurance and run off.

I also couldn't get straight answers about what had been done with Angel's body. Fierro politely but firmly told me that since I wasn't next of kin, it was none of my damn business. And Aiysha, who *was* next of kin, couldn't be reached.

Beyond Angel's mother, everyone was asking questions about whether there would be services. It was an expected part of the grieving process, especially with a death as shocking as this one. Yet there was a dearth of decision-making, or even communication, around the subject.

I felt like, as his best friend—and as Balco's vice president of corporate communications—I had standing to step in.

So I did.

First, I consulted with the pastor of his church. He was a kind, older man who was every bit as vexed by Aiysha's absence as I was. But he also reminded me: "Everyone's grief takes a different path."

I had to respect her need for distance.

We decided that it made sense to do something on Saturday afternoon. That would give his mother and some other family time to come out from Chicago. Plus, a Saturday would make it easier for Balco people to attend.

Since there was no body, this would not be a funeral. To call it a "celebration of life" felt grotesque when the life in question had been so tragically cut short.

No, this would be a memorial service.

The pastor deemed his church too small to accommodate the crowd we were expecting, so we went shopping for a venue. I soon learned about the Cathedral of Christ the Light in downtown Oakland, which had a capacity of eighteen hundred.

Angel wasn't Catholic. But the Diocese of Oakland was willing to make it available to us for a reasonable fee, and Lorne had already volunteered that Balco would cover all related expenses.

I made the short drive up from the Port to check it out, and it was magnificent—truly worthy of the name "cathedral."

The nave was lined by massive wooden slats that were set at an angle and meant to invoke sunlight filtering through redwood trees. At the front of the sanctuary was a fifty-eight-foot-tall aluminum shield with a series of small holes drilled into it.

When the light filtered through the holes, a depiction of Jesus appeared, looking like a pixelated computer image—which felt very appropriate for a church that served a wide swath of Silicon Valley.

It was just very cool. Angel would have approved.

Angel's pastor and I agreed on the flow of the program. We picked out some readings, which we assigned to some of Angel's family and other close friends. Lorne Murphy would give the first eulogy, followed by me, then the pastor. The music would come from the cathedral's majestic 5,298-pipe organ.

With that settled, I delegated a lot of the details to Korynne Vuong and Amy Dietz, our social media manager, who also did some event planning on the side.

The only real curveball came from Sal Salcedo, who insisted that a full security detail be detached outside the church. He promised they would be dressed in black suits, so they would blend in with the other mourners.

I still felt like it was unnecessary.

Really, it was a memorial service happening in broad daylight in the middle of downtown Oakland.

What was he so worried about?

By Friday afternoon, the bulk of the details had been sorted out.

I was mostly just trying to get to the end of the day—and of a hellish first workweek—when an email from Sidney Graves, the CFO, popped up in my inbox.

The subject was "Final FY Budget."

Balco's fiscal year ran from July 1 to June 30. I had a pet peeve about fiscal years not aligning with calendar years, which always seemed to create unnecessary confusion. Though in our corner of the logistics industry, I had to allow that it made a modicum of sense.

Peak shipping season usually started in mid-August, as our clientele began ramping up production for the holiday season, and lasted through mid- to late-autumn. We were sometimes still chasing after them to pay their bills until the end of December and beyond. So, a January 1–December 30 fiscal year might present problems.

Besides, accountants the world over hated to have their holidays wrecked by having to close out the books. And the pencil-pushers usually got their way.

For a July–June fiscal year, May 5 seemed a little late to be submitting a final budget. But maybe that was just how they did things around here.

I clicked on the email.

> Colleagues,
>
> Linked below is the final budget for the coming FY. I apologize for not getting this to you sooner. It was unavoidably delayed due to circumstances beyond our control. You can find it here:
>
> Final-Budget-v2.13
>
> The budget is being presented to the board on Monday. We anticipate a swift approval, as there have been no objections up to this point.

Respectfully Yours,

Sidney

As a private company, Balco was not required to disclose its board of directors. I assumed it consisted of Rig Weiskopf and other investors who had helped launch Balco—and still owned shares—but I didn't really know.

It was the kind of thing I would have asked Angel about.

Shaking off that thought, I clicked on the link that led to the relevant document floating in the Balco cloud.

I had already seen a preliminary version of the budget. It had been included in the information Angel had given me access to in the weeks leading up to my hiring. So I wasn't expecting any big surprises.

Then I scrolled down to the line item for the total Comms Team budget.

It was half of what it was supposed to be.

Almost immediately, I felt my blood pressure rising as I stared at the number in total shock.

Was my budget really being cut by *50 percent*?

And was no one going to even mention it to me?

It was infuriating. And overwhelming.

And impossible. We had some operating expenses that could possibly be trimmed, such as printing costs and contracts with outside vendors. But the bulk of my budget consisted of my team members' salaries. I couldn't conform to this new number without a massive bloodletting.

Layoffs would be necessary. And my understanding was that Balco didn't lay people off.

So, really, what was I supposed to do? Cut everyone's salary, including my own, by 50 percent?

Just to make sure I wasn't mistaken, I checked back in the files that Angel had sent me. Sure enough, the preliminary budget had called for a 3 percent increase, which was in line with what other departments were receiving.

No one had said a word to me about it being otherwise. But I couldn't help but follow the straight line of cause and effect.

On Tuesday morning, I had contradicted the CFO in front of the CEO and the rest of the C-suite. And by Friday afternoon, he had found a way to get his revenge.

This wasn't business. It was personal.

The only question was what I was going to do about it.

My experience in corporate warfare of this sort was nonexistent. I'm sure there were protocols and procedures I was expected to follow—a formal process through which I could register my objections and have my concerns addressed.

Likewise, I'm sure Angel would have told me to proceed with caution and remember who I was dealing with. *Don't trust a word he says. He has no integrity.*

With the board vote set for Monday, I didn't have time for prudence. I also didn't have the patience.

In the newspaper world, if you had a problem with someone, you confronted them directly.

And, often, loudly.

As such, I charged up to the fifth floor with my hair on fire.

CHAPTER 18

SIDNEY GRAVES'S OFFICE occupied the southeast corner of the building.

The wall that faced the hallway was entirely glass—thanks to that good ol' Balco transparency—so I could see him sitting behind his desk as I steamed toward him.

Ignoring his administrative assistant and anything or anyone else who might have slowed me down, I barged through his door without bothering to knock.

"Sidney, what the—"

And then I added a four-letter word.

He looked up at me slowly, curiously, like I was a plant whose genus-species the amateur botanist in him couldn't quite place. His face was pleasantly tanned and unbothered. It gave away nothing.

"Hello there," he said in a faux-friendly tone. "It's Curt, yes?"

"Stop it. You know who I am. And you know damn well what you did to my budget."

He leaned back slowly. As with other power offices at Balco, there was a credenza behind his desk. It was filled with plaques, trophies, and pictures of Sidney on a bike, wearing loudly colored jerseys festooned with company logos.

It figured Sidney Graves was also an amateur cyclist. He was probably typical of the breed found zipping around Northern California: They were essentially terrorists who refused to follow traffic rules; but they also became indignant the moment a car came too close, as if the road belonged solely to them.

I thought maybe he was going to continue to play dumb with me. Instead, he said, "You're new here."

"Yeah? What's that got to do with anything?"

"You're also new to business in general, am I right? You were a journalist if I recall correctly?"

"Again, what's your point?"

"I just think that maybe I need to explain to you how we approach budgeting here at Balco. Do you have a moment for that discussion?"

He was being deliberately pedantic. Between that and the set of his protruding chin—which he held in a way that came off as slightly superior—I pretty much wanted to strangle him.

But I couldn't let him get me that easily.

"Oh, by all means, proceed," I said with a fake smile.

"Wonderful. Do you understand the difference between a cost center and a profit center?"

"Please enlighten me."

"Well, it can be a bit of a confusing concept for new people, because both profit centers and cost centers have costs associated with them, of course. The difference is, a profit center adds money to the top line while a cost center does not. Tell me: What revenue does the Comms Team generate for the company?"

He had me there.

"It doesn't," I admitted.

"Exactly. Ergo, you're a cost center. The board is concerned that Balco has become bloated with too many cost centers and not enough profit centers. My mandate is to shift the balance back in the right direction. It's for the good of the company."

He smirked at me, and I was about to unspool an impassioned defense about how vital we were in support of those profit centers; how *everything* came down to communications, especially now, in the information age; and how only a great fool didn't understand the vital importance of messaging in every aspect of the business.

But I stopped myself. There was no point in trying to justify my team's worth to this vindictive son of a bitch, especially when we both knew this had nothing to do with what was or wasn't good for Balco.

It was about power.

His.

And what he perceived as my lack of it.

Admittedly, he wasn't entirely wrong. As CFO, he outranked me. And we both knew that, without Angel, I had lost my chief protector in the C-suite.

But I wasn't going to just lie there and let him wipe his shoes all over my face like I was some kind of doormat.

"That's very interesting," I allowed. "I really appreciate the education you're providing me. Now, tell me something—based on the definition you've just provided me, isn't the Accounting Team also a cost center?"

His mouth opened, but nothing came out.

I pressed my advantage.

"So you must have also cut your own budget by a considerable amount, yes?"

"Well, now, accounting is a necessary function of—"

"As a matter of fact, your budget is, what, ten times larger than mine? I have to think there are a lot more savings that could be realized if we cut *your* budget by fifty percent."

"That's not—"

"Tell you what, let's take this to Lorne. We can share your deep concerns about cost centers. And then we can look at the Accounting Team budget side by side with the Comms Team budget. How does that sound? You know, for the good of the company."

He straightened his long, Ichabod Crane torso and jutted out his chin just a little farther.

"My budget is not what's under consideration here. But if you'd like to take your concerns about yours to Lorne, I suppose there's nothing I can do to stop you."

"Thanks," I said. "I think I'll do that."

It was not the response I was expecting.

Maybe he just realized he had been outmaneuvered and was admitting defeat.

"You might want to hurry, though," he added. "The board vote is Monday."

I shot him one more disingenuous smile, then left his office.

As I retreated out of sight of Graves's glass office and considered my options, I checked the time.

It was 3:26 p.m.

This put me in the awkward position of being one of the worst types of subordinates: the kind that bothered the CEO with urgent business on a Friday afternoon.

But that was still better than what I might otherwise be: the kind that bothered him over the weekend.

So I rounded the corner and pointed myself toward the CEO suite. Lucas Chandler was in his usual spot, guarding the stainless-steel entryway to Lorne's white-collar man cave.

Lorne wasn't available at the moment. But Lucas chiseled out a slot for me at five thirty. I thanked him, then spent a nervous two hours gathering evidence, rehearsing arguments in my head, thinking of ways to avert this catastrophe.

I didn't dare whisper any of this to the rest of my team. The last thing I wanted to do was set off a panic in the department. This was my problem, and my problem alone.

Shortly after five, I went back up to Lorne's lair; and, after a brief wait, I was let in.

"Curt!" he said warmly. "What can I do for you? I got an email from Sidney saying you were pitchin' a fit about something."

Of course he did.

I'm sure the CFO had done everything he could to poison the pool for me. I just couldn't let it bother me.

"Yeah, I don't know how carefully you looked over the final budget that Sidney sent out, but he cut the Comms Team by fifty percent."

Lorne recoiled a little. "Fifty percent!"

His tone alone told me he found it as outrageous as I did. Emboldened, I began gushing, "I realize there's a concern about cost centers, but when you look at all the ways in which the Comms Team supports the Sales Team, the Marketing Team, and the overall mission of—"

"Hold on, hold on. I didn't hear about anyone's budget getting a cut of that magnitude, and that's something he'd run by me."

"It wasn't in any of the preliminary budgets, only in the final version sent out this afternoon."

I stopped myself from adding: *Sidney made the cut vindictively after I embarrassed him in the meeting the other day*. Saying that would only make me sound petty.

Besides, Lorne would surely make the connection on his own.

"Well, now, Sidney's not the kind of guy to act rashly," Lorne said. "Believe me, that's why he's my CFO. Are you sure? *Fifty percent?*"

I hadn't bothered printing out the budget, which was a huge document. All I had done was look at it online.

"Yeah, hang on," I said, fishing into my pocket for my phone.

I tapped on the link Graves had sent me and gawped in confusion at the screen that came up.

FILE NOT FOUND.

Thinking maybe my clumsy fingers had tapped the wrong thing, I navigated back to my email and, more carefully this time, tapped on the Final-Budget-v2.13 hyperlink.

Again:

FILE NOT FOUND.

Lorne was just sitting there, watching me fumble around. I heard him take in a deep breath, and I could feel his patience wearing thin. It was after five o'clock on a beautiful spring Friday. I was probably the last thing standing between him and a gin and tonic.

"I'm, uhh, I'm having problems bringing up the file," I said. "It's not—"

"Hang on, I got it right here," he said and began manipulating his mouse. "Here you go. As far as I can tell, there's been no cut. Am I missing something?"

He swiveled his screen toward me.

The number was back to what it had been in the preliminary budget I had seen.

With a sinking feeling, I was already putting together exactly what had happened.

Sidney Graves had sent me a fake version of the budget, which he had already eliminated from the cloud. He had sent the "Dear Colleagues" email to himself, using blind carbon copy to hide the distribution list. That had become such standard practice—to help avoid unnecessary Reply-Alls and other such annoyances—that I hadn't even noticed it. I just assumed this was the email sent to everyone.

Really, I had been the only recipient. Lorne and everybody else had received an email that was identical in all ways except that their Final-Budget-v2.13 link sent them to the real version.

Sidney Graves had done this to humiliate me, knowing I would fly off the handle, storm into Lorne's office, and make a fussy fool out of myself.

And I had walked right into the trap.

"Sidney thought maybe you were a little confused about how to read a budget spreadsheet," Lorne said, with a gently paternal tone. "It's okay. I can remember being a little overwhelmed by that sort of thing when I was a greenhorn. Happens to all of us."

Lorne gave me a patient smile.

I had two choices. I could go through the long explanation of how Sidney had set me up—an accusation for which there would be scant evidence.

Or I could just accept that I had been outmaneuvered.

"Yeah, I guess I . . . my eyes must have been playing tricks on me," I said. "It's . . . it's been a long week."

"Don't worry about it. You have a nice night, now."

Red-faced, I just dipped my head and escaped the office with what little was left of my dignity.

I already knew that Sidney Graves was a powerful enemy. Now I was seeing just how insidious he could be. He was a seasoned corporate gladiator who was not going to let some young punk shame him without responding in kind.

Worse, I had the sneaking suspicion he wasn't done punishing me.

CHAPTER 19

SATURDAY DAWNED BRIGHT and clear and quickly revealed itself to be one of those perfect Bay Area spring days: blue skies, low humidity, temperature gradually climbing from the brisk mid-fifties up to the comfortable low-seventies.

It only added to the heartbreak that Angel was missing it.

The memorial service was scheduled for 2:00 p.m., which gave Page and me time to sleep in. After that, we made breakfast and then shambled about the house, moving around furniture only to move it back again, as if that would make it feel more like ours.

I hadn't said anything about what Sidney had done to me the previous afternoon. I told myself it was because she didn't need to worry.

Really, I just wanted to keep my shame to myself.

After a slow morning, Page and I left the house around noon. I had on one of my new suits. She was wearing a long-sleeve square-neck black dress that beautifully hugged her swelling midsection. Her hair was tied back in an elegant chignon. She looked stunning, as usual.

She knew I was nervous about delivering the eulogy, so she volunteered to drive, giving me the chance to run over my notes one more time. As she guided us toward the cathedral, she kept a hand resting gently on my thigh. It was a nice gesture of support.

When we arrived, I got Page settled in the front of the sanctuary, to the immediate right of the altar. We had reserved the first row for Angel's family, and the second row for others involved in the service, including Page and me.

Then I went and checked on the arrangements. The Comms Team really did have its act together. Everything was already in place—or getting there fast.

The programs were printed. The ushers were ready. The organist was practicing a piece by Bach that was so evocative and beautiful, it sent chills rocketing up my spine.

Up front, there were some large photos of Angel that had been printed onto posterboard and set on easels. They were surrounded by a gorgeous display of flowers.

I didn't actually see Sal Salcedo's people at first. Then I began to be able to pick them out, arrayed around the plaza outside and even stationed inside the sanctuary. They were discreet and kept a respectful distance, but they were definitely a presence.

As the mourners began to arrive—first in ones and twos, then in larger numbers—I felt my chest tightening.

I knew so many of the people in Angel's life, because they were the people in my life, too. We had a substantial overlap of friends from college but also, because we had kept in good touch, from other phases of our lives.

There were colleagues from former jobs, business school friends I recognized, people from his church, even just casual acquaintances who still felt close enough to Angel to want to make the drive to Oakland. It was a warm reminder of how many lives Angel had touched.

But what was somehow most poignant to me was that all of Balco was showing up. That started with Rig Weiskopf, who was actually wearing closed-toe shoes, along with a black linen suit and black T-shirt.

But it wasn't just the top brass. There were also truck drivers and warehouse workers and maintenance people and forklift operators and janitors, all of them coming with their families to pay their respects.

Bob Brunato said that Lorne had used Angel as a kind of front man for the company, but it was clear they didn't see him as some aloof boss figure. He really had connected with them.

I was getting so overwhelmed by my emotions that I suspected I was going to have a very hard time getting through even the first sentence of my eulogy.

And then, among the throngs entering, I recognized someone who absolutely didn't belong there.

A man with slicked-back hair and a paunchy face.

It was Rudy Szymanski, the IWW-Local 37 president.

CHAPTER 20

HAD I GIVEN myself even a moment to think, I'm sure I would have practiced some restraint and not risked making a scene at my best friend's memorial service.

Instead, I charged right for the man and intercepted him while he was still standing in line, waiting to be seated.

Crowding his physical space, I growled in a low voice, "You have a lot of nerve showing up here."

"Excuse me?" he asked, clearly taken aback.

I drew even closer.

"My name is Curt Hinton. I'm Balco's vice president of corporate communications and I'm also Angel's best friend. You are not welcome here."

"And why is that?"

I almost spat, *I don't want the man who ordered Angel's murder at his memorial service.*

But I restrained myself. Not because I thought he was innocent. It was because I didn't want him to know I was onto him and I didn't want him or Neil Rees aware that we were closing in on them.

Better to let them think they had gotten away with it.

What I came up with was: "I saw that post on your website. You call him a liar and then you have the nerve to show up here?"

"Take it easy, it's just a post," he said. "Angel was a friend of mine."

"A friend? I seriously doubt that."

"I don't care what you think. I'm just here to pay my respects. Why don't you back off?"

"I will when you get out of here."

"I'm not going anywhere. I have the same right to be here as anyone else."

"I don't care about your rights. Get lost."

"You really want to make this ugly, pal?" he said, stepping close enough that I could smell the coffee on his breath. "I could get a hundred guys with baseball bats out here in a heartbeat. Is that what you want?"

And I could get Sal Salcedo's men to forcibly remove Szymanski and anyone else from IWW who tried to show up.

But there was at least some small part of my functioning brain that told me that wasn't the right play.

I had to get ahold of myself.

Rein it in. Be smart.

Rudy Szymanski was an enemy for another day.

"Just get out of here," I said.

And then, without another word, I turned and stalked back up the main aisle, taking in big gulps of air until my breathing returned to normal.

The pews were rapidly filling up. Toward the front, my eye landed on Sidney Graves. When he saw me, he gave me a quick sneer, then looked away, as if I wasn't even worth his derision.

With petty satisfaction, I noted that he was sitting by himself.

Completing my journey to the front, I sat down with Page. Seeing her helped calm me down, re-center me, and turn my thoughts back toward Angel.

After a quick check-in with her, I said hello to Angel's family—his mother, along with several cousins and some aunts and uncles. I had gone home with Angel for Thanksgiving several times during college, because Chicago was so much closer than Tennessee, so I knew them all.

At 1:56 p.m., I rejoined Page and sat down to wait for the start of the service.

At 1:58 p.m., there was a stir coming from the back of the sanctuary. I turned to see what was happening, then gently squeezed Page's thigh to get her attention.

Aiysha Reddish had just walked into the church.

She made quite the entrance. Dressed head to toe in black, including a black fascinator with a small veil attached to it, she seemed not to notice or care that nearly every eye in the church was on her as she walked up the aisle. Joining in her procession, linked arm in arm with her, was her sister, who I recognized from the wedding.

They settled into the far side of the pew in front of us, next to Angel's family.

Page and I exchanged a look that seemed to pose all the relevant questions: Where had she been? Why hadn't she answered anyone's phone messages? Why was she suddenly showing up now?

There were no obvious answers and this was no time to ask.

Before I could make sense of anything, that magnificent organ was filling the church with haunting notes, and the service had begun.

The next hour or so was a blur. I veered between feelings like bumper cars at a carnival, all while stewing in this fundamental disbelief that any of this was happening.

I just keep staring at those pictures of Angel—Angel laughing; Angel smiling; Angel being his strong, brilliant, beautiful self.

There was one of him in particular that kept grabbing me by the throat.

It was from his bachelor party. Since neither Angel nor I were big partyers, it was a pretty low-key affair. No strippers or anything stupid like that. We chartered a sailboat and took it out on San Francisco Bay—twenty or so guys, enjoying a great time in a gorgeous setting.

The photo was snapped just as the sun was setting. In it, Angel is gazing out at the water and the hills beyond with this look of hope—a young man on the verge of marriage with his whole future ahead of him.

So much talent. So much to give. So much potential.

Such a tragedy that he didn't live to see it through.

I managed to tear my attention away from the photo during Lorne's eulogy, which was, to my ears, perfect. Warm. Touching. A few funny stories. A few serious stories. Lorne had that Texas twang and a way of speaking that he came off like a southern preacher. It was lovely.

My turn came next. My opening paragraph was: "In our culture, men don't say they love each other very often. Angel and I did. All the time. That's the kind of man he was. He led with love."

I'm not even sure what I said after that. I was just trying to keep my composure. I failed more than once. It was a struggle to make it through.

The pastor focused his eulogy around John 11:35, which was known for, among other things, being the shortest verse in the Bible.

It consisted of just two words: "Jesus wept."

The pastor went on to talk about the profound hurt we were all feeling and how—at a time like this—even God was crying.

I was weeping, too. Unabashedly and uncontrollably. I wasn't trying to hold anything back anymore. I just let it all go, all the grief I had been bottling up inside since Tuesday morning.

So did Page. We were clinging tight, leaning against each other for support, bawling.

By the time the organ began playing to mark the close of the ceremony, there wasn't a dry eye in the house.

As the song ended, those who wanted to pay their respects to the family began queuing. Page and I joined them.

When we reached his mother and cousins, there were a lot of hugs. And more tears.

Then I got to the very end of the receiving line, where Aiysha was standing. As I groped for what words I wanted to say to her, I moved toward her.

Maybe I didn't even need to say anything. Maybe I should just give her a hug.

As soon as she saw me closing in, I watched the temperature of her face drop at least fifty degrees in an instant.

From behind her veil, she spoke in a voice that dripped with venom.

"I don't know if you were ever truly Angel's friend," she said. "But you're no friend of mine."

My mouth dropped.

"Aiysha, what are you—"

I was interrupted by a shove from behind. Page was hissing at me, "Keep moving, just keep moving."

Not knowing what else to do, I allowed myself to be pushed out of the way.

On her way past Aiysha, Page offered a quick, terse, "We're very sorry for your loss."

CHAPTER 21

THE TUESDAY AFTER the memorial service, I answered my summons to Rig Weiskopf's Stinson Beach surfing hut.

There was no set agenda for our meeting, at least none I had been made aware of. It was framed only as a get-to-know-you affair; though it was pretty clearly not social. Even though it was scheduled for five o'clock—and arrangements for dinner had been alluded to—there had never been a mention of Page being invited.

This was business. If I was to serve as the mouthpiece for Balco, I needed to better understand the beliefs and principles of its owner.

Rig had things he wanted to say.

Earlier in the day, I had pumped Bob Brunato for a scouting report on Rig. From this, I had managed to learn that, in addition to being a free-spirited surf bum, he was also a lifelong bachelor with no children.

In a different era—and a place less progressive than the Bay Area—the description "lifelong bachelor" would have been polite code for gay.

Bob assured me that wasn't the case here. Rig had been seen with a variety of women on his arm through the years. Most were what Bob deemed to be gold diggers, with fake boobs and lip filler. None had lasted more than a few months.

Really, Rig was married to Balco, and everyone knew it.

His only other lasting relationship was with the waves.

Beyond that, Bob seemed mostly bemused with the idea of my visit. The pilgrimage to the surfing hut was a rite of passage for communications VPs. Every single one of my predecessors had, at some point fairly early on in their tenure, been subjected to it.

Bob's parting thought was, "Rig's a little kooky, but at least he knows it. Just roll with it."

Rig's "hut" turned out to be a gracious home perched at the edge of the beach. While not ostentatious, it was still at least five bedrooms. In this neighborhood, that had to make it worth ten or fifteen million.

There was a short driveway wide enough for two vehicles. I parked next to a Rivian pickup truck with a longboard stowed in back.

I had to walk up a flight of steps to reach the front door, because the house was elevated. I rang the doorbell and Rig soon answered in his usual getup—boardshorts, a T-shirt, flip-flops.

"Come on in," he said slowly, smiling easily.

There was something loose, almost oiled, about his voice. Was he high?

I didn't smell any weed or detect anything else that might have indicated drug use. Maybe he was just more relaxed in his home environment?

As he began talking, he seemed lucid enough, though I still had the sense he was on something. There was no slurring of words, per se; just a certain lugubriousness to his speech.

He led me on a tour of his home, which left me with two basic impressions.

One, Rig liked things neat. Every space was squared away, every surface dustless.

Two, and quite unexpectedly, Rig was into art. There were paintings hung on nearly every available wall surface. Abstract impressionism seemed to be his jam. And he had spared no expense.

At one point, I thought I recognized a Rothko. In another room, he casually waved toward what I was fairly certain was a Jackson Pollock.

These were million-dollar paintings—multimillion-dollar paintings, even. Rig didn't name-check any of them. When he mentioned a work, it was only to talk about how it made him feel, or what emotional state had led him to acquire it. He mentioned several art dealers and "art friends," with whom he bought and sold works. He also donated pieces to museums.

We finished in the living room, where a series of massive picture windows commanded my attention. Through them, I could see over the dunes to the Pacific Ocean, whose waves ended their long journey with an audible crash onto the sandy shoreline.

"Beautiful," I said.

"I never get tired of it," Rig said. Then he explained: "We're pointed southwest right now. If it wasn't for the curvature of the earth, the next thing you'd be able to see is Hawaii, three thousand miles away. Then it would be another five thousand miles of empty ocean and you'd hit Australia. I've got a little cruiser docked in Sausalito that I like to putter around in. But one of these days I'm going island hopping around the Pacific on that baby."

"What's stopping you?" I asked.

Because, really, what was he waiting for?

"I don't know," he said, his eyes fixed on some distant point. "It's always something."

His gaze snapped back to the beach. This launched him on a detailed reportage of where the best waves could be found based on certain underwater features and how they interacted with the winds and tides of any given moment.

He shifted next to local lore, pointing out where Janis Joplin's ashes were said to have been scattered, then the approximate locations of several of the more gory great white shark attacks.

"Do you ever worry about that?" I asked.

He didn't flinch. "Nah. There's certain commonsense stuff you can do. Don't surf at dawn or dusk. That's when great whites feed. Don't surf if there's a colony of seals around. That's what great whites eat. Beyond that, the odds of getting attacked are really small. You have a better chance of being struck by lightning. Really, it's like anything in business. You're never going to eliminate a hundred percent of the danger. You do what you can to mitigate the risks and then you move on."

By this point, we had meandered toward a sitting area at the corner of the house, where all the chairs were pointed toward the spectacular view.

Just short of it, there was a table filled with picture frames. This was the one and only place in the house where the art was personal: They were all photographs of Rig with other people.

But not just anyone.

I picked up a frame of Rig next to a white-haired gentleman who was familiar to *Star Wars* fans the world over.

"George Lucas?" I asked.

"Yeah. He's lived in Marin for years. *Star Wars* was actually created in San Anselmo, just up the road. Same with *Indiana Jones*."

Next to that was Rig with a handsome man who could have been a movie star were he not more familiar in another realm.

"Gavin Newsom?" I asked.

"He went to Redwood High School. It's not far from here. I

contributed to his very first campaign for Board of Supervisors in San Francisco. And probably every campaign since."

I moved onto Rig with his arm around a man with one of the thickest beards I had ever seen. It covered his cheeks so thoroughly it was practically in his eyes. He had on a short-sleeve shirt that showed off arms that were every bit as hairy.

"And who is that?" I asked. "Sasquatch?"

Rig roared with laughter. "No, he's just an art friend."

We went through the rest of the gallery. Rig with politicians. Rig with movie stars. Rig with famous surfers.

Eventually, he led us around to the chairs. Once we were seated, he surprised me with his next question: "Curt, do you like physics?"

"I've never really given it much thought," I admitted. "Though I'm aware it exists whether I like it or not."

He smiled at this. "I dabble in it. I can't pretend to understand it on a deeper level. But I'm fascinated by the theories and their implications. Our existence is so precarious and so wonderful. Did you know that the only reason we came into being at all is that during the big bang, matter just slightly outnumbered antimatter? It's true. There were a billion and one matter particles for every billion antimatter particles. If that hadn't been the case, matter and antimatter would have kept fighting it out forever. They would have annihilated each other with their againstness, and the universe would have amounted to nothing. Instead, because one-billionth of that primordial soup had nothing against it, it was allowed to become matter. And that gave rise to everything you see—the sand, the ocean, the air, those birds, you and I. Everything."

"Wow," was all I could say.

"I know. 'Wow.' But the thing I always wonder is: Why? What made that one-in-a-billion happen here? There were probably a billion other universes that never amounted to anything, but we came into being for some reason. There has to be a purpose to it. I refuse to accept that we're just some glitchy accident."

His eyes were again bolted to the horizon. I was starting to wonder if maybe he wasn't high after all. Maybe his speech was just slower because his brain was weighed down with all these heavy thoughts.

"This is what I was starting to say the other day about againstness. Fundamentally, the entire known universe sprang forth because some small part of it was able to escape againstness. Therefore, if we are to be at harmony in the universe, we must also not engage in againstness. Do you understand?"

I didn't really. Not in the way he wanted. But I said, "I think so, yeah."

"So I know you're hurting because you lost your friend. I'm hurting, too. Angel was a wonderful man. But to go out and try to get revenge like Lorne and Sal want to do, that doesn't serve anything. All it does is create more againstness, which is counter to the very nature of our universe."

He stopped, looked at me with unusual directness, and said, "You're still not convinced."

"I . . . I'm neither convinced nor unconvinced," I said, then immediately cringed at what a meaningless sentence I had just constructed.

"Okay. You're in an absorption phase. I get it," Rig said. "Sometimes I think againstness is easier to understand with simpler physics, Newtonian physics. Think about a tree, just standing there. If you go over and push against the tree, you actually make the tree push back. You cause it to exert a force against you. Whereas if you left the tree alone, there would be no force against you. When you are against things, you cause them to be against you. Whereas if you are for things, they will be for you. Does that make sense?"

I wasn't sure how I was supposed to be for a tree, but I just nodded.

"Maybe a better analogy is surfing," he continued. "When you're a young buck, you think you can overpower the wave. The truth is, the more you battle the wave, the more you make the wave battle you. I don't care how good a surfer you think you are, you'll never be stronger than the ocean. You only become a great surfer when you let go of your againstness and learn to go with the wave. It's the same with everything else. Business. Relationships. Everything."

Surfing as a metaphor for life.

Yes, I was definitely in California.

I thought for sure that, at any moment, he was going to pull out a bong and ask me to smoke with him. Instead, he said, "Anyhow, enough physics. There's dinner set out for us in the kitchen. Let's eat."

CHAPTER 22

AFTER THAT ODD evening, life settled into an unfamiliar—if predictable—new pattern.

I typically arrived at the office by six or six thirty so I could beat the morning traffic and get things done before the day started pulling me in too many directions.

On the back end, I tried to leave by five thirty or six so I could get back to the DreamHouse and spend some quality time with Page. Admittedly, my on-time departure rating probably would not have compared favorably with most major airlines.

On weekends, I worked from home. Eight hours on Saturday. Two hours on Sunday.

Logistics just never stopped.

Nearly everything I encountered felt new, different, or strange. Even with things I had seen before, I was often experiencing them 180 degrees off from what I was used to—because I wasn't the reporter.

I was the flack.

It wasn't my job to create stories anymore.

It was my job to plant them and hope they grew into something wonderful.

Or prune them, if they were harmful.

Or, at the very least, shape them into something more pleasing.

The sneaking sense that chased me everywhere was that I was faking it, and I dreaded the seemingly inevitable moment when I was going to get called out for it.

It would have been different with Angel there to help me. In lieu of that, I just tried my best to remember the things he had drilled into me during the weeks leading up to my start date.

One of his bits of wisdom was to "walk the warehouse" now and then.

You'll learn more about logistics walking the warehouse than you'll ever learn from staring at spreadsheets. Too many of the people here are bean counters. They forget that what we spend all day moving around isn't numbers. It's stuff: actual stuff being moved by actual people. But you only really get a sense of that if you go down and walk the warehouse.

With this in mind, I made it a point to walk the warehouse every couple of days.

In addition to giving me some much-needed exercise, it made for a nice break from some of my other tasks.

One of the main things occupying my time and attention was the impending union vote. Without Angel to serve as the down-to-earth voice of the company, there was a vacuum on our side of the debate.

For as beloved as Lorne Murphy was, it was tough to trot out a multimillionaire and pretend he was a true man of the people.

It was even worse with Rig Weiskopf. He was a multibillionaire.

I was way too new to have any credibility with the rank and file.

When I suggested to Bob Brunato that, owing to his long history with the company, he might be the right person to sway hearts and minds, he just laughed.

"I'd probably lose us votes," he said. "Everyone knows I'm the ultimate company man."

There was really no one quite as effective as Angel—as I'm sure Rudy Szymanski knew.

Regardless of who was or wasn't talking, the subject of the union vote remained nuclear hot. A brawl had broken out between pro-union and anti-union factions in the break room at the Long Beach warehouse. The foreman had to use pepper spray to quell it.

It was either that or call the cops.

There were also more routine matters that were taking up my time. I remained on the steep part of the learning curve with most issues, inhaling knowledge as quickly as I knew how. But that at least meant I was starting each new day a little smarter than the last.

I probably felt best about the job I was doing as a manager. There would be no Comms Team mutinies on my watch. I made an effort to really get to know everyone on the team, figure out how they ticked, and support them as best as I knew how.

Once a week, on Friday afternoons, I gathered everyone for carefully disguised team-building exercises. I called it "Happy Hour," even though there was no drinking involved. Whether it was to play a game or to get everyone off-site at one of the Bay Area's many beautiful places, it was all about giving everyone a shared experience outside work.

Spouses, partners, and significant others were welcome. Page—who still didn't know anyone and was seriously lacking in social outlets—joined us pretty much every time.

There, some funny patterns emerged. Korynne Vuong seemed to avoid her at all costs, while Bob Brunato was drawn to Page like metal shavings to a magnet.

My guess was that Bob had a little crush on her. She said he mostly talked about the romantic things he did for his wife, so it was pretty harmless. Page and I mostly laughed it off.

I didn't blame Bob for having a thing for Page.

Hey, I did, too.

Otherwise, Page was homebound most of the time. Her newfound domesticity was something of a marvel to both of us. Before this, when we both had demanding jobs, tasks like cooking and cleaning had fallen rather evenly between us. Now she was taking the management of the household head-on, with the same gusto as she once attacked her career.

When our belongings arrived on the truck, she dove into unpacking and putting things away. She donated a lot of our old furniture to Goodwill and found proper places for everything else.

She wanted the place perfect for when the baby arrived.

Her energy astonished me. The fatigue of first trimester had given way to this mania for scrubbing and organizing. I'd come home and find her on her hands and knees in a closet, rearranging what looked, to me, like perfectly orderly belongings.

Her nesting instinct, she called it.

She was also experiencing changes to her body. In addition to her expanding midsection, her sense of smell had grown so acute she could make out something rotting in the fridge from down the street. Her mane of red hair had grown even thicker, curlier, and more glamorous.

Between the nose and the hair, she had started referring to herself as She-Wolf.

To be clear: Her husband had not.

In the meantime, the ache of Angel's death remained ever-present. There were so many small moments where I thought of something I wanted to say to him or I found myself reminiscing about a good time we had together.

I still didn't know what to make of Aiysha's comments to me at the memorial service or understand what I had done to incite her ire. She had once again disappeared. And it was quite apparent she didn't plan to come back.

A For Sale sign had gone up at the house.

Everyone's grief takes a different path.

My own grief felt like it was stumbling along. Every morning after I got off the elevator on the fourth floor, I passed this bulletin board that held employee announcements.

The flyer for Angel's celebration of life—with his picture prominent on it—was still posted. In my mind, I greeted him each morning as I entered, then said goodnight in the evening as I exited.

It was silly, maybe. But it made me feel like I was at least doing something to keep him close.

The investigation into his murder was not moving much. Sal Salcedo's people had struck out in their efforts to find additional security footage with a Ford F150 in it. No one's cameras reached as far out as Adeline Street.

Meanwhile, Mando Fierro was waiting for the DNA on the blood in the back of the car and was hoping that would break open the case.

I had the sense that was the limit of what he planned to do. He had already moved onto other cases. Oakland averaged a murder every three days. He couldn't spin his wheels on one of them no matter how important I happened to think the victim was.

Before I knew it, the first half of the month had slid by and a direct deposit from Balco payroll appeared in my bank account. The pay stub that went along with it had numbers that astonished me. Even with deductions for taxes and retirement, I had cleared a little over $10,000.

It would have taken me three months to earn that much in my old job. Yet, unless I got myself fired, I was going to keep taking that home every two weeks for the foreseeable future.

Wild.

It certainly made the steady drumbeat of eleven-hour days feel worthwhile. I still missed journalism and the feeling that I was contributing to the public dialogue, though there was at least one aspect of Balco that replicated my old vocation: You could never quite predict what was going to happen.

That first payday, a Tuesday, was a prime example. I was forcing my way through some truly dreadful copy about greater efficiency in last mile delivery when Bob Brunato appeared in my doorway.

"Hey, I was just up on the fifth floor. Did you hear the news?"

"No, what?"

"Sidney Graves suffered a heart attack while on vacation in Prague," Bob said. "He's in surgery as we speak. His wife isn't sure if he's going to make it."

I was soon summoned to an emergency meeting in the boardroom, where it became evident that there were no details beyond what everyone already knew—Sidney had taken seriously ill—and therefore it was difficult to make any long-term determinations.

The gravity of the situation was underscored by the presence of Rig Weiskopf, who looked like he had been dragged in off Stinson Beach to attend the meeting. There were still grains of sand clinging to his flip-flops.

There was a lot of speculation as to Graves's long-term prognosis. He was fifty-eight, which wasn't that old; but it also wasn't that young. At any age, he'd be facing a long recovery.

That's if he recovered at all.

More than anything, people were in shock. Apparently, Sidney wasn't merely a recreational cyclist. He was a champion, a guy who routinely won his age group in masters road races of forty, fifty, or sixty miles around the Bay Area. No one could fathom that someone in such excellent shape would have heart trouble.

Lorne seemed particularly stricken. And, perhaps because of the CEO's uncharacteristic lack of leadership, a sense of crisis gripped the executive suite. They were already without a COO. The specter of losing the CFO on top of that would put a significant portion of the organization in flux.

I felt a certain amount of guilt throughout the meeting because my only thought on the matter was some form of: *Good riddance.*

But no one was really asking the vice president for communications about his thoughts. It was generally agreed in the room that since Sidney was supposed to be on vacation anyway—and since we didn't know much about what had really happened—we shouldn't say anything publicly for the time being.

That seemed to me to just be delaying the inevitable. But I supposed it didn't hurt to at least wait until there was a little more clarity.

Coming out of that meeting, updates about Sidney's condition remained hard to come by; so much so that Lorne actually considered sending someone from the Accounting Team to the Czech Republic, just so we wouldn't have to rely on Sidney's beleaguered wife, Lisa, for reports.

It took a day or so before Lisa Graves began communicating more, and a fuller story emerged. Sidney had been sitting in a bistro alongside the Vltava River, not far from Charles Bridge, when he started complaining that his left shoulder was bothering him.

Then he collapsed.

He was rushed to a nearby hospital, where it was his luck that their lead cardiothoracic surgeon was available to perform an emergency quadruple bypass.

On Thursday, Lisa shared a photo of Sidney, sitting up in a hospital bed, gamely giving the camera a thumbs-up. His eyes were half-lidded and his complexion underneath his ever-present tan was decidedly gray.

He was topless, with a hospital sheet covering his lower half. A nasal breathing tube snaked across his face. His chest had several patches with wires leading out of them; though, of course, that wasn't what most drew the eye.

It was the raw, ten-inch-long, Frankenstein-like zipper scar running along his sternum where he had been cracked open.

He looked like he had been through hell.

What had come out by then was that Sidney had been suffering from hypertension and had a family history of heart trouble. He had been under orders from his doctor in the States to slow down and find better ways to manage his stress.

Between that and his age, a decision about his future had already been made. Lisa informed Sidney—and the rest of us—that he was retiring immediately.

My last act that Friday afternoon was to write a press release announcing the retirement of Sidney Graves due to health concerns. An interim CFO had been named, and a search for a permanent replacement was already underway.

I sincerely didn't wish him ill, but I couldn't say I would miss him. Where I was concerned, it didn't matter who the new CFO was. They would be better than the one who had just quit.

The incident had mostly faded into my rearview mirror by the middle of the next week, when a new calamity rose up.

It began on a Wednesday afternoon, when Korynne Vuong leaned her head full of shiny black hair into my office.

"There's a reporter from the *San Francisco Chronicle* on the line," she said. "He wants your comment about a video involving Balco."

"What video?"

"I don't know. He won't tell me. He says he needs to talk to you directly."

"Okay," I said. "Put him through."

CHAPTER 23

I FELT A QUICK jolt of energy. Other than the first few days, when Angel was in the news, we didn't get regular inquiries from major media outlets like the *Chronicle.* Most of my focus had been on internal communications, requests for copy from the Marketing Team, and maybe placing a story in a trade publication or two.

But this was certainly what I imagined when I took this job: finding myself on the other side of the notebook, sparring with reporters who inhabited the same seats I once sat in.

I picked up the phone with my best, "Curt Hinton."

"Hello, Mr. Hinton. This is Ron Talbot. I'm the immigration reporter for the *Chronicle.* I was hoping to get your comment on a rather disturbing video that is making its way around the internet."

The immigration reporter? I thought to myself. But what came out of my mouth was: "And what video is that?"

"Check your email. I just sent you a link."

Ron Talbot's message was at the top of my inbox. I clicked, then hit the button to put the video in full-screen mode.

It began with blackness. There was maybe a smudge of light in the upper left corner. That was it.

All I heard was a plaintive female voice squealing in Spanish: "No, please, stop, please, no, help! Help! Help!"

Whoever was shooting this video seemed to be hiding in the dark, behind something or below something. But, slowly, the cameraperson got braver, inching upward and around a corner.

The lighting improved, but only marginally. It was still this eerie, gloomy orange—almost like the safety lighting on the stairs of a movie theater.

Gradually, the image came into focus, and whoever was holding the camera zoomed in on the subject matter.

It was a man. A large man. Lantern jaw. Thick neck. Burly shoulders.

He was on top of a much smaller woman, who looked young, but not too young. Maybe thirty or so. He was pressing her against the shiny concrete floor of a warehouse. He had her arms pinned against her sides. The ferocious rhythm of his thrusting made it revoltingly clear what he was doing to her.

She kept screaming the whole time.

No one came to her rescue.

Her terror was so plain.

It was sickening.

As a reporter, I had witnessed some of the most repellant things human beings could do to one another. This easily ranked up there with the worst of it.

All I could think about was that poor woman and the horror she had experienced.

But I already understood that wasn't why Ron Talbot was calling me.

It's that the clearest thing in the whole video, at least to my eye, was the assailant's hat.

It was navy blue with white lettering: a retro script font that said, "Balco."

Our company logo. It was familiar to anyone who had ever driven on an interstate anywhere from Texas to California, because we plastered it on all our trucks. We also spent tens of millions of dollars a year advertising it, all in the hopes that people would have positive feelings for the company behind it.

And now it was becoming associated with one of the most heinous things I had ever seen.

The man rather quickly finished his task. When he was done, he growled, "You better not say anything. I'll turn you into ICE. *Comprende*, senorita?"

"*Si, si*," she said meekly.

Then the video cut out. It had lasted about forty-five seconds.

That was more than enough.

I felt like I was going to vomit already.

"Oh God," I said, then quickly added, "That's off the record."

"I understand," Talbot said. "You need to play it back?"

"No. I don't ever want to see that thing again."

I exited full screen mode. That's when I saw the title of the video: "Balco driver rapes migrant."

Good Lord.

"I think you can see why I felt the need to call you for comment," Talbot said.

"Yes. Thank you," I said. "Can I ask you some questions off the record?"

"Sure."

"Where did you get this?"

"Are you familiar with the Breathe Free Network?"

I was, only because it had some billboards around the Port. Breathe Free was an advocacy group for undocumented immigrants whose name was derived from the famous inscription on the Statue of Liberty: "Give me your tired, your poor, your huddled masses yearning to breathe free."

"Vaguely, yes," I said.

"It was sent to me by their executive director, a woman named Rose Tyvand. Apparently, she had a volunteer who was given this video by someone—presumably one of Breathe Free's clients, which means it's someone undocumented, though the volunteer refused to say anything about who it was. So I don't know if the volunteer got this from the person who shot the video, or if it was secondhand, or what. For what it's worth, the volunteer checks out as a real person—they're a local flower shop owner who votes, owns a home, all that. And I had an expert look at the video to make sure it wasn't AI-generated. The expert said no, no chance. It's legit. Anyway, the volunteer had first taken the video to the DA's office, and the prosecutor said he couldn't do anything without a victim."

"The volunteer doesn't know who the victim is?"

"Nope. It sounds like the person who shot the video doesn't either. The victim remains unidentified, whereabouts unknown."

I had covered cops and courts long enough that I didn't need Ron Talbot to explain the rest to me. Without a victim to testify, it didn't matter how graphic or repellent this video was. The perpetrator could claim it was all an act; that the sex was a hundred percent consensual; that off-camera the woman had been smiling and happy; and that she only screamed "no, please, help" because she knew it aroused him.

Gross, but true.

"And because of it, a rapist runs free," I said.

"Exactly. The volunteer was livid when they heard that, so they started posting the video publicly to try to shame the DA's office into doing something."

"Oh my."

"Yeah. YouTube, Facebook, TikTok, Instagram, all the big ones. It got taken down pretty fast, but it's definitely out there to a certain degree. There were some people who were able to make their own copies before it got removed, and they've reposted it here and there."

As Talbot was talking, I did a quick image search for "Balco driver rapes migrant."

And, sure enough, there were hits—mostly from what appeared to be porn sites.

Sick.

"Anyway," Talbot continued, "I think the volunteer eventually talked to Rose Tyvand at Breathe Free, and she convinced the volunteer there was a better way to go about this. Are you familiar with the U Visa program?"

"No," I admitted.

"It's for victims of violent crime who are undocumented. Basically, it says if you come forward to cooperate with the authorities to help them prosecute serious crimes—including rape and sexual assault—the DA can line you up with a visa and a work permit. They're hoping if they put this out there along with information about U Visa, the victim will come forward."

"I see."

"Breathe Free is going to be posting this video on its website. They know it's sensitive material, so it'll come with a full trigger warning. They're also blurring parts of it, including the victim, of course. But they still want as much attention on it as they can get in the hopes that the victim hears about it. Rose Tyvand reached out to me with this because we've done stories together in the past, so I've got the exclusive on this, at least for the moment. I'm kind of curious what other outlets will do with it."

So was I.

Though my curiosity was also filled with dread.

"Are you guys planning on posting the video?" I asked.

"I don't know. That's above my pay grade. My editors are meeting about that soon."

"Has anyone identified the guy in the Balco hat?"

"No," Talbot admitted. "We're assuming it's a Balco driver, but of course we don't know that for sure. We're hoping you can tell us who the driver is and then we figured you might want to make a comment beyond that."

I now understood the real reason Ron Talbot was calling. He didn't want my comment. He wanted my help.

There was certainly a school of PR thinking in circumstances like this that said: Deny, deny, deny. Admit nothing. Concede nothing. Threaten that if Talbot wrote the perpetrator was affiliated with Balco, we'd file a defamation suit; and, otherwise, no comment him to death.

Frankly, that school was filled with idiots.

I recognized that Talbot was really offering us a bargain: Cooperate, and he'd make us look like good guys; like part of the solution and not part of the problem.

That meant that helping him was the right thing to do from both a moral *and* public relations standpoint.

Which made the decision pretty easy.

"I'll help in any way I can," I said. "What's your deadline?"

"We're hoping to get it up on the website tonight and in tomorrow's paper. I'd need to hear from you by five."

Five?!? Are you kidding me?

I looked at the time on my screen.

It was 3:47 p.m.

"You do realize Balco has six thousand drivers," I said. "You've just given me a little more than an hour to find a needle in a haystack."

"Is that on the record?"

"No. I'll call you by five."

CHAPTER 24

THE FIRST THING I did was swear explosively, loud enough that Korynne popped up from her cubicle to see what was the matter.

I ignored her for the moment and tried to think.

My impostor syndrome was rearing up again, but I did my best to tamp it down. This was not the moment for self-doubt. I had done this many times before: digging up information that was difficult to find, and doing it under extreme deadline pressure.

It was time to earn that bloated paycheck of mine.

If the assailant was our employee—and it sure looked that way—*someone* at Balco had to be able to identify him.

Once we made a positive ID, I could then call back the *Chronicle* with a statement about how we had terminated the offender for gross misconduct and would fully support law enforcement efforts to hold him accountable for the crimes he had committed.

Maybe we could even find a way to further support Breathe Free's efforts to find the victim. Offer her a job? Or would that come off as gratuitous overcompensation?

Whatever the case, I didn't want what we did to be about the optics. I wanted us to have a real impact.

But first: Find the driver.

I had memorized our organizational chart, in part because I knew my job would inevitably involve crisis management. And in a crisis, you didn't have time to teach yourself how to walk. You had to start at a run.

As a result, I knew this driver reported to a team leader, who reported to an operations manager, who reported to a regional operations manager, who reported to the director of regional operations, who reported to the vice president for transportation, who reported to the COO.

Who was dead.

Lorne Murphy had yet to appoint an interim COO. Rig Weiskopf had come out of retirement to serve in the role for the time being—his island hopping delayed once more.

Rig's four years out of the game had not dulled his abilities much. He had built this business from the first truck on up and knew it inside and out.

Still, I didn't feel like calling Rig. The last thing I needed at the moment was a lecture about the dangers of againstness.

I reached out to Lorne's assistant, Lucas Chandler, who told me Lorne was traveling and would be unavailable for several hours—which were among the last things I wanted to hear.

After ending the call, I swore again.

One of the many problems with the video was that we had no idea where it was filmed. There was nothing unusual about the background, no identifying features. That warehouse could have been anywhere.

(This was yet another reason prosecutors would have been leery about weighing in: They didn't even know whether they had jurisdiction.)

We had two main warehouses in California—Oakland and Long Beach—and four more spread around Mexico, including a facility in Tijuana that actually had more employees than headquarters. Each was considered its own region. Without knowing which region the driver worked in, I didn't know where to start.

Which meant I had to hit all of them at once.

I called Eric Strauss, the vice president for transportation, since he was at my level and all six thousand drivers were under his purview. I briefly explained what was happening and the extreme urgency of the situation. I also stressed the importance of getting the ID correct: If we botched it, we'd be handing one of our employees a defamation suit for the ages.

Thankfully, people in the logistics industry were used to dealing with emergency situations where we absolutely had to get things right.

We agreed that whoever this driver was, his team leader would certainly recognize him; and his operations manager, who was next up the ladder, would maybe recognize him. Beyond that, our chances of getting an ID diminished significantly.

So we had to focus on team leaders and operations managers. Eric had email groups set up that would allow him to email all team leaders and operations managers in just a few keystrokes.

There was no way we could send all those people a video this graphic and disturbing. Whether or not it was legal—and I wasn't entirely sure on that front—Human Resources would have us hung in effigy outside the main entrance.

We would just have to pull a still image of the driver from the video and hope that would be good enough. Eric would disseminate the photo and then we would both start praying that this driver's team leader and/or operations manager was still on the clock.

"Start typing the email," I said. "By the time you're done, I'll have the image for you."

"Got it," he said, and we hung up.

I was out of my chair before I even had the phone down. I rushed out into the hallway and looked a few doors up, through the glass wall, and toward the office of Amy Dietz, our social media manager.

In her mid-forties, Amy was a latter-day hippie who eschewed typical corporate dress, favoring bright colors and fun patterns. She was also a lot faster and better than I was when it came to editing and manipulating video images.

At this point, every minute mattered.

"Hey," I said as I entered her office. "Sorry to barge in. I really need you for something. It's an emergency."

"Sure, what's up?"

"I've got to show you something," I said. Then I started with my trigger warning: "It's really, really, seriously disturbing."

After I described the content, she assured me she could handle it. If anything, she welcomed the chance to help. She was eager to help me nail this creep to the wall.

"What can I do?"

"I need you to zoom in on this video and get the best possible still of this guy's face, and I need you to do it, like, fifteen minutes ago."

"On it," she said.

I hurried back to my office and forwarded Amy the video. She was already watching it when I returned to her office. There were soon tears rolling down her face.

"Oh my God," she said.

"I know."

She lobbed several angry, obscene words in the direction of the truck driver. Then she went to work.

It wasn't going to be easy. The footage was grainy. The lighting was terrible. The angle the video had been shot at wasn't particularly helpful, either. Everything was from the side.

She stopped the video at what looked to be the best moment, magnified the man's face, and captured it. Then she went to a photo editing app that allowed her to sharpen the image.

"Okay, how's this?" she asked, turning her screen toward me.

It was still blurry. In some ways, zooming in hadn't helped, because it had taken his face out of context with the rest of his body, whose girth was certainly an identifying feature. If this were being used as part of a photo array in a trial, a judge might throw it out as inadmissible.

I looked at the time on my phone. 4:09.

It would have to do.

"Great," I said. "Send it to me and Eric Strauss, please."

I immediately called Eric. He confirmed that he had received the image and was already attaching it to the email he had crafted.

"Okay," he said. "It's off."

Eric's office was on the fifth floor. Since his inbox was now the focal point of everything, I started heading there.

On my way, I stopped in to see Bob Brunato. I gave him a quick briefing of what was happening and asked him to loop in HR and start crafting a company-wide email. The last thing I wanted was for our employees to learn about this from the *San Francisco Chronicle*—or from whatever other news outlet might pick up the story.

Bob promised he'd have it done within the hour.

As I stepped into the elevator, I remembered how Angel had warned me about this aspect of working at Balco, and how it would impact my life.

We've got fourteen thousand people. At any given point in time, one of them is probably doing something they shouldn't.

I only wished he were here with me now, backstopping me, helping me figure out what to do. I found myself channeling him.

C'mon, C Note. You got this.

But did I?

If we didn't find this driver, we'd look like a bunch of stonewalling, obfuscating, bloodless corporate henchmen who were only interested in damage control and didn't care about this woman at all. Whatever statement I put out would ring hollow.

And maybe we'd still weather the storm. Or maybe this video would become a flashpoint in the debate about the plight of immigrants in the same way George Floyd changed the discussion around race in this country.

After all, it would prove that, in America, you could be caught on film raping an immigrant and still get away with it.

And a man wearing our company's logo would be the image in everyone's head.

When I arrived in Eric's office, he invited me to sit. Eric was a good fifteen or twenty years older than me. He was another Balco lifer, the son of a truck driver who had started out as a dispatcher and slowly climbed his way up the ladder. He had a table behind his desk that was cluttered with trophies and plaques—awards that either he or Balco had won for their distinguished service and general excellence.

"I take it you haven't heard anything yet," I said.

"Nothing. I'm just going through employee ID photos," he said, tilting his screen so I could see. "It's probably a waste of time. Some of these pictures are really old. But I figured it beat just sitting around and waiting for an email to come in."

"Yeah, I guess."

He clicked through more photos as he spoke. "I also reached out to Sal Salcedo. He has some fancy AI facial recognition software. He's trying to feed in the video and see if it matches with any of his security camera footage."

Balco definitely didn't lack for video surveillance.

"Good thinking," I said.

"My money is still on the human beings. I don't trust any of this AI nonsense."

"I'll take the ID where I can get it," I said.

Eric continued rolling through photos. I had scooted closer to his desk so I could be a second set of eyes on it.

Now and then we'd come across someone who might have been a match, but it was hard to tell. It turned out we had a lot of thick-necked truckers on our payroll. The more photos we looked at, the more everyone started looking the same.

The minutes kept rolling by.

It was now 4:35.

Make it 4:36.

"Hang on," I said, when he clicked through a photo a little too quickly. "Go back to that one."

Eric did as I requested and we both studied a man who may have borne a resemblance to the rapist. I was just starting to convince myself this was the guy—out of hope as much as anything—when Eric said, "Wait a sec. I just got an email."

He clicked over to his inbox. His eyes scanned the screen.

"We got a hit!" he yelped. "A team leader in Long Beach says it's one of his guys."

Eric was already picking up his phone.

"Is he sure?" I asked.

"I'm going to find out."

Eric dialed a number on his desk phone. His voice then dropped an octave as he spoke into the handset: "Hi, this is Eric Strauss from corporate . . . And you're positive? Beyond the shadow of a doubt? . . . We really can't screw this up. You have to be a hundred percent here . . . Okay, if you say so. I'm going to send you this video so you can be extra sure. Just to warn you, it's really bad . . . Okay, I'll hold."

Cradling the phone against his ear, he tapped out a few keystrokes, then clicked SEND.

He looked at me and raised his eyebrows for a moment, then spoke into the phone.

"You got it? . . . Great . . . There aren't any women in the office, are there? . . . Okay, just play it."

He waited.

"Yeah, I know . . . Good, good. Okay, I believe you. Where is he now? . . . Perfect. Bring him in, show him the video, then fire his ass. And make sure you get his ID badge . . . No, we can't arrest him. That's not our job, and at this point he doesn't even have charges against him . . . All right, call me back as soon as it's done."

Eric hung up.

"The driver is named Joseph Manger," he said, pulling up Manger's photo.

I knew from the moment I saw his ham hock of a jaw that we had found the guy. There was also a certain meanness to him that eliminated whatever doubt I might have had.

"He's forty-three," Eric continued. "He's based out of here. He's been with us eight years. He's only about an hour from the warehouse with an FTL headed for Tijuana, but they're recalling him right now. This will be over in no time. I'm going to call Accounting. I don't want this asshole getting another dime of Balco's money."

I looked at my phone.

4:44.

Perfect timing.

I went back to my office, called Ron Talbot, and fed him the name Joseph Manger, along with his company ID photo.

The statement I emailed him expressed the company's disgust at what had happened, its eagerness to help the authorities punish Joseph Manger to the fullest extent of the law, and its deepest sympathies toward the victim—who we urged to come forward so that justice could be served.

Talbot thanked me and scurried off to file his story. He said it would likely hit the *Chronicle*'s website within an hour or two.

Then I sat back and waited to see if this thing was going to blow up in our faces.

CHAPTER 25

THIS TIME, IT was the messenger who signaled the need for the call.

The alert went through the usual channels; and, before long, the messenger was on the phone with Lorne Murphy.

"What's going on?" the CEO asked. "Make it quick. I'm busy."

"You have a situation."

"Do I now?"

"There's a video of one of your people raping a woman making its way around the internet."

"What are you talking about?" Murphy demanded.

The messenger patiently described the video and its contents. He finished with, "My boss is offering our services if you need them."

"No. *No.* Absolutely not. We'll handle it."

"Just like you're handling Gillespie?" the messenger asked.

"You keep bringing up Gillespie. Tell me something: Has he been a problem?"

"We don't like to wait for things to become problems. He's a liability. My boss keeps asking about him."

"Yeah, well, tell your boss to cool it. We handle our business a little differently than you do."

"So you're going to take care of this situation with the driver?"

"Yes."

"How?"

"I don't know," Murphy said. "But that's my deal, not yours. Stay out of it."

CHAPTER 26

AT FIVE THIRTY, around the time that I normally texted Page to tell her I was coming home, I called to say I wasn't leaving anytime soon.

I told her it would be a long night, that I was sorry, that I wasn't sure when I'd be home, and that she shouldn't wait up.

She was mostly a good sport about it. The only thing she really expressed concern about was that I would be driving home after dark.

I didn't need the reminder as to why.

Before the *Chronicle*'s story went live, we sent Bob Brunato's note to the employees as an unsigned message from the Balco Communications Team email account.

Then we waited.

The best-case scenario was that this story would thread what felt like a rather small needle: It would get enough attention that the victim would hear about the U Visa offer, come forward quickly, and put Joseph Manger on his way to a jail cell; but, at the same time, it wouldn't trigger a landslide of other media coverage that would repeatedly put the phrase "Balco driver rapes migrant" in front of the nation's eyeballs.

I kept refreshing the *Chronicle*'s website, anxiously waiting for the first shoe to drop.

At 6:08, Ron Talbot's story finally appeared with the headline: "Bay Area Group Searches for Sexual Assault Victim."

It led with Rose Tyvand, Breathe Free, the U Visa program, and the group's efforts to find the victim of this terrible assault. The video was described but not shared—not even a blurred version—so obviously the *Chronicle*'s editors decided that the content was too graphic for their readership. It was a good call, in my opinion.

The story reported that the video was posted on Breathe Free's website. But it did not link to the video.

Another good call.

Balco was mentioned only sparingly, and only toward the end. Talbot wrote that Manger had been employed by Balco as a truck driver, but that he had been fired. It then generously quoted from my statement, making it very clear the company was on the side of the angels and fully cooperating.

It was as good as we could have hoped for under the circumstances. Honestly, without the video—and the prominent visuals of the Balco hat—the company's involvement felt a lot more tangential.

Joseph Manger could have been a trucker for Hapag-Lloyd or Estes. We were just another easily forgotten detail.

Now that the story was out there, Amy Dietz posted statements of support for Breathe Free's efforts on our social media accounts. Before she departed for the day, she promised she'd monitor the responses from home and call me if anything concerning arose.

On his way out, Bob Brunato said he'd do the same with the Balco Communications Team email, which had already been shipped out and had yet to receive a single reply.

Really, what was there to say?

Shortly after that, I heard from Eric Strauss, who told me that "the situation" was "resolved." I didn't ask for details.

I checked in with Talbot and thanked him for writing a story that was balanced and factually accurate. He thanked me in return for helping him, then told me he had found my bio on the Balco website.

"It doesn't surprise me you used to be one of us," he said. "You're good."

This led to an amicable conversation about the state of the newspaper business—and its seemingly endless decline. I shared how I missed it. He was still a believer.

"I know people get gloomy about how this is a post-truth world and nothing we report matters anymore and all that," he said. "But to me, there's still nothing like public outrage to prompt significant and immediate change. It can be harder to make the needle move. But when you do, it goes faster than ever."

As we wrapped up the call, I asked if he would be updating his story any more this evening. He said that was unlikely.

I gave him my cell number and asked him to keep me in the loop. He promised he would.

By the time all that had unfolded, it was nearing seven o'clock. It felt like the next hour or two would be critical. If other news outlets were picking up the story, it would be a long night. I'd know fairly quickly, because our phones would start going crazy.

It wouldn't take much. The media was nothing if not filled with copycats.

One network TV affiliate including this in its evening broadcast—or the Associated Press deciding to parrot the *Chronicle*'s story and put it out onto the wire—could make this thing metastasize and spread across the country in no time.

It was a content aggregation world and we were just living in it.

I kept doing a variety of online searches to track the story's progress, or lack thereof. The only person left in the office was Korynne, who seemed to be staying for moral support—or maybe because she had nothing better to do.

This had happened the two other times when I had stayed late as well. She just sort of hung around, for no apparent reason other than that I was there. I wasn't even sure what she was doing. I was so busy figuring out my own job I hadn't really had time to delve deep into the details of anyone else's.

Still, she seemed busy with . . . something. Or maybe nothing. Maybe it was like stories I had heard about the famed Japanese salaryman, who couldn't depart the office until the boss had left.

I had never asked Korynne about her personal situation, but she had gone out of her way to tell me about it anyway. She had been briefly married during her mid-twenties to a guy who turned out to be "a scumbag."

Since ending it, she had tried dating a little, but her heart wasn't really in it. So, now that she was in her late twenties, it was just her, alone in an apartment alongside Lake Merritt, a very livable part of downtown Oakland maybe ten minutes away.

No roommates. No pets.

"I don't even have houseplants," she had cheerfully volunteered.

As much to stretch my legs as anything, I got up and wandered out to her desk.

She gazed up at me like she was grateful for the company. She was wearing what I now recognized as fairly standard Korynne Vuong attire: short skirt, sleeveless button-down silk blouse, three-inch heels.

The official dress code for Balco corporate was business casual. The only reason I wore a suit every day is that I never knew what might happen—and whether I might suddenly need to represent the company on camera.

Korynne also seemed to dress a little sharper than was strictly required. Or maybe she was just a person who liked putting extra effort into her appearance.

"Hey, you don't have to stay, you know," I said. "I can handle this on my own."

She looked wounded. "Are you saying you don't want me here?"

"Oh, no, no, no!" I insisted quickly. "I'm grateful for the company. I just . . . I don't want you feeling like you *need* to stay, that's all."

"I know, but if this thing goes viral, you're going to want all the help you can get. Besides, I don't mind. It's not like I have anyone to run home to."

She smiled, showing me a perfect set of teeth.

"Okay, as long as you understand it's your call," I said. "I was probably going to hang around until nine or so. After that, I think we're in the clear for the night."

"Got it. Can I do anything?"

"Nah, from here on out it's just a lot of worrying, but I've got that covered."

She laughed. I returned to my office and kept refreshing my various searches.

Eight o'clock came and went. So did eight thirty. It was starting to look like we were in the clear—at least for the night—and I was thinking about packing up and heading home.

I didn't even hear Korynne padding softly into my office at first. She had taken her shoes off, so her approach was a lot more silent than usual.

She didn't bother stopping at the chairs. Without a word, she walked around to my side of the desk, cleared away the keyboard, and took a seat where it had been.

"Okay, I think it's time to call it," she announced. "You can stop worrying now."

I rolled my chair back to make as much extra room as I could. She fixed me with a dazzling smile.

It was hard not to notice that another button on her blouse had come undone. Her outfit seemed to have been transformed from office attire to something more suitable for the bar after work.

It was also hard not to notice that Korynne was gorgeous. Most of the time, I kept this thought—which served no good purpose whatsoever—as far from my mind as possible. But now it was rather impossible to ignore.

In addition to the extra skin she was suddenly showing, her hair, which she normally kept up, was now down. It was lustrous and cascaded several inches past her shoulders.

She held a bottle of wine in her right hand. In her left, she had two red Solo cups, which she set down on my desk. She filled them both halfway, then handed me one.

"I found this in the break room," she said. "I figured after a day like this, we could use it."

I almost never drank. But somehow I went along with it this time.

"Cheers," she said.

We touched rims and I tilted back the cup. I could feel the wine trace a warm path down my throat and into my empty stomach.

Korynne began a stream of banter. She kept shifting positions, crossing and uncrossing her legs, and flipping her hair. There wasn't a lot of room behind my desk, forcing us into close quarters—closer than we had ever been. This put me well within range of the light, sweet perfume she was wearing.

Now and then, I'd make a joke or a funny comment, and she'd throw her head back and laugh. Somehow, her bare feet had come to rest on the arm of my chair. This gave me a rather close view of her long, strong, lightly tanned legs.

With nothing in my stomach—and without much tolerance for alcohol to start with—the wine was going straight to my head. I reached the bottom of my cup fast, and Korynne was quick to refill me, leaning in quite close to me as she did so.

She was maybe getting a little sloshed, too. As she finished pouring, she lost her balance, causing her to reach out and grab my upper arm for support.

"Sorry," she said, though her hand lingered for a bit. Then she patted my shoulder a little and asked, "Oh, do you work out?"

"A little," I said. "I have a few free weights that I toss about now and then."

"It's nice," she said. "I need to get into weights more. I do yoga and run but sometimes I feel like my arms could use a little more definition, don't you think?"

She was now stretching her arms, which were slender, shapely, and, frankly, about as perfect as the rest of her. She was still standing quite close to me, giving me ample opportunity to examine the rest of her.

I hadn't been single in a while. And even when I was single, I was never much of a player. So I remained totally oblivious as to what was happening.

But as she smiled at me and flipped her hair again, it suddenly occurred to me.

Oh my God, is Korynne Vuong hitting on me?

She's maybe even trying to seduce me.

Is that why she always avoids Page at Happy Hour? Because my wife is the competition?

As soon as these thoughts registered, I stood up in a semi-panic and stepped away from my desk, practically running to the corner of my office.

"Well, this has been fun," I said, putting down the cup of wine. "But I really have to go."

"Are you sure you don't want to stay?" she asked sweetly. "I mean, you should at least finish your wine. Otherwise, it's alcohol abuse, right?"

She giggled.

I was just looking for a graceful escape.

"No, I've got a long drive home. Anyway, thanks for staying late. I really appreciated the support. You know, professionally. The support."

And then I practically ran out.

The only thing that slowed me down was a quick stop in the break room, where I grabbed two Clif Bars, just so I had something to sop up the alcohol in my stomach.

I was so busy and so distracted on my way out, I forgot to say goodnight to Angel's picture in the hallway.

While I didn't think I was anywhere near the legal limit, I still let the Rivian self-driving feature do most of the work on the way back to Marin County, all while keeping a death grip on the wheel.

I was also stewing over what to tell Page. My first thought was that I should just vomit a confession on her and provide a forensic accounting of every detail, every cue I failed to pick up on, every way in which I was culpable for what had occurred.

It would be the guilt talking, of course; and the guilt had a lot to say.

But then the more I thought about it, the more I rationalized that maybe I didn't have anything to be guilty about, and that I hadn't actually done anything wrong.

After all, I hadn't encouraged Korynne. I hadn't asked her to stay late or to get us a cup of wine. I certainly wasn't the one who had taken off her shoes or popped that extra button on her shirt.

It was even possible I was just misreading the situation entirely.

Had she *really* been trying to seduce me? Or was she just a lonely person who didn't feel like going back to an empty apartment? Really, why would someone like Korynne—who clearly wouldn't have trouble attracting male attention—hit on ordinary old me?

It was more likely that she knew I was happily married and therefore felt comfortable letting her guard down around me, because she knew it wasn't going anywhere. There was no interest on her part.

Plus, I was her boss. In this day and age, everyone understood an office romance between people on different rungs of the org chart was a nonstarter. I might as well have been a eunuch.

By the time I finished the drive, I had sobered up significantly. And sober me decided it made more sense to keep this to myself.

Nothing had actually happened. And there was no need to make Page worry every time I had to stay late at the office.

Stress wasn't good for pregnant women. I had seen the research that said high cortisol levels were associated with all kinds of negative outcomes for both mother and child.

Besides, she was now seventeen weeks in and feeling strange in her body as it was being taken over by her rapidly growing passenger. The last thing she needed to hear was her husband talking about some ambiguous interaction with the lithe, single yoga/running enthusiast at the office.

Further solidifying my decision, Page was already asleep by the time I got home. She didn't need to be woken up with something like this.

I quietly slipped into bed beside her and tried to get to sleep.

Though, in truth, it was a long time before I finally managed to drift off.

CHAPTER 27

FROM THE WINDOWLESS room, the call went out not long after the lights went out on the fourth floor at Balco headquarters.

"Hey, he went home," the caller said.

"Yeah? Did our girl get anywhere?"

"I thought she was going to. It looked good for a moment there. But she struck out again."

"He's a tough nut to crack."

"I gotta be honest, I don't know if she's working it hard enough. I mean, I watched the whole thing, and all she took off was her shoes. Unless your boy has a thing for sucking toes, how's that going to get her anywhere?"

"Just be patient. She knows what she's doing."

"You think maybe we should switch it up?" the caller asked. "Send in someone else? What if the gentleman prefers blondes? Or redheads—like that little cherry tart he's got?"

"Nah. I'll talk to her. Get her to up her game."

CHAPTER 28

THURSDAY PASSED WITHOUT any significant acceleration of interest in Ron Talbot's story.

Only one other media outlet—a San Francisco NPR affiliate—did a follow-up.

It sent a reporter to interview Rose Tyvand. The video was mentioned. Balco was not. Joseph Manger was referred to as merely "a local truck driver."

The story was primarily about the dangers that migrants—and, in particular, migrant women—faced in a world where they were afraid to report crimes to law enforcement.

Having public radio weigh in didn't exactly create a feeding frenzy. The overall impact was minimal. The same well-meaning progressives who had read the story in the *Chronicle* now listened to it on NPR. They fretted about it as they sipped their organic ethically sourced fair trade coffee.

But they didn't actually do anything besides stew in their liberal indignation.

No one else touched it.

Maybe it was too nuanced. Or too complicated. Or too difficult.

Or maybe it was that TV, which thrived on visuals, couldn't actually do anything with *this* visual. It was too graphic, too difficult, too likely to stir up FCC complaints.

Whatever the case, the story was showing all the signs of dying down rather than ratcheting up.

As for Korynne, there was no change to her demeanor. She was carrying about as if nothing unusual had happened Wednesday night, which only solidified my thinking that maybe I had been making too big a deal out of it.

She was still there come five thirty on Thursday evening, though, hanging around as usual—maybe even a little expectantly. If I stayed late again, would she stay with me?

I didn't feel like finding out. So I announced my departure loudly, making sure she didn't miss it. She gave me another one of those bright smiles that might have meant anything, up to and including *I'm just trying to suck up to my new boss.*

But then, out of curiosity, I hung out in my car in the parking area beneath the building to see how long she stayed after I left.

Sure enough, two minutes after I departed, she came hurrying out of the elevators toward her car.

Korynne Vuong, salaryman.

The next day, Friday, was again sliding by uneventfully. I had an in-house Happy Hour planned—a silly team-building game we would play. I was mostly just trying to get caught up on a backlog of requests.

Page was making noises about us having some "quality time" over the weekend. She had sketched out the basics—it involved making waffles and having sex, both of which sounded plenty good to me—and I knew I would ignore her at my own peril.

She was increasingly on my case that I was turning into a workaholic, and she wasn't wrong. My unfamiliarity with the logistics business meant that many of the things I did took twice as long as they probably should have.

Even with the extra effort, I was barely keeping my head above water; and the weight of expectations I felt to justify my considerable salary and benefits package was like an anchor, dragging me toward the bottom.

I hadn't shared with Page that the reason I was working so hard was that I was worried about being fired. I had learned more about my predecessor's departure, and it hadn't exactly been reassuring.

Yes, he had been unpopular with the Comms Team, as Angel had told me. But the bigger problem had been that other department heads weren't satisfied with his work, or with the work of the Comms Team in general.

The chief complaint was a damning one: that he didn't truly know the business; and that, therefore, everything he put out, and everything he okayed from his people, was facile, shallow, and reflected his superficial understanding of the underlying issues.

What worried me most was that I felt like this was my biggest weakness, too. For as gallant as my efforts at faking it were, I was surely going to be exposed.

I didn't even know what I didn't know.

How soon until that caught up with me?

So I was engaged in my usual race against my own self-doubt sometime after three o'clock when a call came in on my cell.

It was Ron Talbot.

"Hey, Ron, what's up?"

"We found her," he said.

"The woman from the video?"

"Yeah. I just got done interviewing her. We won't be naming her, naturally. I'll be calling her 'Maria.' It was kind of our luck that she lives locally—in Richmond. I guess she had told a few people who are close to her what had happened. Her aunt, who also lives here, was the one who saw the story and wondered if this was the thing her niece had talked about. Maria said she knew even before she looked at the website that the video was going to be her. She just had no idea someone had been filming it. When she saw the video, she recognized everything, and she immediately reached out to Breathe Free."

"God, I can't imagine what that was like for her, having to rewatch that."

"She actually said that if she had known there was a video, she would have reported it to the police when it first happened," Talbot said. "She just thought that without any hard evidence, the cops wouldn't believe her, so there was no point in taking the risk of coming forward."

"But now she's cooperating?"

"Yeah. Breathe Free connected Maria with the police and she gave them a full statement. The DA is using the complaint to get a warrant for Joseph Manger's arrest as we speak. After she was done with the cops, she talked to me. Her English is pretty good—better than my Spanish. She's undocumented, of course, but she's well-established here. She's got a job at a local restaurant that I won't be naming. She and her boyfriend are talking about getting married. She's been in the country for ten years—since she was nineteen. The aunt I mentioned won the green card lottery a number of years back and a lot of the rest of the family has slowly joined her."

"I guess the narrative of 'brand-new migrant taken advantage of by predator' falls apart a little."

"Well, yes and no. Even people who have been here ten, twenty, thirty years still feel like they need to live in the shadows."

"I guess that's true," I allowed.

"Anyway, there's actually a little bit of an unexpected twist to this, and it's why I'm calling."

"Are we on the record right now?"

"Why don't I just tell you what I need your comment on, and then you can tell me what that comment is?"

"That sounds fair," I said.

"Okay, so here's the deal. Maria actually *was* a new migrant in a way. When she was attacked, she had just been returning from a trip to Mexico. She had gone down there because her cousin was getting married, and she hadn't seen that family in ten years, and her *abuela* is sick, and she had been saving money so she could go down and see everyone."

"Right."

"So she was basically facing the same problem that people without documents have been dealing with for years: It's really easy to leave this country. It's not so easy to come back."

"Can't she just hop on a plane and say she's coming here for a visit?"

"Yeah, but then there would be a record," Talbot said. "When she entered the U.S., she would have to fill out an I-94 Form, which nails down her entry date, her visa status, and—at least in theory—her exit date. The moment she overstays her visa, she's breaking the law. Enforcement is pretty shoddy, admittedly, but it still exists. A record would have been created. If she got caught, she could be deported. Another problem with a violation like that is it makes it really difficult for her to ever get legal status here by any other legitimate means, because Uncle Sam would forever view her as someone who had broken the law."

"I follow you. So how did she do it?"

"Like a lot of people in her circumstance do. She paid a coyote eight thousand bucks to smuggle her safely back into the country."

"Oh."

"Now here's the twist. She says her coyote was the guy who raped her."

"Joseph Manger was a coyote?"

"According to Maria, yes. She says Manger secreted her across the border in his truck and then raped her on the floor of a Balco warehouse. So that's the thing I need comment on: Is Balco aware that one of its drivers was acting as a coyote?"

There was silence on the line for a moment as I tried to digest this.

Like it wasn't bad enough the guy was a rapist. He was smuggling immigrants, too.

"What's your deadline?" I asked.

"Five."

Of course it was.

"Let me get back to you."

CHAPTER 29

I DIDN'T BOTHER calling. I just went straight up to the fifth floor.

When I came across Lucas Chandler, I put on a weary smile.

"Please tell me he's back from Mexico," I said. "It's an emergency."

"He is. Hang on."

Lucas tapped three times on the door behind him, then disappeared behind it for a moment. When he reappeared, he held the door open for me and said, "Go on in."

Balco's CEO was sitting behind his rather substantial cherry desk, which perfectly matched the nearby paneling. The bustling Port of Oakland was visible through the floor-to-ceiling window behind him.

Sal Salcedo was parked on the other side of the desk.

Rig Weiskopf was stretched out on the couch.

"Curt," Lorne said, warmly. "What can I do for you today?"

Lorne had already been fully briefed on the Joseph Manger situation, so all I had to do was update him on the latest development.

When I was through, he leaned back and shook his head.

"Well, now, I'm afraid this isn't the first time with something like this," he said. "By now I think you know a lot of the loads we have coming from Mexico aren't totally full. The stuff we bring back just isn't as bulky as the stuff we bring down, so there's often extra room on the truck. We tell the drivers all the time: Don't you dare take on any unauthorized payload. But some of them just can't resist the temptation. Drugs. People. You can't stop all of it."

He was saying this casually, as if he were talking about a truckload of circuit boards that had accidentally been misrouted.

"The trucks are all equipped with GPS now, and the drivers know it," Sal added. "That's helped us clamp down on some of the freelancing. But not all of it. The drivers will make a stop and claim they were just taking a piss, or they'll say they had to stop because of DOT rules, and it can be hard for us to distinguish between that and an illegitimate stop. Things also just slip between the cracks. We're not omniscient."

"How often has something like this happened?" I asked, feeling naive even as I asked the question.

"Oh, geez, with the drugs? It used to be all the time," Lorne said. "An 18-wheeler is a big place. They'd stash stuff in the spare tire, on the undercarriage somewhere, in the engine manifold, inside the door panels, you name it. We had one guy who had a fake spare truck battery. When you popped the lid, it had been completely hollowed out. One of those dope-sniffing dogs found it and went nuts. Guy must have had fifty kilos of heroin in there."

Sal cut in with: "I'm pretty sure he's *still* locked up."

Lorne laughed at that before he continued.

"The feds have gotten a lot better at searching for that kind of thing, so I think guys are more afraid to take the risk than they used to be. They're also being paid better than ever. When you're making a hundred grand a year doing legitimate work, you don't want to put that at risk. But there's still the lure of the quick score. Coke, heroin, fentanyl, you name it. I can't claim to know the exact figures, but if you can buy something for a buck on the streets of Durango and turn around and sell it for ten on the streets of Los Angeles, you can make a lot of money real fast. Same is true with smuggling people. Five years back, we had a driver—what was his name?"

From the couch, Rig piped up with, "Melvord Finck."

"Melvord Finck," Lorne enthused. "That's right. How could I forget that name? Anyhow, he got caught with twenty or thirty of 'em in his truck. Ol' Melvord swore up and down he had 'no idea, no idea' anyone was back there, like he was shocked—shocked there was gambling in this establishment. The prosecutors were talking real tough with him and with us. Again, these were feds, and they don't mess around. They were going to give Melvord ten years for each offense, which would have put him away for life, and they were going to fine us some crazy amount. They were being pretty ridiculous about it."

"What do you mean, 'ridiculous'?" I asked. "I mean, he was breaking the law, wasn't he?"

Lorne's head tilted a little. "Well, sure, I'm not arguing that. But did they need to throw the book at him? When you think about it from an economic standpoint, Melvord was just providing a service. Some people like to demonize migrants for their own purposes, but I grew up in a border town. I was around these folks all the time as a kid. Those people he had in his truck, they weren't criminals. They were just people trying to live their lives. To me, if someone wants to come here and work hard and contribute to our economy and get their slice of the American Dream, we ought to let them. I don't condone illegal immigration. I think folks ought to do it the right way. But the system we have right now doesn't let them. It isn't working for anyone—not for the migrants or for the businesses that need migrant labor. And sometimes when a system is broken, people make their own system.

"Anyway," Lorne said with a heavy exhale. "There was a federal task force that arrested Melvord. Joint Task Force 1954. They were all over us for a little while, like our other drivers were doing the same thing Melvord was. They had Border Patrol stopping our trucks, harassing us, you name it. We had a pretty big target on us for a little while. Rig was actually the one who saved the day. He went and talked with them and worked out a deal where Melvord agreed to plead guilty and serve eighteen months and we agreed to pay a fine. And then Rig told them if they kept stopping our trucks, he was going to hire a small army of lawyers and sue the hell out of them."

"Not true. I never made any threats," Rig interjected. "All I did was talk to them. It was just a matter of working *with* the task force rather than engaging in againstness."

Lorne looked like a fish trying not to rise to the bait. "Let's not get into that right now," he said. "Long story short, all's well that ends well."

"I guess," I allowed. "Anyhow, what am I supposed to say to the *Chronicle* about Joseph Manger being a coyote?"

"Well, you can't exactly deny it, can you? Just distance us as best you can. Say he was acting on his own, doing this without our knowledge. Say we tell our drivers not to mess with this sort of thing and . . . Christ, I don't know. It's a complex world. The people who think it's simple to control everyone and everything ought to try it for a while and see how it works out for them."

"People who think you can control everything are engaging in a delusion," Rig added. "There is no such thing as control. The universe always has its way in the end."

I chuckled nervously. "Yeah, that might get outside of the scope of what we've been asked to comment on."

"Right," Lorne said. "Point is, don't get yourself too bent out of shape here. I realize it's your job to do damage control, but sometimes I think . . . well, in logistics, damage is part of the business. We factor it into our costs. Let's just make it clear we think this Manger fellow is reprehensible and if people want to take shots at us, let 'em. We'll survive."

"Okay," I said, standing up, because it felt like the conversation was over.

"One more thing, though," Lorne added.

"What's that?"

"That young lady said what happened took place in our warehouse?"

"Uh-huh."

"I don't want us to seem like we're contradicting her, but I studied that video pretty close. That wasn't a Balco warehouse. Wherever this happened, it wasn't at our place."

I wasn't sure how much that actually mattered, but I said, "Okay. I'll correct the record as best I can."

"All right, then," he said.

"Keep up the good work," Sal added.

I returned to the fourth floor. As much as I didn't want to, I played that awful video again, paying closer attention to the background than I had in the past.

Lorne was right. Balco warehouses had sheetrock walls. This wall was corrugated steel.

Also—and I hadn't thought of this part before now—Balco executives were fairly obsessed with lighting, because lighting was considered a safety issue. And Balco executives, like most seasoned logistics professionals, were also obsessed with safety.

Accidents cost money. Safe warehouses were more profitable.

I had bumped across internal memos talking about how brighter spaces were less accident-prone and also improved worker morale and productivity. Our facilities had huge overhead LEDs that bathed the warehouse floors in near sunlight-level radiance.

A Balco facility would never be dark and gloomy like the one in the video. It just wouldn't happen.

Joseph Manger must have stopped somewhere else to unload his human cargo. It made sense that he would want to do it in an enclosed space. Any cop—or even a random citizen with an anti-immigrant bent—who saw a bunch of Hispanic people filing out of an 18-wheeler would surely get suspicious.

The full narrative was forming in my head. Manger probably had his eye on Maria from the moment she boarded the truck in Mexico. He had the whole drive to think about what he wanted to do about it. Then, when they disembarked on the other side of the border—wherever it happened—he pounced.

With that settled in my mind, I came up with some talking points for Ron Talbot, then called him. I was basically repeating what Lorne had said: that this was a Balco driver acting on his own, and that the facility where this terrible deed happened was definitely not ours.

When I was through, Talbot said, "Okay. Thanks for this. Meanwhile, there's one more twist in the story. It might actually just be the end of the story."

"What are you talking about?"

"I just got off the line with the Oakland Police," he said. "When they went to execute that arrest warrant on Joseph Manger, they found him lying dead on his couch. Preliminary indication is self-inflicted gunshot wound to the head. They found a note and everything."

CHAPTER 30

THE MESSENGER HAD the alert sent out. The channels worked as they usually did.

And soon, he and Lorne Murphy were on the phone.

There was no extended greeting this time.

"I told you we'd handle Manger," the CEO said decisively. "And unlike the way y'all do things, no one is asking any questions."

The messenger did not bother hiding his annoyance. "I'm not calling about Manger. We have bigger problems."

"What's that?"

"Gillespie."

"Enough with Gillespie," Murphy burst. "I've told you, we've been watching him. We've had no indication he's—"

"You watch him at work?"

"Yes. Of course."

"You watch him at home?"

"We listen. If a mouse farts in his house, we know it."

"What about when he's not at home or work? Are you following him, watching all the time?"

"Well, now, that sort of thing gets expensive, and there's nothing to—"

"What about when he and his wife took that trip out to Palm Springs over the weekend? They stopped at a Golden Corral on the way. Were you watching him then?"

Murphy had no response.

"You weren't," the messenger said. "And we know you weren't."

"So?"

"He took the bait."

"What are you talking about?"

"We took a page out of your book and had two men approach him, pretending to be FBI. They offered him money, immunity, and witness protection. He practically fell over himself to take the deal."

"Son of a bitch."

"How long until he decides to talk to the FBI for real?" the messenger asked.

Again, Murphy had no answer.

"Deal with it. Now," the messenger said. "If you don't, we will."

CHAPTER 31

Ron Talbot's story was posted on the *Chronicle*'s website on Friday night, and appeared on the front page of Saturday's paper.

It was important, well-executed journalism: the harrowing, real-life story of one woman's attempt to do something most people take for granted—go back home for a wedding and visit family—and how that simple desire made her vulnerable to sexual predation. And, also, how our immigration laws made such horrors possible and, perhaps, even inevitable.

But, like a lot of important, well-executed journalism, it was almost completely ignored.

The piece got zero comments on the website, was not being widely shared on social media, and did not appear to have the legs to carry it any further than it had already gone.

For all Ron Talbot's beliefs about how public outrage could foment change, there was simply no outrage to be found here.

This, sadly, was what the public expected to happen to poor migrant women.

Plus, the bad guy had already been dealt with. Joseph Manger's apparent suicide served as a fitting coda to the whole saga—a confession, conviction, and punishment in one squeeze of the trigger.

There was really nothing more to be said.

With the story fading away, I was able to turn my attention back to all the other things I had ignored the remainder of Friday afternoon while I had been paying attention to the Talbot story. Plus, I had the usual lists of writing tasks to take care of.

This was becoming how I spent my weekends. There were so many interruptions at the office—Comms Team people who had questions or needed approvals, urgent requests, the ever-increasing inrush of email—it was difficult to get any decent writing done there.

On the weekend, when I worked from home, it was easier to find the flow. Our huge back deck had these two sprawling California live oaks looming over it, providing the perfect amount of dappled sunshine throughout the early and middle portions of the day. Later in the day, when the afternoon sun revved up, the deck was shaded by the house itself. It was pleasant all the day long.

While this pleased me well enough, it pissed off Page. She had made it clear that while she could tolerate my long weekdays, weekends should be family time—her time.

I agreed with her.

But that still didn't change that I had a lot to do.

So, as I churned out copy that Saturday, she stewed quietly.

There was no sex or waffles.

By Sunday, the stewing had stopped being so quiet. She made it clear that I was risking a serious spousal explosion if I put her off.

I could also tell she was feeling a bit of cabin fever. Just because *I* delighted in lounging around the Barbie DreamHouse and enjoying its comforts didn't mean she was eager to do the same. She spent every day there already. She wanted to get out and discover the area.

While we enjoyed our view of Mount Tamalpais, the 2,500-foot peak that dominated the skyline of the southern portion of Marin County, we had yet to actually explore "Mount Tam," as it was known by the locals. So we decided that would be our destination. A quick consultation with the internet led us to a hike that was advertised as "moderate" and promised a towering canopy of redwood trees and beautiful views of the ocean.

With Page at eighteen weeks, moderate was all she felt like taking on.

It was going to be a warm day, with highs approaching eighty; so I filled several water bottles and put them in a backpack along with the rest of our picnic. Then we struck out on our little adventure.

The best parking available near the hike was at something called Pantoll Campground. According to the map, the road leading out to Pantoll had a lot of switchbacks, so Page asked if she could drive—windy roads made her nervous. I was happy to acquiesce.

What this led to was me enjoying the view from the passenger seat of something called Panoramic Highway, which was rather aptly named. Over a handful of miles, it traced through a stunning array of ecosystems, with one giving way to the next so suddenly you never knew what was coming next.

There were groves of eucalyptus trees, with their bark dripping off in huge strips in a fashion that made them look haunted; or thick stands of Douglas firs, so dark and primordial you felt like you were in a fairy tale; or sloping meadows of grasslands dotted with wildflowers in every color; or even isolated pockets of manzanita.

Sometimes we'd emerge from the trees to realize we were clinging high to the side of a valley of coastal scrub, which plunged into a jagged V-shape bottom. Other times, we'd get a glimpse of the Pacific Ocean stretching out to blue infinity.

The road was narrow and had a twenty-five-mile-per-hour speed limit, so the going was slow; not that either of us were in a hurry. The other obstacle—seemingly ever-present in Marin County but especially abundant during the weekend—were the cyclists. They almost seemed like part of the local fauna, chugging up the hills in their colorful skintight suits.

There was nowhere near enough width on the road for a bike lane, and passing them was anywhere from challenging to impossible, especially for a driver from the Midwest who was accustomed to longer sightlines. Legitimate straightaways, where you could actually see oncoming traffic for a decent amount of distance, were rare. Depending on where you were in a given switchback, you only had a brief window where you felt safe to zip around them.

We had already passed at least a dozen of them and were working our way past yet another Lycra-clad middle-aged man when I actually gasped.

I recognized this particular biker.

His helmet and glasses obscured his identity a little, but his protruding chin was a dead giveaway.

The thing I couldn't figure out was what Sidney Graves was doing standing on his pedals, hammering away like he was in a mountain stage of the Tour de France.

He was less than two weeks removed from major heart surgery. Based on what I knew about recovery from a procedure like that, he shouldn't have been able to fly home, much less feel like revving his beats-per-minute well past 150 during what was pretty clearly strenuous exercise.

Yet there he was, looking perfectly fit, going as fast as—or faster than—bikers half his age.

By the time I was able to absorb all this, we were already past him. I turned around to look at him through our rear window, just to make sure I hadn't been mistaken.

There was no doubt in my mind.

It was Sidney, with his long, bony body and his sharply cut face.

The champion cyclist on another training ride.

Once we navigated another switchback, we were finally clear of him. But I wasn't ready to move on.

This was too weird for me not to investigate further.

Every so often, there were turnoffs for slower vehicles. As we reached the next one, I asked Page to pull over.

"What?" she asked. "Why?"

"We just passed someone from Balco," I said. "I want to say hi."

"Oh," she said, and obliged me by putting on her turn signal and coming to a stop in the small, crescent-shaped space that had appeared alongside Panoramic Highway.

"Thanks," I said. "I won't be long. Just a quick hello."

Page seemed satisfied with my explanation, and I got out of the car and positioned myself by the side of the road.

After a few minutes, Sidney Graves came huffing and puffing our way. His jersey was unzipped down to his navel, as bikers sometimes did when they needed to cool off.

His chest was smooth and unblemished.

There was no scar anywhere.

And that's when things started to make sense to me.

Sidney Graves never had a quadruple bypass.

He faked that photo.

Just like he faked his heart attack.

But why?

And why go to the Czech Republic to do it?

I stepped out into the middle of the roadway and held up a hand as he approached. Sidney was so intent on his climb, he didn't see me until he was maybe twenty feet away.

When he did, I saw him startle a little.

He obviously recognized me, too.

"Pull over, Sidney," I ordered.

He did as he was told, straddling his bicycle as he came to a stop. His hand immediately went to his zipper, which he yanked upward.

"It's too late for that," I said.

He pulled off his glasses so he could look at me with pleading eyes.

"I'm sorry," he said.

"What the hell?"

I was still too surprised to come up with a more articulate formulation of the question.

"Look, I know you don't owe me anything, but please don't tell anyone you saw me," he said. "I really am sorry about the thing with the budget. That was . . . lousy of me. I was being an ass. Can you please accept my apology and keep this between us?"

Apparently I couldn't, because the first thing that came out of my mouth was, "Screw you, Sidney."

"I know, I know, you hate me. I hate me, too. Look, you're not going to have to see me anymore. We're moving to Montana at the end of the month. I . . . this is my favorite ride. My wife told me not to, but I just had to do it one last time. Can you please not say anything to anyone?"

"Maybe, if you explain to me why you faked your heart attack."

He shook his head.

"I . . . I had to get out," he said. "It was the only way they'd let me go."

"You couldn't have just said, 'Hey, I know I'm only fifty-eight, but I've worked hard and I want to retire a little early'?"

He gazed at the scrub by the side of the road for a moment.

"They wouldn't have gone for it," he assured me. "They'd never let me."

Here was Sidney with his self-importance again.

"Come on. So Lorne would have tried to talk you out of it? So what? Let him."

"Something like that," he said. "Can you please just keep quiet about this? I'll give you money."

"You want to *bribe* me into silence?"

"You're right, that's a terrible idea. Look, I'll do whatever I can for you. I'll . . . I'll owe you one. Anything you need, anything that's in my power to do, I'll do it for you."

"What good is that?" I asked.

He looked me square in the eye. "Trust me, Curt. You never know when you're going to need a favor in this world."

I had no idea what he even meant by that, but I didn't get time to ask him. He had abruptly hopped back onto his saddle and turned his bike in the opposite direction.

He was soon pointed down the mountain, with gravity to speed him along the way.

It was such an odd interaction—and such a strange thing to do, period—I had half a mind to try to go after him and demand more answers.

But being a newspaper reporter had taught me the futility of such efforts.

When people didn't want to talk, you couldn't force them to.

For the rest of the day, I tried to just put it out of my head and focus on my much-neglected wife.

Whatever ploy Sidney Graves was pulling, it wasn't my problem.

As it turned out, I was about to have much bigger problems of my own.

CHAPTER 32

MY PHONE RANG at 5:47 the next morning, just as I was about to leave the house.

I didn't recognize the number. But it had an Oakland area code, so I answered it.

"This is Curt."

What I heard back was a gentle Texas twang informing me: "Hey, it's Lorne."

"Oh. Good morning," I said.

"Not really. There's been an accident. A pretty bad one. One of our trucks was heading southbound on I-5, about halfway between Long Beach and San Diego, when the driver lost control. He barreled through a highway divider and struck a northbound minivan that was carrying a family of five. Four of them were pronounced dead on the scene. There's a fifth one that's been airlifted to the hospital and is clinging to life."

"Good God. Who's the driver?"

"His name is Dan Gillespie."

I pulled out a pad and started writing. "What can you tell me about him?"

"He's been at Balco twenty-one years. No history of any problems. Not even a speeding ticket. That's about all I've got."

"Any idea what went wrong? Was he drunk? Did he fall asleep?"

"I don't know. We can't ask him. He's dead, too."

"What?!?" I asked. "What *happened* down there?"

I had covered more than a few 18-wheeler accidents that involved fatalities. Whatever the death toll in the smaller vehicles, the driver of the truck usually walked away without a scratch. They suffered more physical consequences from the hangover—because so many of these crashes involved alcohol—than from the wreck.

"We don't have a lot of details right now. Long Beach dispatch has just been trying to get everyone out of bed and making them aware of the situation. This only took place about thirty minutes ago. We're still trying to gather information."

"Okay, I understand. What do you need from me?"

"Just get yourself down there ASAP. We used to have a Comms Team presence in Long Beach but we consolidated everything in Oakland as a cost-saving measure a while back. We need boots on the ground down there that know how to deal with the press."

"Of course."

Lorne paused for a moment to collect himself, then said: "This is going to be brutal. These things always are."

"I'm aware."

"No one is going to treat us like the good guys. But if you go down there and show we care, they'll at least look at us like less of the bad guy. You with me?"

"Totally."

"Okay. You're probably going to need some administrative help. I'd suggest you take Korynne Vuong with you and have Bob Brunato hold down the fort for you up here."

"Sounds like a plan. Anything else?"

"No. Get going."

I ended the call. Page was still in bed, dozing. I gently brought her awake and then very quickly explained the situation.

"When will you be back?" she asked.

"No clue. But it won't be today. Probably not tomorrow, either."

"Okay," she said. "Good luck."

After throwing three suits and some underwear in a garment bag, I hurried out. My first call was to Bob Brunato. I asked him to mobilize Korynne for me while I figured out how to get us to Long Beach.

As soon as I reached the highway, I put the Rivian on self-drive and started searching flight options while keeping an eye on the road. I found something on United that left SFO at 8:10 and arrived at LAX at 9:35. I booked tickets for myself and Korynne.

Meanwhile, Bob was monitoring all the Los Angeles news sites and television stations as best he could and kept calling me with updates.

I-5 was completely closed northbound as the California Highway Patrol investigated the crash. CHP had created a temporary ramp that allowed one lane of traffic to be routed around on Old Pacific Highway, but there was already a huge backup building—at least five miles and piling up fast, according to a Los Angeles television station that had its traffic helicopter overhead.

Southbound was actually worse. There were two lanes open, but with the rubbernecking, the delays were at six miles.

What a mess.

There was still no word about the identity of the four family members who had been killed, or about the fifth one who remained alive. CHP had yet to release anything.

Once I arrived at SFO and made it through security, I hunkered down in front of the gate and started doing my own scan of the coverage. Because this was almost exactly halfway between Los Angeles and San Diego, media outlets in both cities were covering the crash.

Several of the local TV stations had traffic helicopters that were providing live footage, giving me my first good glimpse of the crash.

It had happened on a section of I-5 that hugged the Pacific Ocean, south of San Clemente but north of Camp Pendleton, in a rugged, uninhabited part of the coast. The water was to the right, just a few hundred feet down what looked to be a fairly steep bluff.

The southbound truck had veered left, away from the water, which was what put it in the path of the northbound traffic. It had crushed a section of low steel guardrails, the kind you find on more rural stretches of highway.

The only buildings in the area belonged to the San Onofre Nuclear Power Plant, which was just north of the crash site. Several of the stations mentioned this in ominous tones—like somehow one runaway truck could have triggered a nuclear meltdown.

I was just clicking to another station on my laptop when Korynne arrived in the gate area. I waved for her. As soon as she saw me, her face brightened and she came directly toward me. Something about her approach made me want to stand.

Maybe it was just my southern upbringing. You never stayed seated when a woman came to the table.

She put her carry-on luggage down near my feet, wrapped her arms around my shoulders, and hugged me.

It felt a little weird. Who hugs a work colleague? But I didn't say anything about it.

I gave Korynne a briefing of what was happening and she got to work arranging lodging near the Long Beach facility, along with transportation.

We were soon airborne. Our seats were next to each other in coach, and there were a few times when I imagined that Korynne's arm and leg were rubbing against mine more than was strictly necessary.

Then I told myself not to make too much of it. These were small seats. It was hard to avoid each other.

In-flight Wi-Fi allowed me to keep up with developments in the story, which is how I learned some horrifying news via the *Los Angeles Times* website.

The fifth passenger in the minivan, the only survivor of the crash, was a baby.

Just ten months old.

And now she was an orphan.

She had been in a backward-faced car seat, which was the only thing that saved her. The vehicle had crumpled around her, but paramedics had been able to extract her and airlift her to Scripps Memorial Hospital in La Jolla, which had a Level 1 trauma center—the best there was.

Still, her injuries were extensive and her prognosis was uncertain.

I felt a stab to the heart, thinking about that little baby girl, broken and clinging to life.

But that wasn't all.

Selfish though it may have been, there was a certain lens through which I had found myself running everything. And I couldn't stop myself from doing it again here.

What if that had been my baby?

The flight landed a few minutes early, and as soon as I was able to power on my phone, I checked in with Bob Brunato.

He sounded frayed. The backup had topped out at ten miles in each direction and it was promising to be a story that continued to dominate news coverage in Southern California throughout the day.

"CHP just released that the truck was ours," he said. "The phones are going berserk. What do I say?"

I had just looked at the time on my phone. It was 9:32.

The internet had greatly diminished the importance of news cycles, but the cycles still existed. Site traffic and viewership took a dive in the midmorning. The news-obsessed people who provided those much-coveted eyeballs and clicks were now settled into work. They wouldn't come up for air again until lunchtime.

That gave us a brief window to figure out how we were supposed to respond.

"Tell them we'll be putting out a release at eleven thirty," I said.

"You got it."

As soon as we were off the plane, we bolted to the exits. Thanks to Korynne, a car service was waiting to take us to the Long Beach facility. The 405 and the 110 were kind to us—morning rush traffic had cleared out—and we pulled up by ten thirty.

Long Beach was another version of Oakland. Its buildings may have looked different on the outside, but functionally it was the same: one large boxy structure that contained most of the stuff, surrounded by multiple smaller buildings that existed in support of the big one.

Oh. And a lot of security. Sal Salcedo's touch was everywhere.

As soon as we entered, we were greeted by Ken Helms, the operations director at Long Beach. He had ashy blond hair and an eager-to-please disposition.

His first act was to hand me a fob that would provide me universal access to the facility. He took us to what they were calling the "situation room"—really just an empty conference room where they had some televisions tuned to reruns of the same helicopter footage I had already seen. He then steered me over to a small-statured, slump-shouldered man.

"This is Dan Gillespie's team leader," Ken said. "He knows Dan better than anyone."

I pulled out my reporter's pad. Feeling like I was on very familiar ground, I said, "Okay, what can you say about Dan Gillespie?"

"He was a good guy, you know?" the team leader said. "We played on the same softball team, so he was a friend outside of work. I got to know him pretty well."

It was always interesting to me how people's personalities evinced themselves through sports, so I asked: "What kind of player was he?"

"Oh, you know, he was the kind of guy that if he was on the other team, you probably hated him, because he was a little too competitive. This is just beer league stuff, you know? But if he was on your team, you loved him, because he busted his ass. There was no quit in him, you know?"

"So he was pretty fiery?" I asked.

"Yeah, real passionate."

I asked a few more questions about softball, about Dan's family—he had a wife and two grown stepsons—and other off-Balco topics. I knew eventually I would have to write some kind of tribute about Gillespie, and I needed as much material to humanize the man as possible.

Then I turned to his work life.

"Did he have any problems? I know he didn't have an accident history, but were there any red flags with him? Any issues with him as a driver that gave you concern?"

My motivation for asking this question was simple: If Dan Gillespie *did* have anything troubling in his past, I wanted us to know about it before the *Los Angeles Times* did. The last thing we needed was to be blindsided by something; like, say, that he had recently been treated for narcolepsy.

"No," the team leader insisted. "If I could clone a driver, I'd clone Dan. He never missed a shift, never showed up late. We give awards for safe driving every year. Your record needs to be completely clean, no incidents whatsoever. Not even a motorist calling the safety hotline to say they saw you changing lanes improperly. It's not easy, but Dan always got one. The way we do it, we give out the awards for all the drivers who have one year safe, then two years safe, then three, and so on. Dan hit twenty last year. There's only one other guy in the whole company who's got a longer streak. Dan was one of our stars."

"Can you get your hands on his driving record quickly?"

"Yeah, we got the last ten years on the computer. Before that it's hard copy and I'd need to go digging through some filing cabinets. I think they're up in HR somewhere."

"Don't worry about it. If you can email me the last ten years, that'll be good enough for now."

"You got it."

"What about his health?"

"Oh, he was a horse. I can't even remember the last time he took a sick day."

Which didn't necessarily rule out that he might have suffered a heart attack, stroke, or aneurysm, which was the most likely cause of the crash.

As I asked more questions—and received mostly unremarkable

answers—something was creeping its way up through the lower folds and wrinkles of my brain until it finally made it to the top of my mind.

Fiery . . . passionate . . . if he was on the other team, you probably hated him.

"Tell me something," I said. "Had he been vocal when it came to the union vote?"

The team leader cocked his head like this was something new.

"He was a driver, so he wasn't directly involved. But, yeah, he was definitely . . . 'Vocal' would be the right word."

"And which side was he on?"

"Pro-Balco, all the way. His thing was that the company was really good to everyone, and he didn't want to upset the apple cart. He said the people who were voting for the union were just trying to get away with being lazy, because unions only existed to protect lazy people from getting fired."

"Wow," I said. "How did the pro-union people take that?"

"Not well. As a matter of fact, you know that brawl we had down here? The one that started in the break room?"

"Yeah."

"Dan Gillespie was right in the thick of it."

CHAPTER 33

THERE WAS LITTLE time to consider this new revelation.

My conversation with the team leader was cut short by word that a helicopter was ready. A group of us would be flying down to the crash site to tour the devastation firsthand.

Our party included two executives from the operations staff, one of whom was said to know more about our truck fleet than anyone; Balco's chief counsel, a fiftyish woman in a charcoal-gray suit who had arrived from Oakland just after me; and a representative from our insurance carrier, a sour-faced man who had yet to open his mouth.

In some ways, he didn't need to. The human costs notwithstanding, this was going to be expensive for Balco. Even if CHP determined our driver was completely without fault, which felt unlikely, we still had a lot of potential liability here. There would be personal injury lawyers swarming around this crash, and they would pry up every rock and explore every crevice to find that whiff of negligence they needed to cash in.

None of that involved me, per se. My task would simply be to gather as much information as possible so that I could serve as the articulate, knowledgeable voice of Balco at this difficult time.

Before departing, I called Bob Brunato and dictated the bare bones of the press release that I hoped would hold down the midday for us.

The entire Balco family was devastated by the tragic crash and grieving the loss of life. Balco prioritized safety and would be cooperating fully with the investigation but would leave all comment on the details of the accident to California Highway Patrol and other authorities. Dan Gillespie was a veteran driver with a stellar driving record, the details of which we would share judiciously, trying not to sound defensive.

I trusted Bob to flesh it out. He was a pro.

It still might have struck a cynic as a bunch of empty words from the company that appeared to be responsible for the tragedy. But, at the moment, it was all we had.

On my way out, I said farewell to Korynne, who was staying behind in the situation room to continue monitoring coverage and provide other back-office support that became needed.

The helicopter was waiting for us in an empty section of asphalt at the edge of the facility.

Within five minutes, we were loaded in and lifting off. We flew low at first but steadily climbed several thousand feet. It was a bright, clear, sunny day with none of the smog the Los Angeles area was so famous for. The Pacific stretched out below us.

Its beauty felt so at odds with the carnage that had taken place along its shores earlier in the morning. But that was the nature of the world. Hang around a newsroom for more than a few minutes and you'll realize the person taking wedding announcements and the person writing obits are working simultaneously.

A half hour later, we landed at a heliport that served the San Onofre Nuclear Power Plant. It was a short distance from the crash site.

We covered the remaining ground on foot, walking south on the northbound side of the roadway, which was still closed to traffic. It had this apocalyptic feel to it—three completely empty lanes that ought to have been buzzing with traffic.

From the other side of the roadway, I felt the stares of angry motorists who had been waiting for hours just to pass through.

We were soon met by our CHP liaison, who introduced himself as Officer Krempitz. He was our assigned escort, and he handed us bright yellow reflective vests that we all put on.

I wasn't totally aware of the arrangements, but I was under the impression that since Balco owned the truck, we were permitted to oversee the accident investigation, as long as we didn't interfere with the investigators.

Officer Krempitz's main instructions were "stay together" and "don't touch anything."

He led us closer to the crash, which was still abuzz with activity. In addition to CHP, there was a Go Team from the National Traffic Safety Board, which was conducting its own investigation, owing to the substantial loss of life.

Collectively, they would photograph and document every inch of the catastrophe.

The first vehicle we came across was a large red firetruck with several firefighters milling about. I assumed they were there as a precaution at this point. I couldn't imagine anything was still ablaze.

A large wrecker was also on scene. It would be clearing away our truck just as soon as permitted by CHP. I had already heard talk that some of Sal Salcedo's people wanted to perform their own inspection.

But the bigger issue for Balco was the payload. Already, the operations people had been nervously whispering into their phones about how some part of this shipment was urgently needed by a customer in Mexico, who wasn't pleased that it was now stranded on a section of highway in California.

Arrangements were already being made to get those goods back on their way.

Once again, the business of Balco would stop for nothing.

This was life in the logistics industry: Not even death could stop it.

Crass but true.

We were now close enough that I could take in the entirety of the scene.

It was horrifying.

For all the crashes I had covered for various newspapers, it had always been secondhand. There was no need to get to the highway and, in any case, no real ability to—the traffic that was part of the story kept me away. I faithfully reported what other people told me, from a safe distance.

Seeing it up close and personal was something else entirely. The field of debris surrounding the crash was far larger than I imagined it would be, which spoke to the extreme violence of the collision. Most of the pieces were burned, warped, or generally unrecognizable as having ever been part of a car or truck.

One of the only objects I could actually identify was a shoe, just sitting there in the middle of the roadway.

A child's sneaker.

The foot that would have fit in that sneaker was tiny and absolutely no match for the forces involved here.

Just thinking about it made me ill.

I felt even sicker when I saw the minivan.

Or what was left of it.

The entire front of the vehicle—from the front bumper, to the engine block, and into the passenger compartment—was just gone. Disintegrated, really. The impact had broken it into all those small pieces that now littered the roadway.

What remained of the minivan was blackened, mangled, and lying on its side. A whitish substance—whatever the fire department had been using to extinguish the blaze—stained the nearby asphalt.

It had obviously burned for quite a while. The seats, the plastic trim, really the entire interior of the vehicle was either blackened or had simply melted away, leaving only the steel frame in many places.

I really didn't understand how anyone could have survived, much less a baby.

Moving on to the truck, I felt even more puzzled.

It had a dent in the grille where it impacted the minivan, though not much of one. This was, perhaps, to be expected: The truck was so much more massive and built of much more solid materials. In the high-speed highway version of Rochambeau, steel beat plastic every time.

What was weird was that the cab of the truck looked like it had sustained heavy damage. The doors were missing. The windshield had been blown out. The inside was charcoaled. It had caught fire just like the minivan had.

How was that possible? Cars caught fire during cataclysmic crashes when their engines split open, causing the internal combustion to go external.

But what would have caught fire inside this cab? There was no accelerant in there, no highly ignitable fuel source. The truck's fuel tanks, which were in the rear, were completely unscathed.

And it's not like the burning minivan had ignited the truck. The grille was not burned. And there was a portion of the truck—going from behind the grille to just before the cab—that was completely unscathed.

The fire couldn't have leaped over that section, could it?

I felt my bewilderment growing as we got closer and I was able to better see inside the cab. It was a study in destruction. The driver's seat was missing. So was the steering wheel and much of the dashboard. Even the underside of the roof had been buckled upward. I just couldn't imagine how that was possible.

"My God," I said. "It looks like a bomb went off in there."

Officer Krempitz stared at me for a moment, then said, "That's because a bomb *did* go off in there."

This brought our entire party to a halt.

"What are you talking about?"

"The first officers on the scene had the exact same observation you did. They told their superior officer, who called in our bomb squad from San Diego. The bomb squad found the remains of what they described as an improvised explosive device under the driver's seat. It appears to have been triggered by a remote detonator."

I rocked back on my heels, as if feeling an hours-old aftershock from the blast.

That explained why Dan Gillespie hadn't simply walked away from the wreck like every other truck driver I ever covered.

It wasn't the accident that killed him.

And it wasn't a heart attack, stroke, or aneurysm either.

Why do they call him the Mad Bomber?

I'm sure we don't want to know.

CHAPTER 34

AS SOON AS I got myself clear of the rest of the group, I called Sal Salcedo.

This was no longer just a tragic mishap.

It was an attack.

Make that: another attack.

And Balco's chief safety officer needed to know about it.

Sal's assistant gave me a brief runaround until I prevailed on him that, no, he couldn't just take a message; and, no, this *could not* wait.

"What's going on?" Sal asked, sounding hurried.

"I'm down here at the crash site."

"Yeah, I know."

"Okay. Did you know that Dan Gillespie was an anti-union hothead?"

There was a pause.

Then: "No."

"His team manager said he was in the thick of that brawl that happened down in Long Beach last week. It sounds like he had a special talent for annoyance. And it looks like it got him killed."

"What are you talking about?"

"The accident wasn't an accident. Someone put a bomb under Gillespie's seat."

"What?!?"

I walked Sal through what I had seen and what the CHP bomb squad had discovered. "And Neil Rees, Rudy Szymanski's attack dog, is known as the Mad Bomber," I concluded. "I hope I'm not the only one connecting the dots here."

Another pause. "No, you're not."

"Well?" I asked, resisting the urge to add *What are you going to do about it?*

"I just don't see . . . Our trucks are kept in a secure lot when they're not in use," Sal said, already sounding defensive. "There's no way he could have gotten inside the facility to plant an explosive device like that. No way."

"We have a dead family and a huge mess on I-5 that beg to differ."

Angel's words came back to me: *Toughest job at Balco. Everything that you could never anticipate going wrong becomes his fault.*

"Yeah, I know," Sal said, then interjected a string of words that were mostly profane.

"Okay," he said when that was over. "We'll start scouring the security footage. We've got a hundred percent of the facility covered. Some places are double-covered. If Rees snuck in somehow, we'll find him, we'll get it to CHP, and CHP will nail him to the cross. They're not going to let him get away with murdering six people."

"You mean seven," I said. "Don't forget Angel."

I certainly wasn't.

"Right, right, of course," he said. "Sorry."

"Let me know what you find."

"Will do."

Mindful of the officer's instructions to "stay together," I returned to our group, though its attention was now divided. The revelation about the true nature of the cause of the crash had sent everyone to their phones.

I took that as my cue to call Bob and Korynne to let them know a major curve in the story was coming.

Within the hour, CHP released two more pieces of information to the public.

One, that the I-5 crash was now considered a criminal investigation. There was no specific mention of the bomb—that was being withheld for the time being. It was being referred to as "a deliberate act of sabotage."

And, two, that the baby who had been rushed to the hospital had succumbed to her injuries, despite extensive efforts to save her.

The tragedy was now complete.

Korynne told me that one of the anchors for the San Diego ABC affiliate had actually wept on air as he announced it. The station had quickly cut away to commercial, but the footage of him being overcome by emotion was already going viral. Some enterprising social media disaster peddler had packaged it along with aerial pictures of the wreck, and it was making all the algorithms hum.

At some point—probably while we had been in the air toward the crash site—CHP had identified the victims as the McClintock family of Del Mar. Mom and Dad were former high school sweethearts, both thirty-six. The other two kids were five and seven.

They had been on their way to Disneyland for a three-day stay.

The whole thing was gut-wrenching.

And Southern California's Fourth Estate simply couldn't get enough of it.

An hour or so later, the investigators had finished cataloguing the wreckage and the crash site was finally getting cleaned up in anticipation of reopening the roadway. News that the criminal investigation revolved around a suspicious explosion inside the truck had leaked out and was now being freely parroted by outlets whose only source for this news was other media outlets.

Officially, Dan Gillespie was no longer the villain of the story. He was just another unfortunate victim.

Once the last of the debris was cleared and I-5 was flowing again, we returned via helicopter to Long Beach.

As the afternoon progressed, our media relations strategy was to be as open and human as possible. We set up an area just outside the entrance for local TV to set up shop. Any Balco employee who wanted to talk about their personal relationship with Dan Gillespie—or their thoughts about his passing—was free to do so.

I was keeping my suspicions about Neil Rees under wraps. It was hard not to let it slip at times. I kept having to remind myself that until Sal's people found hard evidence, it was just speculation.

It burned in me all the same.

In the meantime, I was gathering more string about Dan Gillespie, talking with colleagues who knew him. I spoke with several reporters who were looking for more background on him.

A few asked if I suspected why anyone would want to kill such a fine, hardworking person. I just gritted my teeth and said, "No comment."

There was still nothing from Sal on the Mad Bomber front. I wondered how long that search would take.

When not obsessing about that or conducting interviews, I ghost-wrote a personal note from Lorne to the employees. It was necessarily different in tone from the one I had written about Angel—because

Lorne didn't know Gillespie personally—but I still tried to infuse it with warmth and sincerity.

Korynne had been by my side for much of the afternoon, pitching in at every turn. By early evening, she convinced me to shift operations to the hotel in downtown Long Beach. She had secured adjoining suites for us on the twenty-first floor that gave us ample room to continue working and also provided a beautiful view of the harbor and the ocean beyond—a vista that I barely even had time to look at, much less appreciate.

It was after nine o'clock by the time I came up for air, feeling worn to a stub. Korynne had been absent for a while but soon appeared at our shared door.

"Knock-knock," she called.

"Come on in," I said, leaning back in my desk chair.

She entered carrying a heavily laden room service tray. She had changed into civilian clothes—a cropped camisole and skintight yoga pants.

This is just how she dresses away from work, I told myself. *Nothing to see here.*

I averted my eyes and tried to focus on the food instead.

"You must be starving," she said, setting the tray down on a table by the window, then taking a seat behind it.

"Famished," I confirmed, getting up from my seat and joining her at the table.

"I didn't know what to order for you, so I got a little of everything. There's a salad, a steak, pasta, bread. I already had some salmon. It was delicious. I could order that for you if you wanted."

"No, no, this is fine."

"You've had quite a day."

"Not as bad as Dan Gillespie and the McClintock family," I said heavily.

Her response was to pull a wineglass and a single-serving bottle of Merlot off the tray. She unscrewed the top, poured the contents into the glass, and held it out for me.

"Oh, no. I couldn't."

"Okay. More for me, I guess," she said. "Cheers."

"Cheers," I said, nodding toward her as I removed the metal lid to a plate that turned out to be a medium rare New York strip steak.

I tore into it, quickly dispatching that and the potatoes that came with it.

Korynne had moved down to the carpeted floor. She had her legs out in front of her and was flopping her entire body forward, grabbing her feet in a long, sumptuous stretch.

She had shifted into small talk, at which she seemed to excel. I could feel her deliberately trying shift attention away from the terrible events of the day and lighten the mood.

Her stretching—it had really turned into a series of yoga poses—was getting more ambitious. Now and then, she'd reach up for her glass of wine on the table and take a long sip.

At several points, she arched her back. This pulled up the hem of the camisole to just under her breasts and allowed me to count every one of her ribs.

Then it was back to the wine.

"You sure you don't want some?" she asked.

"Quite sure, yes."

She responded to this by opening the second mini-bottle and pouring it into her glass.

After I was done eating, I shoved my chair away from the table so

I could extend my legs. The view from the twenty-first floor really was quite something—the sparkling lights of Long Beach ended abruptly at the dark expanse of the Pacific.

I glanced at the time—ten o'clock—which felt like too late to call Page. I missed her. I wished she would suddenly materialize here in my Long Beach hotel room so I could climb into bed next to her.

Korynne was chattering the whole time and, frankly, getting a little tipsy. It didn't bother me. It had been an intense day.

I had been looking out toward the lights of the harbor when suddenly Korynne was on her knees and had positioned herself between my legs. I wasn't totally sure how she had gotten there, but she was staring at me with a pair of rather intense bedroom eyes.

"What if I told you I liked you?" she asked.

She was rubbing my thighs, working rather quickly from the knees up to more sensitive areas.

"I know we work together and I know you're married, but I don't care," she said. "The heart wants what the heart wants. And I've wanted you since the moment I laid eyes on you. I just think you're so, so sexy."

In one flowing gesture, she slipped one strap of her camisole off her shoulder, then the other; then she yanked downward.

She had nothing on underneath. The sight of her momentarily stupefied me. I felt like I couldn't even move. She surged toward me, rubbing her half-naked body against mine as she climbed up the chair. This ended with her breasts in my face and her hand running through the back of my hair.

Her nipples were erect. She was breathing heavily.

"We don't have to tell anyone about this," she said, sinking into me. Her lips settled on my ear, and she took my earlobe between her teeth.

"You can do whatever you want to me," she whispered hotly, her hand now on my crotch. I felt my blood flow surging in that direction.

This, finally, broke my paralysis.

"Whoah, whoah, whoah," I said, grabbing her gently by the shoulders and straightening my arms. "This isn't okay with me."

She responded by rubbing between my legs with even more fervor.

"Come on. It'll be fun. No one has to know."

I managed to get myself disentangled enough from her that I was able to stand up. I averted my eyes from her.

"I would know," I said. "Please put your shirt back on. I'm happily married to a woman I love very much and do *not* want to cheat on."

"It wouldn't be cheating," she purred. "Just think of it as your exercise for the day."

"No thanks. I'm good."

She reached out and touched my hip, causing me to take a step farther away.

"Sorry," she said. "I'm probably just a little drunk and . . . and lonely."

I went to look at her but she was still topless, so I kept my head turned away.

"It's okay. It's been a long day for both of us. A lot of emotion. Just . . . don't worry about it."

"Okay," she said with an exaggerated sigh. "You sure? What about a quick blow job to relieve the stress?"

"No thanks."

She had collected her top from the ground. She still hadn't put it back on.

"You should probably go now," I said.

I was rather pointedly not looking at her, but she just as deliberately invaded my personal space on her way out.

"If you change your mind," she said. "I'll be next door."

CHAPTER 35

FROM THE WINDOWLESS room, there was elation, followed by a lifting of the landline.

"We got him," the caller said.

"Who got whom?"

"Your girl. She finally made her move."

"Oh. Good. How did it go?"

"Great. I mean, it wasn't perfect. He still resisted her. Honestly, I have no idea how. He must be a monk or something. Or gay. But she had her tits out and she was all over him. It went on long enough that it'll serve our purpose."

"But they didn't do the deed?"

"No."

"Well, then, what good is it?"

"You'll see. I'm sending it to you right now," the caller said. "Trust me, there's no way he wants his wife to see something like this. Boy Scout that he is? He'd rather die."

"Okay, let me look."

There was silence on the line for a while. Then: "Oh my."

"See what I mean?" the caller asked.

"You're right. It's not perfect. But it's good enough. We own him."

CHAPTER 36

EXHAUSTED THOUGH I was, I couldn't sleep.

I just lay there in my hotel bed with my heart slamming against my rib cage.

It didn't matter that I had turned the thermostat in the room down as low as it would go or that the air-conditioning was pumping. I was still hot.

The guilt was practically burning a hole in my chest.

Had I encouraged Korynne in some way?

Did I let it go on too long?

What should I do about it?

Several times, I had to fight off the urge to call Page immediately. I went so far as to have my finger hovering over the phone icon next to her name. I just couldn't press it.

I didn't want to wake her, but it was more than that.

Telling Page would make this a capital-T Thing. And I didn't want or need this to be a Thing.

In addition to worrying her, I knew she wouldn't just let it be. She would insist I report this to HR. She would say it was for my protection. No sane wife would let her husband stay quiet about something like this.

The problem was, reporting it would only make this even more of a Thing. A lawyered-up / HR-infested / overly documented Thing.

It would be a massive headache and a huge distraction at a time when I was still just trying to survive in my job.

Maybe it would even force Korynne into a corner and make her lie. What if she said *I* came onto *her*? Or, worse, that I assaulted her?

Really: If something like this came down to he-said, she-said, who would believe the younger, lower-ranking woman had tried to take advantage of her older male boss? When did that ever happen?

And if Korynne went public with it? Forget it. I'd be done.

Even if they decided not to fire me, I'd be forever stained. At a time when I was just trying to establish my reputation in the company as a reliable team player, I'd instead become known as the guy who had that incident with his assistant.

What I really wanted was for this to have never happened. To just disappear.

And the surest way to achieve that outcome was simply to ignore it.

Act like it never happened. With Page and with everyone else, too.

If I didn't say anything, I couldn't imagine Korynne was going to tell anyone.

Her feelings for me would go away when she saw how unavailable I truly was.

All of this would go away.

Still, my heart kept pounding.

After a half hour of lying there, feeling like I was having a panic attack, I hoisted myself out of bed, wanting to do something productive with this surfeit of energy surging through me.

I had been wanting to walk the warehouse at some point during my visit to Long Beach. This seemed to be as good a time as any.

You'll learn more about logistics walking the warehouse than you'll ever learn from staring at spreadsheets.

The suit I had been wearing all day had been tossed haphazardly on a nearby chair. No one at the warehouse this time of night would care that it looked like an elephant sat on it. I tossed it back on, along with the wrinkled shirt that went with it.

Before long, I was striding through the lobby of the hotel. The Long Beach facility was a five-minute Uber ride away, and there were plenty of cars available at this time of night.

It was a typically cool California evening. When I rolled down the window in the back seat, the brackish scent of the nearby ocean filled the car.

I used my badge to open the main gate and had the Uber drop me off at the guard shack—at which point it made a U-turn and departed.

After showing the guards my badge, I continued on foot. I used the fob that Ken Helms had given me to enter the main warehouse.

All Balco facilities were three-shift-a-day operations, with start and end times staggered so as to avoid even the slightest dip in productivity. There was no such thing as downtime in the logistics industry.

Still, at this time of night—it was now after eleven—the staffing was as minimal as it could be. Much of the work was being done by machines, including the small army of autonomous forklifts we had zipping around; but there were still human forklift operators, drivers, and maintenance people moseying about.

It was, as usual, bright as daylight inside, which perked up my senses.

Having done this a few times, I understood why Angel was an evangelist for walking the warehouse. It was exciting.

The inventory alone was something to behold. The shelving racks towered thirty feet in the air—taller than your average house—and the rows of racks stretched seemingly forever.

I watched a few trucks get loaded and unloaded from the bays that lined the north side of the building. It was kind of mesmerizing, especially when I thought about all the gadgets, whatsits, and widgets that would someday be built from the contents of the boxes that were passing in front of me.

So few consumers would be aware that a crucial component in their oven timer, Bluetooth speaker, or smartwatch had spent a portion of its early life in a warehouse in Long Beach, California.

I didn't attract much attention as I walked around. I had my badge clipped to my suit jacket, so people knew I was legitimate. They just nodded at me—or ignored the guy in the suit altogether.

There were a few workers who weren't quite as busy, so I chatted them up, explaining to them who I was and how I wanted to better learn the business. They were unfailingly gracious and helpful.

A few times, when I thought the conversation was going well, I asked nonchalantly—or what I hoped was nonchalantly—about the IWW vote.

This earned me a few noncommittal I-don't-want-to-talk-about-it shrugs. Some shared that the entire subject had become so nuclear hot they were afraid to voice an opinion. Others just clammed up the moment I mentioned it.

I also asked a few times about Dan Gillespie. My hope had been to find someone else who knew him, maybe someone who would let slip that Gillespie had mentioned being threatened, or something similar.

But none of the people I talked to professed to know Gillespie on anything more than a nodding basis, if that.

Once I got my fill of the main warehouse, I gave myself a tour of some of the other buildings, which tended to be quiet at this time of night.

The urge to sleep was slowly creeping up on me, and my heart had finally settled down. Before I ordered an Uber to take me back to the hotel, there was just one last building I hadn't visited.

It was a square, boxy structure set off on its own, toward the edge of the grounds.

There were no markings on the outside. It had just one garage door, which was odd. Like the rest of the third-party logistics industry, Balco thrived on volume. The only reason we could offer our customers such good rates on shipping—cheaper than they could do it themselves—was because we did everything on such a massive scale.

This setup suggested to me the building was reserved for different types of shipments. Was it refrigerated? I wasn't aware of anything we shipped that was perishable. But maybe we dealt with a product or component that needed to stay cold?

I had no idea. For as much as I had been learning, I still didn't know everything about the company yet. Not even close.

The building was dark—another oddity—so I had to use my phone's flashlight until I got up close, when a motion sensor finally registered my presence and turned on a light.

All Balco buildings were labeled with a letter (which corresponded to the facility where they resided) and a number. So, for example, headquarters was K-1—the K standing for Oakland (because I guess they didn't want the "O" to be mistaken for a zero).

This building was L-11, with the L signifying Long Beach.

I climbed a small set of steps up to a landing area, where I touched my fob to the sensor next to the door. The mechanical lock whirred. As I pushed my way in, I expected another motion sensor would trigger and allow me to see where I was going.

But it stayed dark.

It wasn't cold inside, so obviously this wasn't refrigerated. The air was warm and still.

My eyes took a moment to adjust.

When they did, I realized I had seen this place before. I recognized the corrugated steel walls. And the gloomy orange lighting.

And I knew.

This was the building where Maria had been sexually assaulted.

CHAPTER 37

MOMENTARILY FROZEN, I took in the aura of the place.

Knowing what had happened here was deeply unsettling, like visiting a crypt filled with malign spirits.

Whatever this building's regular purpose—which I still couldn't discern—this was where Joseph Manger had decided to bring his quarry.

This out-of-the-way place. With only one loading dock. Where he knew it was unlikely to bump into any other Balco employees. Where he knew he would meet the least possible level of resistance.

It supported the assumption I had made earlier: that this crime was 100 percent premeditated. He had seen Maria when he loaded her in Mexico. He had been thinking about what he wanted to do with her the entire trip. And then he went to the perfect place to make it happen.

This also may have explained why Lorne Murphy believed the assault hadn't taken place at Balco. Unlike Angel, the walk-the-warehouse crusader, Lorne had probably never been to this little building. Or, even if he had, he wouldn't readily recognize it as being ours.

When I finally took a step, it was hesitant. And not just because the lighting was so low.

I still felt like I didn't want to touch anything, like this was a crime scene that should remain undisturbed until the authorities arrived.

Then I reminded myself any useful evidence was long gone.

And, in any event, no one was going to be prosecuting this crime. The defendant had already served justice on himself.

I pointed my flashlight into the opening in front of me, even though it was mostly useless against the darkness, and had a look around.

If there had been a truck in place, it would have been backed up to the loading dock door, which was just the right size to snugly accommodate one trailer. But the door was closed, so obviously nothing was being loaded or unloaded at the moment.

One of our autonomous forklifts was sitting quietly in the corner, unused and inactive. That told me this loading dock had to be fairly active, the current moment notwithstanding. Those forklifts cost somewhere in the neighborhood of $100,000. A company as efficiency minded as Balco would never allow such an expensive piece of equipment to sit idle for long.

I took a few more steps forward. There was safety lighting positioned every dozen feet or so along the walls. That was the source of that gloomy glow.

The ceiling was higher than it perhaps needed to be, though I couldn't guess why. The floor was that same smooth concrete I had seen in the video.

There were maybe ten feet on either side of the door. Standard trailer width was 102 inches—eight-and-a-half feet—so the entire building was roughly thirty feet wide and an equal number of feet deep.

I walked across the space, swiveling my head left and right as I went. I didn't notice any cameras, which was certainly odd for a Balco facility. I guess whatever happened in here didn't need to be watched.

Maybe it was because there were no employees in here. Autonomous forklifts didn't have to be watched, just programmed.

The floor was empty except for one small piece of debris along the far wall. As I got closer, I saw it was a purple bag of Takis Fuego tortilla chips.

Which was strange.

Balco facilities were scrupulously clean. That was an ethic that came from Rig Weiskopf on down.

You never saw trash like this anywhere. Employees could eat whatever they wanted in the break room, but they weren't allowed to bring snacks onto the warehouse floor with them.

Food was known to be a contributing factor in workplace accidents. It also attracted bugs and rodents, two things you definitely didn't want in a warehouse filled with expensive electronics.

Just beyond where the bag sat, I stopped when I reached the spot where, based on my best reckoning, the assault had taken place.

It was just another bare spot of floor. There was no reason to have chosen that particular place, other than that it was where Manger happened to accost Maria.

I was now imagining myself as the cameraperson—who was, I think I could safely assume, another migrant who had paid Manger $8,000 to be secreted across the border. Obviously, the person was undocumented, like Maria; and, therefore, they were frightened, and hoping to get away from this place and disappear into the vast anonymity of America as quickly as possible.

When they heard Maria calling for help, they hadn't interceded. Maybe the cameraperson was also small, like Maria, and didn't feel they could take on a brute like Joseph Manger. Maybe they tried to rally others to come to Maria's rescue and failed.

Or maybe there weren't others. Maybe Joseph Manger had only hidden two migrants in his truck.

Whatever the case, when they heard Maria shouting, they didn't rush to her defense; but they at least had the presence of mind to document what was happening.

As I recalled, the video had been completely dark at first, like the cameraperson had been hiding behind something. I was now looking around for whatever might have shielded them.

There was nothing. At least nothing that was here right now. Had there perhaps been some pallets of freight that had since been cleared away?

As I tried to imagine where they had been standing, my eye traced backward to something I hadn't noticed before.

It was an opening in the floor—just this random hole in the concrete at the midpoint of the wall, with no markings to indicate what it was.

I walked closer and saw it was actually a stairwell, leading down.

Way down. My weak little flashlight didn't reach to the bottom. And there was no safety lighting along these walls.

It suddenly made sense. The cameraperson had been in this dark, recessed stairwell. That's where they had been when the video started, then they got a bit braver and stuck the camera—and perhaps only the camera—up out of the hole to capture what was happening.

When they were done, they slipped back down the stairwell.

Which begged the question: Where did the steps lead?

I started my descent into the darkness, training my flashlight on each step as I went. There was no railing, so I kept my hand along the wall for balance.

A typical staircase going from the second floor of a house down to the first floor has thirteen steps. This was deeper. I hadn't counted the steps, but I was guessing I had gone down thirty of them when I reached a steel door.

I tried the handle. It didn't move. What's more, this door was unlike every other that I had encountered at this facility, in that there was no magnetic reader to accept my ID badge. There wasn't even a keyhole.

It was just this heavy, locked steel door that led . . . where, exactly?

To the sewers? To another Balco building? To a secret room?

There was no telling.

Really, I didn't know what to make of any of this, or what this building was about.

All I knew was that I found it to be extremely strange.

CHAPTER 38

ANOTHER PHONE CALL went out from the windowless room.

"What is it now? I was just about asleep."

"It's the new guy again."

There was a laugh on the other end of the line. "Ah, I guess he's not a monk after all. He go next door and help himself?"

"No. He went on a late-night walk."

Another laugh. "Feeling a little restless, was he?"

"No, you don't understand. He went to L-11."

"What are you talking about?"

"He left his hotel room, and I didn't know where he went. I thought maybe he was just going to get some air. The next thing I knew, he was showing up at Long Beach. I guess he took a cab there or something."

"He took a cab to L-11?"

"No, at first he was just walking around the main warehouse. He does that sometimes in Oakland, too. He just talks to people and, I don't know. It seems harmless enough. Still, I was just keeping an eye on him, following him from one camera to the next, you know?"

"Sure."

"Anyway, after he was done in the warehouse, he went around to some of the other buildings. Then he spent some time in L-11."

"How did he get in?"

"He used his fob."

The man on the other end swore. "His fob worked on L-11?"

"Yep."

"That goddamned Ken Helms."

"What about him?"

"He's an idiot, that's what. He knows that building is supposed to be off-limits. I swear, he just doesn't know how to program the fobs so you only get into certain places."

"No one know how to program the fobs. We really need to replace that whole system. It's terrible."

The man swore again, then said, "Okay, so he went in the building. Then what?"

"Well, he just looked around for a while. Then he, uh, went down the stairs."

"Jesus. Did he go all the way down to the door?"

"Yeah."

"Did he open it?"

"He tried. It was locked."

"Thank goodness for small favors. Then what?"

"He went back up the stairs, looked around a little more, then left."

"There wasn't a truck in place, was there?"

"No."

"You think he has any idea what goes on in there?"

"I don't see how he could. All he saw was an empty building. I think we're good."

"No," the man corrected. "We're not good. All we were is lucky."

CHAPTER 39

SLEEP STILL ELUDED me for a long time after I returned to the hotel.

The next morning, my eyelids didn't flutter open until 7:48, a positively decadent hour for someone who was usually out of the house by six at the latest.

I rolled over in bed and checked my phone. There was nothing particularly pressing among any of the messages that had rolled in overnight.

The only one that demanded an immediate answer was a text from Page, sent at 6:54, that read: YOU ALIVE?

My reply: BARELY.

This earned me a phone call before I had even summoned the gumption to sit up.

I answered with: "Hi."

Even that one short syllable sounded to me like it was ridden with guilt.

"Hey, sweetie. How are you?"

There was forced cheer in her voice.

"Oh, I've been better. But I suppose I've been worse, too."

"Sounds like it was a late night."

"Yeah, I didn't get back to the hotel until after midnight."

Which was true. Sort of.

"Oh, you poor thing. Was it media inquiries or internal stuff?"

"A mix. It was just a hellish day. Not really worth rehashing," I said, hoping that would put an end to any inquiry she might have had—and thus not putting me in the position of having to lie, either by commission or omission.

Eager to change the subject, I asked, "How are you feeling?"

"Fine. I've got my appointment this morning."

I felt an instant stab of remorse. It had been a point of pride for me that I had made it to all her prenatal checkups—both before and after the move. It had been my small contribution to the lip service of this being "our" pregnancy, a concept that felt increasingly absurd as her body was taken over by an ever-more-demanding parasite and mine stayed unchanged.

"Oh, damn, I forgot. I'm sorry I'm missing it."

"What, because you're losing your gold star for perfect attendance?"

"Well, yeah. That and I just wanted to be there for you."

"I'm fine," she said. "Just make sure you're there for the delivery."

It was a cheap shot.

Maybe she was even trying to pick a fight.

But I didn't have any fight in me. And I was feeling like I deserved whatever barbs she wanted to toss my way.

"Of course I will be," I insisted. "C'mon. I'm sorry I had to miss this. Could you FaceTime me or—"

"I'm not holding my phone through the entire appointment," she said definitively. "It's fine. I've basically resigned myself to the fact that I'm raising this baby by myself."

"Page, that's not true—you know that."

"Do I? Because right now I have a husband who is gone for thirteen hours or more every day. And then, on the weekend, when I think he's going to be eager to spend time with me, I basically have to throw a tantrum just to get him to notice me. At the moment, that's what I know."

I couldn't dispute her characterization of my recent work patterns.

"It's just because I'm so new," I said. "Once I get settled in the job, the hours will calm down."

"Will they? Or will it just get worse because everyone will realize they can just heap more work on you and you'll just keep saying 'more please' because Curt Hinton can't let anyone down."

"Page, that's not—"

"I have to hop in the shower," she said. "I'll talk to you later."

"I love you," I replied.

But I was pretty sure she had already hung up.

Which I felt like I deserved.

I showered and dressed and was just starting to contemplate my next move when I heard a small tap on the side door. It was Korynne. She was also fully dressed, thank goodness.

"Hey, just wanted to make sure you were awake," she said in an officious voice, as if nothing was changed between us and nothing unusual had happened the previous evening.

That version of events was fine with me.

I still spent breakfast not making eye contact with her, then made sure to maintain social distancing as we Ubered over to the Long Beach facility.

Diving into the coverage, it became clear to me that the I-5 wreck had all the hallmarks of a one-day story.

With traffic flowing again—and with the victims already fading into the background noise of all the other tragedies in the world—media outlets in Los Angeles and San Diego were looking elsewhere in their relentless search for audience titillation.

There wasn't a single new inquiry.

I checked in with Officer Krempitz from the California Highway Patrol, and he impressed on me that nothing was going to happen very soon. CHP had sent what remained of the improvised explosive device to a lab for further testing, and the expected time frame for results was measured in months, not days or weeks.

Likewise, the NTSB would put out a report in six weeks. But a flack there explained it would be narrowly focused on mechanical issues and the performance of the relevant safety apparatus. The criminal aspects of the crash were not in the NTSB's purview.

I had also received an email from Sal Salcedo sharing the frustrating news that an exhaustive review of footage had tracked the truck from when it had entered the facility until it departed.

There was no sign of Neil Rees or anyone else who didn't belong.

I called Sal to follow up. He told me the only person seen going near the cab was Dan Gillespie. We agreed it seemed unlikely that he had blown himself up.

So how had the explosives gotten onto his truck? It remained a mystery, but Sal said he'd keep working on it.

By midmorning, I was working through the kind of minor brush fires that would have been occupying my attention had I been in Oakland, which had me wondering what I was still doing down in Long Beach.

But just as I was thinking about pulling the plug and finding flights back north, Lorne emailed me saying he thought it made sense for Korynne and me to stick around in Long Beach for "another day or two." He wrote that he would feel more comfortable knowing he had "boots on the ground" in case the story reared back up again. And at $350,000 a year, my boots had to go wherever he said.

I was still working in the situation room, which was now just an empty room. Korynne was in there with me. She had been staring at her laptop screen as if it were extra fascinating.

Really, the only thing that was close to interesting was when Ken Helms popped in on us near lunchtime.

"How's everyone doing in here?" he asked.

"It's been pretty quiet," I reported.

"Well, I guess no news is good news?"

"I would say so."

"Great," he said, and had already turned to leave.

"Actually, Ken, I had a quick question," I said, thinking of my previous evening's meanderings.

He pivoted back toward me and looked at me expectantly.

"I couldn't sleep last night, so I came back here and gave myself a little tour. I stumbled across Building L-11, and I was curious: What's it for? What goes on in there?"

"L-11," he repeated, like he wasn't tracking.

"It's that little building out toward the edge of the property. It just has that one loading bay."

"Oh, right. That's for SSS."

"SSS?"

"Specialized Shipping Services. It's a catchall for a lot of things. Some trucks are marked SSS, and they go there first. There's usually one or two pallets that need to be off-loaded. It might be something extra bulky, or hazardous, or a shipment that really needs to be expedited. Basically, anytime we have something we don't want to get tangled up with the rest of the warehouse or needs to be sequestered for some reason, we send it to SSS. It's handy to have when we need it."

"Oh," I said. "Thanks."

He smiled and departed.

The afternoon came, and then it started dragging.

It wasn't that I was lacking in things to do. The fatigue of the previous day was catching up to me.

Simply to get my blood moving, I announced to Korynne I was going to head down to the warehouse to walk the floor.

She promised to keep an eye on things for me while I was gone and call me if anything broke, even though that seemed increasingly unlikely.

I wandered out into the sunshine, squinting toward Building L-11, which looked a lot like it had the previous night—isolated and unused.

It still haunted me, knowing what had happened in there.

Trying to shake it off, I went into the main warehouse, where I watched with appreciation as a loading dock door opened and a truck backed perfectly into the opening.

A pair of forklifts were waiting for it. As soon as the truck's door opened, they went to work. A fully loaded forty-foot trailer could fit an astonishing amount of stuff, but there were people at Balco who dedicated considerable time and expertise to making sure it could be unloaded as quickly and efficiently as possible.

They aimed for less than thirty minutes with single-stacked pallets, and less than an hour with double-stacked pallets. Stats were kept. Performance was monitored.

Every minute mattered.

I was mostly just admiring the coordination and nonstop motion—it was almost like a ballet—when a man came my way, pushing a wide dust broom across a floor that scarcely seemed to need it, seeing as it was already as clean as a hospital operating theater.

The man had close-cropped salt-and-pepper hair and a neatly tended beard. He was wearing a standard-issue blue jumper with the Balco logo stitched on one breast, and his name on the other.

Not wanting to be in his way, I stepped back, giving him a nod. As he passed, my eye naturally traveled from his face down to his name.

Melvord.

It was a name I had only heard once in my life; a name not easily forgotten.

"Melvord," I blurted. "Melvord Finck?"

He stopped pushing his broom and turned toward me.

"Can I help you?"

I introduced myself.

"Nice to meet you," he said.

"You *work* here?" I asked, dumbfounded.

"Yes, sir," he said, as if there should have been nothing unusual about it.

"I'm sorry, but . . . are you the same Melvord Finck who . . ."

I nearly finished it with, *Who pled guilty to acting as a coyote and spent eighteen months in prison?*

Instead I finished it with, ". . . who used to drive a truck for Balco?"

"Now, why you asking about that?" he asked.

His eyes had narrowed. I could tell he knew exactly why I was asking. There was no point in pretending.

I could have just let it be. You'd probably be hard-pressed to find a large warehouse in America that didn't have an ex-con or two working there.

If Melvord Finck was pushing a broom for Balco, it really didn't have much impact on me as vice president for corporate communications.

But Melvord Finck wasn't just any ex-con where Balco was concerned. And journalistic instincts die hard.

I just had to know: Why would Balco welcome back someone who had so egregiously violated company policy—and incurred a huge potential liability while doing so?

Even though Rig Weiskopf had managed to smooth the waters with the federal task force, that didn't change the fact that Finck had risked disaster while driving a truck with "Balco" on the side. What if those twenty or thirty migrants had suffocated or died from heat stroke while they were stuffed in the back of that truck?

I knew he wasn't driving anymore, but shouldn't someone in Legal or HR still have sounded the alarm? Or had they been overruled by someone higher up?

Perhaps the man at the top?

Lorne Murphy was a soft touch when it came to people. And he had his own opinion morally about what Melvord had done. Still, CEOs were all about mitigating risk, and it was taking a huge chance to bring someone with Melvord's checkered history back in the fold. Especially when there didn't seem to be any payoff.

Something about it just wasn't right.

"Sorry, but . . . they . . . they hired you back after you got out of prison?"

His eyes quickly flitted toward a camera bolted halfway up the wall, then back to me.

"Can't talk about that here," he said. "You have a nice day now."

And then he continued, letting his broom lead the way.

CHAPTER 40

CAN'T TALK ABOUT that *here*.

It was the final word that my brain chose to fixate on as I departed the warehouse. Maybe I was putting too much emphasis on it, but was there something Melvord really wanted to say to me?

Like maybe at his home, away from Balco's prying cameras?

With that in mind, I retreated back to my laptop in the situation room. Korynne was elsewhere, so there was no one to pay me any mind as I pried into his life a little more.

My first effort was a simple Google search, which I probably should have done before this.

That led me rather quickly to a Department of Justice press release saying Melvord Jeremiah Finck was accused of illegally trafficking twenty-eight people. He had been arrested by Joint Task Force 1954, which was a partnership between the DOJ and the Department of Homeland Security to combat human smuggling across the southern border.

I thought maybe 1954 signified the year of some important piece of legislation. But, no, it was because the border between the U.S. and Mexico was 1,954 miles long. Joint Task Force 1954 purported to protect all of it.

It turned out Joint Task Force 1954 had been created relatively recently, during the pandemic, in response to the rise of the criminal trafficking networks that had become a major force in illegal border crossings.

Since then, Joint Task Force 1954 had established a robust presence wherever migrants were found in large numbers, both along the border and in northern cities, where many undocumented people lived. I clicked on a map of office locations and found there was even one not far away—in the U.S. Appraisers Building on Sansome Street in San Francisco, which was also home to a number of other federal agencies.

That was an interesting start, but it didn't tell me much about Melvord himself. I clicked over to our employee management system to see what more I could learn.

I had vice president–level permission, which gave me fairly free rein to get into things that really weren't much of my business.

But, as I quickly discovered, being vice president only got me so far. If I was clicking on one of the people in my own small division, it would tell me anything I wanted to know about them: the hours they worked, how much sick time they had accrued, how much they were putting away in their 401(k), and—most importantly to me at the moment—their home address.

When it came to Melvord Finck, I could only see that he was an active employee in the Long Beach warehouse.

I couldn't access any of his personal information.

So how was I supposed to figure out where he lived?

I sat and stewed for a short while, and then a plan—probably a bad one—began forming in my head.

It had iffy odds of success. But short of trying to follow him as he left the warehouse—which felt pretty daunting since I didn't have a car—I didn't know what else to try.

Before long, I was approaching the open office door of Allison Fairbanks, the director of Human Resources for Long Beach.

One of the survival skills a reporter has to hone is being able to size up people quickly. My instant read on Allison Fairbanks was that she was a people pleaser who would go out of her way to help anyone.

The tip-off was the Halloween-ready bowl of candy on the edge of her desk. It wasn't merely that it was brimming to the top. It's that it included a great diversity of choices: hard candy, chewy candy, chocolate, caramel, mints, gummies, you name it.

Anyone who put that much energy into their candy bowl cared way too much about what other people thought about her.

I tapped lightly on her doorframe.

"Hi, I don't think we've met yet. I'm Curt Hinton. I'm the new VP for corporate communications."

"Oh, hi, yes," she said, looking up from her screen.

"Can I come in? I need a favor."

She brightened at this, further confirming my assessment of her.

"Absolutely," she said. "Sorry it's such a mess in here."

There wasn't a thing in her office that was out of place—right down to the verdant selection of plants behind her that appeared to be getting the perfect amounts of sunlight and water.

"No problem. I'm just doing some follow-up on the Dan Gillespie story."

Her smile broke at the mention of the name. "Oh. That poor man. That poor family. What do you need?"

"I was hoping you could help me track down his full driving record. I'm told he's won a safe driving award every year for the past twenty years, but I have a reporter who wants to see the year-by-year breakdown. As long as everything checks out, it strikes me there's no harm in showing it to her. I've got the last ten years. I'm told anything older than that is in a filing cabinet somewhere around here?"

If she said, *Yes, let me have my assistant get that for you*, I was out of luck.

Instead, she said, "I think I know exactly where that is. Can you give me five minutes?"

"Sure. Appreciate it."

"No problem," she said, already lifting herself from her seat.

The moment she had disappeared from view, I scurried around to her computer; there, three lucky breaks went my way in fairly short order.

The first was that her screen was still live. It hadn't gone to sleep, which would have required me to enter a password.

The second one was that she had a window with the employee management system already up, so I didn't have to log in.

The third was that, as the chief of HR for this facility, she had full access to Melvord Finck's file.

I didn't want to take the time to read it here. I selected the option to print the entire record, and had it sent to the one networked printer whose output I knew I could easily track down—the one right outside my office in Oakland.

Then I hit the PRINT button, and quickly backtracked so her screen was on the exact record where she left off.

I had been back in my chair, on the proper side of the desk, for several minutes by the time she returned.

"I left the original in the filing cabinet and just made you a copy," she said, holding a thin sheath of paper aloft. "Is that okay?"

"It's perfect," I said. "Thanks."

"Happy to help," she assured me.

"Mind if I help myself to your candy bowl?"

She smiled broadly. "Be my guest."

As soon as I was back in the situation room, I called Bob Brunato's cell. I asked him to go to the printer and read off Melvord Finck's address—3842 Oak Avenue, Long Beach—then put the rest of the printout on my desk.

After we ended the call, I looked up 3842 Oak Avenue. It was about fifteen minutes away, up in a section of Long Beach that was labeled as Los Cerritos.

I kept myself busy for the remainder of the afternoon. At five thirty, I shared an Uber with Korynne back to the hotel. I demurred when she asked me to join her for dinner, saying I felt a headache coming on.

Within fifteen minutes of that declaration, I was making the short walk to a nearby car rental place. I forked over my license and a major credit card, and was soon on my way up to Los Cerritos in an anonymous-looking foreign-made sedan that still smelled new.

I took Long Beach Boulevard, which was lined with palm trees and intersected by traffic lights.

Once I passed under the 405, the neighborhood went from middle class to upper middle class. I made a few turns off Long Beach Boulevard to reach Oak Avenue, where the houses were all single-family, surrounded by neatly tended lots, and set back from the road.

This was the nice part of town.

Frankly, a lot nicer than what I expected for a former truck driver who had spent time in federal prison and was now making his way as a janitor.

3842 Oak Avenue was no exception. It was a small slice of suburban heaven, with a low barrier of boxwood shrubs and a small, lush, perfectly weedless lawn.

The house was single story but sprawling. If I had to guess at the square footage, I'd say it was between 2,500 and 3,000, with at least four bedrooms. It had a beautiful bay window to the left of the front door.

I was no real estate agent. But I wouldn't have been surprised if this house was worth something approaching two million dollars.

How was Melvord Finck swinging that on a janitor's salary?

There were two possibilities. One was that Lorne had mentioned Melvord had a wife. Maybe Mrs. Finck was doing a lot better than Mr. Finck.

But I couldn't rule out that he had succeeded in making a whole lot of those migrant shipments—without being caught—before he finally got nabbed. And it had been lucrative.

Very lucrative. Just say he averaged twenty-five migrants per load. At $8,000 a pop, that was $200,000 per trip.

The typical Balco driver did nothing but runs back and forth to Mexico—fifty, a hundred times a year?

I'm sure there were expenses involved—possibly bribing local officials, or paying off whoever was rounding up the migrants. But even if that halved his take, that was still a lot of money he might have been able to squirrel away.

Maybe even enough to pay for a place like this.

Or maybe I had everything wrong. That was one of the lessons being a journalist had taught me: Sometimes, what I thought I knew for certain early on while reporting a story turned out to be dead wrong by the end.

The only way to find the truth was to keep asking questions.

I pulled to the side of the road and parked. 3842 didn't have a driveway or garage—very few of the houses around here did—so there was no telling if anyone was home based on the cars that were or weren't there. I made my way up the short walkway that led to the house and rang the doorbell.

My wait wasn't a long one.

The main door opened, giving way to the sight of Melvord Finck standing behind a screen door. He had ditched his janitor's jumpsuit in favor of sweatpants and a T-shirt.

"What you want?" he asked.

"You made it sound like you didn't want to talk at work. I thought maybe you'd be more comfortable talking here."

"About what?"

"About your history at Balco."

"Why you need to know that?"

I had prepared this explanation:

"I'm new here and I've been reviewing files. When I bumped across what happened with you, it just didn't make sense to me. So I was hoping you could set the record straight."

In my experience, people love to set the record straight.

"Set it straight how?"

"You tell me. According to the file I read, when you got caught with all those migrants in your truck, you swore up, down, left, and sideways that you had no idea they were in there. And then you still pled guilty to the crime. Why plead guilty if you didn't do it?"

Melvord just stood there, looking at me, then down at his white tube socks.

Me. Socks. Me.

"And then, after you served eighteen months, Balco hired you back? Why would they do that after you put the company in jeopardy?"

He studied me a little more, then said, "What does it say in the file?"

"It doesn't," I admitted.

"Then I guess that's your answer," he said.

And then he closed the door on me.

CHAPTER 41

IN THE WINDOWLESS room, the man had almost missed it.

The exchange had been so brief—less than thirty seconds, maybe a dozen quick lines going back and forth.

It took him going back and looking at it again before he realized what had taken place.

He captured the scene, then saved it in a file, which he emailed to his superior.

Then he picked up the phone.

"Yeah?"

"Something you gotta see," the man in the windowless room said. "I just emailed it to you. It's the new guy again."

"Okay. Hang on."

There was silence on the line for a minute or so.

"All right, so he's back in the warehouse. What am I missing?"

"You know who that is, right? The guy who he's talking to?" the man in the windowless room asked.

"No. Who?"

"Melvord Finck."

"You're kidding me."

"I wish."

"I'll be goddamned. Why would Curt Hinton possibly want to talk to Melvord Finck?"

"I don't know. But he wasn't asking for brownie recipes. Whatever Hinton was saying made Melvord uncomfortable. Check out the way he looks up at the camera. He knows we're watching."

"Well, of course he does. What's Hinton up to? First he goes into L-11. Then he talks to Melvord Finck. Do you think he knows?"

"Seems like a pretty big coincidence if he doesn't."

"God*damn*."

"Are you going to do something about it?"

"I don't know. It feels like I have to kick it upstairs."

"Yeah," the man in the windowless room said. "Better safe than sorry."

CHAPTER 42

THE ONLY DEVELOPMENT in the Dan Gillespie story overnight was one I wouldn't be sharing with the media—but it would certainly be of interest to California Highway Patrol's investigators.

Sal Salcedo had written me an email saying his people had solved the mystery of how the explosives had gotten into the cab.

Balco's trucks were tracked by GPS, and when they downloaded the data for Gillespie, it showed he had pulled off the highway at a Carl's Jr. in San Clemente, roughly an hour into the trip.

Their theory was that Neil Rees could have followed Gillespie out of Long Beach and waited until he stopped. Then, while he was in the restaurant—ordering his breakfast, using the restroom, whatever—Rees could have snuck into the truck and planted the device.

That also perfectly explained why the explosion had happened when and where it did. The accident site was all of five minutes from that Carl's Jr.

Rees had waited until he was certain Gillespie was back on I-5 and ripping along at highway speed, then hit the detonator.

Could it be established that Rees was at the Carl's Jr.? That would be beyond Sal's ability to find out. But CHP certainly could investigate.

Our best hope there would be that the restaurant had cameras trained on the parking lot. Maybe Carl's Jr. would volunteer the footage, or maybe CHP would have to file a subpoena. Either way, this could be the break that would make all the difference.

I wrote Sal suggesting he lean on CHP to find out.

He replied immediately, saying he already had.

We would just have to be patient and wait for the investigation to take its course.

Otherwise, it had been a quiet night, at least where Balco and the Southern California media was concerned. This allowed me to convince Lorne that my boots would be perfectly fine on ground that was a lot closer to home.

When he assented, I booked a morning flight for Korynne and me back to SFO.

We rode to the airport together and were seated next to each other on the flight. But it seemed like there was a lot less incidental contact this time around.

Which was good. Maybe her little crush was dissipating now that I had made it clear it wasn't going anywhere.

When we got off the flight, I suggested to her that she could take the rest of the day off—and Thursday as well—as comp time for having put such long hours in on Monday and Tuesday.

She thanked me, but the truth was I had an ulterior motive. I wasn't planning to go straight back to the office myself.

What Sal's people had discovered about Dan Gillespie's fateful breakfast stop had been working its way through my mind the entire flight.

This ended any doubt I may have had about IWW's involvement. Neil Rees had now been in the immediate vicinity of two major crimes. And I couldn't just do nothing about it anymore.

When I was a reporter, I learned that there were times when you needed to tiptoe gently and let the gaps in your knowledge slowly fill in before you made any big moves.

But there were also times when you needed to force a confrontation and make your source squirm, if only to hear what lies they would come up with.

This felt like one of those.

I looked up the address for IWW-Local 37. It was in the Mission District, wedged among the trendy taquerias, tattoo shops, and low-slung residential buildings.

A morning fog was still stretched low across the city as I made the short drive up from SFO.

IWW-Local 37's home could have passed for a high school gymnasium, with a rounded arch for a roof. Across the front of the building, in tall steel letters, were the words "International Warehouse Workers Union-Local 37," with the union's seal bolted next to them.

Peering in from the street, I could see a large open space that really looked like an old-time union hall. But there was also a door leading to a rectangular side of the building where the offices seemed to be, so that's where I went.

At the reception desk, it took a little time to sort out that, no, I didn't have an appointment to meet with Rudy Szymanski; but, yes, I wanted to speak with him anyway.

All the while, I kept my eyes open. This visit was as much about what I would see as what I would hear.

But, at least at first, there was nothing noteworthy. I sat in a reception area with glossy union brochures arrayed on the coffee table in front of me.

Eventually, I was ushered into Szymanski's office. IWW-Local 37's president greeted me smoothly, looking as slicked back as ever. I anticipated that I'd put him on the defensive the moment I began asking questions. Instead, he did something I truly didn't expect.

As soon as the door closed behind me and I settled in across his desk, he started running the meeting.

"Mr. Hinton, I'm really glad you came in today. Really glad," he repeated. "I've been wanting to talk to you ever since the memorial service."

"Oh? And why is that?"

"I've just been wanting to clear the air. You were pissed at me and, looking again at what I wrote, you were right to call me out on it. It was totally uncalled for. I was actually embarrassed when I reread it. Angel was a great guy and a total class act. I've been . . . I've been thinking a lot about it. I've been thinking a lot about how we do everything."

I had no idea where he was going with this. But if being a reporter had taught me one thing, it was that when a source wanted to talk, you let them talk.

"How so?" I asked.

"Look, our members are great, okay? They're the best people. The absolute best. They'll do anything for the right cause. What I told you at the funeral is true. I could get a hundred guys with baseball bats to show up anywhere in a heartbeat," he said, snapping his fingers. "But lately I've been thinking about whether that really serves any good in the long run. Maybe might doesn't make right, you know?"

He cleared his throat. "Or when I looked at that thing I wrote. Look, a lot of the rhetoric we put out is . . . Well, it's just that. It's rhetoric. We make it this big us-versus-them thing, and feel like we have to talk tough and look tough, because it's what our members expect of us. And you guys do the same thing on your side. But underneath, there's a falseness to it. We know that and you know that."

"We do?" I asked.

"Sure you do. Come on. For whatever we say publicly, behind the scenes we both know we're going to have to come together and figure stuff out. I've been thinking about how we need to better align what we say publicly with what we do privately. Maybe that's something you can even help me with. Really, what purpose does it serve to get everyone all riled up? The fact of the matter is, a work stoppage doesn't help anyone put food on the table. At the end of the day, we're going to have to put all that talk aside, go to the negotiating table, and come up with a CBA"—a collective bargaining agreement—"that makes sense for everyone."

"That's if the vote goes your way," I said.

"Well, of course it's going to go our way."

"It is?"

"Sure. We've done polling that shows us winning sixty–forty. Angel knew that."

I felt my face wrinkle. "Then why did he keep banging the drum for the company?"

"That's *exactly* what I'm talking about. That difference between what we say in public and private. He knew what the deal was. Why not be up front about it?"

I must have looked extra skeptical, because Szymanski went to the laptop in front of him. "Here, hang on. I'll show you what I'm talking about. I've got our emails right here."

Behind him, a laser printer started whirring. It spit out a few sheets, which he stapled for me before handing it over.

It was a standard Gmail-style email exchange, with the newest message first, and older messages beneath.

Wanting to read in order, I went all the way down to the first message. It was all about Szymanski's admiration of Balco as a company—for how it had treated its employees, for having never laid anyone off, for putting people first—and how he hoped they could have a productive relationship that would benefit everyone.

In his reply, Angel was his usual gracious, charming self. There was no questioning the authenticity of the email: I recognized a few of his standard self-deprecating jokes.

The tone was open and friendly. He admitted he would still be putting up a fight to state the company's case but concluded with, "I really look forward to working with you."

Szymanski's response was practically a love letter.

"Now I see why I've heard so many good things about you," it began.

He acknowledged that Angel would "of course" have to keeping toeing the company line in public. Then he shared the information about IWW's internal polling.

Angel wrote back that his conversations with employees matched IWW's numbers and conceded that it was "inevitable" that the warehouse workers would vote in favor of unionizing.

Their emails grew less formal—and more friendly—from there. Each one talked in glowing terms about the partnership that was being formed. There were earnest professions on both sides of wanting to work in good faith.

They had actually already started negotiations. Szymanski had acknowledged that Balco's margins were razor thin and that the union would be careful not to "squeeze too hard" with its demands.

"We want to come up with something that is fair and sustainable for all involved," he wrote.

Angel replied that he appreciated that understanding. He warned that there would be little room to budge on benefits but allowed that there might be "some wiggle room" on salaries, "especially in future years, since we're projecting continued revenue growth."

Szymanski agreed that Balco's benefits were already excellent and wouldn't need to be touched. He then volunteered a willingness to compromise on allowing some of the advanced productivity metrics that unions elsewhere had balked on.

"It never makes sense to me when unions stand in the way of improved efficiency, when that only helps everyone long term," he wrote.

Their correspondence was riddled with pleasantries. There was no hint of rancor. The second-to-last email from Szymanski—written Monday afternoon, a few hours before Angel was killed—regarded some legal minutiae about the exact manner in which the vote would be conducted. It also mentioned a lunch date the two had made for Friday in Oakland.

Angel had written back that he was going to take Szymanski to a "knockdown, drag-out GREAT Puerto Rican joint—make sure you come hungry."

Szymanski wrote back, "Amazing! Looking forward to it."

When I was done, I looked back up at Szymanski.

"See?" he said. "What if, instead of all the tough talk, everyone knew *that* was the real rhetoric? Do you think there would still be fights in the break room?"

There probably wouldn't be.

But I also had to acknowledge something else.

These didn't look like the kind of emails that would be sent from someone who wanted to hurt Angel.

Quite the opposite.

On top of that, if IWW knew the vote was going their way—no

matter what Angel said—it hardly made sense to kill him.

"Yeah, it would definitely help to dial things back a bit," I allowed.

"Exactly. And I know that needs to start on our side. But I'm hoping you guys can follow suit in your messaging. Ultimately, we're all going to be on the same team. What's good for Balco is going to be good for IWW, and vice versa. There are no good guys and bad guys here, you know?"

Except there *was* a bad guy.

Neil Rees.

According to that AI facial recognition hit, he was outside Balco headquarters just before Angel was killed.

How did I square that with the backslapping emails between Angel and Szymanski?

Unless Neil Rees was acting on his own? Was it possible the member education specialist was just another person who wasn't aware of the public–private difference in the dialogue and took it upon himself to silence IWW's loudest critic? Just like he had decided to go after Dan Gillespie?

Maybe he was nothing more than a rogue sociopath.

In which case, might Rudy Szymanski actually want to help bring him to justice? To clean up his own shop?

It felt like a risk worth taking.

"I know what you mean," I said. "I still have a question for you, though. It's awkward. No, it's more than awkward. It's downright offensive. But I have to ask it anyway."

"Go ahead," Szymanski said.

"It's about Neil Rees."

"What about him?"

I uncorked the question slowly, carefully, making it clear that I thought Rees could have been doing what I was accusing him of without Szymanski being aware of it. I told him about the facial recognition hit.

"So, putting it plainly, Angel was murdered by someone," I concluded. "Is it possible it was Neil Rees?"

Szymanski made careful eye contact. "Okay, I hear everything you're saying, but . . . before you start jumping to conclusions, just hang on. What day was Angel killed? It was May 1, wasn't it?"

"Yes."

"Then it's not possible that Neil was involved. And I can prove it."

"How?"

"Are you familiar with May Day?"

I felt a crease coming across my brow. "Isn't that a communist thing?"

"Sort of. It's known as International Workers' Day. But you've got the basic idea. All IWW shops—including Local 37—have a big celebration on May Day, capped by their annual awards banquet. Ours started at 7:00 p.m. and didn't get over until ten. Neil was here the whole time. If you don't believe me, you can look on Facebook. We live streamed the whole thing on our page and it's still saved there."

Szymanski turned to his laptop and did a bit more typing. I was soon looking at a video that was labeled "IWW Local-37 May Day Celebration!"

The camera was trained on the front of the union hall I had seen from the street. There were two long tables set on risers. In the middle was a podium with the IWW logo.

As the video began, the people seated at those head tables were already in place. Among the dignitaries, I recognized Szymanski's slicked-back hair; and, a few chairs farther down, the benign math teacher looks of Neil Rees.

"You can watch the whole thing if you want, but Neil never left,"

Szymanski said. "There are time-stamped comments from our members who were logging in remotely that can prove it. He was there the whole time."

Szymanski clicked the video forward to the two-thirds mark, which corresponded roughly to the time Angel was killed.

Sure enough, Neil Rees was there.

But how was that possible?

How could he be in two places at once?

Something wasn't right.

CHAPTER 43

THE MEETING TOOK place in the windowless room.

Three people were in attendance.

Two of them—Sal Salcedo and the technician in the control chair—were accustomed to spending considerable amounts of time there.

The third was not.

Lorne Murphy preferred to have a certain distance from the things that happened in the windowless room.

But Salcedo had taken the unusual step of asking him to be there, saying his presence was required, because "a decision needs to be made."

Still, Murphy was there grudgingly. He walked in and was momentarily taken aback by the sight of all those screens—the ever-flickering mosaic keeping watch over all corners of the Balco empire—before he was able to focus.

"Okay," he said, "what's this about?"

Salcedo got right to the point: "We have a problem with Curt Hinton. I think he knows."

Murphy scowled. "What makes you say that?"

"Three videos," Sal said; then he turned to the technician. "Show him the first."

The technician hit PLAY. On the screen, there was a low-light image of Hinton walking tentatively through a darkened space.

"This is him in L-11 the first night he was down in Long Beach," Salcedo said. "We think he just stumbled on it by accident. Ken Helms admitted to me he screwed up and mistakenly gave Hinton access. Hinton asked him about it the next day, and he gave the usual story. But Hinton knows it exists and I think he knows what goes on there."

"How is that possible?" Murphy asked.

"Because yesterday he was bothering Melvord Finck."

"What?" Murphy demanded.

The screen switched to the brief interaction between Finck and Hinton that took place in the warehouse.

"What are they saying?"

"Nothing. At least according to Melvord. I talked to him this morning," Salcedo said. "But then Hinton showed up at Melvord's house last night."

"How did he know where Melvord lives?"

"We were wondering the same thing. It turns out the head of HR in Long Beach accessed Melvord Finck's personnel record yesterday."

Murphy scowled some more. "What does that have to do with Curt?"

"Because it wasn't the head of HR. It was Hinton. He visited her office, waited until she left, and used her terminal to access Finck's record."

Without prompting, the technician switched to the video that showed what Salcedo had just described.

Murphy watched with a blank face.

Salcedo continued, "Melvord said Hinton was asking him a lot of questions: Why did he plead guilty? Why did Balco rehire him?"

"And how did Melvord answer?"

"Melvord said he didn't tell him anything, just shut the door on him. But even if Hinton hasn't figured it all out yet, he's asking too many questions. He's too curious. I knew it was a mistake to hire a journalist."

"You think we can bring him in the fold?"

"Maybe if it was someone else. But this guy is different. One of my people refers to him as a Boy Scout. It's pretty accurate, if you ask me. Don't you remember what he was like when you first mentioned Melvord Finck? He was pretty self-righteous about it. I believe his exact words were, 'He was breaking the law.'"

Murphy let out a sigh. "Yeah. I guess you're right."

"If he really wanted to be a team player, he'd be coming to us with questions, not running around in the dark, getting into personnel files he has no business being in, visiting employees at their houses. It feels like he's gathering evidence. It scares the hell out of me."

"So what do we do?"

"He needs to disappear."

Murphy immediately shook his head. "I don't like it. In the last month, we've had Reddish, Manger, and Gillespie—a stabbing, a shooting, and a bombing. The body count around here is too high already."

"No, no. I've been thinking about this, and I have a plan. I mean *actually* disappear. Contact the messenger and ask him for help. He has people who are good at that sort of thing."

"You sure you want to get them involved? You know that bell can be hard to unring."

"We need their expertise. Once we're sure he's out of the picture, we can make it look like he decided to run off."

"And why would he do that? He's got a pregnant wife. I thought you said he was a Boy Scout. He's way too square for something like that."

"Ah, but he has a hot new girlfriend and he's *crazy* about her," Salcedo said, smiling broadly under his mustache. "There's one more video you need to see."

Salcedo nodded to the technician, who had enjoyed watching this particular footage more than once. Before long, the screen was showing a half-naked Korynne Vuong climbing all over Curt Hinton.

"We edit this a little bit, then send it anonymously to Hinton's wife, saying, 'Sorry. Curt was having an affair. And now they want to live happily ever after together.' She vanishes, he vanishes. As long as no one finds the bodies, that's the end of the story."

"You really think the police would buy that?" Murphy asked.

"Of course they would. This is a guy who was impulsive enough to quit his job and move across the country on a whim. We'd make him out to be a loose cannon. We don't need incontrovertible evidence here. We just need reasonable doubt. That video is reasonable doubt all by itself."

"And you're sure you want me to get the messenger involved?"

"Yes," Salcedo said definitively. "Make the call."

CHAPTER 44

MY MEETING WITH Rudy Szymanski soon came to an end.

He suggested we keep in touch, both before the union vote—which was now three weeks away—and after. And he took one last chance to express his sincere admiration for Angel.

Which, for the first time, I actually believed.

Once we said goodbye, I went back to my car. During the time I had been inside, the morning haze had burned off and been replaced by a cloudless sky and a bright sun.

Nothing else around me felt as clear.

Going back to the first hours after I learned of Angel's death—and that it was a murder staged as a carjacking—it had seemed so plain to me that IWW had been involved.

The union was the only logical suspect, the one entity he had seemed so adamantly opposed to. At least in public.

When Dan Gillespie turned out to be an anti-union hothead, and also killed under malign circumstances, it was easy to see IWW hiding in the shadows there, too.

It had been so easy for my brain to hop on board with that narrative. After all, who else would want Angel dead? And why kill a truck driver?

But if I was reading the evidence without an anti-IWW bias, what really was there?

Not much.

A video of two unknown armed men in ski masks getting into a car with my best friend shortly before his death.

Some as-yet-unidentified blood in his back seat.

The remains of an explosive device under Dan Gillespie's seat that could have been planted by anyone.

None of it was necessarily tied to IWW.

I had to acknowledge that it was entirely possible Sal Salcedo's facial recognition software had made a mistake, pinning Neil Rees as the person who jumped into that pickup truck and gave chase after Angel.

Yes, it felt like a wild, wild coincidence that of the billions of faces floating out there on the internet, the algorithm had seized on IWW's member education specialist. But maybe Salcedo had biased the search in some way?

There were more questions than answers, and the biggest one of all was:

If IWW didn't kill Angel and Dan Gillespie, who did?

I drove back to the office slowly, feeling the travel fatigue setting in. After badging my way through security, I pulled into my assigned spot on the third story of the parking deck.

The structure was open on all sides, allowing me to see the huge unloading cranes that formed the Port of Oakland's skyline. For a few minutes, I watched them swing back and forth, lifting twenty-foot steel shipping containers like they were toys.

I was struck—and not for the first time—by the mind-boggling intricacy of the system we had devised and of the remarkable results it achieved: that things created in one part of the world, with pieces from still other parts of the world, could be transported across a vast ocean to arrive exactly where and when they were supposed to, into the waiting arms of someone who was ready to receive it and prepared to parcel it out to yet more distant destinations.

This required exquisite planning, extraordinary coordination, and sustained investments in infrastructure. Yet when you thought about it, it wasn't ships or cranes or trucks that made the whole thing go.

It was people.

All the greatest things our species has accomplished, it has done so together.

The very glue that binds the system is shared faith in humanity. You had to believe that someone you didn't know and would likely never meet—from the procurement specialist to the factory worker to the logistics coordinator to the ship captain to the longshoreperson to the trucker to the forklift operator and so on and so forth throughout the entire supply chain—would do their small part to keep the ball bouncing along.

In our current environment, there were those who were losing faith in our systems and the institutions that surrounded them.

Maybe it was because they had unreasonable expectations of perfection—that nothing would *ever* go wrong. Or they lacked a basic understanding of how the systems were supposed to work. Or they were having their minds twisted by others—too often, my former colleagues in the media—who profited by sewing mistrust.

It could be easy to lose faith.

But on a certain level, you had to decide: Do you believe in people or not?

I did.

And this was another time when I needed to maintain that

confidence. I had to be patient and let Oakland PD and CHP, and their respective laboratories, continue their investigations.

They would soon come up with answers. I had to trust in them.

With this resolved, I walked across the footbridge that spanned between the parking deck and the headquarters building, then got in the elevator that took me to the fourth floor.

When I reached the stretch of offices and cubicles occupied by the Comms Team, there was a backlog of minor staff requests waiting for me.

Amy Dietz had a series of Instagram posts to run past me. Our graphic designer needed artwork approval for an updated version of the Employee Handbook. Bob Brunato wanted to go through some talking points for one of our VPs, who had an interview request from *Electronics Weekly*.

When I finally made it back to my office, I flopped in my chair and stared at the black storm of unread email that had gathered in my inbox since I'd last looked at it.

Then I glanced away from the screen, and my eye fell on a document sitting at an odd angle on my desk.

I picked it up.

It was Melvord Finck's personnel file.

Strictly speaking, the information contained in it was none of my business. I shouldn't have accessed it in the first place. And even now that I had, I should have probably just shredded it without giving it a second glance.

And yet.

I couldn't help myself. I was soon thumbing through it, looking at scanned copies of the various state and federal disclosure forms he had signed, his I-9, his emergency contact form, his healthcare plan election.

None of it was unusual or remarkable.

When I reached his pay stub, his address—good old 3842 Oak Avenue—was at the top. I was going to just keep going, but then the number in the bottom right corner caught my eye.

It was his take-home pay. And it had to be wrong. Even given the necessarily inflated salaries of California, I couldn't imagine having to pay a janitor much more than $30 an hour, which worked out to $2,400 every two weeks.

And, yeah, maybe that rate would grow a little higher with seniority and cost-of-living adjustments. But that still wouldn't get you much higher than maybe $3,000.

Melvord Finck's gross pay was $9,230.77.

Was that monthly? Even then, it was a lot. But then I looked at the year-to-date numbers; and, no, this was the same biweekly structure as me and every other Balco employee.

Still unable to believe what I was seeing, I pulled out my calculator to help me with the math.

And, yes, Melvord was being paid $240,000 a year to push a broom for us.

What's more, he was an exempt, salaried employee—as opposed to nonexempt and hourly, which is what I'd expect for a janitor.

Once again, I found myself wondering: What was the deal with Melvord Finck?

I was no closer to solving the mystery—or even figuring out how I would go about doing so—as lunchtime came and went.

It was simply baffling.

I had stuffed the file in my top desk drawer and had managed to move on to other tasks—sort of—but was still pretty distracted by it as I continued mucking my inbox.

Then a new distraction came from my phone.

A text from Page.

She seldom texted me during the day. She said she didn't like the feeling she might be interrupting me or bothering me; and, in any event, most of what she had to tell me could wait until she saw me in the evening.

So it was unusual to hear from her; and the message itself was strange as well:

Will you please come home?

I wrote back immediately: **Is everything okay?**

The little dots danced, telling me she was already composing her reply. It read:

Yes. I just need you to come home.

This was too weird to leave to the equivocations of text messaging. I hit the little phone icon for "call" and was soon hearing the ringing.

"Hey," she answered.

"Hey, what's going on?"

"Nothing. I just need you to come home, that's all."

A small panic was rising in me. "Are you feeling okay? Is it the baby? Because if you're worried about something, don't wait for me. Just call an ambulance and get yourself to the hospital. I'll meet you—"

"The baby is *fine*. Can't a wife just want her husband to come home? You've been gone for two days. I just want to see you."

Was this going to be the start of another one of her . . . what did she call it the other day?

A tantrum.

I trod carefully in my response.

"Uhh, yeah, it's just . . . I do work for a living, you know? I can't just leave in the middle of the afternoon. Can't it wait a few more hours?"

"No, Curt. *Please?*"

Two things about this were unusual. One, she seldom used my name. I was usually "sweetie" or "honey" or something similarly endearing. Two, she wasn't the pleading sort.

Something was clearly off. And I wasn't going to find out until I went home.

"Okay," I said. "I guess I'm coming home."

On my way out, I told Bob Brunato I had to go, saying it was a "minor emergency" at home. Not that he really cared.

Walking down the hallway, I went to say goodbye to Angel, like I usually did. But his picture was no longer there.

Someone had finally taken the poster down.

It was time, I suppose.

I still felt like I was missing something.

Shaking it off, I hopped in my Rivian and made the drive home—wondering the whole time what, exactly, had gotten into Page.

As soon as I pulled into the driveway of 27 Buena Vista Drive, I started to understand.

Page was sitting on the steps to the front porch.

Sitting next to her was Aiysha Reddish.

CHAPTER 45

HAVING BEEN GIVEN the rest of the day off, Korynne Vuong, whose name wasn't really Korynne Vuong, was settled into her Oakland apartment, which was every bit as plant-less, animal-less, and roommate-less as she had described it.

But only because it was a lot more temporary than she had let on.

In truth, she wasn't just coming off a divorce. She had never been married. And she wasn't a seasoned executive assistant.

She was an actress.

Or, to be more accurate, she had trained as an actress. But when it came to supporting herself as one, she had never had the lightning strike of right place, right time, and right contacts to really get herself noticed.

She had gotten into the business of seducing men for blackmail videos by accident. A shady casting agent had approached her and offered her $10,000 to sleep with a CEO whose soon-to-be-ex-wife lived in an at-fault divorce state and didn't have a prenup.

Going by the name Jackie Tran, she posed as a fellow attendee at an out-of-town conference. They went from the bar to her hotel room to her video-monitored bed in less than two hours.

Easy.

The shady casting director soon had more work for her. One job always seemed to lead to another. There was no lack of work. As in any industry, referrals were her lifeblood.

That she kept doing it came down to three things.

One, it was lucrative; a lot more lucrative than bit parts, temp jobs, waitressing, and all the other things she had done to make rent. She had already managed to squirrel away nearly two hundred thousand dollars. She told herself that as long as she stayed in shape, there was no reason she couldn't get to a million.

Two, she was good at it. True, her marks were always older men who were deeply flattered by the attentions of a hot younger woman. But it still took a certain amount of finesse and subtlety. She had to be easy, but not *too* easy. The men couldn't suspect what was happening. She often found herself pretending to have daddy issues—and therefore drawn to rich older men.

Three, she actually enjoyed it. In a way, it was sort of like acting, in that she had to develop a role and then stay in character, no matter what. But, unlike acting, there was no script to follow. It was extended improv. And that, while sometimes terrifying, was also thrilling. She had become addicted to the rush.

Having sex with random men wasn't her favorite, but that part never lasted very long. The hunt always took longer than the kill. And, at least so far, she had a perfect batting average.

That's what made this latest job so frustrating.

She had never come across a man who had resisted her like this. Usually, she could feel them starting to cave after the first hair flip and button pop.

Not this one. Was it just because he was younger and newer at marriage, and therefore harder to tempt? Or was she losing her touch?

She had never contemplated that she might fail at an assignment—or what the consequences would be—so she was relieved by the message she received on her private, encrypted email. It was from Michael Salcedo, and it was titled, "New Job."

> I think we've gotten what we need with Curt Hinton. I have payment for you, and then I'd like to talk about a new job elsewhere in the company. You game for a trip to Mexico?

She was *definitely* game. And she wrote back saying as much. They agreed that he could come over to discuss details that afternoon.

When he arrived, she was lightly perfumed and wearing a floral print sundress, because in this line of work the flirtation never stopped. It was important to keep the clients happy—and maybe just slightly titillated. She planted a kiss on Salcedo's cheek and invited him in.

He was carrying a briefcase and accompanied by two muscly men in tight black T-shirts. Both had Mesoamerican features. Neither opened their mouths as she and Salcedo exchanged friendly greetings.

"Sorry this latest thing hasn't gone quite as planned," Salcedo said, getting them down to business. "I know it's taken a lot longer than we both thought it would."

"No, *I'm* sorry," she insisted. "I've never come across someone so, so . . ."

"Resolutely faithful?"

"I was going to go with 'prude,' but I guess yours works, too," she said.

They exchanged a light chuckle.

He set the briefcase on the kitchen peninsula, dialed the combination for the lock, and started removing bricks of cash, which he placed next to the briefcase.

"We said ten thousand a week, and I believe this is week five, so here's fifty," he said.

She ogled the money. She always loved this part.

"You can count it if you like," Salcedo added.

She was so taken by the sight of the cash, she didn't register the muscly guy moving in behind her until he had already clamped a meaty hand on her mouth, while wrapping his other arm around her midsection.

Her scream disappeared into his palm.

The last thing she saw was Salcedo pulling a syringe out of his jacket pocket and plunging it into her arm.

CHAPTER 46

I DIDN'T BOTHER pulling into the garage. I just stopped the car in the driveway.

Page had been coming down from the front steps and greeted me as soon as I got out.

"Hi," she said, with a tight smile on her face.

She went up on her tiptoes and kissed me quickly. Aiysha was a few steps behind her.

"Aiysha, hi," I said, but the way they were moving didn't make me feel like this was a time for an effusive greeting.

Then, from the street, I heard a car door open. I turned to see a black SUV with two large men in dark suits getting out. They were looking at us expectantly, like they were awaiting orders.

"Who is that?" I asked. "What's going on?"

"Let's take a walk," Page said, grabbing me by the hand and practically dragging me down the driveway. I could tell she had been crying, though her face was now dry.

"Why didn't you just tell me Aiysha was here?" I asked. "I would have come running."

She waited until we were out of the driveway and walking up the street before she quietly said, "Because it's not safe to talk on the phone. It's probably not safe to talk in the house, either."

"What do you mean, 'safe'?"

"They're listening."

"Who is?"

"Let's just walk some more," she said.

I continued next to her, still holding her hand. Aiysha was just behind us. The men in the dark suits were trailing us in the black SUV.

"I'm sorry, who are those guys?" I asked.

"They're Aiysha's security detail."

"Her *security detail*?" I repeated.

"I'll explain in a little bit."

We walked on in silence. Buena Vista Drive curved to the right, out of sight of our house, then dead-ended a short while later at a rutted fire road that led up to an open space preserve, one of the many that covered Marin County. We passed a sign that warned trekkers to be careful of rattlesnakes and other wildlife and kept going until the path bent left and around some shrubby trees, putting us out of sight of the houses that were now below us.

That's where Page finally stopped.

"Okay," she said. "This is good."

We were on a sloped section of gravel and dirt roadway, surrounded by tall grasses that had already dried out due to lack of rain. A few wildflowers poked through, adding small splashes of purple and red in what was otherwise a yellow-brown palette.

Aiysha, who had been lagging behind us, had caught up. She was slightly out of breath. The men in the suits had not joined her.

"Hi," I said to her. "How are you?"

As soon as the question escaped my mouth, I felt like a moron. *Her husband is still dead. How do you think she is?*

So I tacked on a hasty, "How's Elijah?"

"He's fine," Aiysha said. "He's with his grandparents. So was I for a while. Most of the time he seems to be his usual self. Once or twice, he's asked, 'Where's Dada?' And that's pretty rough. But I guess I should appreciate it while it lasts. Before too much longer, he won't remember his father at all. He's too young to make real memories."

The reality of that settled between us like a blob of negative energy, silencing everyone for a moment.

"That has to be . . . it has to be awful," I stammered. "I can't . . . I'm sorry."

"Yeah," she said, staring down at some gravel.

I was trying to be patient, but I finally just blurted, "Okay, so is someone going to tell me what's going on?"

"Can you please explain it the way you did to me?" Page suggested to Aiysha. "I worry that if I tried to summarize everything you've told me, I'd miss things."

Aiysha looked up at the hill we had just barely started climbing for a moment before returning her gaze to me.

"Let me start at the beginning, then," she said. "I think you probably know Angel had been headhunted to Balco, and at first it seemed like this perfect situation. The salary was a nice bump from what he had been making. They gave him this huge signing bonus. The benefits were great, as you know. The first six months was a total honeymoon. Everyone talked about family, and Angel had totally bought in. Lorne Murphy was the dad. Rig Weiskopf was the crazy uncle. They made it clear they were grooming Angel as Lorne's successor. The job was challenging and the hours were long but that was nothing new. Angel was his usual irrepressible self.

"Then something changed. I didn't really notice at first—or maybe I just ignored it—because I had my hands full with Elijah. But Angel was definitely acting different. He seemed to be under this strain. Whenever I tried to ask him about it, he just waved me off or minimized it. I thought it was usual logistics stuff—someone in Panama has a bad day, and the next thing you know the whole world is screwed up, whatever. Then he started carrying a gun."

"Yeah, what was up with that?" I asked. "When the police told me they found a gun with Angel's fingerprints on it, I nearly fell out of my chair. Angel hated guns."

"I know. And when I asked him about it, he just said Oakland was a rough neighborhood. But . . ."

"But he grew up in one of the toughest parts of Chicago, and he never once thought about carrying a gun. He believed guns caused more problems than they solved."

"Which is what I said. He went into this whole thing about how Oakland was different from Chicago, that in Chicago he knew how to keep his head down and that people didn't mess with him because they knew who he was and that he was trying to go places. In Oakland, he felt like a target, walking around in his nice suits. It still seemed . . . out of character."

"For sure," I said.

"He promised he'd get a gun safe for the house and lock it up whenever he was home so Elijah could never run across it. I was still worried about him, though, because it was more than just the gun. He wasn't sleeping well—and Angel could always sleep through anything. He was irritable. There was this stress that seemed to be building and building.

"Then he started taking phone calls at home. That, in itself, was unusual. Angel had this thing about keeping home and work separate. He worked long hours, obviously, but when he was at home, he wanted it to be like a sanctuary. It had to be a real crisis for him to take calls at home. Suddenly, it was a crisis all the time."

She shook her head. "He talked in the den most of the time, because he didn't want to wake the baby or disturb me. But I'd still be able to overhear bits and pieces. A lot of times it was in Spanish, so I didn't understand what he was saying. I could tell he was upset, though."

"Let me guess: He was talking really fast," I said.

Angel had two versions of Spanish. When he was talking to me or someone in a formal setting, he spoke proper Castilian Spanish, making sure to slow down and enunciate everything. When he forgot himself a little—when he was talking with his family, or when he got excited or stressed—his tongue ratcheted up to warp speed. He slurred words, dropped his S's, and swallowed entire syllables until it was pretty much impossible for a non-native speaker to understand him.

"You got it," she said. "Anyway, I couldn't really follow the substance of what he was saying. And I wasn't really trying. But I kept hearing him say this one thing that stuck out to me. *La Tranquila.* Everything was about *La Tranquila.*"

"The quiet woman," I said, translating the phrase literally.

"Right. Do you know who La Tranquila is?"

"No."

"She's the boss of one of the largest drug cartels in Mexico."

My mouth was probably still agape as Aiysha continued.

"At first, I didn't know what to do. I looked up *La Tranquila* online. She heads up the Norteño Cartel. There's definitely a fascination with her, because there aren't a lot of women in her position. I just couldn't believe someone like that had anything to do with my kind, peaceful husband or this seemingly great company he was working for or anything. But then I overheard another conversation he had—actually, I was kind of eavesdropping—and I heard him mention her again. After that, I confronted him and asked him point blank: Are you working with a cartel?"

"What did he say?"

"Well, he denied it, of course. But . . . I knew what I heard and I showed him the stuff I had seen online. And he was still like, 'It's nothing for you to worry about.' And I said, 'If it's nothing to worry about, why did you buy a gun?' He didn't really have an answer to that. We got in a pretty big fight at that point and—"

"Wait, sorry," I said. "I'm still trying to catch up here. I don't want to sound like I'm playing devil's advocate, but . . . Are you sure Angel wasn't just, I don't know, talking about current events or about some operational difficulty Balco was having? The cartels are all over the place in Mexico. It's difficult to avoid them. They've bought off most of the cops and three-quarters of the politicians. They'll block roadways or find other ways to make a nuisance out of themselves. Was it maybe just a disruption like that he was talking about?"

Page quietly said, "Tell him about the PI."

"Yeah, I'm getting to that," Aiysha replied, then turned back to me. "So, after this big fight we had, he was insistent there was nothing happening, and I didn't really believe him. But I also didn't know what to do. It's not like I could go to the police and be like, 'Hey, I think my husband might be secretly working for a cartel.' So I hired a private investigator and asked him for his opinion. He suggested I could secretly record Angel having one of these conversations in Spanish and then have it translated. I thought that sounded like a good next step, so I hired the guy."

Aiysha laughed sardonically. "He came into the house while Angel was at work and went to bug the den. He was going to hide a listening device under the desk and when he was down there, he found another listening device. Someone else's. After that, he did a sweep for bugs. The whole house was full of them. Like, they were in every room. Even our bedroom. He also found a transmitter hidden up in the attic. It was actually using our Wi-Fi network, even though our network is password protected and encrypted and all that. And that's how I knew who it was that was doing the listening."

"Balco," I said. "Because they were the ones who set up the network in the first place."

"Bingo," she said.

I looked at Page and immediately understood why she said our house was "not safe" and that someone was "probably listening."

Because if Balco had done that to Angel's house, they had surely done the same thing to ours.

"So Balco was spying on Angel—and probably us, too," I said. "Why would an ordinary logistics company feel the need to listen to its employees . . . unless it's not actually an ordinary logistics company?"

"Exactly," Aiysha said. "When Angel came home from work that day, I bundled up Elijah and we went for a walk. I told him what I had found. He was pretty pissed and started fuming about Sal Salcedo—"

"He's our chief safety officer," I said, for Page's benefit.

But Page already knew.

"Yeah, him," Aiysha said. "Angel kind of ranted a little bit about how Sal was a creep and a weirdo and probably got off on invading our privacy. I let him go down that hole for a while, but then I steered it back around to the point of all this: Why would *Balco*, this family-oriented logistics company, need to listen to us in the first place? Wasn't surveillance at this level a pretty clear sign that the company was messed up?"

"What did he say to that?"

"He didn't—"

"Stop," Page said suddenly, gripping my arm. "Someone's coming."

We all stiffened. I hadn't heard a thing. Did Page have super hearing to go along with her heightened sense of smell?

Then I made out the sound of footsteps coming our way. Had someone followed us? Someone from Balco . . . or, worse, someone from the cartel? Had they found a way to quietly overwhelm Aiysha's security detail?

What would we do if they had? We had no way of defending ourselves. And I doubted my pregnant wife could outrun anyone at the moment.

I braced myself. Just as my anxiety was spiking, a middle-aged guy with a salt-and-pepper beard and a floppy sun hat rounded the corner.

A hiker. Just a hiker.

All this talk of spying and cartels had set me on edge.

"Anyhow," I said, when I felt like the guy was out of earshot. "What was Angel's answer?"

"Well, he didn't have an explanation for all the bugs. He said we could just have them removed, and we could disable the transmitter, and that he was going to give Salcedo hell about them. But even that didn't wash with me. I mean, you find out your employer has been listening to you at home and your response is to give them a stern talking-to? How does that track? Why wasn't Angel threatening to quit or filing a lawsuit or demanding Lorne fire Salcedo or doing something meaningful?"

"Yeah," I said. "Why wasn't he?"

"Because he knew," she said.

"Knew what?"

"I'm still not sure exactly. But whatever was going on, he was already neck deep in it. The bugs didn't *really* come as a surprise to him. Their existence was confirmation of something he had already contemplated and, to a certain degree, accepted as part of the cost of whatever business he was now in. And he must have understood there wasn't much he could do about the fact that it had been happening; certainly nothing that would risk bringing attention to it. Or at least that's what I've come to believe. At the time, I was still just confused and trying to drag the truth about the cartel out of him."

"Did it work?" I asked.

She gave a little headshake. "Not really. He stopped taking calls at home, so I never could record him. He kind of admitted that, yes, Balco had some discussions that involved La Tranquila, which was why I heard him saying her name. Then he gave me this runaround about how it was this arm's-length thing. He almost made it sound like a protection racket."

"You mean, like, Balco kicked back money to Norteño in exchange for the cartel leaving their trucks and warehouses alone?"

"Maybe. I don't really know. Angel said the less I knew, the better; and it was safer if I stopped asking questions. He also said it was nothing to worry about, which was pretty paradoxical. If it wasn't safe for me to ask questions, how could it be nothing for me to worry about? I was like, 'Are you kidding me with this?' He told me there was no risk to him individually or to our family because the cartel wouldn't dare lay a finger on him."

She looked away at this point. The memory of that conversation obviously haunted her. I'm sure she had replayed it many times in her mind over the last several weeks.

"That was two weeks before he was killed," she managed to say. "Then I got this weird text from him, telling me to take Elijah and run, and the next thing I knew the police were knocking on my door, telling me this awful thing had happened. I knew it had to be La Tranquila."

And I knew she was right.

But in some ways, that wasn't the most shocking part about all of this for me.

It was that, all along, I had assumed Angel was the victim of some nefarious conspiracy.

In reality, he was also a major part of it.

CHAPTER 47

SAL SALCEDO WAS back in the windowless room.

He had left Korynne Vuong's apartment as soon as she lost consciousness, not bothering to stay for the unpleasant business that followed.

As he understood it, her body would be dismembered into small enough pieces that they could be wrapped in plastic, packed into suitcases, and carried out of her building without anyone noticing.

A careful cleanup of her apartment would follow. They would use a blue light to make sure they didn't leave behind any telltale blood spatters.

Her remains would then be disposed of in a way that they would never be found. Whether that involved an incinerator, a deep hole, a deeper ocean—or some combination thereof—Salcedo didn't ask.

It was Norteño's business, not his.

He was now onto his next task. But, already, that wasn't panning out as he planned.

"What do you mean Hinton *went home*?" he demanded of the technician who was sitting at the control terminal. "He never leaves before five thirty or six."

"He got a text from his wife. He called her. And then he went home."

"What did the text say?"

The technician had anticipated this question and already had the readout from Hinton's phone.

Will you please come home?

Is everything okay?

Yes. I just need you to come home.

Before Salcedo could ask, the technician played the conversation, brief as it was. Hinton asked if something was wrong with the baby. The wife assured him the baby was fine. He asked if it could wait. She said it couldn't. He said he was coming.

That was it.

"What the hell is going on?" Salcedo asked.

"I couldn't tell you."

"Well, what did they talk about when they got home? Or did she just want her man home for some afternoon delight? Did you at least hear a little moaning?"

"Nope. Nothing. The house has been quiet all day. The wife listened to some music in the morning. Then it stopped. There's been nothing since then. I don't think she's there. She definitely didn't make the call from the house. I would have heard it."

"But she told him to come home."

"Yeah."

"So did he go home or not?"

"If he did, he didn't make a sound."

"Not even a 'Hi, honey, I'm home'?"

"Nothing."

Salcedo frowned. "Where's Hinton's car?"

The technician switched screens, bringing up a map showing the entire western half of North America with a multitude of blue dots moving across it. A few keystrokes later, he had isolated one blue dot in particular, and zoomed in its map position.

It was sitting in front of 27 Buena Vista Drive. And it wasn't moving.

"So his car is there, but he hasn't entered the house," Salcedo said. "That's weird. Something isn't right."

"Maybe they're just taking a walk around the neighborhood?"

"Or maybe they're taking a walk around the neighborhood with agents from Joint Task Force 1954, and he's telling them about L-11, Melvord Finck, and everything else he's figured out."

Salcedo swore forcefully. This was the scenario that much of Balco's security apparatus—the bugs, the tracking devices, the cameras—had been designed to prevent.

The leak. The mole. The whistleblower. The person of conscience who decided to take their concerns to law enforcement, putting Balco's operations—and all those involved—in grave jeopardy.

Salcedo had planned for this possibility many times, though it was always in the abstract.

Now that it was concrete, he was almost frozen with fear.

Finally, he said, "All right, I'm sending French and Boston out there. We need eyes on that place, not just ears. I want to know what the hell is going on."

CHAPTER 48

AS WE STOOD on that fire road, next to that burned-out grass, with hawks floating on afternoon thermals above us, Aiysha completed her story.

Once the police informed her of Angel's death, she grabbed Elijah and the absolute bare essentials and fled her house. She didn't even bring her cell phone because she wasn't sure if it was bugged, or if it could be used to track her.

She checked into a hotel in downtown San Francisco and hunkered down there. When Elijah got hungry, she ordered room service and had it left outside the door until she was sure the hallway was clear.

Using the hotel room's phone line, she contacted the PI she had already been working with. The PI performed some countersurveillance and confirmed her worst fears: There were two men parked near her house, watching it, seemingly waiting to pounce.

Hearing this, she booked tickets for herself and Elijah on the next flight she could get to Dulles, the closest major airport to her hometown of Staunton, Virginia. On her way to SFO, she had the taxi driver stop at an electronics store so she could buy a burner phone to let her parents know what was happening.

At Dulles, they picked her up and took her to her childhood home, which was tucked onto a quiet street where they still knew everyone. A stranger might as well have come attached to a flashing neon sign. It was easy to track who was coming and going.

They saw nothing unusual. After a few days, Aiysha felt reasonably assured that the cartel didn't know where she was.

Or maybe it simply didn't care. As she thought about it more, she came to two conclusions. One, if the Norteño Cartel had wanted to kill Angel's entire family, it would have done so already. Two, and more relevant, the cartel had no need to kill her or Elijah. Maybe Angel had become a threat to it in some way, but she surely wasn't. She didn't know anything incriminating. She was just someone's clueless wife.

Her instincts were confirmed when the PI told her there were no longer men watching her house. She was still going to exercise caution, but it seemed likely to her the cartel had moved on—or, more likely, was never all that concerned about her in the first place.

With the pressure easing, she was able to consider what her next steps ought to be. She thought about taking her suspicions of Norteño's role in Angel's death to the FBI, to get some justice for her husband.

But, again, she was confronted by her lack of concrete knowledge. The fact that Balco had bugged her house and that she had overheard her husband talking about a cartel boss wasn't really much to go on.

She hadn't really decided what to do. But when she heard that a memorial service for Angel had been scheduled, the part of her that still loved him completely—and was deep in mourning—decided she wanted to return.

With Elijah safe at her parents' house, she and her sister flew back to California and hired a private security detachment to take them to the Cathedral of Christ the Light in Oakland.

At that point, she was still assuming everyone high up at Balco—including me—was aware of the cartel connection. Hence her icy greeting to me at the memorial service.

I don't know if you were ever truly Angel's friend. But you're no friend of mine.

It was only when she returned to the safety of her parents' place in Virginia that she began slowly rethinking things. She realized that even Angel, the COO who was being groomed as the next CEO, had been unaware of the Norteño connection at first.

Things only changed at the six-month mark. That, she surmised, was when Angel had been told that Balco had a working relationship with the cartel.

Therefore, it was reasonable to assume that I was still ignorant about the cartel. And, just like Aiysha had been in the dark, Page didn't know, either.

We weren't the enemy.

If anything, we were in need of rescue.

She was still in regular contact with her PI, who reported that there was still no sign of activity around her house. She also had our place checked out. There was no surveillance on us, either.

Still, she didn't know how to contact us in a way that was safe. She assumed our home and phones were bugged; and that our internet—and, therefore, our email—was also compromised.

She said she considered writing a letter, but she worried even that might be intercepted. The safest and smartest way was to appear in person. So she flew back to SFO, rehired her security detail, and had them take her to our house.

There was also one more reason she had decided to come warn us.

She saw it as completing something Angel had started.

"His last thought was about you, you know," she said.

"What do you mean?" I asked.

"A week or two after the memorial service, the police gave me back his phone. When I opened it, the screen that popped up was a text to you. I'm pretty sure he had been in the midst of composing it when he . . . when he died. The message was basically: Don't take the job. Just run. He was trying to save you."

I let that sink in for a moment.

"It's still okay to be furious with him for bringing you and Page into this craziness," Aiysha added. "I'm furious with him sometimes for not getting himself out of it."

"I'm sure he thought he had it all under control. He was such an optimist—a naive one, yeah. But an optimist, all the same. He believed he could handle La Tranquila and that he could keep Norteño in a little box where it wouldn't hurt anyone. He couldn't see he had a tiger by the tail."

"I know. That's what I tell myself, too. It's ironic, but that was really one of the things that first drew me to him—that can-do attitude, that belief that everything was going to turn out okay. Then there are also times when . . . well, like I said, I'm just pissed."

"There's no contradiction between loving someone and being really pissed at them," I pointed out. "It's the people you love the most who drive you the craziest."

"Yeah. I know. Still, I wanted you to be aware that, at the very end, he realized he had made a mistake with you, and that he was trying to make it right."

"Thanks," I said. "That means . . . something, I guess."

I didn't really have time to sort my feelings about Angel. I had new problems.

A ton of them.

The most immediate was that I had left the office, supposedly with the intention of going home to spend quality time with my wife. And I now knew someone at Balco was listening—Sal Salcedo or whoever he had doing the monitoring.

And, yeah, it was possible they just left it to AI to sniff out disturbing patterns of speech or listen for certain keywords, like that someone was talking to law enforcement about how they suspected their employer was involved with a cartel.

But it was also possible they were doing it the old-fashioned way and would be expecting to hear from us.

With this in mind, we descended back down the fire road. Aiysha's protective detail was waiting for her at the trailhead. We hugged her and thanked her for her bravery. She had taken personal risk to come back here, and she was quite possibly saving our lives in doing so.

We promised to keep in touch once we got ourselves clean phones.

Then we went our separate ways. Once Page and I got back home, we put on a show for whoever might be listening.

"Thanks for the hike," I said. "That was a great idea."

"It's such a beautiful day," Page gushed in return. "Thanks for coming home. I missed you so much while you were gone."

"I missed you, too. You must be tired, though. You want to take a nap?"

That would at least give us some plausible quiet time.

What Page came up with was better: "Actually, I'm pretty hungry after all those steps. There's a burrito place at Corte Madera I've been wanting to try."

I smiled at her quick thinking. Corte Madera was the name of the upscale mall near us. At least there, we'd be able to talk.

"Great, I'm starving," I said. Then I added, "Let's take your car. Mine needs to charge."

I then quickly scribbled on a note, "Assuming my car is bugged. Think yours is, too?"

She just shrugged at me. She didn't know.

There was a lot we didn't know.

We climbed into Page's Honda and, just in case, forced out more superficial banter as we drove to Corte Madera.

After we parked, I left my phone in the car.

If anyone was tracking us, they would see that we had gone to the mall, as advertised. I didn't want them to know where within the complex we were actually going.

Corte Madera did, in fact, have a burrito place. More importantly, it also had several cell phone stores. We walked into the nearest one and signed up for a new family plan. This furnished us with iPhones that neither Balco nor Norteño knew anything about.

As we were walking out, Page turned to me and said, "Hey, you're kinda cute. Can I get your digits?"

"Yeah, sure," I said, rattling them off for her. "But what's the rule these days on how long you're supposed to wait to call?"

She immediately hit SEND and my phone rang.

"Zero minutes. I wanted to make sure you didn't give me a fake number," she said, throwing in a wink.

It felt good to flirt with my wife again. It was certainly a lot better than the tension that had marked so many of our interactions of late.

I programmed in her number. There was something lovely about knowing we were each other's only contact.

We then sat at a lone table outside a coffee shop, where I let Google give me a basic education about this nightmarish threat I had unwittingly stumbled into.

The Norteño Cartel took its name from the folksy, accordion-fueled genre of music that its founder had played in his youth and that was still popular throughout Mexico, especially in rural areas.

Like so many cartel bosses, the founder was known primarily by his nickname: El Conductor—the conductor.

The syndicate got its start in the late 1980s in Baja California. At a time when crack cocaine was still dominating American cities—and the attention of American authorities who were hell-bent on stopping it—Norteño specialized in what was then a relatively new substance: black tar, a smokable form of heroin.

Cheaper and easier to produce than traditional white powder heroin, it allowed Norteño to develop strong supply lines along America's West Coast and become a significant player in the lucrative and strategically critical border city of Tijuana.

From there, Norteño diversified into other drugs, including marijuana and conventional heroin; which, thanks to the opioid epidemic, had supplanted crack cocaine as the drug of choice north of the border in the early 2000s. With business thriving, Norteño spread to Sonora, then down the West Coast of Mexico—one bribe, takeover, and deadly turf war at a time.

Norteño enjoyed grassroots popularity among the Mexican populace, cloaking itself in a Robin Hood–like mythology. It took from the rich—drug-addled Americans—and gave to the poor in Tijuana, Ensenada, Mexicali, and other needy pockets of the country.

In addition to passing out food in rural areas and hosting block parties in the cities, Norteño even went so far as to build community centers and pools. El Conductor was nothing if not generous with his enormous wealth.

What it bought him was near total immunity from the efforts of U.S. authorities to apprehend him. No one wanted to be known as the person who turned El Conductor over to the Americans.

He also remained at large thanks to a fair amount of moral ambiguity regarding his business model. To many Mexicans, Norteño was simply supplying something the marketplace demanded.

Was the product especially healthy for its consumers? Of course not. But neither was McDonald's, and you didn't hear any great clamoring to lock up their executives.

As El Conductor aged and his health declined in the early 2010s, there was a great deal of speculation as to who would take over for him. While he was rumored to have fathered as many as twenty children, only four were recognized as legitimate: three boys and a girl.

The cartel's hierarchy—to say nothing of Mexican culture—was patriarchal by nature, and therefore it was assumed one of El Conductor's sons would someday be given the reins.

Therefore, no one paid much attention to the girl, who was known as La Tranquila.

The quiet woman.

With soft-spoken efficiency, she inserted herself into every aspect of the family business. Her father, impressed by her skills as an administrator and her deft thinking as a strategist, kept giving her more responsibility.

She had U.S. citizenship—how she had obtained it was left unclear in the article I was reading—and she easily moved on both sides of the border, dealing with issues wherever they popped up.

During one particularly bloody year for Norteño, two of her

brothers—eager to prove their leadership mettle—were gunned down in fights with rival cartels. Not long after that, La Tranquila's only surviving brother, who was always seen as the weakest of El Conductor's children, was poisoned.

There was speculation La Tranquila had done the job herself.

It was just one of the ways in which she proved to her father's longtime confederates that, while she did not raise her voice, she had the ruthlessness needed to lead them. When one of her alleged paramours was abducted and held for ransom, she put out word that the kidnappers should not expect a single dime.

She didn't care whether the man lived or died.

She could find another lover.

All the while, she kept promoting her own hand-picked lieutenants into every branch, stem, and leaf of the cartel, filling Norteño's ranks with people whose first loyalty was to her.

When El Conductor finally passed away—the rare cartel leader wily enough to die of natural causes—there was no real question as to who the new boss would be. La Tranquila had already been calling the shots in every way that mattered.

That was a decade ago. Under her leadership, Norteño had only continued to flourish. All the while, she continued to flummox U.S. authorities. They knew full well who she was and the empire of illegality she commanded, yet they had never been able to explicitly link her to any one crime. She kept many layers between herself and the law breaking. And, at least so far, no one had been able to pierce that shield.

I had been quietly narrating this story to Page. After a while, she said, "Okay, that's enough. I don't need to hear any more about La Tranquila. You're not writing an article about this woman. But it sounds like you might be working with her without realizing it. What are you going to do about it?"

"I'm not sure," I admitted. "Can I really just quit?"

"Of course you can. You have to. They didn't hesitate to kill Angel, and he was COO. They'd kill you in a heartbeat. Look, I realize I was the one who pushed you into this job, because I wanted to be able to stay at home with the baby. Can you please, please let me push you out of it? I know we'll be wiped out financially, but I'd rather be bankrupt than dead. This isn't some theoretical threat we're facing. I don't want this baby to join Elijah in growing up without a father."

Her hand had gone to her belly. Her eyes were filling with tears.

"No, you don't understand. I know I have to quit. But I don't think I can just walk away."

"You're right. You should do what Angel was trying to tell you and *run*."

"It's not that easy."

"Why not?"

"The last thing I want to do is to bring myself to the attention of the cartel. If I just suddenly disappear, it will raise a lot of questions. They'd probably think I'm blowing the whistle. I have to make it seem like I had a change of heart about the business. I'll say I miss journalism and am desperate to return. I'll give my two-week notice, and that will be that."

"And we'll spend two weeks walking on eggshells?"

"Maybe Lorne will do me a favor and fire me on the spot. Either way, we'll be out of this soon enough."

"Okay," Page allowed. "I guess you're right."

I glanced at the time on my new phone. "We should go back home. We've taken long enough. Remember: All we were doing is eating burritos."

"And talking about how you wanted to resign."

"Yeah. That, too."

We rose from the table, and before I could get very far, she grabbed me and hugged me with a tenderness and a desperation I had never felt before.

"I can't lose you," is all she said.

As soon as we arrived back at home, I opened my laptop and began crafting my resignation letter.

I wrote that Balco was a wonderful company, but my passion for journalism was simply too strong. I purposefully didn't mention Angel. This was the equivalent of a Dear John letter that said, "It's not you, it's me."

Then I sent it off to Lorne, stared at my laptop screen, and started wearing out the SEND/RECEIVE button on my email as I waited for his reply.

CHAPTER 49

THEY WERE IN their usual positions: Lorne Murphy behind his massive cherrywood desk; Sal Salcedo in the chair on the other side.

Their argument had reached a stalemate.

Murphy had been stating the case for restraint. There was, it seemed, a plausible explanation for Hinton leaving the office, and for the silence that followed. He and his wife had gone out for a hike. Then they left their home to hunt down some burritos at Corte Medera.

French and Boston had intercepted them as they left the mall and reported that the Hintons had driven back to 27 Buena Vista Drive and were now ensconced in their house. There were no federal agents anywhere in sight. Maybe it was all what it seemed.

Then Hinton's resignation email arrived, and it had practically sent Salcedo into a spasm. To the chief safety officer, this was clear-as-day evidence that Hinton was running to the authorities. They had to take him out *now*. They couldn't wait another second.

Murphy wasn't fond of the idea of sending men into an upscale neighborhood for that purpose. Marin County wasn't Oakland. Unusual activity would be noted and reported by the locals.

Then there was the idea of having to send another one of those all-staff emails about the untimely end of another Balco employee. There had been too many of those already.

They had chased their dispute around in circles and were readying for another go when there were three taps on the door.

"Yes, Lucas, what is it?" Murphy asked, knowing he sounded annoyed.

"The messenger is here," Lucas replied solemnly.

The memory of a severed head sent Murphy's hand flying to his neck, a classic gesture of vulnerability.

"What does he want?"

"I don't know. But there are other people with him, including a woman."

Murphy and Salcedo exchanged questioning glances. *A woman? That couldn't be . . .*

"Send them in," Murphy said.

He stood. So did Salcedo.

Which meant they were on their feet, showing the proper respect, when La Tranquila entered.

She was both preceded and followed by members of a six-man security detail. Dressed in a flowing floral print maxi dress, her legs were obscured such that she didn't seem to be walking; but, rather, floating. With sunglasses perched on her head and a hand-stitched leather bag on her shoulder, she came off more like a wealthy suburban woman on a shopping trip than the head of a violent criminal syndicate.

Her mere presence said all that was necessary about the importance of this matter to her. During the five years since Norteño had forced itself into Balco's coyote operation, she had never once spoken directly to anyone at the company.

Now here she was. In the flesh.

And for one reason, which scarcely needed to be explained to Murphy and Salcedo: Curt Hinton going to the authorities might result in her being charged with a crime for the first time in her life. That was a threat to her freedom and her liberty of movement within the United States, two things she cherished.

"I believe you know who I am," she said in the easy English that she acquired at the expensive all-girls California boarding school she had once attended.

"I do," Murphy confirmed.

"I don't like what I've been hearing. It sounds to me like this operation has been compromised."

"Everything is completely under control. We just needed your help to make sure the situation stayed completely contained. You have nothing to worry about."

He forced out his most charming smile, aware that it probably came out lopsided.

She fixed him with a long, cold stare.

By the time she was done, he was no longer smiling.

"This has to end now," she said.

Because she was the quiet woman, she didn't bother adding the two extra words that had already been implied.

Or else.

CHAPTER 50

LORNE'S EMAIL COULDN'T have been more than sixty seconds old when I opened it.

He said he wanted to talk with me in the morning, but that the only time open in his schedule was at 6:00 a.m.

I assured him that wouldn't be a problem.

To keep up pretenses, I read the reply out loud to Page, who made all the right noises in response. It was this bizarre conversation where our mouths were saying one thing even as our eyes said something different.

Then she suggested we play Scrabble. The rest of the night, all Balco's bugs would have heard is Page posting outrageous point totals through the clever use of two-letter words.

Later on, as we lay in bed with neither of us sleeping—but both of us afraid to say anything about why—there were two possibilities going through my head.

The first was that Lorne would try to entice me to stay. Or maybe he would even find some way to threaten me. I would just have to stay firm and accept whatever happened. The truth was, there was nothing he could do to me that was as dire as the consequences of crossing the Norteño Cartel.

The second was that he was just bringing me in so he could quickly and permanently sever my ties to Balco by collecting my ID badge, my phone, and my company-issued laptop. He'd have HR march me out the front gate and I'd have to take an Uber home because they repossessed my Rivian.

Which was fine.

I was ready to leave California and pretend the state had fallen into the ocean.

The next morning, my eyes opened at 4:57, allowing me to shut off the alarm clock three minutes before it was going to ring.

My new phone was next to the clock on my nightstand, but I had already decided I was going to leave it there. I didn't know what Sal Salcedo could do to it, but the surest way to keep it clean of his listening capabilities was to make sure it didn't go near a Balco facility.

After a hot shower, I dressed in my favorite suit, pausing to look at myself in the mirror when I was done.

Curt Hinton. Soon-to-be-ex-corporate stiff.

Unbidden, a random quote from Franklin Delano Roosevelt popped into my head.

Courage isn't the absence of fear. It's the acknowledgment that something else is more important.

I just needed a little more courage and this would be over. As I was having that thought, Page slid up behind me, wrapped her arms around me, and squeezed.

It gave me all the courage I required.

"Hey," I said, cradling one of her forearms and momentarily savoring the feeling of her body against mine.

"Hi, my love," she murmured.

I turned toward her and kissed her. She kept her mouth closed, like she always did when she was worried about her morning breath.

"Go back to bed," I said. "You need your sleep."

"Yeah, no chance. You'll call me as soon as you're done, right?"

"Of course."

She accompanied me to the door that led to the garage, giving me one more kiss before I climbed into the Rivian and quietly drove away.

There was little traffic. But as I crossed over the Richmond Bridge and into the East Bay, a soupy marine layer enveloped me, severely limiting visibility.

The fog was so dense, I had no choice but to slow down a bit. Still, it wasn't much longer until I was waiting for the rolling razor wire fence to complete its journey and allow me entry.

I waved to the security guard, who acknowledged me as he raised the boom barrier. I drove under it and continued up the ramp to the third floor of the parking deck, which was mostly empty, as you'd expect it to be at 5:52 a.m.

The third floor was where the top executives parked, since it was closest to the footbridge that led to the main building. There were just two Rivians there.

Lorne's, I assumed. And someone else's.

As soon as I got out of the car, I checked my phone. I wasn't really expecting any new texts or emails at this hour. It was just habit—a quick tug on my adult pacifier.

There were no texts. But, strangely, my email wouldn't refresh. I studied the phone for a second and realized I had no service.

There were no bars—not even the little "SOS" that told me I could make an emergency call.

Weird. I always had three or four bars when I walked around the facility. Thick as it was, fog didn't do anything to affect cell signals. There was a tower a short distance away.

Maybe it was down.

Shrugging it off, I made my way toward headquarters. The walk from my assigned parking spot to the footbridge was, by now, part of my routine. I had made it dozens of times already during my brief tenure at Balco.

To my left there was a four-foot-high concrete barrier that served as the parking deck wall. Above it, the lights from our facility, muted though they were by the fog, came in through the opening. But, preoccupied as I was by my own thoughts, I really didn't pay attention to my surroundings.

The first thing that brought me back to the present moment was the scuffling of feet on gritty concrete.

A man was approaching me.

He wore jeans and a puffy black jacket with ornate white lettering across the chest. He had a slouched posture and appeared to be of Mexican descent—just your everyday *vato*—but that wasn't what impressed me as being odd about him. A good portion of our warehouse workers were Latino.

It was that his jeans were roomy enough to fit two people.

Loose-fitting clothing was a notorious safety hazard in a warehouse. We had way too much machinery that it could get caught in, to say nothing of the tripping hazard. Baggy jeans had long ago been banned in all Balco facilities.

What's more, the guy was coming from the direction of the warehouse, like he was done with his shift. Even if an ignorant newbie had messed up and worn baggy jeans on his first day, his supervisor would have immediately made him change. An outfit like this wouldn't have been tolerated.

As he got to within about twenty yards, I saw he was also wearing a long, dangly chain around his neck.

Another no-no.

This was definitely not a warehouse worker. And he wasn't a corporate employee, either. Not at this time of the morning. And, besides, I would have recognized him.

My mind was just beginning to puzzle over all the oddities when I heard another scuffling sound from about thirty yards behind me.

Another man. Also Latino. I hadn't seen him when I parked. And I hadn't heard any other car coming in. But he was coming at me from the direction of my car.

Almost like he had been hiding near there.

He was, likewise, wearing generously cut clothing that wouldn't have been allowed anywhere near the warehouse floor.

Strange.

Then, to my right, also about twenty yards away, a third man emerged from behind a column. I watched as it happened. And there was no question he had been hiding there, lying in wait.

Our eyes locked. He actually smiled. Like he was having a good time. His teeth were capped with gold.

Something about his malicious nonchalance made the necessary neurons in my brain fire.

These guys weren't Balco employees. And they weren't random trespassers either. There's no way any of those could have made it past security.

Yet they had been waiting for me, stalking me, and were now closing in on me.

That left one conclusion.

They were from the Norteño Cartel.

They were coming for me.

And they had me cut off from any means of escape.

There was something patient and unhurried about the way they were approaching. They were going low and slow, without any real concern that I could break free. They were just collaring an animal they already had cornered.

I stopped, because any direction I would have gone would have just put me closer to one of them. My messenger bag, with my laptop in it, was hanging from my shoulder. I let it drop.

Something made me want to have my hands free. I couldn't say why. I'm not sure I could have won a fight with even one of these guys, let alone all three.

They didn't appear to have weapons. They didn't need weapons. Maybe they knew they didn't need any to subdue me. They were just going to wrestle me down . . .

And then what?

Nothing good for sure.

They continued inching toward me patiently. Then, from below, I heard a car engine roar to life.

The next thing I knew, a white van had rounded the corner from the second floor of the parking deck, its tires screeching on the rubberized concrete. It came to a stop and three more men jumped out.

Because I hadn't been outnumbered enough.

They joined the first three, forming a semicircle that gradually tightened as they got closer, almost like a noose.

No one had said a word. Whatever was going on, it wasn't something that needed discussion.

They were ten yards away.

The man with the gold caps was closest. I could see now he wasn't truly smiling. It was more accurate to say he had his teeth bared.

I had been backing away slowly but I now had nowhere to go. The barrier was hard against my back. A cool breeze wafted in from the nearby bay.

My options had whittled down to two.

Let them capture me—and do whatever it was they wanted.

That felt like suicide.

Or jump.

That felt like madness.

The third floor of the parking deck was probably thirty or thirty-five feet up. I had no clue if I could survive a fall from that height. And even if I did live, I wasn't going to get very far with a broken leg, a shattered ankle, or whatever other injuries I sustained in the fall.

The odds of success were surely small. But that still felt like a better outcome than standing there and letting La Tranquila's men decide my fate.

With the decision made, I didn't hesitate. I turned and vaulted over the side.

For some fraction of a second, I dangled on the other side, gripping the barrier. There was nothing between my feet and the earth but the early morning gloom.

But as I looked down, it occurred to me I didn't have to fall the whole way. With luck and a little skill, I might be able grab onto the second-level barrier below me. Then I could drop from a much lower height.

I swung myself outward a little bit, so that my top half was angled toward the parking structure and I wasn't falling straight down, then let go.

The second floor came at me faster than I thought it would. I grabbed for it desperately, clawing at it so hard I could feel my fingernails bending backward. I just couldn't get myself to stop. The concrete had been slickened enough by the fog that it was impossible to get a grip.

Either that or I had too much velocity and too little forearm strength.

Nevertheless, I was able to slow my fall substantially; such that when I reached the grassy shrubbery that ringed the parking garage, I wasn't going murderously fast. I did my best to roll through the landing, which I did awkwardly. I still felt a powerful shock wave going up from the dirt to my ankles, then from my knees to my hips.

The pain was dazzling. And the roll itself was far from graceful. When my upper body hit the ground, I could feel the wind being knocked out of me.

This, I imagined, was what it felt like to be hit by a truck.

I didn't stop to assess the damage, though. I couldn't. I just continued through the tumble, awkward though it was, and somehow popped back to my feet.

From above me, there were shouts in Spanish that I didn't bother to parse.

Their tone told me everything I needed to know: They were pissed, and they were coming after me.

I just ran. For my life.

With my arms and legs pumping and the soles of my dress shoes struggling for grip on the asphalt, it was like some version of that nightmare everyone has—the one where something is chasing you, and you can't make yourself go fast enough, and the thing must be gaining on you even though you can't see it.

I must not have broken any bones in my lower half, though; because everything still seemed to be working after that long drop.

Obviously, there was also some adrenaline at work.

With all my strength, I surged away from the parking deck.

I was free. At least for the moment.

But I didn't kid myself about how long the moment would last. I was still trapped in a completely secure facility; surrounded by twelve-foot-high, razor-wire-topped fences; with only one exit and no hope of escape.

From above and behind me, the van engine was roaring, its tires once again screeching as it negotiated the series of tight turns needed to descend from the third floor of the parking deck.

None of the men had jumped after me. They weren't quite as motivated to chase as I was to get away.

Or maybe they knew they didn't need to do anything quite so rash.

It's not like there was anywhere I could go. They had all the time they needed to pursue me—around and around; up, under, and through—until they caught me, I became too exhausted, or I hurt myself so badly I couldn't continue.

Time, numbers, and geography were all on their side.

The only advantage I had was visibility; specifically, the lack of it. The fog at least gave me a chance to get out of their sight—and maybe even out of sight of Sal Salcedo's ubiquitous cameras—and stay that way, if only for a little while.

The corporate offices loomed in front of me but I didn't even give a thought to running inside.

You didn't elude the beast by running into its belly.

No, I only had one real option here, and that was to call in the cavalry. All I had to do was reach into my pocket; pull out my phone, tap the numbers 9, 1, and 1; and wait for the sweet sound of "Nine-one-one, what is your emergency?"

Except as soon as that occurred to me, reality interceded.

My phone had no service.

And it more than likely wasn't because of some glitch with the local tower.

Someone at Balco was jamming the signal. It wasn't hard to see Sal Salcedo's fingerprints on something like that.

My phone was now beyond worthless. It was even a liability. As long as I held onto it, Salcedo could probably use it to track me. He would be able to tell those Norteño thugs exactly where to locate me.

Which meant even if I managed to get away from them, I'd be playing a game of hide-and-seek that I was guaranteed to lose.

Without hesitation, I spiked my phone on the ground, continued around the building, and fixed my course toward the warehouse. Even at this early hour, it would have a smattering of people inside. And the cartel guys wouldn't grab me in front of potential witnesses.

That was my first thought.

My second thought said no.

On the one hand, a small collection of overnight warehouse workers might wonder why a group of sloppily dressed Mexican guys were grabbing the vice president of corporate communications, who was howling that his captors were cartel mercenaries.

On the other hand, they would still be Balco employees, subject to Sal Salcedo's version of the truth. And while I was somewhere in a dark room, gagged and bound with zip ties, Sal could surely tell the one or two or three people who had watched me be taken that I was nothing more than a crazed malcontent.

He was trespassing.

He was stealing.

Or, better yet: *He cannot be trusted because he's a disgruntled ex-employee, spreading lies. See? Here's his resignation letter.*

Still, I might at least be able to find a place to hide in the warehouse. It was just shy of a million square feet. Surely, there had to be somewhere in there I could disappear, at least long enough to be able to weigh my limited options.

Then I remembered the warehouse was rotten with cameras. And there would be no fog to obscure those lenses.

I was now dashing along the side of the warehouse, still with no idea what my destination should even be. The van sounded like it was now out of the parking deck, getting closer.

There may have been men on foot as well. I couldn't see.

Which was good, because that meant they couldn't see me either.

I rounded the edge of the warehouse and kept running. I was now out into an empty stretch of asphalt. I had the dimmest notion that maybe I could point myself toward the truckyard, which was out at the edge of the facility. The trucks that weren't in use were always parked tightly next to each other at an angle. It would maybe give me somewhere to hide.

Perhaps, if I found a good enough spot—and that was certainly a big "if"—I could hitch a ride on one of them out of the facility. It likely wouldn't be too long a wait. Balco trucks were never idle for long.

It was at least a possibility, even if wasn't a great one. The trucks would surely be locked. Security had been tighter than ever after the Dan Gillespie incident.

Maybe I could clamber on top of one of the trucks and hide behind the windbreaker on the roof. Or I could find some part of the undercarriage to hang onto.

I still felt like I'd be pretty exposed out there, especially once the fog burned off in a few hours.

There was also an excellent chance I wouldn't make it. There was only so long I could continue at a full sprint. My lungs were already burning and I could feel the lactic acid making my legs heavier with each stride.

For all the will I could summon to continue, it still might not help. The truckyard was several hundred yards off. The van sounded like it was closing in on me a lot faster than that. The fog may have made me difficult to see, but it didn't make me invisible.

Then another option presented itself.

Perhaps even the only option.

Appearing suddenly to my left, there was a building.

It was numbered as K-12, and it was exactly identical to L-11 at Long Beach. Same boxy shape. Same size—with room for just one truck. Except here it was in Oakland.

Was this Oakland's Specialized Shipping Services building?

And, if that was the case, perhaps K-12 was also like L-11 in two other hugely important ways.

It would be empty.

And there would be no cameras.

It was a snap decision, but it seemed like the best place I was going to find under the circumstances.

The only place, really.

I fished into my pocket for my ID badge, touched it to the magnetic pad beside the door, and pushed my way in.

CHAPTER 51

IN THE WINDOWLESS room, the veins on Sal Salcedo's neck stood out like tiny snakes on a sidewalk.

The reverberations from his shouts filled the air.

"What do you mean you *lost* him?" Salcedo demanded.

The technician wasn't shy about yelling back.

"You can't track what you can't see."

"How is that possible?!? He's a goddamn corporate executive, not Houdini. We've got ten bajillion cameras in this place."

"Yeah, and all ten bajillion of them are useless in fog like this," the technician snarled as he brought up one view after another. "Look: Gray. Gray. Gray. The thermal imaging can't cut through the marine layer when it gets this thick; you know that."

Salcedo swore explosively. Everything had been arranged so flawlessly. Norteño's men were going to grab Hinton, kill him quietly, and make sure no one ever found his body or his car. If the authorities asked questions, Balco's official line would be to stick with the story that Hinton's resignation and disappearance was all part of his plan to run off with his mistress.

Then Salcedo set about making sure nothing went wrong. He had jammed all cell coverage in the immediate area, blocking it with a strong enough signal that Hinton couldn't use his phone to call for help.

Salcedo also made plans to edit the security camera footage and change the security logs, such that they could voluntarily turn it over and say, *See? He resigned and then stopped showing up for work!*

He once again cursed Oakland Police for having ShotSpotter technology. It had prevented the Norteño men from doing what everyone favored: putting a bullet in Hinton's ear as soon as he stepped out of his car.

Now they had this mess on their hands.

And the consequences of failure were altogether clear. La Tranquila was somewhere nearby, getting regular updates from her people.

Those people were, at least in theory, helping Balco. But Salcedo knew it would only take one sentence from La Tranquila for them to turn.

Salcedo lifted his walkie-talkie. With cell signals jammed, this was his only way of communicating with Norteño's crew. He pressed a button to open up the line and switched to Spanish to say, "We still haven't laid eyes on him up here. What about you?"

"We found his cell phone, but not him," Salcedo heard back.

He cursed inwardly this time. He hadn't even thought to check the tracking on Hinton's phone, but already that option had been foreclosed.

"Keep looking," Salcedo said. "He can't get far."

Then he swore again.

He picked up the desk phone and ordered the chief security officer at the front gate to be on the lookout for Vice President of Corporate

Communications Curt Hinton, who should be apprehended on sight, by force if necessary.

Then Salcedo told the officer to halt all traffic exiting from the facility and to stop anyone who tried to defy the order.

"No one leaves. *No one*," Salcedo barked. "I don't care who it is. Even if it's Lorne Murphy. If they give you crap, call me. If they try to leave anyway, shoot them."

"What about entering?"

Salcedo considered this for a moment. He could see no harm in letting trucks come in.

Plus, they were expecting an important shipment.

"That's fine," he said. "Call me the moment you see anything."

He slammed down the phone.

"Still nothing?" he asked the technician.

"I'm trying."

"You're worthless. Try harder."

Salcedo went back to speaking Spanish into the walkie-talkie.

The Norteño men were still flailing. Hinton seemed to have disappeared into the mist.

CHAPTER 52

AS SOON AS I entered K-12, I bent at the waist and sucked in air.

My heart was thrashing. My lungs were pure fire. My thighs felt like they had been filled with concrete.

But I was out of sight.

At least for the moment.

Once my breathing became a little less pained, I straightened and checked myself out a little more thoroughly. Miraculously, the long drop from the parking garage really didn't seem to have left any lasting damage.

I looked around. The room had the familiar orange safety lighting and corrugated steel walls. And when I peered into all the corners—and scanned along the walls—I didn't see any cameras.

K-12 really was a carbon copy of L-11, right down to the autonomous forklift, sitting unused off to the side.

I took a few labored steps into the middle of the space, wiping my brow, which had popped a sweat at some point during my mad dash.

My vulnerabilities were probably too great to list. It was certainly possible that one of Balco's many external cameras had seen me dashing into K-12, in which case my stay here would be very short.

There was also a chance that using my badge to enter had already given me away, and that someone was right now reporting to Sal Salcedo that employee Curt Hinton had entered Building K-12. My only hope was that the magnetic card readers Balco used were relatively ancient, non-digital technology; and that, therefore, that information wasn't readily accessible.

Still, even if I caught a break with the cameras and the badge system, my hiding spot would only be good for so long.

All I had really done was buy myself time. I remained in need of a viable plan.

True escape was almost certainly impossible. I couldn't make it over the razor wire fencing without slicing myself wide open. And the armed guards at the exit had surely been alerted to be on the lookout for me. They would be checking every vehicle that tried to leave this place. Any thought of rolling out while clinging to a truck's undercarriage was, upon further consideration, sheer fantasy.

What's more, the people chasing me would soon stop and reassess the situation. Whether or not they could find me with their extensive surveillance technology, they would soon summon more boots on the ground—Lorne's favorite term—and fan out to search for me, building to building, warehouse aisle to warehouse aisle, and stairwell to stairwell, leaving no inch of the facility unchecked.

Eventually, I would be caught. It was inevitable. Any plan I came up with needed to acknowledge that.

I was coming to the conclusion that I actually had no choice but to surrender myself.

However, when I did, it couldn't be in a nearly empty warehouse. I had to make sure there were as many eyeballs and eardrums nearby me as I could get.

Which meant running back into the belly of the beast.

The headquarters building.

I didn't know if I could make it that far. But if I could, I had to make a huge, loud fuss: that I was being taken against my will by the Norteño Cartel, that what they were doing was illegal, and that someone should call the cops.

This only had a prayer of working if I could wait until after nine o'clock to make my move. By then, headquarters would be humming with supervisors, mid-level managers, even some higher brass.

Yes, Salcedo would tell them I was unhinged, a lunatic.

But if I could state my case to enough of them, surely one of them wouldn't buy the company line. The notion of Balco having a relationship with Norteño would shock them, just as it had shocked me.

I just had to hope that their shock would turn into action; that one of them would be an upstander, rather than a bystander, and heed my pleas to call law enforcement.

Really, it was the only play I had.

With my biorhythms finally dialing back down into the normal range, I completed my walk around the floor of the building. It was scrupulously clean, like all Balco facilities, and there was nothing to hide in, behind, or under.

There was only one place that afforded even a bit of cover.

That odd hole in the floor that led to a stairwell.

K-12 had one, just like L-11 did.

I started climbing down. This time, I counted steps. There were thirty-five of them all the way down to the bottom. Figuring seven inches per step, that put me roughly twenty feet below ground level.

There, I was met with another one of those heavy steel doors. Its handle didn't budge.

Locked.

It had no magnetic reader, no keyhole.

There had to be *some* way to get it to open, but I couldn't divine what that was. As far as my current capabilities and resources were concerned, it was a total dead end.

Nevertheless, this felt like the best place to stay while I waited for the population of potential witnesses to improve. If the Norteño men came through, maybe they wouldn't notice the opening in the concrete that led to the steps.

Or they might not bother to go down the stairs to look for me.

With this thought, I lay down at the very bottom of the stairwell, wedging myself as tight as I could against the last step, and tried to make myself as small as possible.

Without my cell phone, I didn't know what time it was. The building didn't let in any natural light, so it wasn't like I could judge the hour by the gradual brightening of the morning sky as the fog burned off.

I would just have to wait it out for a while, then maybe peek outside when I thought it was after nine.

But that would be a while.

So, for the time being, I just hunkered down, settled in, and waited.

CHAPTER 53

THE FIRST HUNDRED times Sal Salcedo thought about what to do next, he told himself he needed to relax and be patient.

There were twelve cartel men on the search, plus four more Balco security officers who had been pulled off their usual patrol to assist.

They would find Curt Hinton soon enough. For as large as the Oakland facility may have been, it wasn't infinite. Either the men would come across him, or the fog would clear and the cameras would regain sight of him.

There was no way—*no way*—he could have escaped the facility. There was only one exit, and all outbound traffic had been halted.

But then a half hour slipped by.

The men kept coming up empty.

And Salcedo's desperation steadily increased.

It was around the hundred-and-first time when Salcedo allowed himself to entertain the idea that Hinton had escaped.

Maybe he had slipped out through the entrance before Salcedo had been able to close it? Maybe he had found a hole under the fence?

None of it seemed likely, but Salcedo had seen too many times in this business when the impossible had somehow happened.

And if that was the case, Salcedo needed an insurance policy.

With this in mind, Salcedo picked up the desk phone again, dialed a number, and barked out, "French!"

"Yeah, boss?" he said, sounding sleepy.

"You and Boston better still be near Hinton's place."

"Been here all night. Nothing to report."

"Okay. We have a problem here. But you're going to help us solve it."

What Salcedo proposed next was probably madness. But he felt like he had no choice.

Time was running short.

And he was desperate.

CHAPTER 54

THE SWEAT ON my body turned clammy and cool. The concrete ate into my side, forcing me to change positions now and then.

At one point, I heard shouting outside the building—sharp, rapid Spanish that I couldn't quite make out.

I tensed, but nothing came of it.

A little while later, a vehicle cruised past without stopping.

The search was obviously continuing, but Building K-12 was getting no special attention at first.

Then, roughly thirty minutes in, the door opened noisily.

I happened to be facing to the right and upward, so I could see a small change in the light within the building brought on by the opening of the door.

Someone was walking in. I heard them padding softly across the floor.

Then someone else entered behind them, and the door boomed shut.

If it was Balco security, they would be wearing steel-toe boots, and those would be noisier.

These were cartel men.

A flashlight beam strafed the opening at the top of the stairs. Its rays did not penetrate down to where I was hiding; but if the holder of that flashlight decided to come down, I was in trouble.

The beam disappeared for a moment.

Then it flickered back my way.

"*¿Ves algo?*" a male voice asked.

Do you see anything?

There was a pause.

The flashlight beam lingered on the top step for another harrowing moment.

I expected to hear a curious, "*¿Qué es eso?*"

What's that?

But the beam disappeared again.

Then a second voice replied, "*Nada.*"

Nothing.

There was no reply. But the slamming of the door told me I was once again alone in K-12.

It took a while for my breathing to return to normal.

More time passed. Perhaps another half an hour.

I kept straining my ears, but whatever was happening twenty feet above me remained beyond the reach of my senses.

Maybe they were just waiting for the fog to burn off before resuming a more intensive search. They knew they had me bottled up. They were in no hurry.

As I lay on the cold concrete, my thoughts had turned, naturally, to Page. She was expecting to hear from me eventually.

But maybe not yet.

At this point, she probably thought my meeting with Lorne Murphy had just run long.

Or she might be trying to call me or text me, wondering why I wasn't answering, wondering what she should do about it. Would she know I was in danger? Would she do something about it?

Unlikely. When I left this morning, we had no reason to suspect the cartel would come after me like this. She was probably still curled up in bed.

I was somewhere in the midst of picturing that comforting thought when I heard an unexpected sound. It was faint at first. But it was growing louder.

The incessant *beep-beep-beep* of a truck backing up.

It was coming closer. Definitely in the direction of K-12. There was no other building immediately close by.

Then, triggered by nothing I could discern, I heard the hum of an electric motor. Natural light began pouring into the space above me.

The lone dock door at the front of the building was opening.

K-12 was getting an SSS delivery.

It was just like I said on my first day.

The business of Balco will stop for nothing.

Defying the stiffness that had seeped into my body after an hour or so of lying on concrete, I clambered to my feet.

Maybe there was some kind of opportunity to be exploited here.

I crept up the stairs as the backup alarm continued echoing through the building.

The quality of the light coming in through the open dock door indicated that, while the sun hadn't yet poked through, the fog had lifted somewhat. Visibility within the facility would definitely be improved—much to my detriment.

When I was almost to the top, I crouched to keep myself out of sight of anyone who happened to be outside, peering in.

The truck's air brakes moaned and hissed as it eased into its berth. Even without being able to see it, I could tell the back edge of the truck must have been close to the loading dock.

With my legs gathered under me, I poked my head up for the briefest fraction of a second, then immediately brought it back down.

There was an armed Balco guard to the side of the truck, attentively tracking its progress. Whatever thought I had about running out and trying to make contact with the driver was immediately squelched.

I would never make it that far.

As the truck completed its backward journey and came to a stop, the light inside K-12 had once again dimmed. The cloth shelter that surrounded the outer edge of the dock opening had closed around the trailer, forming a seal between the truck and the building.

I descended the steps to get further out of sight, shrinking myself down in case someone came inside to open the truck door.

Instead, I again heard the hum of an electric motor. The truck door was rolling open automatically. I hadn't realized they did that.

I climbed back up the steps again to get a better view, stopping on the eighth one from the top, which allowed me to see what was happening while also giving me the option to duck down and get out of sight if needed.

In the dim light, all I could make out in the back of the truck was a wall of shrink-wrapped boxes with pallets underneath. Since the trailer flatbed and building floor were exactly even, it almost made the truck feel like a continuation of the room.

It looked like any load I had seen coming into the main warehouse. What was specialized enough about it to make it an SSS shipment? Was it just that it had to be turned around faster?

This was not mere idle curiosity. I was already thinking that this cargo might be my ticket out of here. Perhaps I could burrow my way onto one of these pallets? If I managed to conceal myself, would that get me to the next facility—a non-Balco facility—where I would then be able to break free?

Or would I be packed tightly away in another load where I suffocated or dehydrated to death?

Honestly, I was willing to take that risk. No one in either the logistics industry or the customer base Balco served—the electronics industry—made money by letting products and merchandise sit around.

You could go without water for twenty-four hours, couldn't you? Or maybe longer? By then I'd surely be able to free myself.

For a minute or so, nothing happened. Then lights came on in the corner. The autonomous forklift was coming to life.

I had seen the autonomous forklifts in the main warehouse operating, and they always seemed to be one part technology, one part witchcraft. I understood how they operated—they had one main front-facing camera on top and additional cameras on the sides and back to serve as eyes—but it still came off as magic.

Really, how did they know what to do?

It was hard not to get a little mesmerized as the forklift went to work.

The wall of boxes was four pallet-loads wide. I assumed the forklift would start at the side—either the pallet all the way to the left, or the one all the way to the right.

Curiously, it selected the second pallet from the left. There was no reason for this I could discern. But I watched as the forklift raised its arms, slid them into the openings of the pallet, gently lifted up, then came away with the entire load.

From there, the soft rubber tires wheeled backward across the smooth concrete floor until the entire pallet was out of the truck. It backed a little farther, maybe ten feet or so, then set the load down in that spot.

This didn't make any sense, either. Why put this one pallet in the middle of the floor? Wouldn't it just be in the way when the other pallets were unloaded?

The forklift retreated from the pallet, then zipped around it, returning to the truck.

I had thought it would pick up the pallet to either side of the one it had just grabbed and continue to clear the first row of boxes.

Again, I assumed wrong.

It drove itself into the opening it had just made and went for the pallet that was the next row in. It repeated the same maneuver it had done with the first, bringing the pallet away and setting it down in the middle of the floor.

Except, this time, it didn't go back for a third trip.

It just stopped.

I kept waiting for it to go. But, no, it was just sitting there, not moving, its lights and cameras still activated.

Then I heard a light metal-on-metal rasping sound coming from inside the truck. When I looked at where it was coming from, I was surprised to see a small steel door opening.

Why was there a door in the middle of the trailer?

Then I saw the door was part of a larger metal box. There was a container inside the trailer.

From there, my astonishment only grew.

The door hadn't opened on its own.

A man had pushed it open.

He had a duffel bag slung over his shoulder and a rolling suitcase behind him, looking for all the world like any other traveler you might see at an airport.

Having cleared through the doorway, he walked in between the walls of boxes, then into the building and toward the staircase. When he reached the steps, he collapsed the handle on his rolling suitcase, picked it up, and descended the steps.

"*Buenos dias,*" he said, dipping his head as he passed me.

"*Buenos dias,*" I replied, still too shocked by everything that was happening to summon any other response.

But that was really just the start.

Trailing the man was a woman. She also had luggage, like she had been on a trip, and was soon smiling as she passed me.

Then came another man.

And another.

Then a woman.

People were filing out of this hidden container in an orderly fashion, single file, just like they were getting off a bus or plane.

They seemed far less bewildered by me than I was by them. There was this air of routine about them, like emerging from the guts of a forty-foot trailer was the most ordinary thing in the world to be doing.

I had the sense some of them had even done this before.

As the box emptied, I was able to get a better look at its insides. It was certainly cramped, but it appeared to be quite habitable. It was pleasantly lit. There was a metal bench all around the side that gave passengers a place to sit. There was a portable air-conditioning unit attached to a vent in the ceiling.

I had lost count of how many people had passed me, but it was at least a dozen, with more on the way.

One larger man made eye contact with me and had to turn to the side to shimmy by me on the stairs.

"Where are you going?" I asked him in Spanish.

He replied in English, "Don't worry, *amigo*. We're following the plan."

Plan? What plan?

There were now people waiting on many of the steps below me. They were chatting in low tones. None of them seemed upset or impatient. This was just another part of their journey.

I was finally coming to my senses about what was happening here.

The air-conditioned compartment hidden behind two layers of pallets. The "specialized" building. All of the functions being automated, such that no one on this end had to touch a thing—or see a thing.

It had all the hallmarks of high-level planning and coordination, the kind of thing that logistics experts excelled at. And this pretty obviously had happened before.

Many, many times before.

Balco wasn't just bringing electronics back from Mexico.

It was also smuggling human beings.

CHAPTER 55

THEY HAD COME up with the plan hastily.

French thought it was fine. It's not like they had time to grind over details and devise something better. And Salcedo said it was life or death.

Boston still considered it half-cocked.

But he also hadn't offered any alternatives.

As such, French simply left the cramped confines of the Ford Explorer, where he had spent the evening, and strode up to the front porch of 27 Buena Vista Drive.

He rang the doorbell. His fake FBI badge was out of his pocket and glinting in the morning sun that was rising above San Francisco Bay to the east.

Boston trailed by a few paces.

Page Hinton answered the door wearing yoga pants that hugged her thighs and a V-neck T-shirt that barely covered her swelling midsection.

French looked at her lasciviously, feeling excitement stirring below his belt.

"Good morning, Mrs. Hinton. Agent Frisch with the FBI. I'm sure you remember my partner, Agent Bastian."

Boston gave a curt nod.

"We're very sorry to bother you at such an early hour," French said. "Can we come in?"

"May I ask what this is about?" she asked.

French already didn't like that her posture was so defensive. She had not even fully opened the door. She was half-hiding behind it, looking ready to close it at any moment.

This hadn't been part of his plan. He had assumed that Page Hinton would have naive trust in her friendly federal law enforcement agents and would let them inside without question. He didn't want this conversation to be happening in front of the entire neighborhood.

"Yes, of course," he said. "The FBI has developed information about the death of Angel Reddish."

"What is it?"

"It's . . . It's highly sensitive. We're actually . . . You'll need to come with me to my office to see it."

He sounded more faltering than he wanted to.

The Hinton woman met this suggestion with a skeptical expression. "Have you spoken to my husband about this?"

Damnit. This was definitely not going well for French.

"No," he said. "Not yet."

"Why not?"

"We haven't been able to reach him."

At least that was true.

"I'd like to wait for him to get home before I go with you," she said.

"I'm afraid there's no time for that."

"Why not?"

"This is a rapidly developing situation. We have to move."

More skepticism. "Angel was killed weeks ago. How could it now be time sensitive?"

"It just is," he insisted, and immediately wished he could take it back.

Terrible answer.

Boston finally stepped forward to save his foundering partner.

"We've only just had a break in the case," he said, trying to sound authoritative. "There are things we can't reveal here. When we get to the office, it'll all make sense."

"I'm not comfortable doing anything without Curt," she said, and she was already starting to close the door. "You gentlemen are just going to have to wait until—"

French didn't let her finish the sentence. He slammed his shoulder into what was left of the opening between the door and its jam, sending Hinton sprawling backward onto the Persian rug that graced the foyer.

Not giving her a moment to recover—or caring about the life growing inside her—he leaped on top of her with his full weight. In the ensuing struggle, he managed to straddle her, suppressing her efforts to knee him in the groin.

All she could really do was scream. When he pressed his hand on her mouth to stifle the sound, she bit him. He roared as she broke the skin.

"You nasty bitch," he yelled, backhanding her with brutal force.

Then he jammed his hand on her face, clamping down so hard she yelped in pain.

"Help me, you idiot!" he called out.

Boston had been frozen on the front porch. He finally entered the house, closing the door behind himself.

He was moving gingerly, clearly more concerned about hurting a pregnant woman. But he grabbed ahold of her flailing arms and pinned them to her sides.

"You got the zip ties?" French said, grunting with the effort of keeping her pinned down as she continued writhing and bucking.

"Yeah."

"Good. Let's get her rolled over."

It was an effort. She was stronger than she looked and she fought them every inch of the way. But they soon had her bound at the wrists and ankles. To muffle her screaming, they had taken a washcloth from a bathroom and stuffed it into her mouth, then secured it in place with a dish towel from the kitchen.

By the time they had her immobilized and quieted, they were both panting from exertion.

"Get her cell phone off her," Boston said. "Don't want her making any calls on us."

French knelt down and patted the phone compartment in her yoga pants. The woman didn't have the energy to fight him off.

"Hey, she's get two of them," he said.

"Well, get both of them."

"You got it," French said.

Then he ran a hand over her backside. "All right. Now let's have some fun with her."

"What?" Boston said in horror.

"Come on. You know I have a thing for preggos."

"No way. We don't have time for that."

"Oh, it won't take long, believe me." He was already attempting to tug down her yoga pants. Hinton bucked and thrashed in response.

"Knock it off," Boston said, shoving French away from the woman. "We gotta go. We can't stay here. What if the cleaning lady comes or, or, I don't know, a neighbor drops by? It's not worth it."

"Fine," French said, looking at his partner scornfully. "But I'm having a go with her later."

"Whatever. We have to figure out a way to get her out of here without the neighbors seeing us."

"That's easy. We drag her into the garage and take her car."

They split up, searching the house until they found the keys to Page Hinton's Honda CRV. Before long, they had her balled up and stuffed into the well of the back seat. Boston was back there with her, with his feet resting on her shoulders and hips so she couldn't pop back up.

"Where are we taking her?" Boston asked.

"I don't know. Let me call Sal."

French pulled out his phone, tapped at it, then said, "We got her. Where do you want her?"

"Headquarters."

"Roger that. You find her husband yet?"

"No," Salcedo said. "But as long as we've got her, we've got him."

CHAPTER 56

AS PEOPLE CONTINUED emptying from that steel box, certain things began falling into place in my mind.

One of the first lessons about logistics Angel had given me was the difference between FTLs and LTLs—and how it was more profitable to maximize the former and avoid the latter. Among Balco's constant challenges was its tendency to have FTLs heading down to Mexico and LTLs coming back.

The intricacies of FTLs and LTLs aside, Lorne Murphy had put it in more folksy terms during one of our first meetings.

The stuff we bring back just isn't as bulky as the stuff we bring down, so there's often extra room on the truck . . .

That was the story with freight.

With immigration, the issue was reversed.

As Ron Talbot once told me, *It's really easy to leave this country. It's not so easy to come back.*

At a certain point, some clever person at Balco—Lorne? Rig Weiskopf?—had obviously realized that there was a very lucrative way to deal with this discrepancy.

Fill those partially empty trucks with people.

There was certainly plenty of demand—from Mexico, or Venezuela, or Haiti, or any number of places where people's economic prospects simply weren't as bright as they were in the United States, even as undocumented immigrants.

Then there were people like Maria, who probably made up a considerable chunk of the clientele: not new migrants, but established ones. Estimates put their population in this country at well over ten million.

They had been here for many years. They had pressing reasons to go south. But then they wanted to be able to return to the lives they had built here, because this had become home. And, by the way, they had the funds to do it.

They were absolutely willing to pay $8,000 for the service of being delivered back to America.

Other than the occasional tragic exception—like Maria—most of them made it without a scratch.

In a Balco truck, they wouldn't have to face the dangers of exposure during a long trek across the desert; or dodge Border Patrol Agents; or risk being attacked by gangs that preyed on migrants.

They were being delivered comfortably and safely to their destination: L-11 in Long Beach, if they just needed to get across the border; or K-12 in Oakland, if the Bay Area was their final destination—like it had been for Maria, who lived in nearby Richmond.

Even if it was just one shipment a day to each location, with thirty people on each truck, that was roughly twenty thousand people a year—or $160 million in extra revenue.

Multiple shipments meant you could double or triple that number. With more than three million people crossing the border illegally each year, there was certainly no shortage of demand. Whatever Balco was doing still represented just a tiny fraction of the total. The state of Texas was shipping more migrants than that to sanctuary cities all by itself.

How did Norteño get involved in Balco's operation? I could only speculate. But with that kind of money at stake, it wasn't surprising that it would want to assert itself. Cartels tended to get their fingers into just about everything in Mexico. The coyote game was no exception.

Maybe the enterprise had been Norteño's idea all along. The cartel had seen all those Balco trucks and Balco warehouses and realized the company had all the infrastructure needed to smuggle people on a large scale.

Or maybe Balco already had a thriving operation going, and Norteño came along and insisted it get its piece of the action.

That would have made it a lot like a protection racket, as Angel had hinted to Aiysha.

Whatever the case, much of what I had seen during my brief stint at Balco was starting to make more sense.

Joseph Manger wasn't freelancing, as Lorne had said. The driver was just doing his job.

How had he come to realize that there were people in his truck, and that one of those people was a woman he could take advantage of? I couldn't begin to guess.

But it was as obvious as that metal box that Manger wasn't the coyote.

Balco was the coyote.

Then there was Melvord Finck. His initial protestations of innocence were probably accurate: He truly didn't know there were people in the back of his truck.

So why had he changed his mind, agreed to plead guilty, and served eighteen months in federal prison?

Because Balco bought him off.

That was why he was now living in a small slice of suburban heaven and getting paid $240,000 a year—as an exempt, salaried employee—to be a janitor.

What was also now striking to me was that the Melvord Finck episode had been *five years* ago. Balco had been doing this for a long time.

It had obviously learned from that mistake. There had probably been many refinements to the process since then. Improvements. Streamlining. That was the Balco way.

But, as with everything else in logistics, there would always be unexpected wrinkles, things you didn't plan for.

Like that bag of Takis Fuego tortilla chips I had seen down in Long Beach. That hadn't been dropped there by a Balco employee, in defiance of the no-food-outside-the-break-room policy. It had been cast aside by a careless passenger.

That was a small example, of course. And it could be easily cleaned up.

Other wrinkles would be a lot messier.

Like Joseph Manger, an opportunistic predator.

Had Balco really gone five years—from Melvord Finck to Joseph Manger—without an incident that put its illicit operations in danger of exposure?

Or had there, in fact, been many breeches that the company found a way to hide?

I was now wondering if Dan Gillespie was one of those. Had he seen something he wasn't supposed to see? Had he threatened to expose what was happening here?

All of these thoughts were colliding in my mind, making it difficult to work through them all at once. It was like trying to untangle a bunch of knots in a pile of rope.

Then I was jarred by an unexpected noise.

A buzzing sound. It was coming from below me.

I couldn't figure out what it was until I realized the line had started to move.

That's when I figured it out.

The lock on the steel door at the bottom of the stairs had released.

And now the passengers were moving through it.

CHAPTER 57

LORNE MURPHY WAS fuming.

His ire was directed at his chief security officer.

"You . . . you . . . you kidnapped the wife?" he sputtered. "Have you lost your damn mind? That wasn't the plan."

"All our plans went out the window the moment La Tranquila walked into your office," Salcedo shot back. "We have no choice—"

"*We?!?* Don't make this a *we*. If this goes bad, this is not a *we*; this is a *you*."

"News flash: This already has gone bad," Salcedo snapped. "I'm just trying to contain the damage. You were the one who started all of this, remember?"

Murphy had no argument there. He had been the head of Balco's Mexico operation when he recognized that the combination of the empty space on his northbound trucks and America's broken immigration system represented a significant untapped revenue stream.

His proposal had found an enthusiastic supporter in Rig Weiskopf.

Norteño entered the picture—forcibly—later on.

"What I started was a . . . a peaceful business operation," Murphy said, "not a goddamn criminal enterprise."

"Yeah, because transporting illegal immigrants is no different from shipping laptops and Bluetooth speakers."

Murphy huffed. "I did what I had to do."

"Look, none of that matters. We either deal with this Hinton thing, or we're as good as dead. If he runs to the feds, we need leverage to shut him up. This is our leverage."

"Unbelievable," Murphy said. "And what do you plan on doing with her when you're done using her as leverage?"

Salcedo just shrugged unapologetically.

He didn't need to say it.

Murphy threw up his hands. "We can't keep doing this!"

"I don't see where we have a choice."

"And how are you going to get rid of her? You gonna blow her up like you blew up Dan Gillespie? Because *that* worked out just great."

"No, she's going to kill herself," Salcedo said.

"And why is she going to do that?"

"She's distraught her husband has left her for another woman, leaving her to raise a baby by herself. We'll have her leave a note. It'll work."

Murphy stopped to consider this for a moment.

"Actually, that's not bad," he allowed.

"It'll work," Salcedo said. "It will *all* work."

"You just going to have her shoot herself like Manger? That's a little suspicious, don't you think? A woman like that with a gun?"

"No, we're going to give her a bath."

"What are you talking about?"

"The reason people drown when they're submerged in water is that it causes the carbon dioxide levels in their blood to become too high. Eventually, that triggers an involuntary reflex to suck in air. They literally can't resist the urge to breathe. They take in a big lung full of water, and that's it. They're done for.

"So, really, it's pretty simple," Salcedo continued. "We fill a tub with water from the Bay. You hold her head down in it until she takes in a big gulp of water. Once she's dead, drive her car out to some secluded spot by the water, leave it there, and toss her in the drink. Eventually, she washes up somewhere. That's if the sharks don't get her. Either way, her body will be so beat up by the surf, they won't know what happened to her. When they do the autopsy, they find water in her lungs. Cause of death becomes suicide by drowning. Especially when I make her write a note."

Neither spoke for a few moments.

Then Murphy shook his head and said, "No one is going to believe a woman who is pregnant with her first child just up and decided to kill herself. She'd have to be mentally unhinged to do something like that."

"Then we'll give her a history of mental illness."

"And how are we going to do that?"

"I know a shrink who will say anything for twenty grand. Dr. Effinger is his name. He's got an expensive ketamine habit to support. I'll have him tell the cops he had been seeing Mrs. Hinton for several weeks now and that she was having a major depressive episode. I'll make Effinger fake session notes and everything. She was already depressed about having left her job. She hated California. She had no friends here. She was already terrified about raising a child in her depleted condition and the thought of trying to do it without her husband threw her over the edge. Whatever. It'll work."

He paused for a moment, then said, "Or you can just see how it goes when you tell La Tranquila we have no plan, no backup, and no hope because we've lost Hinton."

"I see your point," Murphy said. "Fine. Do what you have to do."

CHAPTER 58

OF THE THIRTY or so people who had climbed off the truck, roughly twenty were ahead of me on the steps, with ten more behind.

I fell in line with them. Wherever they were going, it had to be better than here.

Upon reaching the bottom of the stairs, I passed through the door and into a concrete-lined tunnel.

It was maybe three feet wide—about the same as the doorway we had just passed through—and roughly the same height as the door, which meant there wasn't much head room, but it was at least tall enough that I didn't have to stoop. It had the same orange safety lighting as K-12 did, with one bulb every few feet along the sidewall.

And, again, there were no cameras.

Balco pretty clearly didn't want there to be any footage of this.

The line wasn't moving very fast—more at a shuffle than a walk. I kept looking forward to see where we were going. All I could see was the backs of people's heads.

All chatter had stopped. The only sounds were the scraping of shoes and the squeak of luggage straps.

I just kept putting one foot in front of the other.

At this slow speed, and without being able to take full strides, it was difficult to keep track of how far we were traveling. But this was not a short tunnel. It had already stretched well more than a hundred yards—call it a hundred and fifty—when the procession abruptly came to a halt.

The man in the lead must have stopped, but I couldn't tell why.

Just that we weren't moving anymore.

Then, very slowly, we began to inch forward again.

Progress was far more halting than it had been, even at shuffle speed.

After two minutes or so, I was finally able to make out what was happening.

There was no more tunnel to travel horizontally.

It had turned vertical.

There were rungs buried in the concrete, and the people ahead of me were climbing up what appeared to be a cylindrical utility hole.

When it came my turn, I grasped onto a rung at shoulder height and looked upward.

Roughly twenty feet up, I could make out a small patch of gray-blue sky.

It was just about the most beautiful thing I had ever seen.

Without further hesitation, I began climbing. The going was still quite slow—many people were seriously struggling to make it up, burdened as they were with their belongings.

But eventually, I made it to the surface, where two rectangular metal grates were yawning open, supported by stainless-steel pistons on both ends that kept them open. I could guess these were automatic, just like everything else had been.

One of the men who preceded me was standing at the top, giving everyone a helping hand up.

I gratefully accepted his assistance, then looked around. We were in a kind of alleyway that had been created between two tall stacks of rust-stained shipping containers.

Stepping to the side so others could pass, I filled my lungs with air, like I hadn't been able to breathe free in hours.

No one else seemed to be marking the moment in similar fashion.

They all had places to go. I did, too.

I had to get back home to Page and then we had to run the hell away from here.

There was only one way out of this shipping container canyon that had been created, so I fell back in line with my fellow travelers as we passed between the tall steel walls.

We emerged into an open stretch of asphalt. It was old, cracked, and sun-bleached.

I was still a little disoriented as to where we were. But when I turned around, I saw the cranes from the Port of Oakland looming behind us. We seemed to be exiting from the back side of this container storage lot.

That meant Balco headquarters was also behind us, and we were walking in the opposite direction of the facility.

Which was exactly what I wanted.

There was still no conversation. Everyone was just plodding along like they somehow knew where they were going. We passed a trailer that had been used as an office at some point in the past. Its windows were now covered in a layer of brown-orange dust.

Next came a line of low Jersey barriers that were easy enough to clamber over. Then there were a series of railroad tracks, none of them in use at the moment, that we walked across. Then came another line of Jersey barriers, though we were able to squeeze through the spaces between them.

After that was another set of railroad tracks.

Then came a road.

It was a frontage road for a highway. Cars zipped along in front of us. Now that I had my bearings a little better, I recognized Interstate 880.

When the people in front of me reached the road, they began fanning out. Some turned left, others turned right. There were a few groups of two or three, but mostly people were going it solo.

They were simply disappearing into the vastness of America, as undocumented immigrants in this country had been doing for hundreds of years.

If I had my phone, I would have just pulled up my Uber app and arranged for a ride. That wasn't an option, so I turned left and walked until I reached an intersection with a road that went under a raised portion of the freeway.

Continuing straight would have soon put me on the highway. Going left would send me closer to the Port.

I turned right. After passing under the highway, I departed the industrial landscape of the Port and entered a neighborhood that was just starting to come to life. I turned up what appeared to be a larger avenue and soon came across a bus stop.

The man who had once been leading our procession was waiting there.

"Where does this bus go?" I asked in Spanish.

"The BART station," he said.

BART was Bay Area Rapid Transit, the region's passenger rail system, but that wouldn't do me any good. The BART didn't go to Marin

County.

I was thinking about taking the bus anyway when a gray Hyundai with a "Lyft/Uber" sign on its windshield came up the street. I stepped out into the street, waved, and yelled, "Hey, over here!"

It came to a stop in front of me.

Our negotiations were brief. As soon as the driver realized I didn't have a phone—and that something about me smelled a little desperate—he asked for $100 for the ride to Marin County. It was at least a 30 percent upcharge over the usual rate.

As he swiped my credit card, he had no idea how happy I was to overpay.

With that, I was on my way.

I rode with a powerful sense of hope and dread building within me. The cartel had obviously decided I was a threat in need of elimination.

And that was *before* I had witnessed the full extent of the operation Norteño and Balco were running together.

Given what I now knew, I was even more dangerous to them. All it would take was one phone call to interest law enforcement—like Joint Task Force 1954—to set a chain of events into motion that might very well lead to the implosion of both Balco and Norteño.

It would soon be raining indictments.

That's *if* the feds believed me.

I really had no proof for what I was alleging beyond my own say-so. Would the word of one person be enough to secure search warrants?

Or would the FBI dismiss me as a disgruntled ex-employee making up stories?

That would be a worry for later. For now, the only thing that mattered to me was Page. Had Norteño decided she was also a threat?

My hope was that it hadn't.

My dread was that it had.

And, if so, was I already too late?

As we crossed the Richmond Bridge and entered Marin County, it was 8:06 a.m., more than two hours after my scheduled appointment with Lorne Murphy—a meeting that, I now recognized, was a setup.

That gave the cartel all the time it needed to move in on our house, if it so chose.

My only hope was that if Norteño had decided to leave Aiysha alone, maybe it just wasn't in the business of going after spouses.

That felt like a ludicrous thing to pin my optimism on: a cartel's sense of humanity.

As we neared 27 Buena Vista, I knew it would be foolish to drive straight up to the house. Once Norteño and Balco knew I had made it out of the facility, this would be the first place they'd look for me.

And depending on how quickly they reached that conclusion, they might already be here. I'd be stumbling into a trap.

"Pull over here, if you don't mind," I said to the driver, who immediately complied.

As I prepared to get out of the car, I stopped myself.

This was a sanctuary: a place that was both mobile and anonymous. It was as safe from the cartel as I could imagine myself being.

I suddenly really liked the idea of having it stick around as a backup plan.

Or maybe a primary plan. Even if Page was still safe at home, we wouldn't exactly take her car. We had never determined if it had any listening devices or tracking devices installed on it, and now wasn't the time to find out.

This Hyundai was guaranteed to be bug free.

"How much would it cost me to have you wait for me here?" I asked.

"Another hundred," the driver said.

"How long would that buy me?"

"An hour," he said.

"Deal," I said. "And I might need a ride to the airport after that. I'm not sure."

"That would be another hundred," he said.

"Okay," I said.

We completed the transaction for the first hundred, and I pointed in the direction we had come.

"Turn around so you're facing that way," I instructed. "This is a dead-end street."

And I wanted to get out as quickly as possible.

Though I left that part unspoken.

While the Hyundai completed its K-turn in a nearby driveway, I walked with my head on a swivel up the street, keeping a cautious eye out for a van full of *vatos* lying in wait or anything else that didn't match what I usually saw on Buena Vista Drive.

But nothing seemed out of place. One of the neighbors, who Page and I had met on a walk, waved as she drove past on her way to work.

When I reached the spot where 27 Buena Vista came just into view, I stopped.

The street was still. There were no pedestrians.

A black Ford Explorer that I didn't recognize was parked along the right side, though it was not particularly suspicious. Its un-tinted windows made it easy to see there was no one inside.

The Barbie DreamHouse looked to me like it always did: a bit too large and ostentatious for anything that ought to have housed a newspaper reporter and his stay-at-home wife.

There was a glare on the windows that made it impossible to see inside, so I couldn't say if Page was in there.

Or if there were cartel thugs waiting for me in the living room.

Given this possibility, I wasn't going to approach head-on. I turned right up one of my neighbors' driveways, then walked around into the back of their property, which sloped down and away from the house.

Due to the topography, no one on Buena Vista Drive had a lawn for a backyard; just trees and shrubbery that clung to the hillside.

The vegetation wasn't particularly dense, though. So I was able to easily work my way through the back of their lot, then across three more, until I was staring at the back of our house and the deck on which we had spent so many blissful hours.

It was empty.

For a few minutes, I monitored the house for signs of life. But there was nothing happening outside.

I still couldn't see inside.

Slowly, I crept up to the stairs that led to the deck, trying to stay alert for any noises inside or any signs that there was trouble within.

All I heard was the sound of joists lightly creaking under my weight.

As I neared the top, I stopped and sat on one of the steps, where my eyes were level with the deck surface. I could finally see inside to the family room / dining area / kitchen, which was really one large space.

It was also empty.

Page may have been upstairs in our bedroom.

Or there could be Norteño men waiting in the foyer.

I really had no idea.

It might have been prudent to stay there for a while until the truth revealed itself, but I couldn't stall forever. My Lyft/Uber was going to hang around for an hour, and I had already used twenty minutes of that time.

I simply had to keep moving.

Cautiously.

Gathering myself, I rose from my spot and climbed the last few steps. Then I crept across the deck surface in a low stance. I felt very exposed—and I was ready to turn and run at the first sign of anything awry—but I reached the first of the sliding glass doors without incident.

It wasn't locked. We went in and out of doors so often that we had stopped locking them. This was definitely part of the privilege of living on a quiet street in an upscale neighborhood, and now it was what allowed me to enter quietly into the back of my house.

Leaving the door open behind me, in case I needed to make a very fast exit, I listened for any noise that would betray the house's occupancy status—whether it was Page taking a shower or Norteño men chatting amongst themselves.

All was quiet.

Mindful of the passing of time—but also continuing to exercise prudence—I went quietly, room-by-room, through the entire house. The more of it I covered, the more I came to realize there was simply no one there.

When I checked the garage, I saw Page's car wasn't there.

Where could she have gone? An errand? The gym? I couldn't say I had her daily patterns perfectly memorized so it might have been something mundane.

I completed my sweep of the house with a quick scan upstairs.

When I reached our bedroom, I spied my new phone sitting on my nightstand, exactly where I had left it. I crossed the room and had just picked it up to dial Page's new number when I heard the front door to the house opening.

Thinking it was Page, I walked to the top of the stairs and was about to call out a greeting when I heard a voice.

It wasn't Page.

It belonged to a man.

CHAPTER 59

THIS WAS NOT what French wanted to be doing.

He saw absolutely no reason why he shouldn't have been allowed a go at the pregnant redhead as a reward for all his good work.

They were going to kill her anyway. Why not enjoy her first?

Instead, after delivering her to Salcedo at headquarters, French and Boston had driven another one of the SUVs belonging to Balco security forces back to Marin County.

An increasingly frantic-sounding Sal Salcedo had given them three instructions.

First, they had to retrieve the Ford Explorer, which they had left parked along Buena Vista Drive, just down the street from the Hinton residence.

Second, they had to deliver the note they had forced Page Hinton to write at gunpoint.

Third, they needed to grab some of her personal effects—her purse, her wallet—which needed to be left in her car, for authenticity's sake.

Getting back in the house was easy enough. They had unlocked the front door before they left. So French just walked into the house like he owned the place, with Boston trailing behind.

"Where should we put this thing?" French asked.

He was wearing gloves and delicately holding a single sheet of white paper that he knew he had to treat with care. It had been explained to him that the police would very likely be giving it careful study someday—verifying that the handwriting on it was authentic, dusting it for prints, that sort of thing.

"Not sure," Boston replied. "Where did you put it with Manger?"

"Next to the body."

"Oh."

That wasn't an option here.

"C'mon, you're Mister Manners," French said. "What's Emily Post say about where you leave a suicide note?"

"Kitchen counter?"

"Yeah, yeah, that's good. A woman would leave something important in the kitchen."

"See, there you go, being misogynistic," Boston said.

"Aww, knock it off with that."

French positioned the paper at the edge of the counter and looked at its handwritten contents one more time.

Curt,

I've seen the video of you and that slut Korynne. You disgust me. I can't take any more. Not even Dr. Effinger can help me any more. Don't bother trying to find me. Where I'm going, I'm never coming back.

Page

"Here is good, right?" French asked.

"Yeah, works for me."

"Okay, now where do you think this bitch—"

"C'mon."

"Sorry, where do you think the honorable Mrs. Hinton left her wallet and purse?"

"I dunno. I was hoping it would be somewhere obvious."

They both looked around the kitchen for a moment.

"Aww, hell, nothing's ever easy, is it?" French said. "Let's split up. You take down here, I'll go up there."

"What if it's actually already *in* the car? Did you look?"

"No, but who leaves their stuff in the car? That don't make sense. I'm sure it's around here somewhere."

"Okay. Let me know when—"

Boston was stopped by a noise that suddenly echoed through the house. "Did you hear that?"

The hard look on French's face made it clear he had.

For a moment, neither man spoke. They just listened.

Boston pointed a finger toward the ceiling and mouthed *up there.*

French nodded, slipped a pistol out of his shoulder holster, and moved quietly toward the stairs.

CHAPTER 60

IT TOOK ME a few moments to place the voice.

As soon as I heard the man say, "Where should we put this thing," I knew I had heard him before.

But where?

And who was he?

Then he wisecracked, "What's Emily Post say about where you leave a suicide note?"

And that's when I knew.

It was Agent Frisch of the FBI. He had a distinct New York–area accent.

I also recognized that his partner, Agent Bastian, was the one replying.

Except I now realized neither one of these men were who they said they were.

FBI agents didn't go breaking into houses unannounced. Even if they had a warrant, they knocked first and informed you they were about to perform a search of your premises.

In the rare instances when they had a no-knock warrant, they didn't come in with just two agents. They came in large numbers. And they came in loud.

They also didn't talk about their experiences planting suicide notes, like they had apparently done with Joseph Manger.

Ron Talbot's words came back to me: *Preliminary indication is self-inflicted gunshot wound to the head. They found a note and everything.*

Whose suicide were they faking this time? Mine? Page's?

I really didn't want to know.

But, at the moment, I had an even more immediate problem.

I was trapped here. As long as Frisch and Bastian were on the first floor, all of the exits I might have used—front door, garage door, sliding glass doors—were blocked.

Maybe they would simply plant this fake suicide letter and leave without bothering to check out the rest of the house.

But that hope was quickly dashed when I heard them talk about splitting up to find Page's wallet and purse.

Which meant one of them was coming my way.

I had to make a hasty escape.

And the only way out was through a window.

As quickly and quietly as I could, I moved away from the top of the stairs and back into our bedroom, where there was wall-to-wall carpeting to soften my footfalls.

Our windows were large enough for me to fit through and overlooked the deck, meaning it would be a relatively short drop. After my three-story plunge a few hours earlier, one story felt like nothing.

The main problem were the windows themselves. The Barbie DreamHouse was mid-century modern; and even though that style was all the rage among nostalgic millennials such as my wife, it also meant that some parts of the house weren't truly modern at all.

They were just old—like the windows, which were original and hadn't been replaced by anything vinyl that would open smoothly. They were metal panels set in metal frames, and they slid only with a certain degree of protest.

I positioned myself in front of the window on the left, since that was the one we used every night, when we wanted to let the cool air roll in as we slept.

With one hand on top and the other on the bottom, I tried to ease it open slowly, gently, noiselessly.

It wouldn't budge.

I could feel myself running out of time. One of them would be up here any moment, and I hadn't closed the door to the bedroom. They would see me almost immediately.

Panicked, I simply yanked as hard as I could, resulting in a discordant, metal-on-metal squeal.

From downstairs, Frisch said, "Did you hear that?"

I had been made.

Without further deliberation, I put one leg through the window. There was no screen on the window, because Californians didn't seem to believe in those, so there was nothing to stop me.

For the briefest moment, I straddled the window frame, ducking my head low so I could fit through the opening. Then I pulled myself the rest of the way through, with my other leg trailing behind me.

I fell, hitting the deck with a tremendous thud.

From somewhere inside the house, there was an explosion of shouting, but I was already on the move. I vaulted over the railing, dropping another ten feet to the ground below.

The mature plantings beneath me absorbed some of the punishment from my hard landing. I felt the rest in my feet and knees.

No matter, I kept right on going, even if it seemed to take forever for my dress shoes to gain traction.

My only hope was to reach the safety of my Lyft/Uber Hyundai before Frisch and Bastian reached me. So I plunged into a thicket of scrub to my right.

The tiny branches might as well have been thorns, tearing into my suit jacket, slashing at my hands and face. I ignored the pain as the shouting emerged onto the deck.

All that mattered was putting as much distance—and vegetation—between me and those men as I could. I continued my mad dash through the brush, then around the wide trunk of a California live oak.

I was already onto the property next door when I heard Bastian yelp, "There he is."

This was met by a burst of swearing from Frisch. He was charging down the steps after me.

But that was a lot better than what Bastian was doing.

He started shooting at me wildly. I could hear the bullets banging into tree trunks and burying themselves in the dirt.

His pistol must have been silenced, because its only report was a soft *thump, thump, thump* that wouldn't have alarmed even the most vigilant neighbor. At most they would have thought someone was beating dust out of a rug.

I didn't dare look back to see if his aim was improving. But I did begin zigzagging so he couldn't get a beat on me.

My right foot slipped on some lose dirt, and for a moment I worried I was going to wipe out; but I managed to right myself by grabbing onto a tree trunk and vaulting myself forward.

Already, I was two properties down. Frisch was getting farther back.

I heard more cursing. He was definitely struggling with the underbrush more than me. He wasn't as willing to sacrifice his hands and face.

He also didn't have the same level of fear to propel him forward.

As long as I kept my feet under me, I was going to be fine. Frisch was older than me and overweight. I could outrun him, and I already had a head start.

Bastian was continuing to empty his gun. I was guessing—maybe just praying—it was a fifteen-round magazine and that he'd soon need to reload. I had already counted twelve shots.

Then he let loose with lucky number thirteen. I heard a loud *crack* and then felt something bite me in the ass on the right side.

I roared in pain but didn't dare stop. The muscle was either going to keep functioning and propel me faithfully forward or I'd keel over.

Somehow, it held up, even though I could feel something warm and moist trailing down my leg.

Before long, I was sprinting down the same neighbor's drive that I had run up earlier. Then I was back out on Buena Vista Drive.

The driver was waiting exactly where I had left him. I leaped into the back seat, staying on my uninjured left side, and barked, "Let's get out of here. Go, go, go."

He startled a little, but quickly fired up the Hyundai's engine and got us underway.

The first thing I did was look at my right butt cheek to assess the damage.

I didn't see a bullet wound. But there was a three-inch-long shard of wood that had penetrated my pants and was now sticking out my backside. With determination, I yanked it out, then pressed my hand against the wound to stop the bleeding.

The pain wasn't as bad as I thought. It must have been all the adrenaline rampaging through me.

With my hand still in place, I turned and looked out the rear window behind me. There was no sign of anyone giving chase.

I was bloodied, but I had escaped.

For now.

We turned right at the end of Buena Vista Drive, which was the way back to the highway.

In case Frish and Bastian did try to come after me, I directed the driver down a random side street, to get us off any route they might anticipate we would use.

Then I asked him to pull over.

"Can you wait here a second?" I said. "I need to make a call so I can figure out where we're going."

The driver had already gotten two hundred bucks out of me and probably sensed he was in line for more, so he did as asked.

I got out of the Hyundai and brought up Page's number, which was the only contact currently in my phone.

My wild hope was that I'd interrupt her in the middle of the grocery store; or that she was just coming out of a workout; or that, wherever she was, she'd race to join me, and we'd be able to jet off to someplace that was little more than a name on a map to the Norteño Cartel.

That hope was alive until she answered on the first ring and I heard the panic in her voice: "Curt, I love you, I love you so—"

Then all sound stopped. The insides of my stomach felt like they had just dropped to the sidewalk.

"Page!" I yelped. "Page, where are you? I'm—"

"Hello, Curt," a man's voice cut me off. "How are you?"

It was Sal Salcedo.

"What's going on?" I demanded. "Put Page back on."

"You didn't report for work this morning. We're concerned about you. Where are you right now?"

"Somewhere your thugs won't find me. I want to talk to Page."

"Oh, I'm afraid she doesn't want to come to the phone right now. Don't worry. She's quite safe. She's just a little upset with you. If you want to see her, you're going to have to come to headquarters so we can all have a little chat."

"A little chat. Is that why you allowed those men from Norteño to enter the facility and attack me this morning? So we could have a little chat?"

"I have no idea what you're talking about," he said, and I realized he was acting as if I were recording the conversation.

It figured someone who listened in on everyone would assume that someone else would do the same.

I actually felt cold. I was so terrified by the thought of Page being in their clutches.

But they had to know I was capable of doing some pretty scary things to them, too.

"Look, let's just cut to the chase here," I said. "If you don't let Page go right now, I'm running to Joint Task Force 1954 and telling them exactly what I saw in Building K-12 this morning. I'm telling them about how you've been partnering with Norteño, about how you've been paying off Melvord Finck, and about how you killed Joseph Manger. Do you understand that? If you so much as touch her, I swear I will dedicate every ounce of my energy to making sure you spend the rest of your life in prison—is that clear?"

This was met with a moment's silence; then I realized Salcedo was muffling the speaker.

Then I heard the phone being passed to someone new.

"Curt, buddy, it's Lorne," he said in his best paternalistic voice.

"Listen, no one is going to prison, and no one is going to hurt your missus. Let's just relax here. I think everyone has gotten their wires crossed. What we really wanted to talk to you about today was offering you a piece of the pie. We call it 'the dividend.' There are a few of us here who get it. We'll start you off with a hundred thousand free and clear, just for joining the club. I know you got a baby on the way. A hundred grand buys a lot of diapers. Then we'll start adding to your check every other week. In your case, it would start at two thousand a week—a hundred thousand a year. We added bonuses if we reach certain levels. How does that sound?"

"It sounds like a bribe," I said.

"Well, you can call it whatever you want. I like to think of it as showing you that you're a valued—and trusted—part of this family."

He emphasized the word "trusted."

But I stumbled on a different word.

"Family," I said.

"That's right."

"You have a pretty strange way of treating your family. Trying to kidnap me. Actually kidnapping my wife. Letting Angel get killed."

"What happened to Angel was a tragic, tragic accident. I've communicated with our partners to the south and I can assure you they punished the person responsible. I saw it with my own two eyes. I know that doesn't do anything to bring your friend back, but we're back to business as usual. They've given me assurances nothing like that is ever going to happen again."

"An assurance from a cartel," I said derisively. "That's very comforting."

"Listen, son, I know you're hot right now. And I get it. But you gotta cool off and think about this for a second. What I told you a few weeks back in my office is true. We're providing a service here—an important, valuable service, giving hardworking people safe transport so they can keep on living their lives in peace. Forget what the law says. The law in this case is messed up. Think about the morality of it. Morally, we're in the right here."

"Great. I'm sure that helps you sleep at night," I shot back. "But you do know, in the long run, you're going to get nailed, right? Even if I don't go to the Joint Task Force, something else will happen. There will be another Melvord Finck, another Joseph Manger. Someone like Dan Gillespie will manage to talk before you can silence him. You've been wildly lucky they haven't caught you yet. It's just a matter of time."

"Well, now, there I have to beg to differ," Lorne said. "We learned from what happened to Melvord. That's why we came up with that box you saw. They've got air-conditioning so no one suffocates. They're lined with lead on the inside so the Border Patrol's X-ray can't see the folks moving around in there. They're even collapsible so they don't take up much room in the truck. We just ship 'em back down and then fill 'em right back up again. Oh, and I forgot the best part. We had an image painted in metal on the outside that bounces off the X-ray just right so that it looks like more boxes—and not like a lead-lined box. It's damn ingenious. I got a picture of it saved on my phone. I'm sending it to you right now."

My phone dinged. Sure enough, there was an X-ray of a forty-foot trailer that looked for all the world like it was filled with boxes of electronics.

"You're telling me there were migrants in that truck?" I asked.

"Sure were. But you can't see 'em, can you? And the proof is in the pudding because we've made hundreds—hell, thousands—of runs with those SSS trucks. They've been inspected at the border. They've never come close to catching us. Most of the time, they don't even open up the back. When they do, they see a wall of boxes. And if they look through that, all they see is another wall of boxes. Border Patrol doesn't have the time or resources to go unloading an entire forty-foot trailer. And if something does happen? Well, we weathered one Melvord Finck. We'll weather whatever else comes our way. Trust me, son. We've got this all worked out. Now come on back to the office, get your wife, and let's put this all to rest."

The offer was clear.

Come back to the family.

Take our $100,000 bribe.

Keep raking in your fat paycheck.

It was plenty seductive.

Too bad it was all a lie.

For however friendly Lorne was sounding at the moment, they hadn't sicced those Norteño men on me because they wanted to have a nice chat. And they weren't having Frisch and Bastian plant a suicide note because they wanted to give me a raise.

I had seen enough of how Balco really operated. They would kill me as soon as they saw me. Then they would kill Page. The only reason they were keeping her alive was to use her as bait. They would come up with some kind of story to explain it all.

We'd never be seen again.

But I couldn't tell Lorne and Sal I had figured that out.

They had to think the lie was still alive.

"Let me think about it," I said.

"What's there to think about?" Lorne asked.

The paternalistic sound was gone from his voice.

"Morality," I said.

It was a word I chose purposefully, because Lorne considered morality his strongest argument. If he thought I was stewing over the morals of the situation, he'd assume I'd eventually stumble into his trap.

Really, I was just trying to buy myself time.

"I understand," Lorne said. "How long do you need?"

"I'm not sure. A few hours. Let's just say until the end of the day."

"By which you mean 5:00 p.m."

"Yes."

"And then you'll come in?"

"Probably, yes. You're right that I . . . I mean, I really don't have a choice."

"Okay. We're going to keep your missus here in the meantime. Just to make sure she stays nice and safe. Oh, and Curt?"

"Yes?"

"I wouldn't go running off to the police if I were you. Seeing blue lights flashing outside the facility might make some people here nervous. Your missus might not be safe after all, you follow me?"

"I do."

"Okay. Good man."

CHAPTER 61

LORNE MURPHY HAD taken the call in the windowless room.

Then he and Sal Salcedo decided that whenever French and Boston came back to headquarters, they would move the Hinton woman to a different location within the facility.

It didn't seem right to keep their captive in the middle of their surveillance nerve center.

They decided Building K-5 made sense. It was a storage building, little used and out of the way. No one, they announced loudly, would trip across her there.

In the meantime, they left her under the semi-watchful eye of the technician. She was bound and gagged, so it wasn't like she was going anywhere.

Then Murphy and Salcedo retreated back to the CEO's office to consider what to do next.

Their options weren't great. The most prudent choice—to shut down operations until they knew Hinton was either back in the fold or silenced—wasn't possible.

There were trucks loaded with passengers headed across the border at that very moment. And Norteño always had a line of paying customers waiting to go next. La Tranquila had made it very clear she would not accept hitting the pause button.

If you get caught, that's your problem.

So: Don't get caught.

"Well, what do you think?" Lorne asked.

"I think an 'I told you so' is in order," Salcedo said.

"Not yet. He's going to take the money. You watch."

"You better hope so."

They mulled over this thought for a moment.

Then Lorne said, "Okay, what if I'm wrong? What do we do then?"

Salcedo sighed and petted his mustache. "Well, at this point, Hinton is in the wind. There's no way he'd be stupid enough to go back to his house. French and Boston can keep watch over the wife. She's not going anywhere. The main threat is if Hinton takes what he knows to the Joint Task Force, so that's what we have to guard against. They have a field office in San Francisco. I can have the Norteño men camp out there and try to intercept him before he makes it inside."

"They would just grab him off the streets of San Francisco in broad daylight? That's risky."

"It's less risky than if he actually talks to the task force."

"True," Lorne admitted.

"Don't get me wrong, I'm still holding out hope the hundred grand is enough of an enticement."

Salcedo paused over this, then added: "But I still think you should call Rig, let him know."

"Good idea," Lorne said.

The CEO took out his phone and made the call.

"There's something going on you need to know about," Lorne said, then described the day's events.

When he was done, Rig asked, “So you think he’s going to take his story to the Joint Task Force?”

“He might,” Lorne allowed.

He did not expect Rig’s answer: “That’s fine. Let him.”

“Come again?”

“Let him,” Rig repeated. “There is no need for againstness.”

CHAPTER 62

IT WAS EASY—morally and otherwise—to decide what I needed to do next.

Joint Task Force 1954 had a field office on Sansome Street in San Francisco. I had to go there and tell them everything.

The difficult part was how I'd get them to believe me.

I had no photographs of what I'd seen, no hard evidence. I was just a guy wandering in off the streets and telling them a wild story about migrants pouring out of trucks—and a seemingly legitimate company that had been smuggling people illegally into the country for years without getting caught. They would rightly treat me with suspicion.

Especially when they learned I had just tendered my resignation at Balco, which was something I would have to tell them; because if they found it out on their own, and I hadn't told them, my credibility would be shot.

Even without that conflict of interest, they would probably decide my testimony alone did not rise to the level of probable cause they needed to get a search warrant of Balco's properties.

They would perform their own investigation, and that would take time. Weeks. Months.

Time I didn't have.

I needed them to act quickly and decisively; to marshal the resources of the federal government, obtain a search warrant, and execute it with shock and awe. This wouldn't be a clumsy blue-light effort from the ham-and-egg locals. It had to descend with such speed and surprise that Lorne and Sal would have their hands bound behind their backs before they had time to react.

It was the only way I could think of to keep Page—and our baby—alive.

To get us out of this safely.

To get us out, period.

Just as that thought was traveling through my mind, a cyclist rode past, and I found myself thinking about, of all people, Sidney Graves.

And why he faked his heart attack.

He had said almost the exact same thing.

I had to get out. It was the only way they'd let me go.

At the time, it hadn't made much sense to me. I had turned it into Sidney Graves being typically over-impressed by his own self-importance.

Now I understood.

Just like me, he knew what Balco really was; or at least he had some inkling that it was not merely a logistics company.

Just like me, he was desperate to escape a criminal enterprise he had probably stumbled into quite unwittingly.

And, just like me, Balco and Norteño would never allow him to walk away voluntarily. It would be seen as suspicious, and he would be thought of as a loose end—as someone who might take what he knew to the authorities once he was out of the operation.

But if he had a health problem serious enough that he was physically incapable of continuing? Well, then it wouldn't be seen as voluntary.

They'd let him slink off to Montana with the rest of the California ex-pats and that would be the end of it.

Most importantly for my purposes at the moment, the fact that he wanted to get out—and he was desperate enough to concoct a pretty elaborate scheme to do so—told me he wasn't really *with* them.

He was the law and order guy; the one who wanted to recall what he perceived as a soft-on-crime district attorney. Being part of a scheme that allowed thousands of people to come into the country illegally was repellant to him.

All of that was easy enough to see.

What I didn't yet know was now the most vital question:

Would he help me?

I didn't know where he lived. But a quick search on my phone gave me an address of a Sidney Graves who lived in nearby San Rafael. Also at the residence was Lisa Graves, so I knew I had the right place.

Without little more than a dim plan forming in my head, I asked the driver to point us in that direction. We agreed that another fifty dollars was sufficient for the ride and for him to wait for me while I conducted some business.

As he drove, I looked down at my clothes. In addition to the puncture wound in my seat—and the now-dried blood that went with it—my suit pants had a six-inch rip in the thigh through which I could see a patch of skin. My jacket had several smaller tears. My shirt was missing a button and was smeared with dirt. My silk tie was ruined.

There was nothing I could do about it now. A few turns after the Marin Yacht Club, where I'm sure Sidney had a boat along with the other local titans of industry, we pulled up to a nicely appointed home. The tasteful wooden gate that guarded the short driveway was open, and my driver pulled in.

I rang the doorbell and waited, hopeful that a man who had just retired—and was pretending to be recovering from a heart attack—would be at home and answering his door in the middle of the morning.

Instead, I got something even better.

His wife.

She also appeared to be in her late fifties. Dressed simply in jeans and a T-shirt, she was long and willowy, with steel gray hair and intense blue eyes.

"Hello, can I help you?"

She was looking at me with all the suspicion that a stranger in a tattered suit deserved. Beyond her, I could see an open brown box next to a shelf of knickknacks and framed family photos. The packing for Montana had obviously begun.

"You must be Lisa," I said.

"Yes."

All I did was blurt the truth: "My wife has been kidnapped by Balco, and I need your husband's help."

As I elaborated, I watched the concern in her face turn into a form of outrage. My disheveled appearance actually lent credibility to what I was saying.

A short while later, Sidney joined her at the door. He was also casually dressed in a T-shirt he had gotten at a bike race and cargo shorts. There was something much more down-to-earth about him now that he was no longer Sidney Graves, corporate gladiator.

I caught him up on the relevant events, telling him about my brush with Norteño and what I'd seen in K-12.

"Smuggling immigrants, huh?" he said at one point, punctuating the comment with an ambiguous headshake.

I finished by telling him how Sal Salcedo had taken Page as collateral and making my plea.

"A wise man once told me I'd never know when I'd need a favor in this world," I said. "It turns out that time is now. I kept your secret, Sidney. Will you please help me?"

Before he could say a word, his wife answered for him. "Yes, of course. We'll do whatever we can."

Sidney wrapped an arm around her in solidarity. "Why don't you come inside?"

Over the next half hour or so, Sidney unspooled the entirety of his Balco experience.

He had been vice president of finance at a competitor seven years earlier when a recruiter approached and asked if he'd be interested in becoming CFO at Balco.

The recruiter was honest about a secret that few knew: For whatever image Balco projected, the company was on shaky fiscal ground.

That had actually been part of what lured Sidney in. He thought he could help turn things around.

Once he got in the job, he realized the problems were essentially structural and ran far deeper than he had been led to believe. Whatever advantage Balco had enjoyed as the first logistics company to bet big in Mexico had slowly eroded until it disappeared. Everyone was now in Mexico—including some bigger players, whose size made them ever-so-slightly more efficient, allowing them to undercut Balco on price.

It had been an effort just to keep revenues stagnant. But costs kept growing. Rig's long-standing pride about never laying off anyone, no matter what, certainly didn't help. Eventually, Balco was in the red, hemorrhaging more money with each passing quarter.

No one outside a small circle knew it, of course. Balco's books were private, and Rig projected a veneer of success and prosperity, for however eccentric that image may have been.

Behind the scenes, however, there was considerable discontent.

"Not many people know this, but Rig Weiskopf is actually not the majority owner," Sidney explained. "In addition to his initial investors, he had to sell off parts of the company to keep it afloat through those early years. He only owns about thirty-five percent of the shares."

"Yeah, he told me about the roulette table, betting it all on seventeen."

Sidney frowned. "I don't know why Lorne makes him tell that story. Especially because it's a lie. Rig admitted it to me one time when he was tripping. He actually stole the story from the founder of FedEx—except the FedEx guy did it with blackjack, not roulette, I think. You know how Rig raised the money to keep Balco going? He took a truck down to Tijuana, loaded it up with pot and coke and heroin, and paid off a rancher he knew down there to let him drive the truck across an open section of border in the desert. I guess Rig knew dealers from surfing—there are a lot of drugs on the beach—and he sold it to them for a nice profit. That's how he got the thirty grand or whatever it was he needed for that rent payment."

"So what about all that man on the mountain, 'don't be against this, don't be against that' stuff? That doesn't seem to square with a guy who would sell drugs to keep his company going."

"As I understand it, that came later," Sidney said. "It's a lot easier to be philosophical when you've got millions of dollars in the bank."

"Don't you mean billions?"

"Not exactly. I don't want to make him sound like he's living hand-to-mouth, but Rig isn't as wealthy as you might think. Growing Balco was this obsession for him. There were a lot of years when he took almost all of Balco's profits and reinvested them to keep that growth happening. You might say he was company rich but cash poor. So, when the profits dried up, he didn't have a lot to fall back on. And the other owners weren't interested in going into debt just to cover operating expenses.

"Which gets me back to what I was saying: Rig is actually minority owner. Most of the time, his thirty-five percent was enough to keep him in charge, because the other sixty-five percent wasn't owned by a cohesive block of people. But after enough unprofitable quarters in a row, Balco was about to burn through the last of its operating reserves. That meant Rig and the other investors were either going to have to borrow money or start cutting checks to keep the company afloat. If I've learned nothing else from years in finance, it's that rich people hate cutting checks. The rest of the investors got together and delivered Rig an ultimatum: turn Balco around, or they would find a buyer and sell all their shares to someone who would then be majority owner."

"Meaning Rig was going to lose his baby," I said.

"Exactly. He couldn't stand to see everything he had built get hacked up into pieces. And—I really believe this—he also knew it would be bad for all the people who worked there, people he truly cares about. That part is real for him—and for Lorne, who at that point was running the show in Mexico. Those two are very different, obviously, but if there's one thing that unites them it's this . . . kind of pathological need to be liked, I guess. I told them repeatedly the only way to survive was to cut head count, and they just wouldn't hear of it. They said they'd figure out something.

"The next thing I knew, there was suddenly all this extra money coming in from Mexico. And it was all in cash. Lorne called them 'microshipments' and created this whole thing about how it was coming from this new division, Specialized Shipping Services. Everything about SSS was made to look aboveboard. There were invoices and everything. I suspected . . . well, I knew it was fraudulent somehow. But they put just enough paperwork around it to give it a veneer of legitimacy. We were quite scrupulous about treating it like normal revenue and continuing to report it. We came up with accounting codes for it and everything. That's the funny thing about the IRS, of course. As long as you report all your income, they don't care where it's coming from. So we were very lawful about our illegal activities and I just . . . I just went along with it. I mean, hey, we were back in the black. We didn't have to do layoffs. Life was good, right?"

He smiled crookedly for a moment, then looked down at his hands, as if they had blood on them.

Lisa put her hand on her husband's back. "Sidney was kind of like the frog in the pot being slowly brought to a boil. He just didn't realize how hot the water was until it was too late."

"As time went along, I became aware we had this . . . relationship, I guess you could say, with Norteño," Sidney continued. "Then Rig stepped down as CEO and Lorne took over. Part of it was that Rig was just ready to retire and spend more time surfing. Part of it was that Rig knew he needed to focus more on being chairman of the board and making sure the other investors stayed happy. And part of it was a reward to Lorne for creating SSS. Honestly, I thought this whole time we were just laundering money for Norteño. Up until what you just told me, I never knew it was immigrants. I knew we had the SSS trucks, but I thought that was just for show—like the fake invoices. That's how good they were at hiding it."

"How big *is* SSS?" I asked.

"Big enough that it made up the budget hole we were in and also accounts for all of Balco's profits. From a revenue standpoint, it's around three hundred million a year, with twenty-five percent going to expenses. That's part of how I knew it was fake right away. The math was too simple. Each microshipment brings in eight thousand dollars, with two thousand in expenses. I'm now realizing, of course, that a microshipment is really a person—which means Balco keeps seventy-five percent, and kicks back twenty-five percent to Norteño. From what I understood, Norteño was trying to up it to thirty, but Lorne wasn't having it."

"Oh God," I said. "*Veinticinco* and *Treinta*."

"Excuse me?"

I told him about how I had found Johnny at the scene of the carjacking; and how, over a breakfast burrito, Johnny had told me what he overheard during Angel's abduction.

Twenty-five and thirty.

Angel wasn't just spouting random numbers. He was referencing a negotiation that had become contentious.

I let that wash over me for a sickening second or two.

My best friend had been killed over an additional 5 percent.

As I mulled that, Sidney—ever the accountant—had gone to work with the calculator on his phone and tossing out numbers. Three hundred million was a staggering 37,500 people a year.

Divided by 365—because there were shipments every day, and the business of Balco will stop for nothing—that was a little more than a hundred people a day.

Or four SSS shipments.

They comprised a small percentage of the total trucks we had going in and out, and they hid in plain sight.

Maybe three went to Long Beach and one went to Oakland. Maybe it was two and two. Maybe some times of year—like when crops needed harvesting—were busier and some times of year there were fewer shipments.

Whatever the case, they were loaded in Mexico—perhaps in secret, perhaps not. I couldn't imagine there were as many qualms about the legality of it on that side of the border.

They were then brought north and unloaded on this side without the need for any human hands to be involved. It was easy enough to have them slip in amidst all the other shipments. They were essentially hidden by volume.

Once he had worked that out, Sidney put away his calculator and finished his own story.

"I hated knowing that we were working with a cartel in any capacity. I had told Rig and Lorne I wanted out, but they wouldn't hear it. They said I knew too much, and La Tranquila would never let me walk away."

"Were you getting the dividend?" I asked out of curiosity as much as anything.

"Shamefully, yes. It was one of the ways they kept me in the fold. It's maybe a little disingenuous to say they forced it on me. But they didn't really give me a choice. As long as I was accepting the money, it kept me complicit, which is what they wanted. I was still desperate to get out. Angel's murder was really the last straw, or the wake-up call, or whatever you want to call it. I knew I couldn't keep on keeping on."

Lisa rubbed his back some more as he continued. "Finally, I went to Lorne and Sal and said I was leaving no matter what La Tranquila had to say about it. As what you might call my insurance policy, I made copies of all the documents relating to SSS, then provided a detailed explanation of what they really meant so a forensic accountant could follow everything. I have one copy here, but I put another copy in a safe deposit box. I told them that if anything suspicious happened to me—anything other than dying of very, very natural causes—my will stated that the documents should be sent to the authorities.

"It was actually Sal's idea to fake the heart attack. He had me go to the Czech Republic and pay off a doctor to generate the medical records. He figured that would be far enough away that it was out of the cartel's reach. Then I hired a professional makeup person—there are a lot of movies shot in Prague, apparently—who made me look like a heart attack victim with a big scar. Everyone still acted like it was real, of course. It was all about giving a plausible story to La Tranquila. I think that's why I took the risk of going on that bike ride. Even if I got seen by someone at Balco, they would just say something to Sal or Lorne, who already knew the truth. But I guess more than anything, I hoped that if we disappeared to Montana, Norteño and La Tranquila would eventually just forget about me."

In the time it had taken Sidney to unburden himself, I realized I had actually grown to like him; so much that it was actually hard to utter what I had to say next.

But I needed him to see the truth as I saw it.

"So you know they might . . . but they also might not," I said.

"We've thought about that many times," he said, looking again at Lisa. "In the end, we decided it was worth the risk. Anything was better than staying at Balco and feeling like I was constantly in the crosshairs."

"You know there's really only one way to keep you safe forever. And that's to get the entire operation shut down for good."

"The thought has definitely occurred to me," Sidney said. "But I just didn't have the courage to take this to law enforcement myself. I feel like I'd just be drawing a big target on my back if Norteño found out I was the one who snitched. And I don't trust the feds to protect my identity."

And then he looked at me meaningfully and said: "But if someone else snitched, I'd certainly give them a copy of the SSS documents, as long as they didn't say where they got them from. That person would still be taking a big risk, though."

"They have my wife," I said. "It's a risk I'm willing to take."

CHAPTER 63

THE RELEVANT DOCUMENTS filled a large banker's box.

Once Sidney had retrieved it from a hiding spot in the attic, he walked me through the summary he had written so I understood it and could translate it for someone without an accounting background.

Then he and Lisa walked me back to the car and wished me luck.

Another hundred dollars later, we were pointed toward San Francisco and the U.S. Appraisers Building, home to Joint Task Force 1954. It was ten thirty in the morning, so traffic was light.

It still felt like five o'clock was coming altogether too fast.

As we merged on 101 south, I did some scouting of our destination on my phone, looking at all the potential approaches on Google Maps street view.

I was assuming that Sal Salcedo knew where Joint Task Force 1954 was located, too. Between the Norteño men and Frisch and Bastian, someone might be looking for me there. I needed to be prepared for it.

There was one main entrance on Sansome Street. Like a lot of federal buildings, it had stout concrete stanchions outside—so no one could drive a vehicle laden with explosives into the lobby.

Federal buildings had long been considered targets.

But maybe I could use that to my advantage.

We crossed over the Golden Gate Bridge and made our way to Sansome Street, which was at the edge of Chinatown. As we neared the U.S. Appraisers Building, I asked the driver if he wouldn't mind doing a quick spin around the block, so I could get a sense if anyone was looking for me.

I ducked low in the back seat as we circled. There were long lines of people queued up alongside the building, which also housed ICE, U.S. Customs and Immigrations Services, and a host of other government agencies that excelled at making people wait a long time for things.

There didn't seem to be anything suspicious about anyone until I got a little farther from the entrance.

Then, on the southwest corner, at the end of one of the lines, I spotted a few familiar-looking *vatos* hiding under their stiff-brimmed hats.

On the northwest corner, it was the same thing. There was also a white van parked in a nearby loading spot with its flashers going.

It was the same white van that was supposed to collect me earlier in the day.

They were obviously hoping I'd approach the building on foot—and unawares—and planned to snatch me before I made it inside.

But they weren't getting too close to the entrance, and I already knew why. There was a metal detector staffed by federal marshals just inside. The marshals would get suspicious if they saw the same shady characters hanging around out there all day.

The *vatos* didn't like too much attention. Especially attention from federal authorities. That's what I would exploit.

As we completed our circumnavigation of the building, my driver asked, "What now?"

"For another hundred bucks, would you pull up on the curb by those concrete stanchions and start honking your horn like crazy?"

He assured me he could. And for another hundred beyond that, he was willing to wait for me for an hour. We exchanged phone numbers in case I was still inside and needed to buy more time beyond that.

The driver executed the plan to perfection. As soon as he began beeping the horn, everyone in line was quite naturally staring at us.

About ten seconds after that, two marshals emerged from the building to find out what the hell was going on.

Little did they know it—they were my escorts.

"Okay, you can stop honking," I said. "I'll text you when I'm coming out. You can meet me here."

I got out of the car with my banker's box. My driver pulled away. The marshals—two guys in blue blazers—were now looking at me like they weren't sure what to do about me.

"Don't mind him," I said, nodding toward the Hyundai. "His horn gets a little stuck."

My box and I passed through security easily enough. Thankfully, there was nothing in their regulations about forbidding entry to men in ripped suits.

I was shunted to a security desk, where I told another marshal that I had a matter of concern for Joint Task Force 1954 and wanted to talk to one of their agents. He made a phone call and told me someone would be down soon.

After a ten-minute wait, I was riding an elevator up to the eighth floor with a barrel-chested guy a few inches taller than me. He introduced himself as Agent Matthew Kirkwood.

As I entered the small lobby for Joint Task Force 1954, I was greeted by two rows of official portraits of people in suits. The top row consisted of the United States president, the vice president, and the attorney general.

They're very big on their chain of command in the executive branch.

Kirkwood led me into a conference room, where he introduced me to Agent Adam Marcia, a smaller man with sapphire blue eyes.

Setting my box down in front of me, I began talking. The words poured out of me quickly. I told them I was vice president for corporate communications at Bay Area Logistics Company, aka Balco, which was located near the Port of Oakland, and that it had been perpetrating a major, years-long scheme to smuggle tens of thousands of undocumented people into the country illegally.

I then described the Specialized Shipping Services trailers and how they had been outfitted to elude detection by Border Patrol and anyone else who might decide to inspect them.

Then I told them about L-11 and K-12, the tunnels that led out of them, and the scores of people who made the trip every day.

I thought this revelation would be incendiary; something that would really set them on fire. I couldn't say I knew much about Joint Task Force 1954, but I had seen the press releases on its website.

They touted arrests of people like Melvord Finck, who was responsible for smuggling a mere twenty-eight people. Other operations were larger—fifty, a hundred, five hundred.

There was nothing in the thousands. And here I was, telling them about a ring responsible for tens of thousands.

Yet Kirkwood and Marcia seemed oddly disinterested. At times, I wasn't even sure if they were listening.

Was I too keyed up? Was I talking too fast? Was it my ragtag appearance that made them think I was somewhere between unreliable and mentally ill?

I moved on to the documents next.

These were really my smoking gun, the evidence that went beyond mere storytelling and really established the scheme in undeniable black and white.

It didn't move Kirkwood or Marcia any more than my narrative had.

They let me finish. Then Kirkwood informed me, "We appreciate your information, Mr. Hinton. Our office has looked into Balco in the past. There's really nothing there."

I swore something inside me was going to burst.

"No, no, you don't get it. That was the Melvord Finck case. I know all about that. My understanding is they convinced you guys to back off. But they've gotten much, much more sophisticated since then. That was really just the tiny tip of a huge iceberg."

"Yes, sir, we understand," Marcia said.

He shot a glance at Kirkwood and allowed, "We'll look into this."

"And what does that mean?"

"We're not prepared to discuss our investigative strategies with you, sir," Kirkwood said, clearly annoyed. "When we say we'll look into this, it means we'll look into it."

Marcia's sapphire eyes might as well have been stone walls now.

I wasn't getting anywhere with these guys.

"Well, okay," I said, then gestured to the box. "Would you like me to . . . Can I at least leave this with you and ask you to have a forensic accountant look into it? I think they'll . . . I think they'll find it very compelling."

"That's kind of you, sir, thank you," Kirkwood said. "If we feel that's necessary, we'll certainly reach out."

The next thing I knew, they were shooing me out of the office like they were in a hurry to get rid of me.

As I passed back out into their lobby, it was all I could do not to yell at the portrait of the president.

This is why you'll never be able to get a handle on illegal immigration.

I was baffled.

Then, for the first time, I looked at the second row of portraits.

All it took was seeing one image to understand what was really going on.

The director of Joint Task Force 1954, pictured in that second row, was a man named Patrick Dee.

He had a woolly beard that covered the entirety of his face.

Just like Sasquatch.

It was the man I had seen in that picture at Rig Weiskopf's surfing hut.

CHAPTER 64

AFTER MOVING THE Hinton woman to Building K-5, French and Boston had settled in and were trying to make themselves comfortable.

French was sitting on a box.

Boston had found an old folding chair.

Their captive was on the ground, still bound and gagged.

"Well, here we are, hanging out with the pregnant bitch again," French announced.

Boston just shook his head.

They returned to silence, which was broken when they heard a door opening and footsteps coming their way.

An older man with side-parted gray hair and a loose-fitting blazer was approaching.

"Who are you?" French asked, standing.

"Bob Brunato," he said. "I'm the public and media relations director. Sal told me you guys were in here with her."

"What do you want?"

"My car is parked right outside," he said, then jerked his head toward Hinton. "Help me get her loaded in my trunk."

"And why are we doing that?" French asked.

"Because I'm the one who's going to kill her and make sure her body is never found," Brunato replied, matter-of-factly. "You really need all the gory details?"

"I guess not," French said. "But I got something I need to do with her first."

"What's that?"

French made a thrusting motion with his pelvis.

"Oh, come on," Brunato said, jamming his fists in his sides. "I don't have time for that."

French pulled a pistol out of his pocket and pointed it at Brunato.

"Yeah, you do," he said, then gestured with the gun. "Give us a little space, please. I don't like to be crowded."

Brunato immediately backed away.

"You can watch if you want," French added. "Don't worry, it won't take me long."

The woman screamed into her gag, but that did little good. If anything, it only made French more excited as he unbuckled his belt.

Then he knelt next to the woman and began tugging at her yoga pants. She writhed and squirmed, making it as difficult for him as possible.

He was putting such an effort into disrobing her that he didn't notice that Boston had walked up behind him.

Or that Boston had unholstered his pistol and aimed it at his partner's head.

Boston pulled the trigger twice.

The gun emitted a muted *thump, thump*.

French slumped forward.

Page screamed into her gag.

Brunato stood frozen in place as he waited for Boston's next move.

But the man just returned his gun to his holster.

"Why did you do that?" Brunato asked. "I'm going to have to kill her anyway. Who cares if he rapes her?"

"You do what you have to do. That's not on me. I just couldn't stand back and watch him do that to her."

And then he added, "My daughter has red hair."

Brunato nodded. "Mind helping me carry her out?"

"Sure."

It didn't take them long. Soon, Brunato was driving out of the facility, with the woman in his trunk.

He waved to the guard, who didn't think anything about it.

Bob Brunato coming and going was nothing unusual.

He had been doing it for years.

About a mile down the road, Brunato pulled off to the side.

He removed a utility knife out of his glove compartment and went around to his trunk, which he opened.

Hinton's eyes went wide when she saw the knife.

"Relax, I'm not going to hurt you," he said. "I'm rescuing you."

And then he began cutting away her restraints.

"That was crazy back there. I didn't know if they'd buy my story or not. When that ape started talking about how he wanted to have his way with you . . . I was freaked out."

He gently cut away the rope that had kept the gag in place and removed the cloth they had stuffed in her mouth to keep her quiet.

She coughed a few times, then managed, "How did you realize I was in trouble? How did you even know where to find me?"

"I had been trying to get ahold of Curt all morning. He wasn't answering his phone or his email," Brunato said. "That put me on alert that something was off. Curt is as reliable as sunrise. I don't want to say I was already assuming the worst, but . . . well, I pay attention. Between Angel and Dan Gillespie and even that creep Joseph Manger, a lot of people have been dying. Plus, I saw those strange Mexican guys running around. I've been wondering what the heck is going on for a while now. When I saw those goons taking you into Building K-5, I just knew something terrible was happening. So I acted."

"I don't even know what to . . . How can I ever thank you?"

"I just did what anyone would have done," he said as he helped her climb out of the trunk.

"Still, I—"

"You know one of the first things I told your husband when I met him? Family is everything," Bob said. "You getting to be with your family? That's thanks enough for me."

He escorted her around to the passenger's side of the car, holding open the door for her.

Once she was settled into her seat, he held out her cell phone, which she gratefully accepted.

"Now why don't you call Curt," he said. "Let's get you two kids reunited."

"Shouldn't we call the police?" she asked.

"Well, of course, eventually. But let's find Curt first."

CHAPTER 65

AS I TEXTED my driver to meet me out front—and under the watchful eye of the federal marshals—everything fell into place in my mind.

Rig had even told me what was going on, in his own Rig way, when I first learned about Melvord Finck. I just hadn't understood him at the time.

It was just a matter of working with *the task force rather than engaging in againstness.*

Five years ago, Rig had persuaded the director of Joint Task Force 1954 to be with him, to give Melvord Finck a nice plea deal, and to leave Balco trucks alone.

But I sincerely doubted Patrick Dee had done this out of the kindness of his heart or a belief that it was okay to let a few thousand migrants slip through because it was good for an American logistics company.

Rig had bribed him.

How much had it cost? Did it involve sacks of cash? Or gold bars? Did Dee get a bounty for every truck or a flat annual fee?

I would only be guessing.

What was clear was that Rig had kept it secret from everyone at Balco—his CSO, the CFO, even the CEO.

La Tranquila and the rest of the cartel didn't know, either. They wouldn't have been so worried about me slipping into the U.S. Appraisers Building if they did.

It may have been that Rig didn't trust any of these people with the knowledge that he was bribing a high-level government official. It may have been part of his deal with Dee.

But I think it was more than that. Rig still wanted Balco to carry forth with ultimate caution. The company had to keep acting like it couldn't afford to slip up or get caught.

Really, the bribe was just an additional safeguard—like lighting in the warehouse, or Rig's approach to shark attacks.

You do what you can to mitigate the risks and then you move on.

Having figured this out still didn't help me plan my next move.

With the federal task force compromised, where could I turn? To Mando Fierro and the Oakland Police? No. I honestly didn't have much confidence in an under-resourced, overextended local police force that wouldn't know where to start.

To another federal agency? Maybe. But which one? And how would I know Rig hadn't bribed them, too?

I was already at the front entrance to the building. When I saw the Hyundai pull up, I made a run for it as best I could while lugging my box.

"Where to?" my driver asked as soon as the door was shut.

"Just go."

As we zoomed along the streets, driving toward nowhere, I realized I had to stop thinking about Balco and its immigration scheme.

All that really mattered was Page.

How was I going to get her out of the grip of people who wouldn't hesitate to do her harm? And do it by my five o'clock deadline?

Should I just offer to trade myself for her?

After all, I was the threat, the one who had seen too much and knew too much.

Could I leverage the documents that were riding along with me in the back seat?

That might work. As long as they didn't know how terribly uninterested Joint Task Force 1954 was in having them.

But how could I assure that Page would be able to get away safely?

I was still trying to come up with something when my phone rang. I looked down and felt a jolt when I saw what came up on the screen.

It was my phone's one and only contact.

"Hello?" I said unsteadily, thinking it was Salcedo calling to troll me or threaten me or make some new demand.

Instead, I heard the sweetest, most beautiful sound in the entire world.

"Hello, my love," Page said.

"Page!" I practically shouted. "What's going on? Are you okay?"

Once I stopped gushing questions at her, she told me the harrowing tale of how Bob Brunato had heroically helped her escape—from his intuition that she was in trouble, to his daring intervention in Building K-5, to how she was saved from sexual assault by Bastian's sudden attack of conscience, to the way Brunato secreted her out in his trunk under the guise that he was going to kill her.

It was thrilling.

And incredible.

And I might have been ready to name our unborn child after Bob, except for one thing.

It had been too easy.

There was no way Bob Brunato, of all people, should have been able to just stroll in and walk out with such an important hostage.

And then toss her in the trunk of his car.

And then drive out.

Without anyone noticing or saying anything?

Shouldn't the thugs have interrogated Bob a little more? Wouldn't they have deemed it odd that the director of public and media relations was also the company's go-to hit man?

More than anything, these weren't men who were hired to think on their own. The first thing they would have done under strange circumstances was call Sal Salcedo. That was their training, to say nothing of their instincts and their default position.

Yet Sal had never been consulted?

Not once?

It struck me that the whole thing had been orchestrated to make Page *think* she was being rescued.

Really, it was just their clever way of getting her out into the world and "free" so she could lead them straight to me.

The scheme nearly worked because, of course, they thought I would trust Bob Brunato.

But, really, should I?

Who had been the first person to tell me that IWW-Local 37 was behind Angel's killing—a trail that proved to be false?

Bob Brunato.

He had probably been taking orders from Sal Salcedo all along, feeding me false information that I eagerly gobbled up like the most gullible of cub reporters.

The whole story of IWW-Local 37 had been concocted by Salcedo so that I would blame someone else for Angel's death and not interrogate the situation too closely.

After all, Neil Rees hadn't really been in two places at once. The only say-so I had that Neil Rees had been caught by supposed AI facial recognition software had come from Sal.

It was a lie.

Really, the man whose legs I saw running toward that pickup truck wasn't a member education specialist. He was a cartel thug.

Likewise, the story about Dan Gillespie's truck stopping at a Carl's Jr.—where the explosives had supposedly been planted—had come straight from Sal. Wasn't it a lot more plausible that the bomb had been planted in the hours while the truck was at the Balco facility rather than the minutes it was at Carl's Jr.?

For that matter—and this was just now dawning on me for the first time—when had those minutes happened? Rig had called me at 5:47 a.m. The accident had taken place roughly thirty minutes before.

I was more familiar with Carl's Jr.'s more easterly cousin, Hardee's, where I sometimes had breakfast when I was a reporter. But a quick search confirmed for me there was something Hardee's and Carl's Jr. shared beyond their yellow star logo.

Neither one opened until 6:00 a.m.

Dan Gillespie had never stopped at a Carl's Jr.

Sal had invented that detail.

And who had told me about the nickname "Mad Bomber" in the first place? Again, Sal.

So this "rescue" of Page was really Bob Brunato doing Sal's bidding. In his own way, Bob had even once admitted it to me: *Everyone knows I'm the ultimate company man.*

The real tip-off that the story was a false front was that Page had called me from her phone.

If Bob Brunato was sneaking her out of the facility, how would he possibly have gotten her phone back? The last people to have it were Sal and Lorne. There was no reason they would have given it to Bob.

As I finished reasoning this through, Page had been gushing about how selfless and brave Bob had been.

I couldn't tell her that I had figured out the whole thing was a sham. There was too great a chance that Bob would overhear it, and I didn't want Sal and his thugs to be aware that I was onto them.

My only advantage here was surprise.

It was clear this was a trap.

Now I had to figure out a way to get us out of it.

I needed time to think, so I interrupted Page's extolling of Bob.

"Hey, honey, my phone is about to run out of battery," I lied. "If we get cut off, it might take me a moment or two to find a place to charge it. I'm on foot right now."

"On foot?"

"Yeah, it's a long story."

"Okay, quickly then, just tell us where to meet you."

"Yeah, sure," I began. "I'm in—"

And then I pressed the END CALL button.

CHAPTER 66

BOB BRUNATO HAD his hands fixed at ten and two on the steering wheel, ever the model of a responsible driver.

Of all the things he had been asked to do in his thirty-three years at Balco, this had to be the strangest.

But they offered him a generous bonus. Something that would cover the trip to the Polynesian Islands his wife had been talking about.

After he heard that, he wasn't going to ask too many questions.

He seldom did.

Mostly, he just wanted to get this over with.

He looked over at the Hinton woman, who was staring at her phone like it had betrayed her.

"His battery died," she said.

"You're kidding."

"I wish I was."

"Do you guys have location sharing on with the Find My Phone app?" he suggested.

"These are brand-new phones. We hadn't set that up yet."

Brunato grunted. "Well, we shouldn't just stay here. Balco is going to notice you're gone and then they'll sound the alarm."

"Yeah, for sure."

"Where do you think Curt would have gone?"

"He said he was on foot. So he couldn't have gotten too far. Maybe just drive around?"

"Sure."

He hefted a sigh. Then he glanced in his rearview mirror.

Two vans were there, ready to follow him, hanging back so it wouldn't be too obvious.

Who were the men in those vans?

One more question he wouldn't be asking.

He eased the car away and pointed north, so they would be in one of the neighborhoods near the freeway. He was careful not to make any radical turns or anything that made him difficult to follow. He also mostly kept his eyes forward, so it wouldn't seem like he was checking the rearview mirror every few seconds.

It was stressful. His hands stayed at ten and two the whole time.

Fifteen minutes passed.

Then twenty.

"I'm just going to pull over here," he said, when he reached a straightaway with ample parking—for him and the vans. "They won't be able to find us here."

"Sure," the Hinton woman said.

"I wonder what's taking him so long?"

"Who knows? I just hope he's okay."

"I'm sure he's fine."

He brought the car to a stop, then allowed his eyes to flit up to the mirror for a moment.

The vans were still there.

This would be worth it when they made it to Bora Bora.

The Hinton woman began chattering about Balco and peppering him with questions. He professed not to know anything.

Finally, her phone rang.

"It's him!" she proclaimed.

She answered the call, listened intently for a moment, then said, "He's in San Francisco. He said he'll meet us at the statue in Union Square."

CHAPTER 67

I ENDED THE call with Page quickly, on the pretense that I wanted to preserve what scant battery I had left.

In reality, it was too nerve-wracking, keeping up a stream of fake dialogue for Bob Brunato's benefit.

Also, I needed to make sure everything was in place.

I was already at Union Square. My driver was nearby, ready to go if need be, having been well-compensated for his continued patience.

My hope was that everything would go as planned and I wouldn't need him much longer.

Union Square was looking the part, filled with the usual mix of tourists, unhoused people, and shoppers from all over the planet. They were arrayed on the steps, sitting at the tables stationed around the plaza, eating leisurely lunches.

The temperature was in the upper sixties, which was balmy for San Francisco, and the sun worshippers were making the most of it.

Nearby, people traipsed in and out of the Macy's, the Saks Fifth Avenue, the Nieman Marcus, the Tiffany & Co., and all the other monuments to consumerism that ringed the square.

There were no cops anywhere, because this was liberal San Francisco, and an overt police presence had long been unpopular with the populace. Stores that wanted to deter shoplifters hired their own private security forces.

What this meant was, for better or worse, what was about to happen would take place without interruption from law enforcement.

I had stationed myself at the base of the statue. It was in the middle of the plaza, which was elevated and had a covering of trees around the edges that prevented me from seeing what was taking place on the streets below.

Without knowing what direction Page would be coming from, I just kept shifting my attention between the four corners of the plaza, where there were stairs that provided entry to the space.

How much longer would it take her to show up?

I had already checked traffic on my phone. The Bay Bridge appeared in green, with only a few spots of yellow near the exits, which told me it was rolling along smoothly.

They should have been here by now, shouldn't they?

Had something gone wrong?

The minutes dragged by with agonizing slowness. I felt like my whole body was one big aneurysm on the verge of bursting.

If I lost Page—if this didn't work—I would probably beg for an end that was quick.

I was trying to keep myself focused on what I had to do, but images of her kept floating in and out of my head.

Her swatting my butt as I teased her before my first day at Balco.

Her looking serenely at me while sitting at the kitchen island, with the lights above catching the highlights in her hair.

Her lying in bed that morning, which was the last time I saw her.

I should have just grabbed her and ran as far away as possible.

Page was my world. Our baby was my world. I had always known that, but somehow I had let them both out of my sight during all those thirteen-hour days and work weekends.

It was a mistake I wouldn't make again.

If only I'd get a second chance.

I continued scanning the crowd around me, hoping and praying I would see that dancer's stride of hers coming my way.

Finally, there she was, about forty yards away, coming up the steps. She was scanning the crowd for me.

Bob Brunato was just behind her.

For a moment, I thought perhaps they were alone and I had been wrong about Bob's treachery.

But no.

Not far behind her, hanging just a little farther back, were several men from Norteño. I recognized the gold-toothed one who had been grinning at me so maliciously earlier in the day. He had a hat on and was making an effort to blend with the crowd, but his real purpose was perfectly clear.

He and his confederates were ready to pounce.

Which is what I had expected.

"Page," I shouted.

Her head swiveled toward me.

She rewarded me with the smile that had been melting my heart since our first date.

Then I did something that probably made no sense to her.

I held my hands over my head and clapped four times.

She was now walking toward me faster than before, all determination and direction.

That's when I felt a hand on my shoulder.

"Don't worry. We're here," I heard a man say.

It was Neil Rees, the IWW member education specialist, who I had recently met for the first time.

He was carrying a baseball bat. Immediately behind him were six other members of IWW-Local 37, who also looked like they were ready for a company softball game.

Five more union men were coming in from my left, from a table where they had been sitting.

Plus another ten from my right, from a hiding spot under some trees.

And that was only the start.

It was my good fortune that Rudy Szymanski had not been one to exaggerate. He really *could* get a hundred guys with baseball bats to show up anywhere in a heartbeat.

And when he heard that the people who killed Angel Reddish had also kidnapped my wife, he was eager to help. It certainly helped that, as a union president, he wasn't a fan of anything that smacked of an effort to import cheap labor into the country.

In actuality, the force he mustered numbered about seventy. But that was plenty enough. They were now pouring in from every direction.

All of them had bats, or clubs, or tire irons. And they were gripping their weapons in a way that suggested they were comfortable using them.

Sometimes might did make right.

The Norteño men were faltering.

They hadn't been expecting any resistance, much less a coordinated effort. This had led to confusion in the ranks. They were at a standstill.

Plus, they were outnumbered at least five to one, maybe more.

As soon as Page reached me, the IWW people formed a clump around us.

"What's going on?" she asked.

"I made some friends. I'll explain later."

Bob Brunato had stopped walking a few strides short of us. This obviously wasn't what he had been expecting, either. He was just looking on curiously as more union members continued to gather, forming a protective shield of humanity around us that was now several layers thick.

Then he did a very Bob Brunato thing.

He shoved his hands in his pockets, put his head down, and walked away like this hadn't been his deal to start with. He was taking no responsibility for whatever happened next.

I just let him go.

Bob was the least of my concerns.

"All right, guys, let's move out," I called.

More or less in unison, we started making our way south. Page had entered from the north. That's where the Norteño men remained, still stalled by indecision.

They didn't come after us.

It would have been futile.

Our destination was only four blocks away. My driver was following us, rolling along slowly with his flashers on. He knew there was another hundred bucks waiting for him once we made it to our destination.

Before long, we were there: the entrance of the *San Francisco Chronicle* building.

I was done with appeals to law enforcement. I didn't know who would help me or who was in Rig's ample pocket.

The Fourth Estate was the one institution I knew I could trust.

I stopped at the car, took out the banker's box filled with financial documents, and paid my driver the last of the money that I owed him.

Then I walked into the lobby and asked the front desk to tell Ron Talbot I was here, and that I was ready to start talking. I had promised him the scoop of a lifetime, and I was ready to deliver.

Once upon a time, I might have tried to write all this myself. But it wasn't my job to create stories anymore.

It was my job to plant them and hope they grew into something wonderful.

Because I was the flack.

CHAPTER 68

OVER THE COMING days and weeks, it all came out.

Unlike Ron Talbot's stories about Maria, which were barely noticed, his Balco series prompted public outrage that brought about rapid results.

This was no longer merely about immigration.

It was about public corruption of the highest order.

Sidney Graves's documents—which established a paper trail of thousands of illegal crossings—formed the backbone of Talbot's first piece, which ran on A1, above the fold, and at the top of the *Chronicle*'s website.

Ron also interviewed members of Joint Task Force 1954, giving them anonymity so they could speak freely. They reported they had been specifically instructed by Patrick Dee to leave Balco trucks alone.

Dee told his people it was because Balco had threatened legal action after the Melvord Finck case and he didn't want to further antagonize a legitimate company when there were so many other targets for the task force to take aim at.

But, really, Balco's free pass was bought and paid for, just as I suspected.

After Talbot's first story hit, federal agents raided Patrick Dee's townhouse in northwest Washington, D.C. They didn't find any sacks of cash or gold bars.

But they did find paintings.

A Rothko. Two Andy Warhols. A Jackson Pollock. There were also some lesser known artists that were still plenty valuable.

Rig had been bribing Dee with art; which was, in many ways, the ultimate untraceable currency.

High-end auction houses were altogether too happy to keep sellers' names anonymous and direct the proceeds to their Swiss bank of choice, their numbered account in the Caribbean, or any other place where the wealthy sheltered their money from scrutiny.

At the same time that the FBI moved in on Patrick Dee in Washington, Lorne Murphy and Sal Salcedo were arrested in California.

Both began almost immediately cooperating with the authorities, informing on each other in hopes of negotiating a better deal.

There was also a warrant executed on Balco's facilities in Long Beach and Oakland. The SSS buildings, L-11 and K-12, were extensively photographed. The hands-free nature of their inner workings was laid bare—along with the tunnels, which were easily discovered.

In the days that followed, the FBI's Financial Crimes Unit turned out to be a lot more interested in Sidney Graves's SSS documents than Joint Task Force 1954 had been.

The resulting charging documents went on for many pages.

A warrant for La Tranquila was also issued.

She was charged with, among other things, the murder of Angel Reddish, which Lorne and Sal pinned squarely on her.

To me, this was justice for my best friend.

To law enforcement, it was even more important. For all the deaths she was likely accountable for, this was the first time she had been tied directly to blood being spilled on U.S. soil.

Whether Mexican authorities would ever be able—or willing—to execute the warrant was still an open question. Supposedly, the search for her was on.

So far, they hadn't had any more success finding her than American authorities did with Rig Weiskopf.

Not coincidentally, his "little cruiser"—which turned out to be an eighty-foot yacht—was missing from its slip in Sausalito.

It wasn't hard to imagine that this had been his exit plan all along. He would spend the rest of his life motoring between remote islands in the South Pacific, living off the money he had likely squirreled away in foreign accounts for just such a purpose, making a determined effort never to be found.

It was just like everything else I had encountered during my years as a reporter.

One way or another, the rich almost always get away unscathed.

He was not entirely silent, though. As Ron Talbot's stories about the scandal continued to fill the front page, he wrote a letter to the editor, railing against the Immigration and Naturalization Act, which granted a mere 675,000 permanent visas each year in a country that had a demonstrated need for at least three or four times that number.

In true Rig fashion, he argued that we shouldn't be against migrants; that we should be for the vibrant contributions they made to our economy and our way of life.

As he put it, "If you think you've eaten a piece of chicken in the last thirty years in this country that wasn't processed by a migrant worker, think again."

I'm not sure how many people he persuaded. In this country, immigration had become one of those intractable hot-button issues: People had their opinions, and because those opinions were often untethered from facts, it was difficult to change their minds.

Balco, meanwhile, was put up for sale by the remaining investors, who were eager to cash out as quickly as possible.

Two other logistics companies made acquisition bids, with plans to merge Balco's operations into their own.

Balco would soon cease to exist.

Many of the top executives would likely be purged. But at least the rank and file—the drivers and warehouse workers who, in fact, had voted to accept membership in IWW-Local 37—would get to keep their jobs.

I wouldn't be one of them. I had already resigned.

And it was just as well. No matter who owned it, I wasn't going anywhere near that company ever again.

As all this unfolded, Page and I continued to move about carefully. None of Ron Talbot's stories mentioned me by name. And law enforcement promised to protected my identity.

I still worried someone might come after me, but we never had any indication that was happening. Getting rid of me wouldn't help Norteño or La Tranquila legally. With Lorne and Sal telling all, the FBI didn't need my testimony. I wasn't even listed anonymously in the indictment as a confidential informant.

Nevertheless, Page and I lived in an empty room at the *San Francisco Chronicle*'s building on Mission Street for the first few days as we waited to see how everything sorted itself out. The paper had laid off so many reporters that there was plenty of space for us.

Eventually, we shifted to a nearby hotel. Then, when it became clear we were no longer needed in the Bay Area, we fled to Page's parents' house.

They lived in a gated neighborhood just outside Atlanta.

That seemed to be enough security for the time being.

I didn't know what my next career move would be. But for the first time since I learned of my admission to Northwestern University—and I began dreaming in earnest of a life as a journalist—I was okay with being unsure.

We would figure it out.

What remained even less settled were my feelings toward Angel. The word "ambivalence" has come to be associated with uncertainty or indecisiveness. But its original definition has to do with maintaining simultaneous but conflicting feelings.

That rather perfectly summed up where I was at the moment, and probably would be for some time.

Nothing that happened in the past few months had changed the many years we had spent together. He was my best man, my best friend, my brother.

He had also made a mistake, one born of unrealistic optimism and excessive self-confidence. It had cost him more than it cost me, but it had still upended my existence pretty thoroughly, too.

Page and I had discussed this a fair amount—we had plenty of time to talk these days. She pointed out that even though things went badly awry, Angel's intentions had always been good. He legitimately thought he was helping us by bringing us out to California and giving us a new start.

In some ways, he had probably done me a favor, getting me out of the newspaper business.

You couldn't ride a dinosaur past its extinction. I was going to have to leave that dying industry eventually; and if I hadn't jumped, I would have been pushed. At least now I could figure out my next step at an age when I had some options.

In that way, Angel had come to represent a complex set of feelings and emotions in both of us. He was optimism and pain and imperfection and joy, all at the same time.

I would always love him, even as I recognized his flaws. It was complicated, for sure.

Anyone who thinks love is simple probably hasn't lived much.

In the end, we couldn't dwell on what had happened.

Page was too busy growing a new person, who we were going to have to figure out how to take care of.

For as nervous as we were about that prospect, Page was thrilled by the idea that her parents could now be active participants in the baby's first months. Atlanta was also a lot closer to my mother in Tennessee.

For all his duplicity, Bob Brunato wasn't wrong about one thing.

Family is everything.

One of the first things we did after arriving in Atlanta was find a new obstetrician, who promptly scheduled Page's twenty-week ultrasound. Ironically, thanks to COBRA, Balco was still covering our health insurance.

Even though I had already lost my gold star for perfect attendance with doctors' visits, there was nothing keeping me away this time, so I joined Page at her appointment.

The new obstetrician did a full intake with Page, who earnestly described her prenatal vitamin intake, her avoidance of fish that might contain mercury, and all the other good-mommy practices she had been committed to.

"Wonderful," the obstetrician said. "Let's have a look, shall we?"

Page was soon hoisting herself up on an examining table, lowering her pants just a little, and lifting her shirt. She took in a quick breath as the obstetrician squirted cold goo on her midsection.

The doctor applied the wand just below Page's navel, and then I sort of lost my mind for a moment.

An image had appeared on the monitor to her right, and I suddenly found myself face-to-face with our miracle.

I marveled at the round curve of a skull, the exquisite architecture of a tiny ear, a rib cage that reminded me of piano keys.

This was our baby. Our beautiful, beautiful baby.

Page quickly reached for my hand, then crushed it in her grip.

She already had tears in her eyes.

Mine were wet, too.

"Oh, honey," she said.

I was having too hard a time breathing to respond. I just bent down and kissed her forehead.

"Everything is looking great, just great," the obstetrician narrated. "All the organs are exactly where they're supposed to be. We've got ten fingers and ten toes. Brain looks good. Heart looks good. You've got yourself a very healthy-looking baby here."

The gratitude I felt at that moment immediately swamped every other emotion I had struggled with over the last few months.

"Do you want to know the sex?" the doctor asked.

We had already discussed this, and we decided there were too many unknowns in our lives at the moment. We wanted more certainty wherever we could get it.

"Yes," we said simultaneously.

"Okay, hang on," the doctor said, moving the wand to change our view. Then she said: "Congratulations, you're having a boy."

She pointed to the spot in the ultrasound that made this abundantly obvious.

Page squeezed my hand again.

"I've been thinking," she said, "that if it was a boy, we should name him Angel. That will be our reminder that things may not be perfect, but we should always maintain our sense of hope."

The moisture that had been welling in my eyes was now spilling down my cheeks.

"Yes," I said. "That sounds just about right."

ACKNOWLEDGMENTS

After thirteen novels, you might think I have grown tired of acknowledging the readers, booksellers, librarians, writers, reviewers, bloggers, Instagrammers, Booktubers, Goodreaders—and all the other people who make up the book universe as we know it.

Instead, my gratitude toward you only grows.

Being an author is a great privilege. But an author doesn't get to keep publishing without an audience. You have a thousand other things—and a million other books—that you might spend your time on. I so humbly appreciate that you chose to give my story a few hours of your attention and emotional energy.

On a more practical level, I need to thank a person who helped informed these pages with an education into the logistics industry. Due to certain agreements, I can't name them. The best I can do is put into print their fervent wish that someday the Texas A&M University football team wins a national championship.

I'd also like to thank Lee Randall and the rest of the folks at Oceanview, including marketing director Robert Rogers, copyeditor Michael Fedison, and designer Christian Storm. Thanks for making these pages better and bringing them to a wider audience.

My agent, Alice Martell, remains my stalwart supporter and a dear friend. She "got me" after ten minutes yet has put up with me for ten years. I appreciate her every day.

Finally, I need to acknowledge my family. My children were very small the first time I published a novel and are now on the verge of leaving the nest, a sentence I can't type without feeling a certain tightness in the chest. Watching them grow and thrive alongside my wife, Melissa, is the greatest joy I have.